The
REALM
OF THE
UNBELIEF

Pilgrim Voyage
Press

<u>Dedication</u>

To Jennifer, my wife and partner in perseverance

TABLE OF CONTENTS

"His life was on the other side of probability; there he lived, there he breathed, there he ventured, in reliance upon God – he, the most sensible of all!"

-Soren Kierkegaard

CHAPTER ONE
CORNELIUS

Inside the casket is the best friend a boy could ever hope for; the best friend an old man would never forget.

Three crestfallen gravediggers lower the casket into the ground beneath a tower window where a man, an old man with a long white beard, long and white and ancient, sits and watches. He appears afraid, this old man, afraid and confounded, sitting at a table in his chamber overlooking the palace courtyard where the ground is swallowing the dead. It has been many years since his boyhood, but the memories of those days are as clear to him now as ever. His wrinkly brow is sweating beads of trepidation. He picks up his pen. His hand trembles with age and longing. It is a longing for the past, a longing born from his present fear.

The setting sun begins to duck behind the orchards to the south, creating a shadow over the courtyard where the casket is being dropped, and casting a pinkish glow upon the distant, eastern hills. It is upon these hills, these plush, swooning hills, that the old man turns his reluctant gaze to study the formation of an army. In all his years he has never seen an army so intimidating, an army like mounting waves of the sea, a dark cloud of bodies hovering atop the hills, like a shadow, like death itself. The old man knows that by morning the army will be upon Port Fectia like a ball of fire and hate, and without the leadership of the man in the casket, Port Fectia will likely be taken.

Port Fectia is a village by the sea. It is a beautiful little place, more beautiful than you could ever imagine. It sits nestled among golden meadows and pink horizons and the softest fields a child will ever explore. At the water's edge sits the King's palace, magnificent and eternal with a stretch of supple sand falling out behind it, disappearing into the silent sea. The village sprawls out from there with daring stone huts and happy villagers and livestock and fields of plenty. Stone

7

paths lead from one hut to another, from one field to another. There are neither fences nor walls. Even the palace is left unfortified. There is an air of both freedom and peace, two irreconcilable virtues in most countries, but in Port Fectia, as common as the sun.

The man in the casket is Cornelius Van. He was the governor of Port Fectia, second only to the King himself. Although you will never meet anyone more loyal than a Port Fectian, Cornelius was the most loyal of them all. He was a true and faithful leader, as true as the sea was calm, and the Port Fectia sea never a tempest was. His death is a catastrophe beyond measure - completely unexpected. In fact, that very morning the entire palace was awakened by the mournful cries of the governess as she discovered her husband lifeless in his bed. Oh the cries! They were agonizing cries, penetrating cries, desperate, helpless, resonating cries, cries that shook the very foundation of the palace, echoing throughout the village, carrying sorrow like a stiff wind carries a cold chill down the streets, like a whisper carries a rumor. There is no corner; there is no bend in which you could have hidden from those sorrowful, burning cries. The old man of which we speak was the first to find her there in her bed, Cornelius in her arms, and a hole in her heart as big as the sky. Eighty six years was still young for a Port Fectian in those days. Cornelius died before the world was ready, and not a soul knows why.

The old man sits quietly, looking and thinking and feeling. He knows that soon he will be fighting. The enemy waits. The village sighs and prepares best they can. He holds his pen because he is determined to write. He lights a candle as darkness begins to settle across the land. He is committed to preserving the legacy of his best friend, the governor of Port Fectia, Cornelius Van. He is going to record the account of how he and Cornelius came to this village. It is a story he considers of greater worth than all the rainbows by the sea, a story which he wishes he would have written years ago. For that reason the old man holds his pen in hand, knowing full well that he will trade it in tomorrow for a sword, and in the candle light he begins:

I, Osgood Esemblion, Chief Advisor to our late Governor, Cornelius Van, do declare that the following story is true against all the adversaries who would swear against it. I am a witness to these events. This is the story of Cornelius Van. More specifically, this is the story of how one young man, when confronted with the imminence of doom, was given the task, in a world of uncertainty, to discover for himself what is true. I, by the will of the King, was allowed to accompany him. While my hours are short, let my record begin the day on which everything changed.

That was no ordinary day because school was cancelled. School was always cancelled on the opening day of brawlball season. It was like a holiday. Brawlball was the most wonderful game in the world. The morning light struck my eyelids like a slap to the face, the rays finding a seam in the fog, penetrating through my window. I was jolted from my sleep because the light came suddenly, like an explosion. It did that all the time. That was how the people of Giltlegard knew it was time to wake up. My father, who was a lightmaker, sat at the highest point of the factory and flipped the switch that generated the burst of light which set the city aglow. Giltlegard had no natural light. We had to manufacture light. My father was an important man. He had to make that daily trek back and forth from the factory, clanging his pelzors in utter darkness, with a simple candle to light his steps. If he failed in his work, the city would remain in darkness. Nightfall came in the same manner. When my father was ready, he would flip back the switch, and the entire city would immediately, without warning, be consumed by darkness.

The light was not particularly bright. It was just light. But compared to the darkness, it was persuasive. On any given day, once the light switched on, the clanging sound of pelzors echoed unmercifully throughout the city. Pelzors were steel boots. Everyone over eighteen years of age wore them unless you were a brawler. If the light did not wake you, the clanging sound of the pelzors undoubtedly would. The sound created a jungle of noise that lasted from lights on to lights off. On this day, I was not yet eighteen, so I popped out of

9

bed unhindered and hurried myself to get ready. I would not miss the brawlball match for anything. It was a special day, but little did I know exactly how special it would actually become.

I was supposed to meet Cornelius before the match, so I darted from my house into the steel streets of the city. Yes, the streets were made of steel. They were steely and cold. The streets were cold. The air was cold. The air was foggy and cold and gray. Practically everything in Giltlegard was made of steel. The houses were steel. The streets were steel. The chairs and the beds and the tables were steel. Everything was steely and cold, and the clanging sound of pelzors was the sound of steel on steel. I was supposed to meet Cornelius in the market square outside of Pattick's.

The Market Square filled up quickly in the mornings. Giltlegardians had very little else to do. Cornelius and I would be among the first to arrive being that we had no pelzors to slow us down. On this day, I arrived before Cornelius. Mr. Gilactus stood outside his fruit stand waving at passersby and waving at me, rotating from left to right like a machine, a retractable smile barely visible under his mustache. Mr. Gilactus was about as friendly a Giltlegardian as I had ever met, a rarity indeed. He never seemed to mind me and Cornelius loitering near his business. I swiped a couple of frizbos when I thought he wasn't looking. "Get your lumpkus! Get your blumes! Get your frizbos here! Two baskets for the price of one!" He pretended not to notice me, so I swiped two more and stuffed my pockets full. I always wished I could push a button to make him stop rotating. He made me feel dizzy.

In addition to Mr. Gilactus's fruit stand, the market square played host to jewelry shops, cooking shops, toy shops and sword shops. There were doorknob shops and trinket shops and pelzor shops and razor shops. There was even one shop which sold nothing but adding machines. And then there was Bloody Pattick's shop. Pattick's was where the brawlsticks were sold. Bloody Pattick formed them himself. Bloody Pattick was widely considered the greatest brawler who ever lived. He was Cornelius's hero. He had a new stick on display, a broad handle with a flat trunk as opposed to the customary rounded variety. I knew Cornelius would drool over it. I was drooling myself. The difference was that I could afford it and I knew that Cornelius could not. My father, the lightmaker, was one of the wealthiest men in Giltlegard. On the contrary, Cornelius's father was a simple, dirty miner. I was about to inquire from Pattick a price when I caught a glimpse of trouble forging a path through the market square. It was Cornelius followed by some neighborhood scoundrels, some kids we knew. They could never seem to leave Cornelius alone. Mostly, Cornelius ignored them. Occasionally, he struck them, but only when they stood in his way. Even when he would knock them upside their heads and bloody their noses with his fist they always came back.

On this particular morning, he just walked on while they heckled him from behind. "Look, there goes The Freak's boy," they would say, or "Hey Cornelius, is Mommy still alive?" or "Why don't you just go back home to Mommy?" or "Where's The Freak?" The ridicule usually centered on his mother who was commonly referred to as The Freak because of her strange and chronic sickliness, although most believed, as I did, that she was really better off than she led on. I was just not foolish enough to say anything. His mother was the dearest thing in the entire world to him, and though he sought help for her, no one ever seemed to know the cause of her ailments. She was weak. She was discolored. She gagged on her own throat more often than she spoke from it. Many medicine experts observed her and offered various opinions on remedies, none of which worked. Some just looked at her and said, "What she really needs is to die." Some joked about magic potions. "What you really need to do, boy, is find the magic healing potion. That is your mother's only hope. Otherwise, she will surely die." Then they would laugh and leave her to fate. For Cornelius, however, this was no laughing matter. Once he heard the words "magic potion", he believed. Though it was but a joke to the medicine experts, to Cornelius it was real.

Cornelius dreamed large dreams. His mind was full of myth. His feet were fast. His balance was good. His motives were mischievous. He could handle a brawl stick like no other his age. He was boyish even for a boy, yet was so close to becoming a man. His freckled face was well formed, and his eyes were bright and bold and blue and trustworthy. To most, however, he was more than a bit strange. He carried a small steel baton in the sash around his waist. He dropped out of school to care for his sickly mother, and when he was not doing that, he was probably at brawlball matches watching from his secret vantage point beneath the rink. He studied the brawler's every move. He practiced relentlessly. He knew what he wanted from life, and his eighteenth birthday, like mine, was quickly approaching.

Outside Pattick's, the ridicule would not cease. A hulking boy named Heel emerged clumsily from the wild pack and jostled Cornelius on the shoulder. Cornelius turned around and faced his mocker.

"What do you mean by this?" Cornelius asked.

The whole world stood still for a moment. There was a crowd beginning to form in the market square, although it was still early. The crowd mainly consisted of Cornelius and me and Heel's gang and a handful of citizens in Pelzors who halted their shopping to observe the confrontation and a few shopkeepers and a pretty little flower girl who sold her goods in the market square. Bloody Pattick heard the sudden stir of silence and stepped outside his shop to investigate, for silence in Giltlegard was so rare it usually meant something was amiss.

"Is he your body guard?" Heel asked, referring to Bloody Pattick. "I got no qualms with you, Bloody. My qualms are with Van here."

"I don't need a body to guard me against the likes of you, Heel," replied Cornelius. "What's your difference with me? I have no difference with you. I just wish you would leave me alone. That's all."

"You stole my watch. I know you did. I want it back."

Heel pulled a knife from a pocket on the inside of his jacket. He pointed it toward Cornelius who didn't flinch.

"So what if I did? What difference is it to you?" Cornelius pulled a steel framed watch from his trousers. "Is this it? I found it right where you left it, on the gate to your house. I was passing by and found it. I believe it's mine now."

"It was on my gate," Heel blurted. "It's mine." Heel began spitting in his anger. He drew closer to Cornelius, his blade pointed

12

and fierce. Cornelius took a step closer until Heel's knife was firmly pressed against his chest. He held out the watch.

"I am not interested in fighting you, Heel, though I'm certain I would beat you. I just want you to leave me alone, that's all. Here, take this watch if that's what you want. You know as well as I do that it's not yours anymore. It's mine now according to our customs. But it means nothing to me. Here take it. Take it!" Slowly, Heel lowered his weapon and took the watch from Cornelius's hand.

"There, now go," Cornelius demanded.

As he turned around to greet me, Heel raised his blade and lunged at Cornelius, slicing him across the back of his neck. Cornelius turned, wiping the blood with his finger. Heel was raging with hate. He was so volatile that his head appeared ready to explode. Cornelius possessed amazing restraint for a boy his age, but he was volatile himself. His will was made as much from steel as the street upon which he stood, and all it took was a decision on his part, a positive, calculated decision to release his own rage, and it would be done. His rage did not show on his face. His rage was bottled up inside. All he needed to do was twist the top from the bottle and his own rage would fly forth like a ball from a catapult. As I watched him, I saw him twisting that top off of the bottle.

"Van, don't do it!" I cried.

"Cornelius, no!" screamed the flower girl. She closed her eyes at what was about to happen.

In a flash, Cornelius whipped out the baton from his sash just as eight rowdy boys pounced on him, driving him down upon the steel street. I could not stand by and watch my friend get pummeled to death, so I joined the raucous. Cornelius was no ordinary boy. He fought them off from the bottom of the pile. Every so often he would emerge from the tussle and punish one of them hardily, only to be dragged back in again. We fought hard, blow for blow, but eight against two are difficult odds to be sure. We were stabbed and poked and prodded and cut and beaten and yanked, and we were taking an unusual amount of bruising. Yet, for whatever we took, we gave out double. Finally, we came to our feet. It was four against two. Heel held his blade firmly in his right hand. Cornelius clutched his baton. We circled each other. Then, with one quick blow, as quick as the switch of a light, Cornelius knocked Heel in the nose and sent him sprawling upon the ground. The other three boys backed off. Cornelius extended his arm toward Heel as if meaning to help him up, but when there was no reciprocation, he instead rummaged through Heel's coat pocket and repossessed the watch. He returned it to his pants and left the bloody Heel to tend to his own wounds.

"Just leave me alone," Cornelius said, walking away. We both knew they would not. They never did.

"Wonderful work, youngsters," said Bloody Pattick. "I thought for a moment that I was going to have to jump in there myself. Come over here. Let me show you the new brawl stick I made. It has a flat trunk. I think you'll really like it."

The pretty little flower girl had her eyes wide open. They were fixed directly upon a very battered Cornelius Van.

CHAPTER TWO
GILTLEGARD

Giltlegard was a cold and foggy place, but I never realized then just how cold and foggy it actually was. It was foggy and gray with icy air and the haunting clamor of pelzors echoing throughout the city. Individuals trudged along the steel streets with their burdens upon their feet, trudging along as if they were hauling an enormous block of steel, aimless and smiling. They almost always smiled. It was an empty, unfortunate smile. Every smile was the same. Cornelius often joked that they were painted on all the faces.

I always thought pelzors were wonderful shoes. The way they glistened in the light and the way they sounded against the steel streets or when climbing steps was the source of much gladness for me. I could not wait until I turned eighteen so that I could have my very own pair. My brother was fitted into his when I was fifteen, and I thought they were the most beautiful shoes in the world. They were square at the toe and rounded at the heel. They raised you about a hand's width off the ground. They were sleek and shiny. It was the rite of passage into adulthood. Sure, you could no longer run in them. They made you tired just from walking to the market square and back. Certainly, you could never remove them, for that would be nearly impossible. Once they were fitted around your feet, they were clamped on so tightly that it cut into your skin. It would take a few days to get used to it. Then, over time, your skin would begin to grow over the top of the boots and eventually fuse into the steel. Despite the restriction, pelzors came with great benefits. They made you a respected member of society. Most boys, once they were fitted for pelzors, were considered ready for a career in the steel factory. The factory was our fate. Either you became a brawler and postponed your fate for a few more years, that is, if you did not die first, or you became a merchant, or you worked in the factory. The first two options merited very few opportunities. The factory, with its production of steel and light, provided the vast amount of employment.

The factory, an erect monument of smooth, glistening steel, towered above the entire city so that its top could not even be seen from the ground. Horizontally, it covered eight city blocks, pyramid shaped, jettisoning upward through the fog and, from what my father told me, coming together at a point in the midst of the clouds. The factory was a sight to behold and the center of industry in Giltlegard. The factory always needed workers. It was considered a rite of passage to work in the factory. It was there that the steel was extracted from beneath the surface of the ground and forged with fire from the depths of the underworld, all taking place in some pit maybe a thousand, maybe a million body lengths deep. Those who braved the depths were the miners like Cornelius's father, and that most likely would have been Cornelius's fate as well. I only know such things from my father the lightmaker, for I never made it into the factory myself. I never reached my eighteenth birthday in Giltlegard.

At the time, life in Giltlegard seemed perfect. There were no wars of which to speak. In fact, there were no laws either. There was just an understanding. Every person was expected to tolerate the next person and any conflict was expected to be dealt with in whichever manner seemed best in the eyes of the parties involved. Conflicts were considered personal. Though they did exist, they were just not allowed to become a burden upon the Giltlegardian way of life. In short, any form of behavior could be justified as long as it did not disrupt the production of the factory.

Looking back, I loved my life in Giltlegard. I could come and go as I pleased. I was not forced to answer to anybody. My father was wealthy and could afford anything my heart desired. I eagerly anticipated my eighteenth birthday when I would become a genuine man. I had a best friend, Cornelius Van, and we went everywhere together. In fact, my only fear of wearing those pelzors was what it would do to Cornelius and me. I was afraid it might tug at our friendship. I was afraid he would be laboring away in the depth of the

16

ground or forging steel and I would be a lightmaker's apprentice. I was afraid he might resent me. I was afraid we would not see each other anymore. There would be no more running through the market square, no more sneaking into brawlball matches, and no more stealing fruit from Mr. Gilactus. There would be no more sitting together beneath the Great Wall. Yes, the Great Wall. In Giltlegard, despite the splendor of the city with its steel streets and buildings and houses and its factory reaching to the clouds in enormity and grandeur, despite the steel which sprawled out across the landscape and everything you touched, despite the pelzors and the fog and the wonderful liberty under which we all lived, there was one thing and one thing only which stood out among them all – the Great Wall.

The Great Wall enclosed the city on all four sides. The Great Wall rendered Giltlegard utterly self-contained. These walls were steel. These walls were so high that they disappeared into the clouds. The Great Wall was an accepted characteristic of our city. In fact, nobody even considered the possibility that life could exist on the other side of the wall. Furthermore, nobody ever suggested that there even was another side to the wall. As far as anybody knew, life was Giltlegard, and Giltlegard was life. My father, who worked atop the highest point of the factory, swore he never saw the top of the walls. The walls were so high that anyone who tried to climb them would die of old age, yet nobody ever found reason to attempt such a climb. The walls were so thick that I suppose nobody could ever burst through it, not even with the strongest steel pillars and all the muscle force in the city, yet nobody ever found reason to attempt such a breakthrough. Giltlegardians were perfectly content within those four walls, trudging along the steel streets with smiling faces and heavy feet, bathed in the world which was their city. To me, it was paradise. To Cornelius, it was all wrong.

Cornelius, remember, dreamed large dreams. To most, remember, Cornelius was a bit strange. Cornelius was different from me. He was focused. He was diligent. He had no time for those who did not understand him. Why he took a liking to me, I will never know. Maybe it was because I took a liking to him. We were friends from the

17

dawn of my memory. He could never resolve himself to a life in the factory. He wanted to become a brawler. I reminded him of the risks, but it was the danger that seduced him. He dedicated himself to its strategy. He practiced whenever he could. He finagled me into practicing with him on occasion at which time I would usually end up with a bruised jaw or a bloodied skull. It was terrible I must admit. I had not the courage that Cornelius had. I was much too sober minded. I once asked him what he would do if he did not qualify as a brawler. "Then I'll craft sticks and other weapons, just like Bloody Pattick," he replied. Actually, to describe Cornelius as focused is probably an understatement. He longed for adventure not because he coveted wealth or fame, but rather because he so despised the thought of a mundane existence and cherished every moment that was not occupied caring for his sickly mother. Cornelius despised the factory. Cornelius despised the pelzors. Cornelius was the only one who ever dared wonder what sort of life might actually exist on the other side of the Great Wall.

CHAPTER THREE
BRAWL BALL

Cornelius and I left Bloody Pattick's and headed toward the brawlball arena. I saw the flower girl watch us as we left. She was pushing her flower cart up and down the street in front of the other shops but staying close to Pattick's. I think she wanted to speak to us. I noticed her countenance fall as we distanced ourselves, but she made no effort to catch us. Soon, she was out of sight, caught up in the emerging crowds.

We raced down the street, passing countless people with pelzors until we came to the courtyard of the temple. Cornelius stopped running and watched. The Ponderers were out. Like most everything else in Giltlegard, Cornelius despised the Ponderers. The Ponderers, seven in all, were the wisest men in Giltlegard. These men, with their long gray beards and flowing white gowns and black pointed hats spent each day walking the courtyard of the temple at the center of the city, pondering. They rarely spoke. They simply pondered. They meandered about, heads down, with the appearance of purpose. They pondered for anyone to see. They pondered from lights on until lights out. They preferred to ponder outside the temple lest anyone forget they were busy pondering. Citizens were forbidden to enter the temple. It was consecrated for the Ponderers alone. It was a place for ideas. Whenever one of the Ponderers was struck with an idea, they would all go inside the temple to discuss the idea. When they emerged, sometimes things would change. It was the Ponderers who thought of the idea of pelzors so very long ago before anyone who was alive could even remember. It was the Ponderers who decided that as the steel landscape pushed the vegetation farther and farther outside the city toward the Great Wall, that the people should find their

19

nutrients from the dirt of the ground. It was the Ponderers who created the laws of tolerance and who advanced the teaching that the mind and conscience were the great enemies of freedom and individuality. Day after day, they could be found in the courtyard of the empty temple pondering, and nobody ever found reason to dispute their ideas, and nobody ever dared to even think about disturbing these noble sages, nobody that is except Cornelius who often joked about ripping away their gray beards and white flowing gowns and discovering underneath little boys on stilts. For the rest of us, however, the general feeling was that their thoughts were too valuable to the life of Giltlegard to disturb them. After all, if they were distracted from pondering, who knows what travesty might befall the city.

Regardless of his disdain, Cornelius was fascinated by the Ponderers. He stood and watched them. They meandered in the shape of the number eight. Then, after a while, they reversed direction. Sometimes they would follow each other in the path of eight. Sometimes they would disperse and each form their own path of eight so as to make seven eights in the courtyard. I could not understand how Cornelius found this so amusing. He laughed at them. When one put his hand on his chin as if to convey deep thought, Cornelius laughed. When one stopped and gazed up into the sky for answers, Cornelius laughed. When one stumbled along the path of eight and caught himself before he hit the ground, Cornelius laughed. He was making me nervous. The Ponderers would not take lightly to mockery. He caught the attention of one. The Ponderer peered at Cornelius with beady black eyes under his black pointed hat. He raised his hand and pointed at Cornelius with a long, spindly finger. "Beware to you, Cornelius, son of Dunbar Van."

"Let's get out of here," I said, "This is creepy."

"Wait!" he said, "What did he say to me?"

"He said beware. Now let's get out of here."

"No. I think he called me son of Dunbar Van. Hey Ponderer, what did you say to me? What did you call me?"

Now I was convinced that Cornelius had gone crazy in his head. He was challenging a Ponderer to his face. He was not just thinking it. He was not just joking about it. He was actually doing it. He started to move closer toward the courtyard. I tried to restrain him.

"Van, think about what you're doing. This is crazy. You can't go in there. You can't go after a Ponderer. He will have you killed."

Cornelius complied. I took my arms down from around his neck. He did not take his fiery eyes off the Ponderer. The Ponderer stared back. Slowly, he lowered his pointing finger and tucked it back inside his robe. His face was old and stern. He was frightfully old. He was old and disturbing.

"Did you hear what he called me, Os? He called me by my father's name."

"That is your name, Van. Cornelius Van."

"No, he called me Son of Dunbar Van."

Cornelius despised his father almost as much as he despised the factory. His father was a hard working miner and well respected, but he was a terrible father and an even worse husband to his mother. It was because of his father's dedication to the factory that he was rarely at home during waking hours. When he was not at the factory, he was at the social house. On the rare occasion that he was home, he was too drunk to remember. Cornelius tried to separate himself from anything that had to do with his father. He would have left home long ago if his mother had not needed him so. Cornelius was the only one in Giltlegard who would care for her, and I never once heard him complain.

Cornelius and the Ponderer broke their engagement. The Ponderer returned to his pondering in the path of eight. Cornelius slowly turned to go. Then, as he took no more than ten paces, he suddenly turned back and faced the courtyard.

"Curse you, Ponderer! Curse to you!" Then he spat upon the ground. The Ponderer raised his spindly finger once again as Cornelius and I dashed out of sight.

I told him that he was going to get me killed and that I did not know why I continued to be his friend. He laughed at me and said he

21

was sorry but that he could not be mocked that way. Then he said he was glad that I was his friend, and I let it go.

We arrived at the arena. A long line was forming outside, but we never accessed through conventional means. We did not buy tickets. We snuck in through the back. Guards stood watch around the facility for that very reason, especially for the first match of the season when practically the entire city would be attending. Carefully, we snuck to the rear of the arena where the compactor was located. This was our secret entrance - through the compactor - but we had to be careful. There was the danger of being seen as well as the danger of being compacted.

Behind the arena was a dark alley with a wall on one side separating the arena from some houses. We noticed two guards patrolling the rear of the arena. That was highly unusual. In fact I do not recall ever seeing guards patrolling the back alley before that morning. Why would they need to guard the compactor unless they were expecting us? We needed a place to hide.

The compactor at the arena was set to automatically activate every so often, so we needed to wait for our chance. Compactors were all over the city. They were used for crushing trash and dead bodies and compacting them into small square cubes. Then they would be filed away into small steel storage containers and inserted into the proper openings in the storage facilities. The trash was inserted into the waste facility while the dead bodies were placed in the mausoleum. There was only one mausoleum, across from the temple courtyard, and it was five stories high, but there were numerous waste facilities scattered throughout the city. They were small cube shaped buildings about the size of one of the shops in the market square, maybe smaller, with drawers on every side for inserting the compacted trash. Giltlegard was kept clean, to be sure. Smooth, smooth steel was all you could find anywhere except for only a few remaining trees. One of those waste facilities was kept in the alley behind the arena. We figured that if we could slip in behind one of those that we could hide out until the compactor opened, so we did, but there was still the problem about the guards.

The waste facility was positioned close to the wall behind the alley, so when we climbed the wall and stood on top of it we could lift ourselves up and peer over the top of our hiding place and monitor the activity of the guards. After a while, it became apparent what we needed to do.

"We have to attack the guards," said Cornelius, "Here. I brought a baton for you."

"What? Why don't we just try a different way in?"

"There is no other way unless you want to get caught."

"We can't attack the guards. They have swords. I'm still hurting pretty bad from our last encounter and now you want to go and get us more hurt?"

"Look, the compactor already opened twice since we've been here. We can't wait around all day or we're going to miss the match."

"Why don't we just go get in line like everybody else this time. I'll talk to my mother. She'll get us the…"

"No!" Cornelius interrupted, "That's not how we do it. Now look. The guards are walking along the back wall separately and coming back together at the compactor. Now we have got to get to them when they are together, so it'll be two on two, not one on one, you with me?"

"We still have to wait for the compactor. What happens if someone else finds them lying around before we get inside. Then what?"

"That's why we have to put on their vests and drag their bodies here behind this waster. Ready? They're coming back together now. We've got to get them when their backs are to each other, just when they're getting ready to separate again. Ready? There they go. Let's go!"

"Wait, they have swords. Wait!" I groaned. Quick as a flash he was gone, and I was left trying to get down off the wall and catch up. My leg was stinging pretty badly from our earlier encounter and my face hurt and my whole body was sore and I was not anticipating any more fighting that day, but I had come to expect the unexpected with Cornelius.

We were upon the guards in a rush, catching them by surprise, but not unprepared. Cornelius took the left flank and struck the first blow, cracking his enemy across the face with his baton, sending him straight to the floor, but he held tight to his sword. He raised it toward Cornelius and sprung back to his feet. The second guard was about to strike Cornelius from the back side just as I arrived, and I walloped the back of his skull in one mighty shot, knocking him completely into an altered state. That left two on one. The guard waved his sword about him. Cornelius studied him carefully. Suddenly, Cornelius sprung toward his legs and tackled him around the thighs. I immediately reacted by grabbing his hand which held the sword, and we all three tumbled upon the steel ground. I took hold of his hand and pounded it into the steel until he released his grip on the sword. Procuring his sword, I held it to his throat.

"Good work, Os," said Cornelius, "See, you had it in you all along. Now let's rough him up a bit and get these vests on."

We never had to. Just as he said that the compactor slowly opened its ferocious jaws. Our opportunity had arrived. It would hold open long enough to fill the lower portion with waste before clamping back down upon itself, but this time it was not being fed. We did not want to enter too quickly lest the guard follow us inside, so we waited. We waited with the sword to our adversary. We waited for what seemed like time standing still. We waited until Cornelius shouted "Come on!" and we darted toward the compactor and dove right through the opening and into the arena clearing the trash pit easily as the compactor closed behind us. It was not a pretty dive, and falling onto a steel floor is never comfortable, but we were inside nonetheless. We jumped to our feet and scurried down the cold, empty corridor. We heard the cacophony of pelzors echoing throughout the arena as the crowd lumbered in from the main doors, taking their seats among the spectators. We were headed for somewhere completely contrary. We were headed for our own secret chamber.

We came to a door and took some stairs down and came to another door and swung it open. Inside was our dark retreat, our secret world. It was the basement under the rink. It was from here that we would watch the event. We would climb atop a stack of steel barrels and see everything up close from two holes in the corner of the rink near the rink floor, holes small enough that no one really noticed yet large enough that we had a wonderful view. Cornelius drilled those holes years ago and we had been visiting that perch ever since.

Finally, we could relax. It seemed like we had been on the move all morning. I said my leg and my shoulder were throbbing. Cornelius said the back of his neck was burning. The blood had dried, but there was swelling and redness.

The basement under the rink was dark and cluttered with old uniforms and brawl sticks and helmets. Brawlers wore steel helmets and pads upon their knees and elbows. The uniforms consisted of colored straps crossing the chest and back in the form of the letter X and short black trousers which cut off before the knee and running boots. The way the competition was arranged, the teams were to represent the various segments of society. For instance, on that day, the miners, wearing the red straps, were to compete against the merchants in the brown straps. The brawlers were not really miners and merchants, but merely represented them in order to give the spectators a cheering interest. The fierce competition played out not only on the rink, but in the stands as well, as one group of spectators would very often rise up against another in the cause of defending their team. Brawlball was conducive to feeding the frenzy of rage and violence that was already burning in the bosoms of so many Giltlegardians.

The air of excitement could not be contained in the arena. The players took their positions. The game was played using a steel ball, small enough to fit in the palm of an older child's hand. A mediator tossed the ball into the air in the center of the rink, and the match was on. Both sides rushed for the ball, slamming into one another in an attempt to take possession of the steel. The game was rather simple. There were very few rules. There were seven men on each team to represent the seven Ponderers. At each end of the rink, a red square was painted onto the steel wall. The object of the game was to take possession of the steel ball and advance it to your opponent's end of

25

the rink in an attempt to shoot the steel making contact with the opponent's red square. The steel could be advanced in any manner whatsoever, but a point could only be obtained if the steel struck the red square as a direct result of being struck first by a brawlstick. Play was continual, even after a point had been scored. The first team to score ten points was declared the winner. Sometimes the match would last all day, sometimes half a day, but it never lacked for entertainment.

The players were broad shouldered and rough, strapping chests and muscular arms, thick necks and powerful thighs. They were machines, the nastiest and toughest that Giltlegard had to offer. They were warriors. They attacked each other like wild men, whooping and hollering and knocking each other down and trampling one another under foot. It was not uncommon for men to die. It was all part of the game. Such was life in Giltlegard. The roar of the crowd was deafening. The spirit of violence rose up. Down in our chamber beneath it all, Cornelius sat fixated upon the demolition. He did not cheer for any particular team. He cheered for the skill and the strength. Despite all the brutality, the best brawlers were the smartest brawlers, and the most successful were skilled with the stick. Cornelius fidgeted with excitement, and after a long while, I made the mistake of asking him about his mother.

"She's getting worse," he answered. His fixation with the match was broken. He climbed down the stack of barrels and leaned up against the side of them. "I'm worried about her. She's pale. She's cold. Always shivering. She curls up into a ball and just lays there on the floor. I wish I knew what's wrong with her. Listen, Os, do you believe in magic potions?"

I could not bear to say no, but I could not truthfully say yes, so I just shrugged.

"Well, I do. I believe there must be a cure for her somewhere. I don't know what I have to do, if I have to go digging under the ground for it or something, but I have to find it. There must be something, Os. I can't just let her die without trying."

"What does your father say?"

26

Cornelius lifted his head. His gaze was frozen. His eyes narrowed. His jaw tightened.

"You know my father. No, I haven't seen my father in a few days. He hasn't even come home drunk. I guess he's been staying elsewhere. Maybe at the factory. Maybe not."

Yes, I did know his father too well. I remember one time I was with Cornelius in his house for dinner. I, Cornelius, and Mrs. Van were sitting together around a meal of worms and lumpkus. We were waiting for Mr. Van to come home from the social house. Mrs. Van, tired and thin, sat upright in a chair across the table from myself. I remember this particular occasion well because I remember her lips quivering and I remember Cornelius helping her lift the drinking cup to her mouth. We ate together with scarcely a word, but I was comfortable there at that table, just the three of us. It felt like something good.

Then Mr. Van arrived. When I addressed him he ignored me. He grabbed Cornelius by the collar of his shirt and ripped him clean out of the chair and plopped himself in his stead. "I'm famished," he growled. He devoured the remaining morsels from his son's plate. Then he snatched the bowl from before his wife and finished hers as well. Then he took a breath.

"How dare you all start dinner before I get home. You know better than that, woman," he said.

Mrs. Van tried to explain by saying "I'm sorry, it's just that it is getting late and Osgood is with us tonight..." but Mr. Van would not let her finish before starting in on a tirade about the price of liquor.

"That blasted Lampus Proel raised his brew five more lumps per cup."

He started in on his own portion like a starving child. Then he pointed at me. "And your old man never has to pay a lick," he complained, "Lucky crank...Cornelius!"

Cornelius answered, "Yes Father?"

"Quit your standing around...What'd you accomplish today? Dancing around like a sissy? Carrying that stupid stick around with you? Lying around at your momma's feet all day? You're gonna be a

27

man soon so you need to start acting like one. Now leave me alone. Can't you see I'm trying to relax?"

Cornelius backed quietly away into the shadows of the room. He was seething. He wanted so badly to make his father proud, but he was not willing to pay his father's price. He was not going to concede his life to the factory, especially since he knew first hand in his father the type of man which the factory seemed to produce.

Mrs. Van came to Cornelius and took him into her frail, motherly arms while Mr. Van licked his plate before closing his eyes.

"It'll be alright, Son," she whispered, "Go on now, before your father loses his temper."

"But mother..."

"Go on, Son. You've done well for me today."

Cornelius helped her back to the table. We listened from down the hall. Mr. Van ordered Mrs. Van to polish his pelzors. Mr. Van complained that the lumpkus were too ripe and the worms were too dry. Then we heard the sound of Mrs. Van upon the floor scrubbing his steel boots and he went on and on about how hard the factory life was and scolded his wife for making Cornelius feel that he had to quit school to care for her all the time and this and that and this and that. We heard him rise from the table so we scampered off so that he would not see us and I remember him mumbling as he forged his way down the hall toward his bed, "I'm trying to become somebody at the factory, my dear, and how am I ever going to succeed if I have to worry about caring for my wife all the time. I deserve more than this. I deserve a little respect. If only I could get the respect in my own home like I do at work, then I'd truly be a happy man." His voice carried off into unintelligible murmurs, and Cornelius hung his head in shame.

Cornelius had the reputation of being a malcontent, a trouble maker, but that is only because he truly loved his mother and despised the factory machine. He did not want to become like his father. Giltlegard was a city of conformity, and Cornelius, I think, understood something that no one else did. He understood that for some reason, life in the city was not quite right.

Yes, I knew his father too well. I could understand why Cornelius was so angry, but at that moment in the basement under the rink, I began to fear for him. He had a certain determination in his eyes. A scowl crept across his brow. I was afraid *for* him and I was afraid *of* him.

"Os, you know what I'm going to do? If my father comes home tonight, I'm going to kill him. I am. I swear it. And if he doesn't come home tonight, then I'm going to find him and then kill him. Yeah, that's what I'm going to do. I'm going to kill him. How does that sound? Don't worry, I won't ask you to help me or anything. But yeah, that's what I need to do."

His countenance moved from a state of anger to a state of resolve, of contentment. I could not say a word to him. I could not possibly at that moment even begin to know what to say. But I feared for his father, that much I knew. Cornelius found some pads lying around the basement floor and strapped them on. He took up a brawl stick, and skillfully darted back and forth across the basement. He fought phantoms. He fought ghosts. He fought whatever came into his head. He ran about like a wild man. I watched him. I caught glimpses of hate in his eyes. I knew he was imagining his father right then and there as he came to a halt in the corner of the basement and unleashed a fury of strikes against a tired old practice dummy he spotted upon the floor. Relentless, his stick must have come down upon that poor victim at least thirty times before the head fell off and rolled away and Cornelius stood still, breathing heavily. I could barely make out his figure in the darkness. I climbed down.

I came to him timidly. His head was down, but there were no tears. I laid my arm across his shoulders. Together we stood, both our heads hanging in the darkness of that cold and wonderful place. The commotion of the crowd raged above, cheers of triumph and moans of desperation. Cornelius turned to me.

"I'm sorry you had to see that."

"Don't worry about it," I replied.

We returned to the pinnacle of the steel barrels and continued watching the match through the eyeholes.

29

He turned to me. "Os, I want you to know that I'm serious. If my father comes home tonight, I'm really going to kill him."

"I believe you," I said.

Little did we know, together beneath the fray, that later that day a stranger would appear who would change the course of the world.

CHAPTER FOUR
THE GREAT WALL

The match lasted well into the latter half of the day, and afterwards, we escaped unnoticed into the gray haze of the city streets. We decided to visit the Great Wall. We made our way to the market square. We swiped a pocketful of blumes from the unsuspecting Mr. Gilactus as he stood in front of his shop.

"Fruit baskets here! Get your lumpkus! Get your blumes! Two baskets for the price of one." Then he turned and spotted us just as we snatched another handful.

"How was the match this morning, Sonnies?"

"Wonderful, Mr. Gilactus. Two more were killed today. It went to the merchants ten to five."

"Wonderful indeed, wonderful indeed. Blumes here. Pomberries. Two for the price of one!"

We passed through the market square and down some streets and past some rusty houses near the outskirts of town where the steel fades into festering brush and grass barely survives in the thickness of the gray. Our mouths dripped with blume juice, that pink sour fruit, and we were drawn to a tree, a lonely dry tree with yellow leaves and a twisted figure. We sprawled out underneath that tree in the cool of the tall, dying grass. I closed my eyes and let some more blume juice drizzle down my chin and propped my head up against the trunk of the old survivor. I was tired and sore. My eyes felt as heavy as the air.

Before us, not more than twenty paces away, stood the great steel wall. It was a behemoth of a wall. Cornelius liked to come here sometimes. He liked to look at it. He liked to pick up stones and hurl them at it and listen to the faint *ping* sound that it made. I picked a piece of straw from the ground and held it in my mouth and chewed

31

upon it. I was feeling sick from too many blumes. Cornelius sat down beside me, his back against the tree.

"Os, look at that wall. Can you honestly tell me that you don't think there is anything on the other side?"

"Yes, I can honestly tell you that there is nothing on the other side."

"How can you be sure?"

"The same way I'm sure about anything else, I suppose. How long has that wall been there? Then why hasn't anyone discovered the other side yet? Not every question has an answer you know."

"Then what about all the other walls? They all have two sides, don't they?"

"This wall may very well have two sides, but it doesn't mean that there is anything *on* the other side."

"So what are you saying, then? That the world ends here at this wall? That if I were to make it to the other side I would be floating in thin air?"

"Yes, that is what I am saying. That is what people have been saying all my life and all the lives before that. Everyone knows that there is nothing on the other side of that wall. The world exists inside these four walls. That's the way it's always been. You are the only one who thinks any differently. What makes you right and all the other millions of people wrong?"

"Well, I don't think it's the end of the world. I think there is a whole other world on the other side."

"Like what?"

"I don't know. Maybe there are two of us. Maybe there are two of everything, one on this side and one on that side."

"No wonder people think you're weird. You talk crazy. You're lucky you have any friends at all. You're lucky I don't just ignore everything you say altogether. You think too much. You're all caught up in this imagination business. It's useless, you know. It's going to get you in trouble someday, your imagination. I promise it will."

"You can just keep your promises, then. I just can't imagine a world without a cure for my mother. I think it's on the other side of that wall. I need to somehow get on the other side of that wall. Come on, follow me."

I refused to follow him. I watched as he trotted over to the Great Wall and touched it. He looked up before it, a monster from out of the sky. It was like an enormous steel foot planted firmly upon the ground by some creature of the mist, some creature that was so big that we were but specks of dirt under its toenail. Then I realized that I too was thinking too much. Cornelius poked and prodded the wall. He got down upon his knees and dug around in the dirt at the base of the wall. Then he stopped and looked up once again. Then he looked to his left and then to his right. The wall was vast and impossible. It would take one man a lifetime just to walk around and poke at it the way Cornelius was doing. He returned to where I was under the tree.

"Alright," he said, "That may not be the best way of going about it, but I won't give up. There must be a way."

"If you insist," I replied. "Van, aren't you the least bit happy? I know your father is a crank and all that, but aren't you content here? I mean, it is the way it is. You might not like the factory, but the factory keeps us from dying. Without it, we couldn't survive."

"We all die anyway, Os."

"True, but just think of how good we have it. This is a happy place. Sure there are a lot of dangers, but not that many. We are free to do as we please. Anything is ours if we want it badly enough. As long as you don't get the wrong people upset with you, we are free men. Nobody is forcing you to go to work or go to school. We have this glorious steel and strength everywhere you look. We have light during the day. We have darkness at night. All the brawlball you want. What more could you want? Seriously. What else is there?"

"I don't know, Os. There is just something not right about this place, that's all."

"That's all? That's all you can say, that's all?"

"That's all."

"Well, you can have your other worlds. I'll take Giltlegard."

We lay in silence for a while, chewing on straw and spitting it back out. I thought about the future of Giltlegard. I wondered what would

33

happen once the city expanded all the way to the wall. I guess they will just keep building up, I thought. If they keep building up, I wondered, could they ever build to the top of the wall? They would have to build much higher than the factory for certain. But could they do it? It would take much longer than my lifetime, I reasoned. Then it struck me. Who built the Great Wall? Whoever it was must have been to the top. And if whoever it was had been to the top, then certainly they must have seen the other side. Right? I wondered. Or maybe the Great Wall had always been. Maybe it was never built in the first place. I knew then I was thinking too much again. That Cornelius, he just could not leave well enough alone.

"Van, what do you think of the flower girl?" I asked.

"You mean the one that pushes that cart up and down the market square?"

"Yeah, that one. What do you think of her?"

"I don't know. She seems like she does alright for herself. She doesn't bother anybody. Her flowers are nice, I guess. Why do you ask?"

"I like her."

"You like *what*?"

"I like *her*."

"Suit yourself, then. Do you want to marry her?"

"I don't know. Maybe. She watched our scuffle today. You know, the one with Heel. She was afraid for you. She yelled your name, Cornelius."

"Really? Why? She should have known I was going to pound him."

"Well, I need to get married sometime. I can't be hanging around the likes of you for the rest of my life. I'll probably wind up dead before I can even be fitted for pelzors."

"Don't remind me. For me, that's in a few weeks."

"Wow, do you think you can become a brawler in time?"

"I hope so. I sure hope so."

"So do you think you will get married soon?"

"Me? No way. I have way too much adventure left inside me to take on a wife. Besides, I've seen my father. Women deserve much better than that."

"You honestly think you're like your father? Come on. I know you too well. You are nothing like him."

"Maybe not, but it scares me just the same."

"I think reality is going to set in for you a lot quicker than you think, Van."

Suddenly, I sensed an intrusion upon our solitude.

"We're not alone," I whispered.

Cornelius sat up into a crouch. I lay still, watching and listening. There was something about us. The faint sounds of Giltlegard echoed in the distance, but there was something much closer. It wasn't so much the sounds that startled me, but the feeling. There was a presence about. Just then, four daunting figures emerged from out of the fog and closed in around us by the tree. Their yellow vests revealed that they were guards. They came bearing knives and clubs. I recognized one as the poor fellow we left on the ground outside the arena with a sword to his throat.

"We have come to arrest you," said one sour mouthed brute.

"By whose authority?" inquired Cornelius.

"By the authority of the Ponderers," came the reply.

"On what charge?" he pressed further.

"On the charge of aggravating the peace," came the response.

The guards were employed by the Ponderers. They were to preserve the peace in the city. They were identifiable by the yellow vests that they wore. They could be found patrolling the market square or the city streets, but many times they operated undercover, masquerading as shopkeepers or factory workers or bums in the alley. They were regular people. They lived amongst everyone else, yet they were bound to a calling much higher than the average man. They were proud men, devoted men, though they carried no authority other than what was given to them by the Ponderers. It was very difficult to enforce anything in Giltlegard because there was no law except that of tolerance.

"Tell me how I have aggravated the peace," demanded Cornelius.

"You have assaulted two of our own and left one of them crippled from a blow to his head."

"That is no reason. That's no crime. I demand to know what this is about."

"You have cursed a Ponderer to his face."

"And what is that but a bruise to his pride?"

"It is a capital offense. It has been determined this day through consultation in the temple. If you refuse to come of your own volition, we will take you by force."

"Take us then!"

The guards encircled the tree where we stood. Slowly, cautiously, they moved in. My steel baton lay on the ground at the base of the tree. Cornelius clutched his in his hand. As they converged, they split us wide by moving between Cornelius and me. From that moment onward, our encounter was but a flash in my memory. I truly thought that I had an appointment with death. I remember blunt objects striking the back of my head. I remember rolling about in the thick, sharp grass. I remember a razor cutting my arm and hardly finding the strength to breathe. I remember the world spinning about me and the grabbing and the clutching and precise moments of pain, each one isolated from the others. And I remember fighting back. But I cannot remember the sequence of events. All I know is that somehow, in the midst of my appointment with death, I found myself clutching a knife, straddling my adversary with one hand upon his throat and one knee upon his chest, and the noise suddenly stopped pulsating inside my head. I was sane again, or so I thought. Still clutching his throat, and squeezing unbeknownst to me, I scanned the clearing for my friend. I noticed him in a familiar spot, his challengers subdued, pinned to the tree with their own knives, crying like lost children. Granted, Cornelius had taken a beating as well. A gash over his right eye released a thin trail of blood down his cheek. His cloak was tattered, his sash loosened. He favored his left hip as he stood. But his focus was fierce. His captives were barely recognizable. I have no words for them. They were simply barren, a wasteland of mediocrity. It

36

appeared that their very lives had already been siphoned from them. They hung from the tree, their heads dripping with shame, their faces unrecognizable, their esteem wrenched away. The fourth guard must have fled, for I only counted three, including my own captive. I watched my friend approach the pitiful bodies. His eyes glared with a hatred that far surpassed that which he had reserved for his own father upon that night. His countenance was as steely as Giltlegard herself. Cornelius clutched his knife so that his fingers and forearm pulsated with pink and white ripples. Slowly, he brought his weapon skyward, the blade pointed down, until his arm stretched as far as possible above his head.

"No!" I shouted, and I tried to stand, but my legs were weak. In my haste, I forgot the man who lay beneath me.

"Van! Stop! Van, no!"

My words had no meaning.

His blade came crashing down upon his victim's skull, and I wish every night that I could find some place in the world where that memory would be blotted out. Even now, I cannot bear the misery of my own two eyes. But what he did stirred me inside, and I could not pull my eyes away. I watched as he executed his second victim in the same manner. I could not stop him. His resolve was too great. I had, by this time, given up trying to make him stop. Instead, as his two victims hung lifeless upon the tree, I turned my attention upon my own captive as I now stood over him. He tried to reach for my knife that I held loosely in my grip, for he was too tired to run. I smacked his hand away. He was still trying to win. Any pity I had was gone, and now I, too, became a villain. I knelt back down upon him and watched his eyes tighten as I thrust my knife deep into his side. Then he breathed his last, and our aggressors had been defeated.

That moment was not really a moment but an eternity. Even now, so much of my memory is but a haunting instance. We dared not speak of it then. We pretended that it never happened. We left the bodies there. We hobbled back to the market square. My companion was as cold as the city streets, and I walked beside him. We were one in spirit. I kept telling myself that it was self-defense and that the mind and conscience, after all, were the great enemies of individuality. I don't know what Cornelius thought. I was afraid to ask. But we did not dwell on it long.

As we entered the market square bloody and spent, a sweet face greeted us in our despair, a sweet face with the scent of flowers and eyes like a ray of light through the fog.

CHAPTER FIVE
THE FLOWER GIRL

"My goodness, what a disaster you two are, an absolute catastrophe. Come sit down, let me help you. Come on now. Here, have a drink of water."

The flower girl led us to a steel bench outside a candle shop where she proceeded to dress our wounds. She tore the apron off her dress and tore it into smaller pieces and wrapped our wounds from head to toe after treating them with an ointment she obtained from her flower cart.

"It's dandy root," she explained, "It will help you to heal quicker. Poor boys, two fights in one day, what sort of trouble have you been getting yourselves into?"

"Three," Cornelius said.

"Excuse me?" she asked.

"Three. Three fights. Not two."

"Boys will be boys," she sighed.

Her dark, sympathetic eyes fell softly upon Cornelius's wounded face. She brushed his sandy hair away from his brow and he met her with surprise in his countenance. For a moment he was pleased with her.

"Thank you," he said, and I said the same.

She put us back together and was preparing her cart for business when I caught her before she went.

"What is your name?" I asked.

"Aza-liel," she replied, "Would either of you be interested in purchasing a flower for someone you love?"

Love. The way she said love was like a song in a deep, dark well.

In Giltlegard, there was no art. Art was not even a word. Beauty was a word, but it meant majestic, the way the factory was majestic.

Some might call the factory beautiful with its smooth, powerful steel and its overwhelming enormity. Loveliness was not understood. Our culture was so caught up in the production of steel and light that we had not the occasion to worry ourselves over whether or not something was lovely. In Giltlegard, there was very little dancing. There was very little singing. There was no painting. There was no literature. There was no loveliness. Frankly, there was no love. I think maybe that is why Aza-liel was so appealing to me. She was unconventional. She actually cared about beauty, and she was not afraid to show it. She was the closest thing to a culture of loveliness that I could fix my restless eyes upon. I think that she and Cornelius had something wonderful in common that I could not match. They both embodied dissatisfaction with Giltlegardian life even if they could not quite understand why. Cornelius longed for more adventure whereas Aza-liel just wanted to push her flower cart up and down the market square and add a little bit of color to all the gray. I admired them both.

"Well, Aza-liel, My name is Osgood and I think you already know that this is Cornelius, and I think your flowers are very pretty. What do you call that orange one there?"

"That is a flaming sideon. Notice how the inner petals have these tiny red dots and the outer petals are bright orange. Sideons come in many varieties – flaming sideons, white sideons, bronze, yellow, rainbow..."

"Rainbow? What's rainbow?"

She pulled a rainbow sideon from among her ensemble. Its dazzling colors were explosive and fine. Each prominent color dazzled in its own way yet came together with the other colors to form a bright, bold color all its own.

"My grandmother told me a story once about the rainbow," the flower girl explained. "She heard it from her own grandmother who probably heard it from hers. A rainbow was a light in the sky, she said. It had wonderful colors all in a row across the sky, like a bow or an arch. It stretched from the surface up into the sky and across the sky and back down to the surface again and everyone could see it but nobody could find it because if you tried to get close it would just

40

disappear. It sounds beautiful. But that was long ago, she said. That was before the factory and the fog. It was like another world, I suppose, when sideons covered the countryside like a warm, bright blanket and the light in the city descended from the stars in the sky."

"That's all well and good," I said, "A wonderful story, but you know it isn't true, right? I mean, there was never a time like that, without fog and light from the tower. My Father told me so. The lightmakers would know, if anybody would. What are stars, anyhow?"

"Stars are great balls of light in the sky. They light up the whole world."

I wanted to change the subject. I thought there must have been something wrong inside her pretty little head. Her naivety was close to embarrassing, but it was so lovely. It was just so refreshing to see the sincerity in her eyes when she spoke. She spoke like she believed every word, but I knew better. I knew she was mistaken. Her grandmother must have been telling her fables. I just could not find it in myself to expose her any further. Then I looked at Cornelius, and it was like a light switched on in his head, like one of those rainbows or star contraptions burst inside his brain. He was hanging on the flower girl's every word.

"I know this might sound strange to you," she continued, "But I really believe my grandmother when she tells those stories. Stars, rainbows, cherubs, all those things existed once, but have somehow disappeared. I think it was when the factory came, and the fog, and the steel, and the brawlball, and…"

"Wait a minute," Cornelius interrupted, "Leave brawlball out of this. Brawlball is the best thing that has ever happened to this city. It is the only thing worth living for here. The only thing."

"No, hold on Van," I said, "First things first. You're getting way ahead of yourself. Cherubs? What in the world is a cherub?"

"Gentlemen, I am afraid I have flustered you. First of all, I adore brawlball. I truly do. And I know for a fact, Cornelius, that you will be a great brawler one day."

"How do you know that?" asked Cornelius abruptly.

41

"Secondly, cherubs are not of this world. They are from another world altogether."

Great. Here we go again, I thought to myself. I have just come across the female version of my best friend. They both believe in things no one has ever seen. I was beginning to become irritated. Cornelius, on the other hand, had brawlball on his mind.

"How did you know I play?" he inquired again. "You've never seen me play. How did you know? Who are you?"

The flower girl began packing away her things in her cart. She locked away her flowers. She tied her cart to the leg of the steel bench and locked that as well.

"Well, you're right," said Cornelius, "I am going to be a great brawler. The greatest that's ever been."

"What's a cherub?" I said again. I needed to know.

Once her things were secure, she said, "Follow me." She started toward a row of shops in the market square. Her pace was quick and graceful. Her eyes were sure. Her lips were gentle with her speech.

"A cherub is a messenger from above. A helper from somewhere among the stars. It has the ability to shine bright like the stars, but also can look much like a beast of the ground. It has great, mighty wings, six of them, and can soar to worlds unknown to human eyes. It has five legs like a beast, but feet and hands like a man. It has arms like a man and great fingers and a snout upon its face and hair and many, many, many eyes upon its wings."

"Have you seen one?" asked Cornelius.

"Only in my dreams," she answered. "And only since my grandmother told me all about them."

"Has she seen one?"

"No. Nobody has that I know of. Not a live one anyway."

"Nobody has because they don't exist," I corrected. Aza-liel shot me a look of disfavor and I cowered a little, not wanting to upset my beautiful new flower friend. Then Cornelius asked the question that I was afraid he might ask once he got his mind off of brawlball.

"Do you believe there is another world on the other side of the great wall, Aza-liel?" He saw me roll my eyes at him, so he punched my shoulder when the girl was not looking. Still, she did not answer. She escorted us inside the jewelry shop where a fat, old, bald-headed man sulked behind the counter. When he saw Aza-liel, he straightened his posture. A look of displeasure crept across his sour brow. I could tell they had met before. He raised his hand as a motion for her to stop, but she paid him no attention.

"That's it. Oh! Isn't it gorgeous!" she cooed. "Pestero, I must hold it. I brought my friends to see it. May I please hold it?"

"I told you that you are not welcome here. Now get!" said the man she called Pestero.

"Oh Pestero, please," she pleaded. "For Grandmother's sake. Please. You know it is my favorite in the whole world."

"I know your grandmother no longer," came the reply.

"Oh Pestero, shall lovers be so cruel?"

She never looked at the man she called Pestero. She was too smitten by the necklace beneath the glass counter. She drew us close to see what she so admired. The chain held a medallion, a circle, engraved with a picture too strange to understand.

"This, gentlemen, is the cherub of which you mock."

After she said that, I began to see. The image was of a beast enveloped by eye-covered wings. It had indeed the hands and the feet of a man. It stood upon five legs and had a tail and a strong, bare back. Its face was both menacing and comforting at the same time. Lines went out from it signifying rays of light. Its gaze was upward, mysterious, like it longed for something greater, like it was not alone. It really was a beautiful necklace. I think when I saw that medallion it was the second time I ever truly saw art. Watching the passion in Aza-liel's face when she explained rainbows was the first time. Suddenly, a thought occurred to me. That necklace could not have been from Giltlegard.

"Ok, you've seen it, now scram!"

"Oh, Pestero, I just want to hold it. May I hold it? Please, Pestero?"

43

The fat man grew impatient. His jaw line began to bulge. He stammered when he tried to speak. Aza-liel was mesmerized by the engraving. She began to pout with her mouth.

"Just once. Let me hold it just once. I will never ask you again. You know me, Pestero. You know my family. What am I going to do? Break it? Steal it? Come now, I just want to touch it. Please?"

"I am sorry, but you cannot touch it. It has been sold. I am merely holding it until the owner comes to take it away. Now you must forget it. I have many, many other necklaces, rings, bracelets for your ankles, your wrists, whatever else you want. I have things you can actually afford with the money you earn from your flowers. If you have no interest in those things, then I have no interest in you being in my shop. Now scram!"

"Sold? Did you say sold?" Real tears formed in the corners of her defeated eyes. "How many days have I been coming to your shop? How many weeks? How many years? How many flowers have I sold? How much money have I saved in hopes of buying that necklace, Pestero? That was my necklace, Pestero. You were to save it for me. Ever since I was a little girl, that was my necklace, Pestero. I have wanted nothing else. I have dreamed of nothing else. How many times did I sit upon your knee at my grandmother's house and tell you of the day when I would buy that necklace?"

"That was only a dream, young lady, the dream of a little girl. This necklace is the most expensive piece of jewelry in my shop. You were only a little girl in love with a dream."

"That was my proof of another world, Pestero. And you have torn it from me. You have torn it from me, Pestero! Despite what you might think of my grandmother, you have torn it from me, Pestero!"

Her tears turned into sobs, falling upon the glass counter. Her body began to shake, twitch, weaken. Cornelius supported her so that she did not faint from grief. She would not take her eyes away from the cherub necklace until she looked upon the man she called Pestero for the first time since her arrival in the shop.

"Who bought it? I demand to know. Who bought it?"

The fat man shook his head.

44

"I hate you!" she screamed. "I hate you, Pestero! You are a pathetic, fat man! I despise you and your bald little head!"

The flower girl broke away from Cornelius and burst out of the shop and into the crowded street, crying. She was crying real tears of real sorrow. She was angry and sad, forsaken and betrayed. That is how she cried. She cried like one who had lost everything she had worked for. I could not understand it, but it was lovely nonetheless. It was lovely and passionate and completely unreasonable. I wished I could comfort her, but I dared not. She raced back to her flower cart and turned as to hide her face. She wept softly now as we approached, and we watched. Finally, it was too much to bear.

"Please don't cry," said Cornelius softly. He reached out his hand upon her shoulder and touched her tentatively. She did not refuse him. She wiped her eyes and turned around and giggled embarrassingly and sat down upon the bench.

"It's only a necklace," said Cornelius.

"I only wanted to touch it," she explained. "I wasn't going to steal it. I guess I'd better get back to work, though it seems I have nothing to work for any longer."

"Wait," said Cornelius, suddenly filled with compassion, "I was going to buy something. A flower for someone I love, remember. I liked that flaming sideon."

A smile emerged on the flower girl's face. Her eyes were red. Her cheeks were flushed. Her eyes were sad but sorry. What she was sorry for, she did not say, but I could see it in her embarrassment.

"See," she said to me, "I told you. Cherubs." Then she pulled a stemmed flaming sideon from her arrangement and handed it to Cornelius. "Three lumps," she said.

Cornelius dug around in his pocket and came up with only two lumps. He looked at me. I dug around in my pocket and came up with one more.

"Who is the lucky lady?" asked the flower girl.

"My mother," answered Cornelius. "She's not feeling well."

"I'm sorry," she said. "I mean, I'm sorry to hear about your mother. And for..." she cut herself off without saying it. I do not think she was sorry for her outburst. I think she was sorry that we watched it. She lowered her voice, almost to a whisper.

"I hate Pestero," she said. "I think he is far too cruel and intolerant. I could just kill him. I mean, if I knew how. Do you know what I mean? I mean, if I had some way to do it. If there was someone, maybe, who would do it for me..."

She turned her face directly at Cornelius. She looked him in the eye. She was serious. Cornelius was flustered. His eyes moved away from her. She spoke softly in his ear. I heard every word.

"If there was someone who wouldn't mind doing it. Someone I could trust. Someone brave and strong, like a brawler. Someone who isn't afraid to kill. Someone with your kind of skills, Cornelius. Someone just like you. Pestero deserves to die. He betrayed me, Cornelius. He needs to die."

"How do you know about me?" Cornelius asked.

"Promise me that you will do it," she pleaded.

"Answer my question first."

"Will you do it? I know how to make you a brawler. Will you do it?"

"Answer my question."

"My brother can make you a brawler. All I have to do is ask him."

"Who is your brother?"

Aza-liel turned her eyes toward the market square. There was Bloody Pattick's shop. Standing outside was Bloody Pattick. He was looking for something - or someone. A little commotion began to stir in the market square. Folks began to shuffle about. Crowds began to move. Bloody Pattick spotted us from afar and pushed his way through the formidable congregation heading in our direction. When he arrived, he greeted us; first Cornelius, then me, then Aza-liel.

"There you are, Sis, I've been looking all over for you. You know these two misfits?"

"Actually, we just met," answered Aza-liel. "Cornelius was just telling me about how much he wants to be a brawler, but he just needs someone to back him as a sponsor."

Cornelius was as surprised as I was about the relation. Bloody Pattick looked at Cornelius and then at his sister and smiled stupidly as if he was the victim of some rotten joke. The noise of the crowds grew louder. There was definitely something amiss.

"You always tell me how talented he is," confessed the flower girl. Bloody Pattick did not deny it. "All he needs is a chance. All he needs is someone to give him a little push."

"Listen Sis," said Pattick, "There is something going on here. This isn't the time. I need you to come with me. People are getting restless. I don't want you getting hurt."

"What do you say, Rod?" she pleaded. "For Cornelius. He only has but a few weeks. What do you say? Please? For me?"

"Alright," he said, "I will help him. Cornelius, it's a partnership, a business. Now we must go, we'll talk later."

Bloody Pattick was hurried, but he did not want to seem rude. He took the flower girl by the arm and led her away into the direction of the moving crowd. She broke away and rushed back to Cornelius.

"I gave you my answer, now give me yours."

Cornelius was still surprised by the transaction. He could not believe he was going to be a brawler. He could not believe this little girl was the great Bloody Pattick's sister. He could not believe that she actually talked about other worlds in the same manner that he did. But more than all this, he could not believe that she actually wanted him to kill the man she called Pestero.

"My answer?" he stalled.

"Your answer!"

"I'm sorry, but my answer is no."

"Aza-liel!" called Pattick from out of the crowd, "Get back here now! You must not leave me!"

"Think about it," she said.

Despondent, Aza-liel slipped away into the crowd, blowing a kiss to Cornelius as she disappeared. The city streets were filling as quickly with excitement and fervor as with bodies and pelzors. There was something terribly frightful happening. Folks were moving as rapidly as they could, grasping onto one another, pushing and shoving. There was talk being bantered about. Words about a stranger. An intruder. An alien. As the crowds cleared out of the market square, we saw him. He was a stranger indeed, and the crowds followed him as he strode into the cold, steel city.

CHAPTER SIX
THE STRANGER

The commotion only increased. Like everyone else, we understood the significance of such an event. Strangers did not visit Giltlegard. It was impossible. Where could he have come from? It should be no surprise that the arrival of a stranger would bring such fantastic curiosity to the citizens of Giltlegard, and yet his arrival in itself was only the beginning of the fascination. The stranger was simply extraordinary.

Despite the soreness in our bones, we raced to the front of the crowd, bumping aside men and women alike, anyone who blocked our path. The crowd followed him like a plague. As he entered the city, the crowds parted like the opening of two doors, and he carved his way through us like a knife through flesh. It was difficult for those in pelzors to maintain his rapid pace. His strides were enormous. He was a giant among the people. He was a colossal man. His hat was tall and deeply purple and feathered with purple feathers. His flamboyant face was long and his chin was pronounced. His eyes looked neither to the left nor to the right. He was extravagantly dressed in reds and purples, a sash around his waist and an impeccably sewn skirt which flowed to the top of his peculiar, tall black boots, and he glided with importance to his stride. A long, daring sword, as long as most men, lay fastened to his hip. The crowd, mesmerized by his confident manners and bold entrance, received his passage like they were receiving a king. He spoke not a word. He walked with purpose and direction. He seemed to know exactly where he wanted to go, paying little attention to his following. As he turned down steel street after steel street, the crowd stayed with him as best as they were able, although many fell behind. More and more citizens were added to the number the further into the city he ventured. Homes emptied. Mothers carried babies. Drunkards left the social houses. The factory gave up its own. Buyers stopped buying and joined the parade. Sellers stopped selling. Guards stopped guarding. Brawlers stopped brawling. The world was in the train of the stranger.

Where is he going? I thought. He passed the market square. He turned down residential streets. He strode by the factory without offering even as much as a glance at it. Finally, still without a word, he made his way to the neighborhood of the Ponderers and stood outside the courtyard of the temple. He was as tall as a tree. The Ponderers stopped pondering in paths of eight. The stranger looked down at the old, gray beards in the flowing white gowns and pointed black hats, but said not a word. He climbed over the fence into the sacred courtyard. The Ponderers did not try to stop him. He reached the doors of the temple. Would he enter the sacred place, I wondered? But he did not. He climbed the walls of the temple onto the roof. There he stood. He stood like a tower atop the temple, facing the factory in the distance with the entire population of Giltlegard sprawled out before him. He raised his arms like tree trunks above his proud head. He was mysterious and haunting, crazy and important. There was not one gray headed man, not one fine, young gentleman, not one dainty headed lady, not one suckling babe that was not waiting for something to be said, for some command or some meaningful gesture. We all waited together, without sound, without purpose, without breath. When he raised his arms, he loomed over us like the branches of a one thousand year old tree, and nobody dared proceed another step. Giltlegard had never before been so still while the lights were on. I wondered about my father. Did even he descend his proud perch to witness this monumental event? I never learned the answer to that.

Cornelius and I stood near the front of the crowd, looking up at the powerful stranger. The Ponderers took their place at the head of the congregation, seven gray beards with flowing white gowns and black pointed hats all in a row, like a curtain, like a shield to protect us from this intruder. They, too, did not move, yet their presence, it seemed, being that they were so well respected throughout the city, lent a sense of comfort to the citizens who waited anxiously for what the stranger was about to do.

The citizens were lined up behind us and around us farther than I could physically see, like a blanket of bodies and heads. There was hardly room enough to move let alone breathe, but since Cornelius and I were near the front, we could see him clearly, like a purple light in the fog.

The stranger lowered his arms once he was sure he had the attention of the city. All eyes remained fixated upon the looming figure atop the temple roof. He had chosen a preeminent location at which to address the population. It was the Ponderer's domain. I had no doubt that he had chosen it purposefully, probably with the intention of making the Ponderers feel small, as if to say, "You are no Lords over this land!" And they did feel small. I could see it in their trembling fingers. They were just as intimidated as the rest of us.

Then he spoke, and when he spoke, it was like a demolition of steel, like the crashing of a steel pillar upon the steel streets. He spoke with no ordinary voice of a man, not like any creature imaginable. He spoke with authority, and it took only one word for me to feel as impotent as dust.

"Leaders and citizens of Giltlegard," he bellowed. "I come to you from beyond the great wall, from the village of Port Fectia, far west by the sea. I have traveled a great distance to speak to you this day. I have come with terrible news."

Murmurs began to rise, but the stranger raised his hands, and we were silent.

"You are deceived!" he bellowed. "I am afraid that you are but prisoners in your own land. You are not free. You are slaves. You live miserable lives, and you are prisoners of your own misery, every one of you, from the strongest man to the smallest child. You are to be pitied above all creatures for you live in a pitiful city and live pitiful lives. You are dreadful creatures, and your misery is truly dreadful! That is what I have come to inform you of today. I have come to tell you how wretched you are because you are victims of this horrible, wretched place."

The murmurs resumed and soon turned to restlessness. The restlessness turned to discontentment. The discontentment turned to rage. The stranger looked on. He looked down upon a people who were frightened by his size and his strangeness and the authority in his voice. But the words, the words we did not heed. It was as if he spoke blasphemy from the top of our sacred structure. He looked down upon us all and cursed us all. The fear which we had turned upon its head and bitterness and anger grew out of the depth of the congregation until the stranger was met with the defiant cries of indignation and unity. The cries grew stronger. The cries grew together. Fists were shook, and the mob began to move forward toward the temple courtyard. The stranger stood tall and bold. He would not shrink back at the voice of the Giltlegardian resolve. The Ponderers smiled amongst themselves. The resonance of the cries must have been music to their ears, and they stood satisfied in their long, gray beards and flowing white gowns and black pointed hats, and they turned to the crowd and raised their fists in unison against the stranger, and the crowd erupted in frenzy and shouted in unison, "WE ARE FREE. WE ARE FREE." The stranger again raised his hands to silence the crowd, but this time they would not listen. I joined my voice with the rest, but Cornelius only watched in amazement.

Our shouts grew louder and stronger and angrier, and we would not heed the gestures of the stranger, cursing and spitting and gnashing our teeth. The crowd moved forward, nearly spilling into the temple courtyard, then the stranger lost patience.

"SILENCE!" he erupted, his voice literally shaking the foundations of the city. His power immediately subdued the voice of the crowd. The stranger glared out across the expanse of bodies, and his own silence was indeed frightening, and again he spoke.

"I can surely account with my own senses that you, the citizens of Giltlegard, are indeed a passionate people. But in all your passion, you are an ignorant people. You are ignorant of your own miserable lives. You may claim your own freedom, but I am not lying when I say that you are by no means free, for certainly you do not even know what this freedom of which you claim looks like. Look at you. You work every day as a slave to your own ignorance. You revel in your own pleasures. You have utter disregard for life. You take what is not yours. You have not even the light of the sun to shine upon your city. You live in darkness. There is no light here. The only light you know is that of your own making. You are prisoners in this place. You march along as captives in your own city. The weight of your steel shoes is enough to hold you down. You have not the freedom that you think you have. You slave day after day to erect these buildings of steel. And for what? To satisfy your own misery! You are a miserable people, poor citizens of Giltlegard! You have been deceived! Look around you. You are surrounded by a great wall. You are trapped inside your own land. You cannot even escape. You are so deceived that you do not even desire to escape. You are miserable indeed. I come from the great village of Port Fectia, where the people are truly free. In Port Fectia, the people know the truth. In Port Fectia, the people live in genuine peace. And I have come to tell you that you are prisoners in your own land. You have never known truth. You are trapped, you are miserable, and the worst of it is that you cannot escape. You will never know that truth which lies on the other side of the wall."

The crowd was now choking on its own silence, suffocating, drowning. There was a terrible ache in my stomach. Giltlegard was clutching a collective ache in her stomach. The people had no rebuttal. They had no cry, no uproar, no complaint. They merely had sadness, distress, and this terrible, sickening silence. Silence. Silence was all we had. I was sick and silent. Cornelius was silent. Could it be true? Could it be true that I and my great city were nothing more than prisoners, nothing more than slaves to our own impressions of the world that we see every day? I did not want to believe it, but I could not help but to be persuaded. Cornelius was mesmerized by the stranger, and I could tell that he believed it too.

"Citizens of Giltlegard," continued the stranger, his voice now like a whisper on the wind. "I am the bearer of terrible news. The reason you are deceived is because this city is the only life that you have ever known. You only know what you have observed, and you have only observed that which you see every day. But I have been sent to you

53

today by the King of Port Fectia to inform you that there is more that exists beyond these walls, more to life than you have ever known. The problem is, dear citizens, that you are prisoners here, and you will never know the other life of which I speak."

With those words, the stranger disappeared into the shadows of the fog. We, on the contrary, were left with the terrible knowledge of our own helplessness. The Ponderers themselves were speechless. They were left in the courtyard of the temple with nothing but their white robes and gray beards and their own thoughts, and they did not even attempt to contradict the stranger's words. Suddenly, the happy city of Giltlegard was not so happy anymore. And me, Cornelius, and no doubt every other citizen who stood trapped not only within the confines of the great wall but also within the thick mire of bodies, longed for something more than what we had experienced for so long. We longed for something beyond the wall.

CHAPTER SEVEN
THE PANDEMONIUM

There are some moments in life that seem as if they occurred only yesterday. These moments are so profound, so life altering, that they burn an impression upon your brain, upon your memory, like a hot steel prong upon your skin. This was one of those moments.

I remember it as if it was yesterday because it seemed to go on forever. There we were, the entire population of Giltlegard, crowded together on the steel streets, knitted together like a large quilt, knitted so tightly that you were warmed by the breath of those around you, so many people yet so alone. We were irrevocably alone.

In the silence, I tried to find reason to doubt the revelation. He was only one man, I thought. He was a stranger. Why should we believe him? Even if it is true that we are trapped inside the walls, what difference does it make? Why could we not go on living as we always had? It was not that bad, I assured myself. Yet, for some reason, once enlightened to the truth, no matter how terrible it is, it becomes impossible to return to old ways. Any attempt to ignore the revelation would be merely contrived, and it seemed to me that to force one's self to live as if the revelation did not exist would be more torturous than conceding to the hopelessness of knowing.

I looked around. Suddenly, the steel was really steel, cold and hard. The fog was really fog, thick and gray. A chill crept over my skin, causing me to shiver, and I knew it had been there all along. It seemed darker than usual, but it was not. The light from the tip of the factory was actually just as dim as it always was. I began to panic. Suddenly, the eternal silence was broken by panic. There was a panic throughout the city. There was a pandemonium.

In a flash, like the switch of a light, the union of bodies was dispersed into fragments of insanity, darting in every possible direction.

The only thing Cornelius said was, "My mother!"

Then, in a ball of fury, he was off.

"Wait for me!" I cried, but I realized that if I did not want to lose him, then it was up to me to stay with him.

We wove our way in and out and around and through the pandemonium and passed droves of frantic people, mourning or hurting or wailing or desperately trying to run but whose pelzors weighed them down. The factory was empty of its workers. I kept an eye out for my father as we ran. The market square was in shambles, blown through by an army of lunatics. As we passed by, I caught the glimpse of something horrifying outside Mr. Gilactus' fruit stand, but we had no time to stop. People were collapsing all around us, but we would not help. Others lay prostrate upon the cold, steel floor of the city, trampled upon, beaten down, lifeless, already forgotten. Around every corner of every street on which we turned waited another tragic story. Children were left alone to cry in the street. Many were trampled underfoot by crazed Giltlegardians. Many were left to die. I saw old ladies and old men throwing themselves off of rooftops, the spirit of living having left them, splattering their bodies upon the steel ground.

People were dying all around us. Some men were fist fighting in the street as a desperate means of retaining the pride that had just been torn from them by the words of the stranger. Others were looting homes or robbing women or creating general havoc in the streets out of madness and vengeance. Death seemed glamorous no longer.

Finally, we reached the Van home. Cornelius did not even break stride, exploding through the front door with the force of ten men. When I arrived but a moment later, he was already upon the floor, hovering over his mother's shivering, crawling body. My stomach sank at the sight of her helplessness.

"Mother, what are you doing on the floor?" Cornelius cried.

"Must-g'out," she whispered, "Must-scape. Words-ter'ble." She was still trying to crawl toward the door.

"Heard-voice. Fright'ning. Too-ter'ble," she continued. I had to strain my ears just to hear her over the wailing noises outside.

"Am-prison," she moaned, "Dear son-help-scape." Her tired voice faded. She closed her eyes. We carried her back to her bed and laid her down.

"I know, Mother. I heard it too," said Cornelius calmly. "We all heard it. The whole city heard it. It is terrible news, I know. But it is madness outside, Mother. You cannot go out there. It's too dangerous."

It took all of her strength just to open her eyes again. "Need-out! Need-scape! Hor'ble-city! Get-m'out! Need-scape!"

In her sickness, Mrs. Van was obstinate and brave. Kneeling beside her bed, Cornelius took her hand in his and gently squeezed. Her eyes closed again. She smiled faintly.

"Son-my son. Get-m'out." She trembled. Even in the warmth of her bed, she trembled. I could barely stand the sight of her. "Bed-feels-hard. Steel. Never-so hard." Cornelius looked upon her with compassion. His eyes were deep and loyal and good, but his heart was breaking, I could tell. I saw that in his good, sad eyes.

"I will, Mother. I will get you out, but not yet. It's too dangerous right now. You need to stay here in our house where it's safe. Understand? I will find a way out of here. I promise. And when I do, when I make it beyond the Great Wall, I will find the truth. I will find the medicine to make you well. I will come back for you, I promise, but right now, you must stay in the house. Understand?"

Cornelius spoke with calm confidence, and I believe that he meant what he said. Mrs. Van rested. Her trembling ceased, but she labored with every breath.

"Your father...loves me. Does...truly. I wait...for him. Will come."

Cornelius could not bear to answer. He situated her blankets and kissed her forehead and pulled from his sash the flaming sideon which he had bought and placed it in her hand, folding her fingers around the stem. He made sure that she had ample food beside her and bid her farewell. We left the house together to the sound of her pleading, desperate voice.

We had no time for conversation. Chaos was everywhere. We ran together. We had no direction. We just ran. Again, we passed the market square, and I remembered what I saw earlier.

"Van, over here!" I led him to Mr. Gilactus' fruit stand. There, on the ground in the doorway, lay a chubby lump of flesh. It was Mr. Gilactus' body. He had a noose around his neck. I turned his face to look upon him. His head was so flimsy that I thought it might roll right off of his shoulders onto the ground. His eyes were wide open with fright. I spoke up.

"He was still hanging when we passed by the first time. Someone must have cut him down."

"Poor man," said Cornelius, "I guess he couldn't bear the burden. The weight of those pelzors must have caused his neck to snap like a twig."

I shut his eyes. I removed the noose from his neck and pulled his body inside the store and left him there. His shop had been ransacked. All his fruit was missing. He certainly did not deserve that, not that way. I almost felt sorry for him. At least now he would not have to listen to the cries.

As we scoured the market square, the carnage was breathtaking. Every shop had been looted. Many merchants lay dead on the street. Most people were clearing away from the center of town. They were headed toward the Great Wall. We spotted Pattick's shop, and headed there, stepping over and around dead body after dead body. Some were stabbed to death, others beaten, others suicides like Mr. Gilactus. Arriving at Pattick's, we were afraid of what we might find inside.

We found something inside, for sure, but it was not what we anticipated. It was Heel and two of his conspirators. They did not hear us come in. They were busy procuring as much merchandise as they could carry.

"Where is Pattick?" asked Cornelius.

Startled, they spun around and dropped everything that they had so carefully obtained.

"How should we know?" came the reply.

"Since you have your hands all over his things, I thought maybe you might know where he is." We started to move in closer toward the back of the shop.

"Look Van, I don't want any trouble. I'm just trying to survive here. You know, like everyone else. What? I bet you have the same idea, don't you. Look at all this stuff. I bet you'd like to get your meddling little hands on this stuff, wouldn't you? I know you, Van. You came in here with the same idea I had. Let's not bother with each other, now. Look, I take what I want and you take what you want. I'll even let you have first choice. I don't want any trouble now. What do you say?"

"Heel, it's madness out there. What am I going to do with this stuff?" Heel was visibly on edge as we approached. His partners flanked him carefully, watching, waiting for us to make a move, but we did not.

"Then I suppose you won't mind us going back to our business, will you?"

Just then, from the corner of my eye, I caught a glimpse of a brawl stick. It was the new broad handled stick with the flat trunk. I nudged Cornelius, and he noticed it too. Then Heel and his gang noticed that we noticed it. Suddenly, it was a mad dash to the take hold of the stick. Cornelius grabbed it first but was immediately thumped on the back of the head by Heel and dashed to the ground. Without delay, he was back on his feet, madly swinging that stick like an ax, and his adversaries backed away. With menacing stares, they backed away. With an air of contempt, they backed away until they were completely gone from the store.

"What do you want to take?" I asked Cornelius.

He took another brawl stick, one with a barreled trunk, out of the display case and handed it to me.

"This is a good one," he said. "This is all we need."

We left Pattick's carefully. For all we knew, Heel and his gang were waiting somewhere in ambush. We walked like we were mad, our heads jerking back and forth, our eyes everywhere at once, carefully walking, studying our surroundings. We quickened our pace across the market square. Then we quickened it a little more. Then I tripped on something outside the jewelry shop that sent me sprawling upon the ground. It was the jeweler. It was the man called Pestero. He was lying on the ground, a knife in his back, blood trickling from the corner of his mouth. The strange thing, however, was that his right arm was completely torn from his body and nowhere to be found, and he had an enormous gouge in his right side. His flesh was open and seething. His bald head was warm. He could not have been this way long. He was still breathing, although faintly.

"Who did this to you?" I asked.

He tried to speak, but it was too much for him. His fingers twitched. His eyes slowly closed. He grunted. He moaned quietly. We watched him suffer.

"Well, Van, I guess you don't have to think about it," I quipped.

Then we thought, the necklace!

Inside the shop, the glass counters were shattered. Everything was gone. Everything. We tried once more to prolong any remnants of life from the fat, bald jeweler.

"Think, Pestero, think! Speak, Pestero, speak! Who did this? Who stabbed you? Who stole the cherub? Who? Who was it?"

Slowly and painfully, he lifted his head, but he could not sustain it, so I held it for him. His lips began to move. His lips began to quiver. Sounds began to form into words, and we listened ever so carefully.

"Be...bare," he mumbled.

"What? Be what?" we asked.

"Be...bare...uf...thark...uf thark."

With that, the man called Pestero drifted away.

We decided to duck into a narrow alley, away from the violent commotion, to rest and to think. The brutality upon the jeweler was too much to speak about.

We sat upon the hard ground of the alley behind the market square, resting our backs against the building, holding our brawlsticks as if our lives depended on it. The air seemed grayer than I could ever recall, and the ground felt colder. A cacophony of ill sounds echoed in the distance. I looked about at the smooth steel walls of the buildings around us and began to wonder if they were really round, or if they were even walls at all, or if they were even truly steel. I stood up and kicked one just to make sure, and pain resonated from my toes to my knee and Cornelius looked at me strangely, and I slid back down the wall onto the steel ground.

"We need to find the way out," Cornelius said.

"Did you not hear what the stranger said?" I asked. "He said there was no way out. We're trapped. Prisoners. There is no escape."

"I don't believe it."

"You don't believe that we are trapped?"

"I don't believe that there is no way out. There must be a way out. He just doesn't want us to find it."

"If that's true, then someone would have known about by now."

"No one has ever looked," he said.

"Van, you can't just pick and choose what you want to believe. If you believe the stranger when he says that we are miserable, if you believe him when he says that we are ignorant slaves, then why wouldn't you believe him when he says there is no escape?"

"Because if there isn't a way out, then there isn't a reason to live!" he shouted. "Just look at Mr. Gilactus. Just look at everybody."

"Eventually, this will die down," I said. "People will need to survive. People will go back to the factory. People will go back to the brawlball. People will live. They will live as prisoners, but they will live. They will live in the miserable experience of knowing what they really are, but they will live. They will live always wondering what could be on the other side of the wall, but they will live. Life will go on, and people will live - guilt, misery, pelzors and all."

"That's not living," said Cornelius curtly. "That's dying slowly."

Cornelius was right. Even if there really was no escape, we had to believe that there was. Most people believed that there was. If not, they would not be rushing off toward the Great Wall like so many of them were. There seemed to be only three types of people. There were those who had no hope and became resolved to that fact and therefore committed suicide.   There were those who felt hopeless enough to be distraught, but found enough comfort in their own distress to live a purposeless existence of constant misery. Those were the maniacal sorts wandering the streets aimlessly, killing, stealing, and maiming. Then there were those who wanted to believe that there was a way out and fled to the Great Wall in hopes of finding a door.

"If there is no door, no portal," Cornelius added, "Then how did the stranger get inside the walls to begin with? And if there is no escape, then where did he go when he left?"

I had no answers, only questions.

"Do you believe everything he said?" I asked. "I mean, that we have been deceived all this time; that we have never known the truth about ourselves?"

"I think it's self-evident," he replied. "I didn't see it before, but I do now. I think he spoke the truth, all right. And since he spoke the truth, that which was once hidden now seems clear...sort of."

"But what is the truth?" I asked. "Isn't it possible that he's wrong? Isn't it possible that he was sent here to confuse us and to destroy us? Isn't it possible that we have an enemy out there on the other side of the wall?"

"So are you saying that you think he's false?"

I thought about that, but my own experience condemned me. I thought he was too powerful to be false. He was too powerful and too awesome. He spoke with too much authority. I could not deny his power. Yet, I was not certain. I wanted so badly to be certain, but I conceded my doubt.

"I suppose not," I admitted. "I think he's probably genuine...I think."

"So we agree then. That's a start. The next thing to do is find our way out of this prison."

"Van?"

"What?"

"What do you think Pestero was trying to tell us?"

"I wish I knew. I wish I knew who took the necklace. It could have been anyone."

"What is be bare uf thark?"

We thought for a moment.

"I think he meant 'Beware of Thark'," suggested Cornelius.

"Thark? Who is Thark?"

Suddenly, a loud cry penetrated the alley. Its sound rose above the sounds of death. It was the sound of deep sorrow. We looked, and at the far end of the alley, in the middle of the street, was the figure of a girl kneeling. She was bent over upon her knees, her head in her hands, weeping and wailing. The cry was frightening at first, and then pitiful, a contrast to the cries of desperation which rose up from the rest of the city. It was the cry of caring. It was a lamentation. As we watched, the wailing died into a whimper, a most simple form of sadness, yet no less powerful. The figure knelt and cried and buried her face and her hair fell down upon the steel street. Curious, we went to her.

"You there, why do you cry that way?" Cornelius called out as we approached. She did not answer, nor did she look up, so we watched her. We clutched our sticks and studied our position in case it was a trap, and we watched her cry. She wept softly. I remembered that I had heard that cry before. Commotion boxed us in on every side. People fought. People screamed. Men, women, children, it did not matter; the hopelessness bit one and all. People beat themselves and others, running into walls and gouging at their own skin. There was no sanity in that place except for this one girl kneeling and crying, her long hair hiding her face.

"What's wrong?" we asked. "Why do you cry this way?" Head down, buried in sorrow, she pointed. There, in the direction of her gesture, a man lay bloodied on the side of the street, beaten. As we approached, it was obvious that he was dead, trampled upon, and Cornelius recognized him immediately.

"Bloody Pattick!" he gasped. He looked at me, saddened. Then he looked as if a light had been turned on in his head and immediately rushed back to the girl.

"Aza-liel?" he asked.

63

CHAPTER EIGHT
THE ESCAPE

The girl looked up. Sure enough, it was Aza-tiel. She wiped her face, smearing her tears. She rubbed her eyes, and she forced a smile. She smiled like she had finally found a friend. Cornelius pulled her to her feet. She wobbled and stood.

"Ouch!" she squealed. "You hurt me!"

"Come along," Cornelius demanded, clutching her arm. "This is no place for a lady. We must get you out of here."

The three of us hurried away, just like everyone else, not sure exactly where we needed to go, but going nonetheless, headed toward the Great Wall.

We passed the tree where we earlier had fought. Sure enough, the bodies of the guards were still there, but they no longer hung upon the tree. They were mere lumps of flesh, discarded, utterly ignored, lying limp upon the ground. Someone had taken the knives that held them up, letting the bodies fall. I could not even look at my victim lest the feeling of guilt haunt me worse than I was already haunted by the words of the stranger. Then, as we hurried past the sorry scene, my eyes caught the sight of something much more terrible, and I knew to where the guard's knives had disappeared.

Upon the ground sat a man whom I recognized. He was my neighbor. Around him were his two sons and his daughter. They were tending to him. Behind him was his wife. She looked away from him. She was screaming, her hands to her face, distraught, terrified. The man was blind in one eye, and for that reason he had been rejected by the factory. He earned his keep by sweeping the city streets. They were a poor family, that much I knew, and I realized that I had never before cared to know him. His sons were no older than ten, and his daughter was not much older than they, and they were dirty most of the time and hungry. Never had I shared with them a hello nor looked upon them longer than I felt comfortable. The thought of my indifference caused me to feel shame in addition to my guilt, and I hated them for it. I despised that poor family for bringing to light my true nature, and I despised the stranger for doing the same. I thought how much easier it had been only a short time ago when actions had very little consequences.

However, the horror upon which my eyes had fallen lay not in the way this family made me feel about myself, but rather, in what they were doing to themselves. The man's wife could not bear to watch as her eldest son took hold of the knife and sawed away at his father's shin, just above his ankle. The boy had tears in his eyes. The father clenched his fists and his jaw in agony. His daughter wiped the blood away with her dress. The boy grew weary and passed the knife to his younger brother and he finished the job and the man's foot fell from his leg onto the ground, his pelzor still attached. He screamed and he bled and he offered his sons his other foot, and reluctantly they took to sawing that one as well. His wife could not bear the sight, but the sounds of the man's agony shook her to the thralls of despair, and she threw herself upon the ground and beat the ground and then sprung back up and seized the knife from her son and began cutting her husband's leg herself. Then, as if utterly possessed, when she had finished that job, she started in on her own feet. The children backed away from her insanity.

No matter what one's reaction to the terrible news of the stranger, I think all Giltlegardians had one thing in common - they realized that their own perceptions of what was real were probably false perceptions. That kind of revelation is shocking. It is shocking to suddenly realize that everything you always believed is false. It is depressing to realize the truth about yourself. It is even more depressing to realize that a better life lies just out of reach and that you will never be able to grasp it. The words of the stranger kept haunting me, those words which said, "You will never know that truth which lies on the other side of the wall."

With this revelation, one's primary burden was to individually search for this truth. The news affected each one personally. Suddenly, people felt alone. The truth was that we were really alone all along, the difference being that now we felt it. But we did not merely feel it – we knew it. Since the terrible news affected each person individually, the quest for the truth became an individual quest. Each person felt the need to experience this other world for themselves. If not, a person could not rest. That was the new state of affairs in our once happy city. Each person needed more than anything to somehow get themselves on the other side of the wall. It was this dilemma that caused the pandemonium.

As we wandered aimlessly on the outskirts of the city, headed toward the Great Wall, I noticed how the dull, grassy fields had been trampled under a million disoriented feet and I could scarcely even find a piece of ground to call my own. The wall was saturated with desperate bodies huddling together at the foot of the wall like insects in a cage. Some tried to find a secret passage by feeling the wall as if their hand would strike against some secret panel so that the wall would open up into freedom. Some worked together to climb the wall, hoisting one another upon their shoulders, climbing up one another's backs, forming towers and pyramids, but it was futile. The pelzors were too heavy and the wall was impossibly high and I realized how easily people lose their rationality under desperate situations. In the same way as I had witnessed my neighbors doing, others tried cutting off their feet and mutilating themselves. Some, out of desperation, chopped down the trees in order to create battering rams in an attempt to knock the wall down. The confusion went out from where we stood. It extended miles around the entire city, on all four walls. There was no section of wall not touched by the miserable search for freedom. Despite all the effort, cries of desperation echoed relentlessly throughout the land, pounding at my brain like a hammer. The three of us stood befuddled by the loud insanity. I had never felt more helpless than I did at that moment. I had never felt more trapped. I had never felt more panicked. I began to think that death was the only way out. Then Cornelius had an idea.

"What if there really is a way out," he suggested, "But it's not at the wall?"

"What do you mean?" I asked.

"What if the way out is somewhere in the sky, or under a rock, or up a tree?"

I looked at him in a funny way. I figured his desperation was affecting his rationality as well. Aza-liel giggled quietly.

"I'm serious," he said.

"Van, the wall is here. It's all around the city. We need to get to the other side. How is that going to happen by climbing a tree?"

"Listen," he explained. "Maybe the way out isn't the obvious way. Maybe we need to look where no one else is looking. Maybe the way out makes no sense at all. After all, with everything we just learned, isn't it possible that maybe the way out of this place is hidden somewhere outside of our senses?"

"You're crazy," I replied.

"But what if it's true?"

"What if a lot of things are true? Does that mean we should waste our time investigating every possible scenario when the true way out of this place could be right in front of our faces?"

"Look around, Os. Where is this truth in front of our faces? Besides, time isn't going anywhere. It can't be wasted."

Cornelius was right. Although I could not accept his idea that our true escape would be found by way of the absurd, I had to agree with him that certainly it was not going to be found by way of the obvious.

"What if there is no way out, like the stranger said?" I asked.

Suddenly, he turned crass.

"Then go kill yourself. As for me, I'm going back to the city, and I won't rest until I find the way out of this place. I refuse to be a prisoner here any longer, Os. My mother's life depends on it. Come on, Aza-liel. Let's go."

Together, they left. I watched them go. I stood for a moment. I watched them some more. He did not look back. He walked on. He walked on with Aza-liel. They came to the streets of the city. I hesitated, but then I went. I ran and caught them. He was my companion. He might have been crazy, but he was resolved, and it was that resolve which I always admired. I needed that. So we entered the city together.

"So what now?" I asked.

"I don't know," he answered. "Just look around."

We looked around and we looked around. We walked on, and we looked around. Just like he said, we looked. There were the same buildings and the same houses and the same brawlball arena. The factory still stretched to the sky, and the streets were still as steely as ever. The streets turned their familiar directions and the Ponderers still pondered in paths of eight in the courtyard of the temple with their long gray beards and flowing white gowns and pointed black hats. We stopped to watch their activity. They pondered as if nothing had changed. They meandered about with the same sagacity they always had. Heads down, they pondered. They were not frantic. They were not upset. They looked as if they were in complete control. Then it struck me. What appeared to be serenity was really purposelessness. For them, nothing had changed. Their lives were just as meaningless now as they had been before the stranger arrived. They were meaningless all along. For them, the courtyard was their prison and their pondering was their escape. We moved on in the mayhem.

We crossed the street in front of the social house when a familiar voice called out to us through the crowd. "Cornelius! Cornelius!" We looked around us, but there was too much confusion. "Cornelius!" it cried again, "Cornelius!" The call grew louder and closer, but we still could not see. Suddenly, emerging from a cluster of frantic people in front of the social house was Mr. Van.

"Cornelius, my boy, I'm so glad I found you. I'm so glad you're alive."

He tried to embrace his son, but Cornelius pulled away. His breath smelled like liquor. His hair was frazzled. His clothes were tattered. He was a pathetic sight. He resembled a beggar more than a father, but Cornelius let him speak.

"Son, I've been home. Your mother. She's safe in bed. I just thought you would like to know that."

"You're drunk," replied Cornelius. "How could you drink at a time like this? You probably didn't have to worry about the price this time, did you? Have you finally had enough? The world as we know it is over and all you can do is hide out and drink yourself to death?"

Mr. Van mumbled incoherently. Shame fell like a shadow on his face. He was saddened, then speechless, then embarrassed. At that moment, the father was intimidated by the son. Mr. Van wanted understanding, but Cornelius gave him none at all.

"What's the matter, Father? Have you nothing to say?"

"I-I...I just needed a little drink, that's all. I just needed a little something to clear my head. I'm so confused, my boy, so confused."

"I was going to kill you today," said Cornelius.

Mr. Van lifted his head from the ruins of his life and looked directly at his son with wide eyes and quivering lips.

"But I suppose it will have to wait," Cornelius continued. "Now is not a good time."

We left Mr. Van standing stupidly in the cold, steel streets. For once, I pitied the poor man. I thought maybe we should bring him with us if we ever found a way out, but I did not dare suggest it to my friend in this instance for I still valued my own life enough not to risk it for foolery. As we turned a corner onto a crowded street, the desperate cries of, "Cornelius, don't leave me alone!" faded into the bleating of the city's deathly demise and suddenly Mr. Van was no more.

To this day I never understood the coldness that Cornelius showed toward his father at that moment. I knew he was serious when he said he wanted to kill him, but maybe I thought that in the current circumstances he would forget. Cornelius' only interest in that moment was for his mother's health. Not for his father. Not for Mr. Gilactus or anyone else he might know. Not for the children dying in the streets. Not for Aza-liel. And I began to doubt if it was even for me. I do not think it was even for himself. It was for the interest of his mother that he wanted to escape. It was for the sake of a better life that he thought by going back into the heart of the city that somehow he was going to find us a way out of that horrible place.

Then it happened. We hurried aimlessly back through the market square and down one alley and then another, the whole time just looking around and looking around. We found ourselves in an alley on a side of the brawlball arena, the opposite side from where we were used to sneaking in. The alley was dark and long and we came to an opened door to a building opposite the arena. That particular door had never been left ajar as long as we could remember, and Cornelius and I had been loitering around the arena since we were old enough to walk. The door was part of a small building that once had been used by the factory as storage for steel blocks which would be melted down into various tools for the factory. The strange thing was, however, that the factory had not used that building in many years. In fact, it was vacant.

"Someone must be in there," I said.

Carefully, we peeked inside. There were no windows. It was dark. We opened the door wider to let in as much light as possible.

"I don't think we should go in," I said. "There could be anyone in there. There's crazy people all over the place."

Suddenly, a voice spoke from out of the darkness.

"Cornelius Van, come in through the door."

With that I was certain we should not enter. I backed away. Cornelius stood still. Aza-liel gripped his arm.

"Cornelius Van, you heard what I said."

"Who are you?" Cornelius asked.

"Cornelius Van, come in through the door."

"Let's go," I said.

"No, wait. I need to find out who it is."

"It could be a trap."

"Who would be trapping people at a time like this?"

"Crazy people. Desperate people. People like Heel and his gang."

Against my advice, Cornelius took a step inside. He stood in the doorway looking inside. It was dark as night. Aza-liel stayed back. I rushed forward to grab him, but he pushed me aside.

"That voice," he said. "Listen to that voice."

"Come forward, Cornelius Van. Come in through the door."

70

Cornelius stepped all the way through the doorway, lured in by the voice. Aza-liel and I followed closely behind until we were all inside. The darkness enveloped us, the only light dimly sneaking in through the doorway behind us, but it was a weak light, the light of a dark alley.

"Identify yourself or I will leave immediately," Cornelius demanded.

"Close the door," said the voice.

"Not a chance," Cornelius replied.

"Close the door," said the voice.

"Who are you?" Cornelius asked.

"Close the door," said the voice.

I reached behind me and slowly took hold of the handle. My instinct was to bolt out the door and into the foggy light of day where at least my senses were before me, but my hand was compelled by an altogether different persuasion, and I slowly shut the door until the last glimmer of light vanished with the click of a locking door. The voice became a whisper.

"Come closer," it said. "Do not be afraid. Come to me. Over here."

We drew near to the voice. We clutched one another anxiously. We were a pod moving through the darkness. We were the only thing left for each other in the world besides this strange, compelling, familiar voice. Yes, it was familiar, but we did not know why. We clutched one another anxiously and tightly, for if we let go, we would most certainly be lost forever. That is how it felt.

"A little further," said the whisper. "Good. A little more. Now stop."

Suddenly, a light beamed in the corner of the room from the end of a rod, like a torch. A looming figure held the rod against the back wall to the left of where we stood. From what I could see, the ceilings were high, and the room was smallish and empty. The door we entered was behind us, and there were two others; one straight ahead of where we stood and another to the right of the entry door. The

71

figure was almost as tall as the ceiling, cast in the shadows of his own light, his face still hidden in the darkness.

"Tell me who you are and what you want with us," Cornelius bravely demanded.

"I am the one that you are looking for."

At those words, I knew who he was. His voice was familiar indeed. It was not as booming as when we first heard it, but it was just as forceful. The figure approached us in the darkness and his face shone in the light of his rod and my suspicions were confirmed and he was tall and his hat was tall and feathered and nearly scraped the ceiling as he moved. He was the stranger. He was a frightening sight, to be sure. He was flamboyant in his cloak and his sash and his skirt and his boots. He loomed over us like a steel pillar. We melted in our very bones at the sight of his presence, and Aza-liel let out a short squeak as he approached. Immediately Cornelius threw himself prostrate upon the cold, steel floor.

"Arise!" the stranger bellowed, and Cornelius obeyed. "Cornelius Van, I happen to know that you turned away your own father when he was in need. I was afraid that might happen. But no matter. Here you are. I have other ways to accomplish my purposes. I suppose you would like to escape this dreadful place. Come, sit down."

He led us to the back corner where three chairs were situated, and we took them. We dared not speak lest we incur his wrath. Anyhow, we had no words.

"I am not your enemy," he assured us. "I am but a messenger. I speak the truth, something of which you have never known until now, and there is still so much more to learn. There is but one way out of this city, and I have come to reveal it to you. But you must be prepared for a great and difficult journey. Who is willing?"

"I am willing," said Cornelius fervently.

"So am I," I said.

Then the stranger leaned forward and took a long look at sweet Aza-liel. She was but a child before him, not more than an infant. She seemed so innocent. She seemed so frightened.

"And who might you be, young lady?" he inquired.

"A friend," she kindly answered.

The stranger studied her in the darkness, like he was surprised to find her there, like he was not sure what to make of her.

"These boys rescued me when my brother died."

The stranger did not seem fully satisfied with her answer. He looked at her long and hard. He studied her face. He studied her eyes. He held the rod of light close to her body in order to study her in the darkness. Aza-liel barely moved. She moved only her eyes as the stranger looked her over, her eyes darting frantically in every direction, like a cry for help, like an uncomfortable situation, yet she remained brave. Finally, the stranger returned to the shadows of the corner.

"Well, then, young lady, are you ready to encounter a great and difficult journey?"

"I am, sir."

"Good, because for those who escape this dreadful city, an altogether different kind of world awaits them."

I could feel his presence even more than I could see it through the darkened room and the solemnity of his voice impressed me as did the rigidity of his chin when he spoke.

"The journey is one in search of the truth. You have been deceived for so long," he continued. "It is a journey to the village of Port Fectia. There, you will find the King, and you will find truth. Beyond the Great Wall, freedom awaits. But there is something else which awaits. Something deeply evil. Something strongly infectious. Something waiting to capture your mind and your will. It is called the Realm of the Unbelief. It is they who conquered Giltlegard long ago, and it is they who desire to conquer Port Fectia as well. They will seduce you, and you must resist. Are you afraid?"

"No Sir," Cornelius answered, once again flinging himself onto the steel floor at the foot of the stranger.

"Stand up, foolish boy!" ordered the stranger. Cornelius again scrambled to his feet.

"You are a brave boy, young Cornelius. But you are still but a fool, too easily enticed by your own passions. Be careful, young man, or the Realm will use it against you. They will devour you along with your zeal. Pay attention now. This is your journey. The King has called you. Remember, I am but a messenger. Now sit down."

The stranger turned his attention toward me. "Osgood Esemblion," he said.

"I'm here," I answered, trembling with fear.

"Osgood, you have been invited to accompany your friend in his quest for the truth. You are to serve as his eyes and his ears. You will be a true companion, lest you also slip and fall into the clutches of the Realm. Do you understand?"

"Yes, Sir," I replied eagerly. "I will be honored."

Finally, the stranger turned his attention back upon the flower girl.

"Young lady."

"Yes?"

"I am not sure what your intentions are with these two young men, but you are here nonetheless. What is it you seek?"

"I'm just afraid, Sir."

"Do you know how to love?"

"I am sure I do, Sir, but I have lost everyone I love."

"Love is a dangerous yet rewarding venture. Your love will be much needed. Are you prepared for that?"

"I am not quite sure what you mean, Sir."

"Do you love? Do you love even after your loss? Do you love these boys?"

"I'm just afraid...I'm afraid."

"In your case, young lady, time will surely reveal what questions never will. I will allow you to accompany these young men on their journey. But you must not cause them trouble. You must be a helper to them. This is a great and difficult task. Do you understand?"

"Yes, Sir." Even in the darkness she beamed with light. "I'm sure I can do it."

The stranger seemed to turn to himself at that moment, as if he was trying to conjure some distant memory. He turned his head upward and emerged from the shadow and breathed a deep and lasting breath. I heard nothing but the troubled sound of his breathing and those horrible, hopeless cries of misery coming from the streets of the city, now little more than a droning in my ear. The rod of light cast its simple gaze upon us, but the darkness was too imposing to feel truly safe, even at the foot of the stranger. He spoke as a friend, but I could not help but wonder how trustworthy he really was. Then I realized that the issue was not so much whether or not he was trustworthy, but whether or not we were willing to trust him. Were we really willing to trust this so-called King whom we had never met? The stranger kept his eye on Aza-liel and seemed to be preoccupied with her being there. I sensed her nervousness. She grew restless, sitting politely, so sweetly. I wondered if she loved my friend. The stranger seemed to imply as much. As he studied the expression on her face, we dared not speak out of turn. The stranger made his way to the door at the back of the room across from where we sat.

"Stand," he commanded, so we did.

"Before you go," he continued, "You must learn what you need to do. I will not send you beyond the wall without direction. I will not leave you to yourselves to find your way in the world, for if I did, you would surely be devoured by the many enemies which lurk along the path. You must trust no one that you meet along the way. Trust not even yourselves. Trust only my direction. Do not accept gifts of any kind. Do not make allegiances with anyone outside your party. Believe only what is true. Believe nothing which is false. Travel away from the Great Wall, toward the sea. That is west. The mountains will be to the north, and the orchards to the south. Keep Giltlegard behind you, to the east. Remember loyalty, honesty, and self-control. Travel only along the ponds and meadows. Avoid the roads. Stay away from the mountains. And remember that very little good happens in the cities. Port Fectia rests against the sea, nestled in a bed of lush fields of exuberant colors. You cannot miss it, for there is nothing more beautiful in all your imaginations. However, you must first enter a cave of dead bones. It is near the village on the north. It is the only way into the community. Remember these words, for I come with the truth. Cornelius, approach, for I have something for you."

75

As Cornelius went to him, the stranger removed a sheath from his sash containing a magnificent sword. Amazed, Cornelius pulled it out of the sheath to examine it. It sparkled at certain angles in the light of the stranger's rod. Cornelius proudly fastened it to his own sash, opposite his brawl stick and baton.

"You will need that," the stranger said, "But bear in mind that the day will come when victory will be found apart from the sword. Osgood, come forward."

I stood next to Cornelius as the stranger presented me with a horn and a canteen.

"Osgood, this horn is to be used as a warning against danger. Use it wisely. The canteen is to be kept full from the water in the ponds so that you may stay fresh and alert."

Next, he beckoned to Aza-liel, and she came to him. He placed a wreath of flowers upon her head.

"Wear this," he said, "As a reminder of faithfulness and restraint. Let your beauty be evident from within, and refrain from vanity. Then you will be of service to your friends." Aza-liel wore it gladly upon her brow, a fitting gift for a flower girl.

"Go now on your journey," the stranger continued. "Escape this dreadful place. Leave the sounds of misery. Be deceived no more. Find rest and peace and truth. Find it well, and heed my words. Know that what I say here is true. Cornelius, do you see this door behind me?"

"Yes," he replied.

"Then open the door and be free."

Cornelius hesitated. He was not sure as to what the stranger meant. Neither was I. How could we be free to embark upon our journey unless he showed us the way out of the city? Surely he could not have expected us to believe that by opening up a door inside of a dark, steel room in the middle of the city that we would end up on the opposite side of the Great Wall. But, despite the absurdity of it all, Cornelius nevertheless opened the door, and after one last glance at the stranger, we entered through the doorway, and as we did, I realized why Cornelius, and not I, had been the chosen one for the journey,

76

because it was Cornelius who had enough imagination to believe such a crazy notion, and it was Cornelius who thought that maybe, just maybe, the way out of the city would be found up a tree. And although it was not up a tree that we went, it was through a doorway in the middle of a dark, steel room, and as we entered through it, we arrived on the opposite side of the Great Wall, with an entire world all around us and the stranger nowhere in sight.

CHAPTER NINE
THE OTHER SIDE

Suddenly, the world was quiet. Suddenly, there was peace. It was a strange sound, this quiet was. It was not silence. It was just quiet.

The Great wall stood just as profoundly as before, yet Giltlegard was worlds away. We were really on the other side. I looked behind me to find the door, but there was no door. There was no more gray. Except for the wall, there was no more steel. There was no more chill. There was no more fog obstructing our view. I ascended the wall with my eyes as far as I could see, but instead of disappearing into a haze, the wall seemed to disappear into a bright, blue sky. I was so small beneath it. The brightness of the new world pained my eyes after being in that dark room. It took me a few minutes to adjust, but when I did, I was awestruck.

We stood atop a small knoll. We stood in a shadow cast by the Great Wall. The shadow extended as far as the eye could see, angling south, as the stranger called it, for it stretched across a great formation of orchards. Before us, to what he called west, sprawled meadows vast and vivid. The green grass was rich and ripe and accentuated with fascinating colors and sprinkled with flowers and trees and I wondered if that was what truth looked like. Strange creatures flew across the sky like winged darts, calling out to us with the sound of a whistle. In fact, the world was littered with sounds. Sweet sounds. Quiet sounds. The sky seemed to sing with sounds. The trees made their own sounds, like a rustling, like a lullaby. Even the grass whispered beneath our feet. I reached down to touch it. It was soft and alive, a drastic contrast to the dying landscape on the outskirts of Giltlegard. It called to me, so I lay down. I stretched my legs in the coolness of the grass. It was softer than any bed I had ever laid upon before. Freedom, I thought.

Freedom. How could I have ever doubted? I listened carefully to the sounds. I tried to listen for the sounds of Giltlegard. I tried to listen for the sounds of clanging pelzors. I tried to listen for the sounds of wailing misery, but all I could hear was quiet. I sprang to my feet and went to the wall. I put my ear close to the steel and listened. I heard something faint. It was but a murmur. It was the cries of Giltlegard drowned out by the thickness of the wall. I could hear something if I listened hard enough. It was but a light buzzing in my ear, but it was definite. I began to feel pity for the ones we left behind.

"Oh! Isn't it wonderful?" exclaimed Aza-liel. "It is so...so...wonderful! Oh, look at it. Just look at it!"

I found a blume tree close by. Its branches were heavy with fruit, each one twice the size of any blume I had ever seen. I took one and ate. Its flavor was richer and sweeter. Its juice was more abundant. It drizzled down my chin, and I plucked another from the tree and ate some more. It caused me to think of Mr. Gilactus, and I pitied him as well, not only because he was dead but because of all the fruit he ever sold, not one was as satisfying as these. I pitied him because he was a fruit man and as a fruit man he had never experienced the true pleasure of fruit.

"Van," I said, "Come taste these blumes. They're delicious."

There was no answer. I turned to look, and my friends were gone. I spotted them a little way down the knoll. They had emerged from the shadow into the fullness of the light. They were looking westward, pointing at something in the sky. I ran to join them.

"Look, Os, it's a rainbow!"

Sure enough, it was. We could not take our eyes off of it. It started at the base of the mountains to the north and rose and arched and stretched across the sky, descending and disappearing into a cluster of trees to the south. It was a sight to behold. A yellow streak dominated the bow, but a bright orange and red faded into the yellow and an assortment of blues and purples blended together below the yellow. I never believed it could be true. I let my eyes move from the rainbow to Aza-liel, and her countenance was just as bright and her smile was big and proud. She was so lovely that I thought she could have been a child of the rainbow.

"Do you think it's a sign?" I asked.

"Of what?" replied Cornelius.

"Of Port Fectia, of course. The village is supposed to lie over there somewhere. It's like a sign pointing us in the direction that we're supposed to go."

"Maybe."

"Maybe? That's all you can say is maybe?"

"Maybe."

"Well, we need to find this Port Fectia. I think we should just start walking and see where we end up. That's west, toward the rainbow, so let's follow it."

"Maybe. The stranger didn't say anything about a rainbow."

"But that's west. I know it is. And it's beautiful. There are probably all kinds of rainbows in Port Fectia. This is the direction that the stranger pointed us in. This is how we were facing when we stepped out of the city. So let's go straight ahead and just keep on walking."

I sat down in the soft grass and closed my eyes, trying to rehearse the words of the stranger. I could not imagine that Port Fectia could be any more beautiful than where we were. It was warm there in the cool grass. It was enveloping warmth, like arms around you. I realized how cold I had been for all those years. I opened my eyes. The trees seemed to go on forever. I looked up and was nearly blinded by what I saw. In the sky, where the top of the wall intersected with the bright blue expanse, was a great ball of light. It sat like a beacon atop the Great Wall. The wall must end, I thought, for there is certainly light above it. The ball of light was magnificent. I could not gaze at it for more than a moment without my eyes being scorched by its brilliance, but there was no doubt that the light came from somewhere over the Great Wall and was casting the enormous shadow at an angle to the south.

"Van! Van! Look at that! Look at the light! Up in the sky!"

80

I looked about, but my friends had once again deserted me. I stood and looked and spotted them. They appeared but the size of pebbles in the distance, chasing one another back and forth across the fields. I heard laughter in the distance and shouts of joy and the sweet, vibrant singing of Aza-liel. There was a sparkling light shining in the meadow near where they played. Aza-liel skipped along toward the light and disappeared inside of it. I called to them, but they were either too far away to hear me or they paid me no attention.

I went toward them across the fields. As I approached, I saw that the sparkling light was but a reflection upon the water. There, in the meadow, was a great pond, and the water sparkled in the light of day. Aza-liel was bent over the bank of the pond drinking when Cornelius came up alongside of her and together they drank. The water was pure and undefiled, unlike any water I had ever seen. Cornelius noticed me approaching.

"Os! It is about time you showed up. Come taste this water. It's perfect!"

I came to the pond, and I drank. I drank and I drank. I cupped my hands together and lifted the cool, pure water to my mouth again and again. Then I abandoned that method and bent down with my face in the water and drank directly from the pond. Aza-liel giggled and ran away. Cornelius chased her down, tackling her in a bed of tall, purple flowers. I could not help but smile. Cornelius was not the type of boy to fancy himself so quickly to a lady, but I think that his new found freedom conjured his giddiness. Aza-liel was very pretty. Although she was mostly soft spoken, she seemed to bask in attention. I could not forget the manner in which she behaved toward the man she called Pestero, acting like a spoiled child. She was still young, I supposed. I supposed also that we all are flawed in many ways. I thought that if she could become a spring of laughter for a hard, bitter boy like Cornelius, then maybe she would prove to be a valuable asset to our journey. Maybe that is why the stranger allowed her to accompany us. However, it was also apparent to me that it was not intended for her to be here, at least that is the impression I received from watching the behavior of the stranger. He seemed hesitant in allowing her to come. I wondered why.

From the bank of the pond, I watched my friends frolicking about the purple flowers. Aza-liel wrestled away from my companion's grasp and raced off, but Cornelius ignored her and came to where I was sitting. Aza-liel called to him, but he did not answer, so she pouted and occupied herself amongst the flowers of the field, picking them and basking in the rays of the natural light and singing. Then she looked up and discovered what I had already found, the ball of light in the sky atop the Great Wall, now in the distance. The ball of light appeared large and powerful.

"A star!" she shouted. We all looked, but it was too bright to gaze upon.

"A star," I said to Cornelius.

"Imagine that," he replied, "A star."

I filled my canteen in the blue, sparkling pool. Cornelius lay beside me in the tall grass. The meadows screamed with an array of colors. Aza-liel went around picking flowers and identifying them in song. Pink crotes, blue and white sideons, red fuzzles and golden daggels. She made up a song about them all. She was a flower in her own right. She was the loveliest of them all.

There was so much to say that I did not know where to begin. I had so many questions that I could not articulate them coherently. We just sat together like we used to do under the tree by the Great Wall in Giltlegard. Although a day had not yet passed since we last sat together under that tree, it felt to me as a lifetime ago. We sat together and said nothing. Cornelius drew his sword and admired it further. He ran his finger gently over the blade and drew blood. It was sharp as a razor and beautiful. I looked all about, but there was no sign of civilization as far as I could see. I concluded that our journey must be great indeed. We watched Aza-liel play and skip about and sing. We liked her song.

"You know what?" Cornelius asked, finally breaking the silence.

"What?" I said.

82

"This is nothing like what I imagined on the other side of the wall. I guess, deep down inside, this is what I hoped for, but I could never imagine it, not in a lifetime. I always pictured it as more of the same, only without walls, without a factory, and without pelzors. I never imagined that a world could exist with so much...so much..."

"Beauty?" I said.

"Yes. Beauty. That's it. I never imagined a world with so much beauty. I'm not sure what to make of everything the stranger said, Os, but I think that I like this place. Look at it. If it wasn't for my mother, I'd be tempted to say that we build ourselves a little home right here in the meadow, or maybe somewhere close by, and just live. But I'm convinced that there's a healing potion for my mother out here somewhere. There has to be, and I will not rest until I find it. In fact, I think we've been wasting time long enough."

Restless, Cornelius started heading west.

"Come on, Aza-liel, it's time to move on."

Aza-liel dropped her flowers and sprinted on ahead, her dress kicking up and flowing in the breeze. Cornelius darted after her. When Aza-liel saw him chasing, she changed direction, stumbling as he approached. Then, as she fell, Cornelius tripped over her rolling body and they rolled together and laughed. I must admit, I began to feel a spark of jealously rising within me, and I immediately recognized it, and I squelched it right away. I smiled again at my two friends as I left them to play, continuing westward toward the sea. When they realized that I was moving on, they caught up to me, and together we walked along the ponds and meadows in the direction of the rainbow until the great ball of light shone directly above us and continued its way southward, slowly, across the sky. It was funny how the farther we traveled toward the rainbow it always stayed the same distance away. Finally, it faded and disappeared altogether. Eventually the great ball of light did the same, ducking behind the orchards to the south, and a tinge of darkness began to set in. To the north lay a dense forest, so we decided to establish camp near a pond on the outskirts of the woods.

The darkness was different than what we were used to. It came slowly and was incomplete, and there were lights in the sky. Aza-liel explained that those are stars because that is what her grandmother told her. I disagreed and said, "Then why are they so much smaller than the star that fell in the south?" She explained that stars come in all different sizes and distances. She supposed that the great star must have been much closer than the others, but I was feeling disagreeable so I asked, "Then where did the great star go? Will there ever be another daylight? Must we wait for one of these distant stars to approach before we are able to see again?" She did not know how to answer that, so I was satisfied. She knew so much about a world she had never seen before, all because her grandmother told her so that I was pleased to finally confuse her. However, when I considered the consequence of my question, it gave me no comfort to think that we may have no more light to bring forth the day. At least in Giltlegard, another day of light was as sure as another day of fog.

We gathered some sticks and, after some trial and error, built a fire. We ate lumpkus we had gathered earlier off the trees. They were even more savory than the blumes. We sat together, warming ourselves as the night grew darker and colder. But even the cold was not as cold as the bitter air of Giltlegard. I thought about the people we left behind. I thought about my mother and father and brother. I wondered if they were still alive. I thought about my neighbors who were mutilating themselves and about the dead bodies scattered throughout the market square. So many were dead, yet here we were. We were allowed to escape. Were we really any better than the rest? I thought about Mr. Gilactus and how we stole from him when he was alive and now that he is dead, we are allowed our freedom. I thought about the man called Pestero. I wondered how he met his own fate.

"Van?" I asked, "Who you think Thark was?"

"Thark? Oh yes. Whoever he was, we don't have to worry about him anymore."

"Yeah, that's for sure."

"Thark?" asked Aza-liel. "I don't understand."

"Thark is the one Pestero..." Then I caught myself. Cornelius looked at me. Aza-liel took interest.

"You saw Pestero? Where? What did he say? How was he? Did he have...?"

Aza-liel stopped short of asking what we both knew she was trying to ask.

"Pestero is dead," Cornelius answered.

"Dead?" She seemed surprised, yet pleased. "Did you..? I mean...You really..?"

"No, Aza-liel. We certainly did not. We found him. He was just about to die. He told us to beware of Thark."

"Thark? Who is Thark? Well, no matter. But if Thark did kill him, then I owe him my gratitude. Me and my grandmother both."

I thought to change the subject.

"Well, Van, I assumed you were crazy, but I guess you were right. Imagination isn't so worthless after all."

"Even so, there's something that's been bothering me all day. I mean, I love the feeling of being here and the fields and the fruit and the water and all the creatures scampering everywhere, but I'm not sure that this freedom thing is necessarily right."

"Why not?"

"Well, for starters, how do we really know that the stranger spoke the truth?"

"He said he did, for one thing. He said 'Know that what I say to you is true'. Remember?"

"Oh, so you're his apologist all of the sudden. Earlier you were trying to say that he was false, and now all of the sudden he can say no wrong. Make up your mind, Os. Anyhow, I agree with you that we need to find this Port Fectia place..."

"Then what are you trying to say? I mean, we're here aren't we? Just like he said."

"True, but that's not convincing enough. The only thing I'm sure about right now is that I was a prisoner in Giltlegard, and now I'm not. But I'm still not sure I really know anything about myself or where he's even sending us. I just need to find a cure for my mother and get back to her as soon as possible. If I can find the cure in Port Fectia, then great. Let's go there. But if not, then show me where it's at. That's why I'm here, to help my mother. I guess I just don't want to grow to love my freedom so much that I forget about her, that's all. I'm sure if we find this King, whoever he is, then he will have the answers. But then again, that's only if the stranger told us the truth."

I understood what he meant. I felt it too. Just because we were freed from Giltlegard did not mean we knew anything for certain, but I had grown to trust the stranger.

"I think that we have no choice but to listen to the stranger," I said. "After all, he helped us escape."

"But that's the whole point, Os. It wasn't long ago that we were saying what a happy life we had there. Then all of the sudden, we want to leave just because some strange man comes and tells us how bad we are? Think about it. That in itself is absurd. But the odd thing is that once he said it, it made sense. I understood. And the whole city understood. And we listened, and here we are. We listened to a stranger, and now here we are, away from home, and we suspect that we're free from the life we thought was so happy not even a day ago. That's why I'm more confused than ever. I thought we were supposed to find what was true out here, and I'm only growing more confused."

"That's why we have to find this village, Van. To find the truth."

"I don't think my mother has that much time."

A small voice piped up across the flickering flame.

"What is truth?" asked Aza-liel.

We looked at her, this little thing in the starlight, boldly speaking from out of the fire. I could not gather where she found the audacity to speak her opinion being that the only reason she was there with us was that Cornelius saved her from danger and she happened to be with us when the stranger called. We continued to warm ourselves, the flames casting a familiar glow, reminding me of the dark room where we left the stranger. Why did the stranger not come with us if he wanted us to find Port Fectia, I wondered? Surely, he could have led us there. My mind grew as tired as my eyes, but my belly was as full as my wonder. Since Aza-liel was not rebuked, she continued.

"I think maybe we should forget about Port Fectia. I wouldn't be surprised if it didn't exist."

Immediately, Cornelius and I erupted in laughter. We were sure she was joking. She smiled, but looked offended.

"Who told you that?" Cornelius said, "Your grandmother?"

That sent our laughter to another level. I tried to stop, but could not. The smile faded from Aza-liel's face. The fire became a chasm between us. She looked as if she would cry, so with an effort, we subsided. We took a moment to catch our breath.

"How can you say that?" Cornelius asked. "What proof do you have?"

"I have no proof, but what proof do you have that it does? You've never seen it. All you know is some fable about it. What happens when we arrive at this place and find out that it's not really there at all? Then what? Have you even considered that?"

"What are you suggesting, Aza-liel?" Cornelius asked.

"Please, I don't mean to cause trouble, but you speak of Port Fectia as if it is a particular place..."

"It is," I replied. "It lies by the sea to the west."

"What I am suggesting is that we put the past behind us and find our own truth here in the present. Our old life has passed away. My brother whom I loved has passed away. I watched him die a terrible death. This is a new world. Can't you see? This is the truth. I agree that we have to find the truth, but maybe the stranger brought us here to forge a new truth - to make our own Port Fectia near our own sea."

"You speak blasphemy!" Cornelius cried.

"Wait just a minute," I said, "Earlier, you said yourself..."

"Never mind what I said earlier! It means nothing. That was before I...Just never mind."

I thought about what Aza-liel said. I understood her concern. If we trust this stranger, and it turns out that he himself has deceived us, than we are worse off than before. We are no freer than we were in Giltlegard. Our walls might be gone, but our reason for living would elude us. We could never be sure of anything again. If we reach our destination, and it proves false, then we will only be the worse off for it because we would maintain the weight of the misery without the hope of peace.

Cornelius's temper, however, flared like the fire.

"Explain to me, little girl, if you be so smart, how it is that this little plan of yours is going to keep my mother alive? Tempt me not, for you are but dust to me. I will not have such nonsense in my presence. Maybe you feel no weight upon those dainty little shoulders of yours. Maybe you think that because you know all about the sky that you have no need for solid ground, but I for one, won't have it. I will not go around all day picking flowers and call that freedom. The stranger's words lay heavy upon my head. His words crushed me back there. Even though we have left the prison, the prison has yet to leave us."

"Cornelius, please, I only meant..."

"Aza-liel, you don't seem to understand. My mother is dying. I need to be alone. I need to think."

Cornelius marched off into the darkness of the woods. Aza-liel watched him walk away. Quietly, she began to cry.

Aza-liel spoke well for a flower girl, almost convincingly. Still, I felt we had no choice but to heed the words of the stranger. Without his direction, we would be completely lost. We had to at least see for ourselves if it was true.

"Oh Cornelius," she cried, "Don't be upset. I'm so sorry. I was just thinking out loud."

She called for him, but he did not return.

"Let him go," I said. "Just let him go."

Crying, Aza-liel ignored me and followed Cornelius into the woods and disappeared into the thickness of the trees. After a while, after her cries faded into the night, I realized that I should go after them in order to satisfy my concern.

CHAPTER TEN
THE DARKNESS

The forest grew denser the farther into the woods that I ventured. The starlight vanished behind the tops of the trees until I could barely see five paces ahead.

I called out to the others but with no response. I was not comfortable venturing this far from the meadows, but I could not leave my two companions in the forest alone. Where could they have disappeared to so quickly in such a dense, dark forest? It was Aza-liel's fault, I thought. The stranger specifically warned her not to cause trouble, and she had already succeeded in driving Cornelius away in frustration and challenging his faith - not the kind of helper I imagined the stranger had in mind. Before long, as I plodded through the darkness and brambles, I doubted if I could even find my way back to the camp fire if I were to try. Furthermore, I felt like I was not alone.

With every step I heard the patter of someone else's feet around me. With every breath I felt the breath of someone else upon me. But I could no longer even see my hand in front of my face. I groped my way like a blind man without a cane, as I had left my brawlstick lying somewhere near the fire. I heard sounds like the chattering of teeth. The threat of the unknown haunted me and the darkness became darker with each forward step. I felt tree trunks and branches, thickets and leaves brushing my face. My hand would touch them or my feet would bump them and I would shuffle around them and smack into some other obstacle. I felt as if I was moving about in one constant location. The forest seemed to grab at me as I pressed on. Then, as I groped in the darkness, I felt other things, things quite unlike trees and branches and thickets and leaves. I felt warm things, moving things, living things. I wanted to turn back, and I would have if I thought I could find the way, for I knew not whether I had already traveled ten paces or one hundred. My toes inched forward, leading my feet. My arm extended straight ahead, leading my fears. I wondered if I would soon step off the edge of the world. That is how dark it was. The chattering of teeth continued until I wondered if it was my own teeth. The pattering of feet continued until I wondered if it was my own feet. I heard the rustling of leaves. I felt something wet crawl over my fingers. Tree branches, pulsating and twitching, prodded my face as if they were alive, as if they were mocking me. Where were my friends? Had they escaped the horrors of the unknown which ensnared me? Or had they been captured? If the latter was true, I certainly could not leave them alone in such a place. To do so would be cruel.

Suddenly, what felt like a slimy hand grabbed at my neck and startled me into a yelp. I flailed my arms about me. I must have been spinning around. I lost my sense of direction completely. I felt trapped and suffocated. Someone or something was unmistakably about me, but I could not see who or what it was. I tried to control myself. I stopped moving about and stood as still as I could and experienced that feeling synonymous with imminent death. The chattering increased and whispers joined in. I knew then that I had more than one visitor. I was trapped more completely than I ever was in Giltlegard.

"Who's there?" I asked. I waited. No response. "Speak or let me be. Let me pass. I need to find my friends...whoever you are...they're lost."

The chattering and whispering and heavy breathing were joined by a symphony of slurping and gargling, intensifying at the pace of my beating chest. I was touched and prodded. The slurping and gargling was in my ear. Whatever it was closed in upon me, it being no farther from me than my own limbs. I needed a light, but all I had was the horn that the stranger had given me, strapped across my shoulder. Of course! The horn! Not knowing what else to do, I took hold of it and blew. I blew loudly and forcefully. I turned and blew it all about me. Then I stopped and listened. I heard something scurrying away from me. The strange noises slowly faded from my ears. I was afraid to

90

move lest I entice them to return, so I glanced up into the night sky in hopes of finding a clue as to which direction I should turn, but the forest was too thick to reveal even one small patch of sky, so instead I sat down upon the wet, slimy ground and fumbled around for a solid piece of tree to hold on to, and I held it like it was my only friend. I took a moment to think. I was amazed that the stranger's horn had driven the aggressors from my midst. His gift had actually saved me from the horrors of the unknown. I called out to my friends, but again, there was no reply. Again, I was utterly alone.

Just then, out of nowhere, a strong wind cut through the place where I was sitting and I needed to clutch even tighter to my dear tree in order to keep from being blown flat onto my back, but as I looked up, the tops of the trees began to part and starlight, however dim, crept into the thicket like an old friend, and I could finally see, albeit barely, but sufficiently, if only for a moment until the wind died as quickly as it had come and the blackness of the night once again enclosed about me. But the wind was a blessing nonetheless as it provided a brief opportunity to recognize my surroundings. From what I could tell, a wall of trees, with tall thick trunks ordered side by side, lay to the right of me. To my left lay a dense overgrowth of smaller trees with wild branches, similar to that through which I had already passed. I decided to turn to the right and press on in the darkness toward the wall of thick trunks. These trunks were so close together they nearly formed one solid wall. I approached this wall upon my hands and knees because at chest level the branches intertwined forming a woven barrier, making ground level the path of least resistance. The slurping and gargling and heavy breathing had disappeared.

I crawled ahead, groping about as I went. I felt the wall of tree trunks. It was firm and dense, but to my left was a glow of light, a ray of hope finding a crease in the mass of trees. I followed the light. Sure enough, there was an opening between trunks, not much larger than the size of my head. On the other side of the wall of trees was a clearing. If I could just squeeze myself through the opening, I would be in a place of sight once again. My head fit through properly, but my shoulders became problematic. I found it difficult to breathe. I

91

pushed forward with all the strength of my legs, but my shoulders would not fit. My chest had difficulty expanding. I began to suffocate, so I pulled back out. Then I tried it again, this time arms first, then my head, then my shoulders. I twisted my body. I saw the light. I pushed toward it. I held my breath. My shoulders contracted. I pushed one last time and was stuck. My head poked into the clearing, but my upper body could not move, and I looked up into the clearing, and there, in the distance, kneeling before a tree stump, weeping, was Cornelius. I had just enough breath to call to him.

"Help! Help me!"

He turned and looked. He wiped his eyes. He came to me. He tugged at my head, but that proved ineffective, only stretching my neck and nothing more. He grabbed my hands and pulled me by the arms, but the tension was too great on my shoulders and I winced in pain. He stopped to rest and amused himself with my predicament, a head and arms protruding from a thicket of trees. His tears turned into laughter, but my breath was growing fainter.

"Why didn't you just go through that other opening over there?" he asked.

He positioned himself on the ground before my situation and secured both his feet upon the crown of my head. Then, with all his might, he pushed. He pushed me right back out from where I came, into the blackness of the unknown, into the smothering density of the trees.

"Go to your left!" I heard him say.

I went to my left, following the wall of tree trunks along the ground. I kept one hand upon them as a guide and the other hand outstretched as a feeler.

"Can you see me?" he shouted. "I'm poking my head through the other opening. Can you see?"

I could not see, nor could I bother to answer. I came to a thick armory of brush, but I resolved that it would not hinder my advance. I pushed my way through the brush, entangling myself severely. Thistles scourged my face. My head, my hands, my side were numb and bleeding. I pushed my way toward the friendly voice, snapping branches beneath my weight and plowing through the unseen thicket like knives upon my skin. Finally, I burst through the bushes into a dim light to find Cornelius waving at me like a shadow in the darkness, his head poking through another opening in the wall of tree trunks.

He helped me into a small clearing in the midst of the forest. I collapsed onto a cool patch of wild grass, the darkness of the night still dominant, but light enough to see that the world around me still existed. I never valued the light as much as I did then. I realized that it was not my eyes which produced sight, but rather, the light of my path. I understood then that the unknown is a terrible place to be.

I laid for a while and rested. My skin burned with lacerations in many places and my joints pounded with pain, but I could see and I could stretch out. There were stumps and fallen trees and twigs and leaves scattered about the ground. The stars were visible in the sky once again. All around us were walls of wooded terrain.

"Where's Aza-liel?" I asked.

"I haven't seen her. I was about to ask you the same thing."

"But she followed you."

"I never saw her."

"This forest is a monster."

"Well, perhaps we should look for her."

"Look for her? How? The forest is dark and unforgiving. We'll never find her."

"It's not so bad."

"Did you not come from the same place I did?"

"No, I came from elsewhere."

"You didn't hear me calling for you from the thickets?"

"No."

"Did you not hear the horn blow?"

"No. You blew the horn? I never heard it."

"What about the wind? Did you feel that sudden gust of wind?"

"There was no wind, Os. Os, are you alright?"

"Van, I called for you. I blew the horn. I blew it loud. Surely you must have heard it. I was lost. There was something after me."

"I heard no horn. What was after you?"

93

"I don't know. Something terrible. A menace. This forest is a monster. You shouldn't have come in here."

"I'm sorry. I was angry."

"Van, why were you crying?"

"I wasn't crying."

"I saw you myself. You were crying. You were kneeling by that stump and crying."

"I don't know what you're talking about."

"I thought it might have had to do with Aza-liel. I was afraid for her."

"I told you I don't know what became of Aza-liel. Besides, I was crying for something else."

"So you *were* crying."

"Maybe."

"What, then?"

"It was nothing. Can't a man cry in peace without having to explain it? Anyway, I wasn't crying very much."

"I've never seen you cry before as long as I've known you. Don't tell me it was nothing."

"I was thinking about those two guards I killed. I didn't have to do that. I didn't have to kill them. It's the truth, Os. It's the truth that haunts me."

I noticed through the darkness that his eyes filled with tears. He turned from me, thinking I could not see. I grabbed onto a log and pulled myself up into a sitting position. I watched him. He was heavy with sorrow.

"Van, I know that I'm not one to tell you to be strong, but you must. You must. I'm counting on you to be strong. I need you to be strong. Don't let those things that Aza-liel said..."

"It's not about Aza-liel! Os, I'm not strong. Can't you see? I was strong in Giltlegard. That was before the stranger. I don't know what to do with myself anymore. I killed two men today. I was going to kill my own father. What does that mean, Os? If I really think about it, I'm not even worth those lives that I took today. It's not just about what's true and what's false. It's not just about what's real and

94

pretend. It's more than that. It's about me. It's about what I am. I'm a killer, Os. I think I've always wanted to be a killer for as long as I can remember. I guess I'm just crying over the lives that I took. It's just part of the misery. It's too much for me to bear."

"But they were guards," I argued, "They came to kill us. They didn't deserve to live. They tried to kill us first, remember?"

"Maybe so," he said, "But I wanted them dead. That's the thing of it. When the Stranger said that we're all prisoners, he didn't just mean in Giltlegard."

Finally, I understood. I think I was too afraid to personalize it. Cornelius was not afraid, however. He was honest with himself. That is why he was a better man than I. Finally, he stood back up, and I saw his soiled face. This time he came to me and placed his hand upon my shoulder.

"You're a good friend," he said, "But you're no different than me. That's why we're both here."

"We're here to find the truth," I replied.

"Yes, you're right. The truth. I'm afraid I've already found it. My misery is the truth. My wretchedness is the truth. Not being who I thought I was is the truth. I was going to be a great brawler. Now I realize that I'm just lost in the woods. I'm afraid that Aza-liel might be more right than we know. What if she is right? What if there is no real place called Port Fectia? All I have left is the knowledge of who I am. That scares me. I need to find that medicine and cure my mother. It's my only purpose for living."

What he said depressed me, but he was right. I was no different. I killed a man as well. In fact, I did many awful things that in Giltlegard only seemed natural. But in my heart of hearts, I could not fully concur with my friend. I just felt that there was more out there than misery. And if I did not know it, then I simply believed it. But that belief was enough for me.

"Don't stop trusting the stranger," I said. "If we believed him about Giltlegard, we should believe him about Port Fectia as well. Besides, I used the horn. It worked."

"What do you mean, it worked?"

95

"It worked. There was something awful, something around me, something..."

Suddenly, a terrible shriek pierced the darkness like a sword. It came to us there in our misery, and we heard it, and we stood still, discerning the direction from where it came. Then it came again, in horror and desperation, a cry for help in the blackness of night.

"Aza-liel!" we cried. "Hurry!"

We raced in the direction of the shrieking voice. We darted in and out amongst the trees, the starlight our only guide. "Aza-liel! Aza-liel! We're coming! Aza-liel! Where are you?"

"Over here!" she called, "On the cliff!" We followed her voice through a maze of gullies and bushes, trees both upright and fallen, across rocks and creeks. Cornelius used his sword to slice through foliage as we ran. The painful sores on my body ached with each stride. We came to an abyss beyond a formation of extremely large rocks, an abyss so black we dared not take another step forward. We heard her calling repeatedly.

"We're here Aza-liel. Where are you? We're coming."

"Over here! Please hurry! Hurry, I'm slipping! I'm gonna fall!"

We climbed to the top of the rocks and looked down over the other side. We scurried down to the place where she seemed to be. We looked about, but could not find her in the darkness. Her voice led us further ahead, over the rocks, and we came to an abrupt halt. There, before us, hidden in the darkness of night, was the edge of a cliff and another abyss as dark and unknown as the first. We saw the figure of Aza-liel, not far, clinging desperately to the root of a tree jutting out from the side of the cliff. She hung on for her life. She was but a few paces away from us and more than an arm's length down the side of the cliff.

"Help me please, I'm losing strength. I can't hold on."

"Os, here, grab my stick. I'm going down after her. Hold this end. There. Lower me down and pull us up together. It's the only way. Hold on tight."

Cornelius took the end of the brawlstick with the slapper and I took the handle. He climbed down over the edge of the rocks. I held on best I could with both hands wrapped intensely around the end of the stick. I couldn't even see down the cliff from where I laid. I tried to anchor my feet onto the base of the tree for support, but there was no use. My weight was not balanced. My shoulders, not my feet, carried the burden, and my shoulders were already nearly torn to shreds from my previous ordeal.

In desperation, I carefully switched positions. I buried my shoulders into the ground, only inches from the ledge, using one of the large, fixed rocks as leverage for my feet, my face wrenched to the side so as not to suffocate myself in the dirt. Twisted and tried, I held on like a starving boy to his bread. I would not let them drop. It was my duty.

"Grab onto me," Cornelius commanded Aza-liel. "Good. Alright. Os, pull! Pull as hard as you can!"

I did. I pulled as hard as I could, my weight inching ever closer to the edge myself. I pulled until my arms were nearly severed from my body, but I pulled nonetheless. I pulled until all the pain of my lacerated arms and face merged into the pain of exertion. Suddenly, I felt the tension ease. Cornelius reached one hand up onto the top of the cliff, still clutching his end of the stick with the other, and Aza-liel, clutching onto him for dear life, still panicked. Finally, with one last tug, my friends were safe, crawling over the top of the ledge and rolling away to safety. All three of us lay there, near the assembly of rocks, like dead bodies. We could not move. We could barely breathe. My arms were on fire, or so it felt.

Finally, after what seemed like all night, we began to move. Cornelius crawled over to Aza-liel who was only but an arm's length away. He touched her forehead. She turned her head to look at him.

"Oh Cornelius, it was awful. I was following you, and I must have gotten lost. Then, this creature came upon me. He chased me toward the cliff. I had no idea it was there. Then I stumbled. I tried to get up and I slipped off the side. That branch was the only thing that stopped me from falling to the bottom. The creature drove me there. He wanted me to fall. I'm sure of it. And if I didn't trip, then I wouldn't be here now because I would have run right off the edge to my death.

Oh. Cornelius, I'm so sorry. I'm so sorry I doubted you. I only wanted to find you. I'll never speak against you again. I promise."

Aza-liel wept softly, partly relieved and partly sorry. She ran her hand across the top of her head. "My wreath...It fell off." Cornelius said not a word, but he drew her close like a friend. He looked at me, but I could not read his thoughts. He was a broken man.

"She's right, Van," I said. "There are strange creatures in these woods. That's what I was trying to tell you. They surrounded me earlier. I couldn't see them. It was too dark. I could hear them and feel them. But I had to blow the horn in order to scare them off."

Tired, we made our way back to the clearing near the stump where I had found Cornelius. We thought it best not to try to navigate any further in the dark for we all had enough trouble for one night. We huddled together best we could like a pile of rocks and slept. Cornelius kept one hand upon his sword just in case the creatures decided to return.

CHAPTER ELEVEN
THREE FRIENDS

When the daylight broke through the trees, we awoke and made our way back to camp. I recognized the wall of tree trunks and the tightly woven branches and bushes, but light provided a fresh perspective to my earlier plight. I realized that what felt the night before as a terrible distance was not really more than one hundred paces. I recognized the place where the creatures came upon me. I noticed what looked like tracks in the dirt flaring off in every direction, and I showed the others. They seemed interested. The daylight made me feel foolish for having been so afraid. The forest was dense, to be sure, but when given sight, it was quite easy to navigate.

We arrived at camp in very little time at all. Our fire barely smoldered. Aza-liel gently cleaned our wounds, dabbing the edge of her dress in the water from the canteen and applying it to our skin. She had wounds of her own of which she did the same. We gathered our few belongings, and set out westward along the ponds and meadows.

The great star warmed our shoulders and the back of our necks. Our bodies ached, but there was joy in our steps. At least we were still together and alive. I lagged behind slightly, observing my two companions. Aza-liel made it no secret that she was disheartened to have lost her wreath of flowers. I think she felt an inadequate companion because of that. She stayed close to Cornelius's side. I think he was beginning to feel responsible for her. They were becoming a pair. She walked in the place where I had frequently walked, and it felt strange to share my friend with a girl. She was part of us now. I figured that I just needed to accept it for what it was, even though I was not quite sure what that meant. We were all supposedly looking for the same place together. I was not bothered by Aza-liel's company. In fact, any jealousy I may have had toward her was changing into sympathy. She was a good girl. Her affinity for Cornelius, though I did not understand it, appeared evident. I was uncertain, however, if he shared her regards. He appeared annoyed with her at times, like when she sang too loudly or spoke too often, but she also made him smile. She was like the light to his fog. He carried this irreconcilable guilt with him, and she made his burden a little bit lighter. They seemed at home together. I lagged a few paces behind, watching and thinking. My duty, I remembered, was to be the eyes and the ears for my friend. I was resolved to that end. Maybe I was not as dependent upon him as I thought. After all, I saw his weakness. I saw him cry. Although I, too, was aware of my own misery, to me it was not something to satisfy. I simply wanted to find the truth of which the stranger spoke. I wanted to find Port Fectia. For Cornelius, however, the journey seemed so much greater, so much more complex that I could not quite put my finger on it, something profound and personal. That was the main difference between me and him. To Cornelius, our journey was about Cornelius. To me, it was about finding this special village. He may have understood something I did not, for that was usually the case, after all.

Aza-liel, on the other hand, I was unsure about. What was she really doing there? What did she really want? Did she desire to find Port Fectia? I had my doubts. I think she just had nowhere else to go. Although I enjoyed her company, I had difficulty trusting her intentions. I tried pushing those thoughts to the deepest regions of my mind in order to concentrate on her virtues. She was lovable in a naive sort of way. She may have confused our journey for a vacation, but that made me feel comfortable. Her long, chestnut hair blew in the breeze as we walked. Her dainty nose wrinkled up in the sun. Her eyes glistened. She was as happy as the morning was bright, a sight to behold. She had a tendency of running off through the meadows and picking flowers. We called, "Hurry up, Aza-liel. You're slowing us down!" She picked so many flowers along the way that she almost needed her flower cart from Giltlegard just to carry them all.

We walked all morning, stopping every so often to fill up the canteen. I wanted to make sure we had plenty to drink. The waters were as pure and clear as the sky was blue and tasted exquisite. We were three friends, together. By mid-day, the great star radiated waves of heat, but the breeze kept us cool. To the north, the mountains loomed across the horizon. To the south, endless meadows and scattered fruit trees decorated the plain. There was no sign of the sea. There was no sign of civilization, either.

We did find creatures, however. They were quite tame, nothing like the mysterious intruders in the forest. Smallish, four-legged furry creatures chased each other up and down the bountiful lumpkus trees. Sometimes they would scurry to the ponds and take a drink and scurry back to the shade. There were larger animals, black and brown in color with stubby legs and crooked backs and wrinkled faces grazing together in groups. They also went upon four legs. We were unable to observe them closely, however, for as we approached, they rushed off in the orchards to the south. Some other creatures flew about the sky with proud wings and noble colors, landing upon the branches of the trees and taking off again, making a spectacle of their speed and skill. These creatures provided entertainment. Aza-liel was enamored with such an array of beauty and vitality that her sense of wonder provided another source of entertainment altogether. Her joy was contagious.

These are the things I remember thinking about as we walked together.

We continued on until the heat beat down upon our heads to the point that we rested ourselves under a shade tree, eating fruit and sipping pond water from the canteen. Our surroundings were as beautiful as I could imagine. I had trouble imagining how Port Fectia could be any prettier.

"We've been traveling all day," Cornelius said. "I don't see the signs of civilization anywhere. Not a single building. Not a single person."

"Well," I responded, "The stranger didn't say how far we had to travel. I suppose this journey could go on for days or even weeks. I wouldn't be surprised. After all, he said that it would be great and difficult, didn't he?"

"I believe he did."

"These lumpkus are wonderful, aren't they?"

"Delicious."

"Yeah, 'licious," mumbled Aza-liel, her mouth stuffed full. Juices ran down her chin onto the collar of her dress.

"Yuck," Cornelius said, turning away.

Aza-liel giggled. She preferred the details in life, I could tell. It was not all the talk about finding Port Fectia and meeting the King that she loved, but it was the taste of the lumpkus. It was the sweetness in the air. It was the cool of the grass. It was the shade of the tree. It was the strand of hair in her eyes that she whisked to the side. It was the speck of dirt on Cornelius's forehead that she rubbed off. Those were the things which delighted her, and the more I watched her the more I began to understand who she was. It was the pleasure of selling beautiful flowers on the street corner that created that happiness. As I thought about it, it had not been since the episode with the man she called Pestero that she had complained about anything. So much had happened since then, though it was only one day prior. Our day seemed to extend once we stepped outside the Great Wall. It was as if a whole new day had begun.

Then I realized, as I watched her under the shade tree plucking the petals off of a golden daggle, so perfectly simple, that I loved her. I knew for sure that I was no longer jealous of her. In fact, strangely enough, I was not even jealous *for* her. It was because of the way she looked at Cornelius, her eyes fluttering like wings, her smile shy but large, that I knew she was fond of him, but I did not care. If he did not love her, then I would love her for him. That is how I felt there in the shade of the tree and the dazzling meadow. I was in love with the flower girl. At that moment, I wanted more than ever to press on toward the sea and discover Port Fectia and speak with the King, for this feeling I harbored seemed empty without fully understanding it in the context of truth and freedom.

"You know what?" Cornelius said. "I need a bath."

Immediately, he sprung to his feet and flung down his sword and brawlstick and bounded across the pasture, fumbling with his shirt and his boots as he went, Aza-liel laughing incessantly with lumpkus juice still covering her chin. Cornelius splashed into the cool of the pond wearing only his pants. He popped his head up from the surface of the clear, blue pool, and called out to us. "Ahhhh! It burns! It stings my cuts!" After a moment, his pain subsided. "Ah, that's better. Come in, the water feels great!"

Aza-liel and I looked at one another, eyes wide open in humor. I left my boots and canteen under the tree and bolted for the water, yelling as I went, but as I approached the pond, I entered cautiously and felt the slow burning upon my skin as the water seeped into my sores and cleaned them thoroughly. I kept my clothes on for I thought they needed every bit the washing that I did. After a moment, as I waded in up to my neck, the coolness of the pond began to sooth my skin like a healing element and I relaxed. We began splashing and playing and wrestling about. We laughed and we wrestled and we laughed some more, dunking one another with wild fury like the boys that we were. During this time, Aza-liel had slipped unnoticed into the far end of the pond among some tall, green, wiry stemmed plants which grew up out of the water and bathed herself quietly. When we finally noticed her, our revelry came to an immediate halt. We felt embarrassed and looked away, for we were gentlemen after all.

Then, something extraordinary caught my eye. Off in the distance, in the midst of the meadow, was a beast unlike any I had ever before seen. Its silky brown coat glistened in the daylight. It went upon four legs, its head held high.

"Look," I said.

Cornelius and I watched as it grazed upon the pasture, so noble and so strong. Yet I was afraid. Could that be one of the creatures which haunted me in the forest and that tried to drive Aza-liel off the cliff? Could it be that such a bold and beautiful beast is really nothing more than a monster? Quietly, we crept out of the water onto the bank of the pond. The creature did not notice us. We left Aza-liel in the water and moved slowly to get a better look. As we approached, the

103

beast did not look up but rather called out with a sound unknown to us. This caught Aza-liel's attention from the water, and she gasped. At that, the beast shook his great head and bellowed a curious, flapping grunt in our direction. Then his gaze fell upon us, and we stopped. Suddenly, another beast emerged from behind the first. The second was slightly smaller in stature but just as amazing. Its coat was a lighter brown and it had a strip of white from its belly to its chest and upon its nose. We dared to move closer. The beasts were not afraid. There is no doubt they were aware of us, yet they barely moved. They stood proudly in the light of day. Were they challenging us to a duel? We could not be sure, but Cornelius, who was always thinking, had a bold idea emerge from his dangerous brain.

"What if they're friendly?" he said. "What if we could master them and ride upon their broad backs to the place where we want to go? Wouldn't that be ideal? We could rest easier, and we could arrive faster. I'm sure, with four legs, they must travel at least twice as fast as we can, don't you think?"

His idea was bold and exciting. I nodded, and we cautiously went forward. Aza-liel had emerged from her bath and watched from the bank of the pond, her hand covering her mouth in either fear or astonishment. The beasts stood like statues upon the ground, strong and dignified, but that grunting sound which they made seemed altogether too similar to the slurping sounds that I heard in the forest. However, I trusted Cornelius as I had so many other times in the past. As we came to them, I expected them to speak, but they did not. They simply grunted. Neither did they run away. Cornelius reached his hand toward the larger, and it did not even flinch. He touched its coat. He stroked it. It made that strange noise and then it grunted, but it did not run. It stayed. It let Cornelius touch it. He stroked its back and its head. Its eyes were large and brown and trusting. Bravely, I went to the smaller and cautiously touched its side and its back. Its coat was smooth and soft, its muscles defined.

Suddenly, Cornelius stepped back a few paces to get a running start. Without as much as a word, he ran at the beast and sprung forward into the air and grabbed hold of the beast's sturdy neck, whipping his legs over the top of its back, and he mounted it. Just like that, he mounted it. There he proudly sat atop his beast, like a king himself, like a conqueror, and the beast never moved. It let him do it, as if it was there for him, as if it was waiting for him all along. After he mounted, the beast rose up, standing majestically upon its hind legs, hollering that crazy cry, and crashing back down with such powerful force that it shook the ground upon which I stood.

Cornelius motioned for me to try my own mount, so I did. I stepped back from the smaller, and just as I had seen my companion do, I ran and lunged forward into the air, kicking my feet to the side, but my distance was lacking. I fell unfortunately and awkwardly from the air to the solid ground at the foot of my failed conquest. I heard Aza-liel giggling uncontrollably from somewhere behind me. Cornelius laughed at my incompetence from atop his success. Everyone mocked my failure but the beast. It grunted and looked toward the horizon, but it did not laugh and it did not move. I got up and scowled at Cornelius, and I tried it again.

This time, I started farther back so as to gain more speed. When I leapt, I leapt higher and closer; and this time, when I landed, I managed, just barely, to kick my right leg over the back of the beast, clutching feverishly to its broad neck, pulling myself to the mount, and there I sat. It was a struggle, to be sure, and I knew that I would have to practice lest Aza-liel think me a fool, but I conquered it nonetheless. The beasts responded to our direction. We nudged them slightly forward, and away we went. We guided them down to the bank of the pond where Aza-liel stood, fully dressed, holding the rest of our clothes in one hand and some of the long, wiry stemmed plants in the other. Her wet hair glistened like her smile.

"What in the world have you done?" she exclaimed. "And what in the world are these beasts?"

"They are cherubs," Cornelius insisted.

"Hardly," Aza-liel explained.

"Then I will call them brownbacks," Cornelius replied. "They will carry us to Port Fectia."

"They're beautiful," said Aza-liel, "But there are only two of them and there are three of us. Should I run behind?"

"Come here, I'll help you," he said, "In exchange for my clothes."

She handed us our belongings and we dressed ourselves, balancing atop the brownbacks. Cornelius took her arm and gently helped her. She took her place on the back of the beast behind Cornelius, clasping her arms around his waist, sending a slight, sinking pain to my stomach which I promptly ignored, and together we rode away, the great star still beating down, but with a breeze more forceful than before. The brownbacks needed little direction. In fact, they more often than not guided us instead of the other way around. They seemed to know where we wanted to go, so we let them lead the way. They traveled much faster than we anticipated, so fast that they seemed to carry eight legs instead of four. Aza-liel looked proud as she rode, her hair flying with the wind, her face perfect, and her singing calm and sweet.

We traveled in that manner for three more days, stopping along the ponds, eating the fruit, and camping out under the light of the stars and the shelter of the trees. Still, we had failed to come upon civilization. We were growing weary of the daily routine. The brownbacks carried us well and fast. I called mine Danger Foot because upon his back I felt invincible. Cornelius called his Magic Healer as a reminder of what he was looking for. Aza-liel explained that she believed that the stems she carried from out of the pond were dandy root, a healing herb in which Cornelius immediately took interest until Aza-liel explained that they had the power to heal wounds by rubbing them on the skin, but not the power to heal sickness. Still, the dandy root gave Cornelius reason to hope for a cure for his mother. Aza-liel used the stems to fashion a new wreath for her head. We traveled with relative ease. The journey already seemed quite great, but difficult it had not yet been. In fact, we journeyed so well that we began to question the wisdom of the stranger. Nobody mentioned it, but since we had gone three days upon our beasts without even a hint of civilization, doubt began to creep in, at least a little bit. Still, we pressed on and after another three days of riding and talking and doubting and Aza-liel holding on to Cornelius even tighter than before, things began to change.

CHAPTER TWELVE
CIRA MAIN

Upon the eighth day of our journey, as the great star had moved over half way to the south, our canteen was almost empty, and we had not come across a pond or a fruit tree since the previous evening. Aza-liel was tired and thirsty. She was having difficulty maintaining her balance as we rode.

"Can't we stop?" she complained. Her voice was barely audible. "I'm afraid I'm about to faint."

Her arms slid off of Cornelius' waist. She almost fell off of Magic Healer, so Cornelius came to a halt. We had become much better riders by that time. He turned and grabbed Aza-liel to keep her from altogether sliding off. I dismounted and rushed over to catch her fall, guiding her gently to the ground. I put the canteen to her lips, and she drank down our last drops, lying like an invalid in the thirsty meadow. She was practically incoherent. We positioned the brownbacks between her and the great star in order to create some shade. The meadows that only yesterday wove their colorful schemes across the landscape had somehow turned brown and parched. There were no more flowers either. Trees were sparse. Water sources were nowhere to be found. Aza-liel moaned faintly. Her eyes were heavy.

"We can't stay here," Cornelius said, "This is no place for a camp."

"But we can't go on with her like this," I replied. "I think we need to stop for a while and let her rest."

"No way, Os. We must go on. Let's lay her across my lap. She'll be fine there. We need to find some more water and a better place to camp for nightfall."

I helped lift her and lay her across his lap. The meadow seemed vast and endless. The great star was on its way downward, so it brought some comfort knowing the air was growing cooler, for the heat of the day was more than she could bear. Suddenly, our new found freedom did not seem quite as perfect as it had originally seemed. Cornelius was right. That was no place to set up camp. However, I was worried about Aza-liel. Who knew how much farther we had to travel before we would find any water, food or shelter? Cornelius took her in like a soldier. I noticed how she lay limp, folded over on her stomach in front of his lap. She made a few unintelligible sounds from her lips, parted and cracked. Her skin was reddish and dry. Did Cornelius care for her out of duty or out of love? I wondered. It was difficult to tell. He did not seem to get annoyed with her as often as he used to, if that was any clue. He was already accustomed to a kind of servitude in caring for his mother so I suspected that he probably took a measure of pity upon Aza-liel, and because he was so kind-hearted toward those in need, he naturally gravitated toward helping her. I, on the other hand, was not so matter of fact. I wanted to take her upon my own brownback, Danger Foot, and lay her across my own lap, not merely as an act of loyalty, but because I wanted to nurse her back to health the way she had done for us. I wanted her to finally open her eyes and to see only me and smile. Then I got an idea.

"Van, wait."

I took the wreath from her head. It was wound tightly, well fashioned. I pulled it apart. I took the long, wiry stem and pricked it. Some fluid oozed out. It was mostly dried out from being in the heat, but not completely. I put it to her lips, and she weakly suckled the vine.

"Great idea, Os." Cornelius watched intently, no doubt eager for the outcome. If the dandy root proved effective in restoring Aza-liel's strength, then he knew that he was that much closer to finding a cure for his mother.

After the first stem was dried up, I tried another, then another. I went through the entire handful of stems which Aza-liel brought with her, putting each one to her lips and letting her suckle them and when she grew tired I squeezed them into her mouth until there was no more left. It was not a lot, but it was something.

Cornelius was pleased. "Let's go," he said.

Whether or not Cornelius felt love for Aza-liel, I did not know. What was clear, however, is that he felt responsible for her. He acted as if she had been entrusted into his care. To Cornelius, responsibility was a serious thing. Furthermore, Cornelius had always been proud. Life was a game, a challenge. I thought that maybe in the case of Aza-liel that he did not like the idea of losing an admirer. I think he secretly liked the attention, therefore, he bore with her. He certainly cared about her. He enjoyed her company and her affections, but I did not think in a million years that he would ever want to make her his wife. But I did. I told him that the last time we lay together under the tree at the foot of the Great Wall. Who was I, anyhow? This was not my journey. What I felt meant nothing. I was but eyes and ears. That was my own duty. I may not have been as principled as Cornelius, but I knew enough to not linger where I did not belong, especially when it came to my best friend's pride.

We rode on into the latter part of the day as quickly as possible with Aza-liel unresponsive. Cornelius barely said a word. He was determined to find water, and I knew he would not stop until he did, even if it meant traveling all night. The sweltering heat slowly subsided as the great star closed in on the horizon, forming a pink hue over the dulling sky.

Then, just as darkness began to descend from afar, Cornelius proved himself right once again.

We raced up a hilly incline and came to a sudden stop on a large summit overlooking a plush valley and civilization. I was beginning to think that we were the only three people in the entire new world. There, decorating the valley like a picture, was a city. We paraded down the slope in excitement. It was farther than it seemed. Aza-liel opened her eyes slowly. She murmured something quietly. She began to stir. Darkness fell gradually upon the mammoth oasis, and as we approached the boundary of the city, I brought Danger Foot to a halt, remembering a warning that at that moment seemed like ages ago but stayed with me nonetheless. Cornelius, racing ahead, noticed my hesitation and returned to question my intentions.

"Remember what the stranger said about cities?" I asked.

"If I remember correctly," Cornelius answered, "The stranger said that little good happens in the cities, or something like that. Am I wrong?"

"No, I believe you're right. He did say to stay away from the cities."

"No, actually, he didn't say to stay away from the cities. He said that little good happens in the cities. That's not the same thing as staying away."

"Van, he said that because he wants us to avoid the cities. Why would he tell us that little good happens there if he didn't want us to avoid them?"

"By his saying that little good happens there, he implied obviously that some good happens there. So why should we avoid the whole thing altogether if some good can come out of it? Look at the girl. She needs attention. She needs water. We can help her. Then we'll leave."

We had arrived at an obvious disagreement. We needed a place to stay, it was true. It was also true that Aza-liel needed attention. She needed water. She needed food. We all did. She continued to stir. The air was cooler. Though she was still weak, the dandy root appeared to be active within her. She was alert with her eyes. She lifted her head and Cornelius gently, without a word, guided it back down to rest. She closed her eyes again.

I studied her. She was famished. She was ill. She needed help, but was it wise to seek that help in a place where little good happens? Was the dandy root not sufficient to keep her well enough until we came across a pond, in which case we could bypass the city altogether? Then again, who knew how long it would be until we found water if we bypassed the city? Could the stranger really expect us to follow his instructions with our companion's life hanging in the balance? Surely he would expect us to be prudent. The stranger spoke of loyalty. How loyal would it be to forsake our beloved Aza-liel just so we could say that we followed his words perfectly? Reason persuaded me to agree with Cornelius, but something terrible prodded my conscience.

"I understand the implications," I said. "I just don't feel right about going in there."

Suddenly, something like a violent spirit must have entered my friend because he spoke to me like never before, with a fury, with a fire, with his usual resolve, but with contempt.

"Are you crazy!" he cried. "Look at the girl! Do you want to kill her? Just a while ago we decided not to set up camp because we had no water. Yet you wanted to stay and rest. Now we find water, and you want to continue on. I think you have it in for her, Os. Do you want her dead?"

His eyes were fierce and grave. I wanted to punch him because he dared question my intentions toward the girl, but I did nothing but concede.

"Yes, you're right," I said meekly, "Let's go in."

Without further delay, Cornelius started Magic Healer into the city with Aza-liel draped across his lap like a blanket, and I followed. Nightfall arrived. Though darkness enveloped the land, the city lights burned bright and activity brewed all around us in mighty contrast to Giltlegard as we guided our brownbacks down the stony street. Looking for water, we came to a man.

He was scraggly faced and bent and filthy. He had a scar across his right cheek. He had an untrustworthy way about him. He was dressed in a baggy shirt and pants, barefoot, strings of beads laced around his neck. He carried a colorful purse strapped over his shoulder. As we observed our surroundings, it was apparent that he was not altogether unlike the others who reveled about the streets at night.

"Where's yas all goin's, if yas don't minds my askins?"

"We're looking for water," Cornelius answered. "The girl needs water."

The man studied Aza-liel for a moment before turning his attention to the brownbacks.

"Them's some pretty nice horses yas got theres, if yas don't minds my sayins so."

112

"These? I'm sorry, you must be mistaken. These are brownbacks. They are wild creatures that we discovered and tamed. They have carried us for many days."

"Brownbacks, yas say?" The man looked over the creatures like he had missed something the first time, then he smiled an untrustworthy smile. "Brownbacks, eh? Well Ize be blind if theys don't looks exactly like horses. Ize means, Ize should knows, 'cause Ize deals with horses all the times. Ize guess Ize whats you would calls a horse dealers. Ize buys 'em, Ize sells 'em, and Ize trades 'em. Yes sirs, thems might be brownbacks to yas, but thems are horses to meze."

"Horses, you say?"

"Yes sirs, horses. Come'eres."

Befuddled, we followed the man into the darkness, set just off the roadside along a rocky path. We were staring at a dilapidated structure with large double doors secured only by a tree branch laced through the two door handles. The sound of snorting and knocking could be heard. The man removed the branch and pried upon the double doors until they swung open revealing a much more severe darkness. Unsure, Cornelius clutched the handle of his sword. The man entered the shadows. We waited. He emerged leading five creatures by ropes out of the darkness and into the starlight where we could faintly see them. They were five brownbacks, it appeared. He led them back down the path to the street where we could cast a more certain eye upon them. It was true. Brownbacks they were, only they were not all brown. One was black and one was white.

"Horses," he said, "Yes indeeds, these is horses."

Cornelius and I looked at each other with astonishment and a new found clarity. We had difficulty containing our laughter.

"Horses," Cornelius agreed. "I stand corrected. Now, will you kindly direct us to some water. Our horses need to drink. So does the girl."

"Hows much moneys does yas have?" asked the man.

"Surely you don't charge a price for water, do you?"

"Yas has no moneys, does yas?"

"We have nothing at all. No money. Will you help us or not? We haven't much time."

"Ize cans gets yas some moneys. Ize deals in horses, ya knows. Ize gives yas ten coggles for one a thems horses. Ten coggles Ize gives yas. Thens yas can still travels togethers and haves some moneys too. What's yas says? Ten coggles."

The man's way was growing more untrustworthy the more we spoke to him. The way his eyes molested our brownbacks caused distaste in my mouth. Cornelius looked at me. I shook my head back at him.

"No, thank you," Cornelius answered. "They are not for sale."

"Comes now. Be reasons'ble. How's yas gonna eats?"

"We'll manage. Now, show me where I can find some water. I'm losing patience."

The man pointed down the street. "Middles a towns. There's a wells."

We turned to go, but Cornelius turned back. "One more thing, sir. Have you ever heard anything about a magical healing potion?"

The man did not answer. He looked confused. He secured his barn. He watched us leave. His untrustworthy gaze followed us as long as it could. I felt it. I felt it in the same way that I felt something wrong about this city. We found the well in the middle of the city, just like he said.

There were people all around us. It had been over a week since we had seen anyone, and now our senses were filled with the sights and sounds of living. The natives spoke strangely, just like the horse dealer. Their hair was wild and colored or they wore fascinating hats and adorned themselves in colorful clothing and beads and scarves and colorful sacks or purses. Some of them even rode upon what they called horses, just as we did. There was nothing particular happening, but the natives were loud and restless and meandering back and forth across the stony streets, entertaining themselves with laughter and drink. It was strange to see buildings made of something other than steel. They used soil and sticks and grass and wood. Some of the more splendid buildings were made from stone. Regardless of the

114

material, the craftsmanship was beautiful and creative, like nothing we had ever seen, as if purposeful design went into every cut and corner. I can think of no other way to describe it but that the city took pride in its way of life.

We rested Aza-liel on the ground next to the well and drew the water in a hurry and drank it up as if we were drinking up life. Aza-liel was too weak to drink, so we poured the water over the outside of her full, dry lips, and she parted them just enough to entertain her thirst. Water never tasted as delicious as then, being weary from the pounding of the great star, so dry and faint. We drew enough water for our brownbacks, and they drank it eagerly. Still, Aza-liel slept, but her eyelids slowly quivered with life as we sat with her. Cornelius held her upright as we rested with our backs against the well. He was conscious of her, more so than the activity around us. I got the impression that Cornelius felt like he owned her. It was strange to watch him this way.

"You weren't really considering selling one of our brownbacks...I mean horses, were you?" I asked.

Cornelius worried me when he failed to answer promptly. He looked as if he was ashamed.

"Were you?" I asked.

"I thought maybe, for a moment, that it might be a good idea. But our brownbacks have been so valuable to us. I couldn't imagine not having them. I just thought we might need some money down the road, that's all. But no, I don't think I could sell the brownbacks...I mean horses."

"Do you remember that the stranger said not to make any deals with others?" I asked.

"I guess so, but come on, Os. I mean, if we need money then we need money. If it's safe, then why not?"

"Don't you think he would have given us money if he thought we needed money?"

"We needed water, didn't we, and he let us go an entire day in the heat without it."

"Well, just don't do anything stupid," I said.

Cornelius looked sour, and turned his attention back to the flower girl. She was stirring. We gave her some more of the dandy root, rubbing on the inside of her mouth. She licked it up with her tongue.

After a while, the crowds began to disperse and Aza-liel began to move. She made no sound, but her fingers stretched and she tried opening her eyes. Cornelius cradled her like a father would a newborn, carefully, as if she was a glass vase. He tucked her head down upon his chest with one arm under her neck, and he never once looked at me. It was as if I was not even there. My heart began to break. It ached and ached all the more. It was like an illness that I felt, and I fought against the jealousy that began simmering once again inside my skin, but this time the jealousy was aimed toward Cornelius. I began to think that maybe, just maybe, he actually loved the one that I loved. His face was warm and tender. He was not himself. From time to time, he would pour more water over her tired lips or hold a wet cloth up so she could drink. Eventually, her lips parted wider and she drank on her own. She whimpered a bit and began to move ever so slightly, outstretched upon the rocky surface. The aching in my heart moved into my stomach. I wanted to grab her and hold her the way Cornelius was.

Finally, Aza-liel woke. She calmly looked up at her hero, like a child in his arms. She did not speak but rather smiled as if she was looking up into the face of a dream, and she held her gaze, so strong and yet so weak.

"Well," I said, standing up. I wanted to make a suggestion, but I had nothing to suggest.

"What?" Cornelius asked, acting as though I startled him from a trance.

"Nothing," I muttered. "It looks like she's all right."

"Yeah, so it does. We need food." Cornelius helped her to her feet, and she struggled to regain her balance.

We left our brownbacks near the well. Across the street, inside a shop, was the sound of music and laughing. Much of the revelry had since moved indoors. We went inside looking for food.

They knew we were outsiders by the way we were dressed. We wore dull, faded browns and grays and cloaks and sashes that paled in comparison to the bold, radiant colors of the native gowns and dresses and striking vests and hats. The music was so loud that I could hardly talk to myself let alone my friends. The atmosphere was festive and fun, and people sat around tables and drank and ate foods and many danced and laughed and jested.

We found three empty chairs and sat ourselves down at the bar amongst some black bearded men with rosy cheeks and red knitted hats and large bellies. They winked and raised their glasses in our direction, so we returned a friendly smile, and sat down in the empty chairs, the three of us in a row, our backs to the crowd.

"We're hungry," Cornelius announced, and in no time a heaping plate full of the most wonderful smelling delicacies we could have ever imagined was set before us, roasted and savory. It was accompanied by the strange, oblong head of an animal with crunchy, pointed ears, a round snout, and a thick, meaty brow which they called a caroo. We pulled its face apart and ravished it like savages. We searched our pockets for the last of our money and laid it upon the bar. We carried a little more than we led the horse dealer to believe. During the meal, Aza-liel quickly improved. Our bellies filled fast. The black beards mistook our hunger for a form of entertainment. Their own bellies bubbled with laughter as we ate. We must have appeared to them as lost, starving runaways, for one of them pressed us for an explanation.

"It seems that yas comes a longs way. Where's yas comes from?"

"Giltlegard," I answered. Cornelius kept his nose in his meal, pretending not to hear the question.

The jolly fellow gave consideration to the name Giltlegard. "Hmmm," he grunted, and looked at his friends momentarily before returning to the conversation. "I've heards of it. Just thems stories. It musts be fars away. I can'ts recall seens it." He looked as if he was trying to conjure up some profound thought. He went back to consult with his friends. I watched curiously as they bantered back and forth. Finally, the plump man returned.

"Hmmm," he groaned. "I thoughts about it. I knows why Ize heards it. I meets a man from thars once. I know he saids heze from thars."

"Sir, that's impossible," I replied. "No one can get in and no one can get out. It's protected. By a gigantic wall."

"Is that's so. Hmmm. Then howds yas gets out?"

"The stranger showed us the way."

"Strangers? Whats kinds of strangers?"

I wondered why this black bearded reveler was so interested in Giltlegard and how he could possibly have met any other Giltlegardians besides ourselves. I would have told him about the stranger and secret passage in the middle of the city, but I caught myself. I remembered the stranger's words warning us not to trust anyone, not even ourselves, and not to make allegiances with anyone outside of our own party, so I diverted the question.

"Who was it that you met?" I asked.

"He was a mans. A lonely, sads look'n mans. I'm sures of it. He saids was from...umm...whatevers that place you saids was."

"Giltlegard?"

"Yeahs. That's its. Heze saids heze from thars. Saids he couldn't says much more. Heze liked our brews. Wores these steels shoes. Funni'st things Ize ever seens. Could'nst walks very wells either."

Pelzors? I was speechless. Certainly a man could not make up a story like that. I was certain he was telling the truth. We were not the only ones freed from other side of the wall.

"Where's yas headin?" asked the black beard.

"Port Fectia," I replied. "Do you happen to know where that is? We've been traveling for days. How much farther?"

The man's eyes grew wide, and his mouth fell opened. He turned and nudged his partners excitedly before addressing me. A strange blush fell across the fullness of his face as he searched for words.

"Hmmm...well...uh...uh..."

"What is it?" I asked.

"Ports Fectias," he said.

"So you've heard of it?" I was quite pleased at this. At that, Cornelius pulled his head from out of his plate and fixed his attention upon the black bearded man who leaned in with a whisper.

"No, Ize nots heards of it. Ize no ideas wheres t'sat."

"Then why do you look so surprised that we want to get there, if you don't mind my asking?"

"Fer sures," he replied, "Ports Fectias the samous place thats other mans who comes from yas town was looks'n for too. Ize never heards the place though."

Cornelius and I looked at one another in disbelief, but Aza-liel, now perky and satisfied as ever, was too busy amusing herself by watching the dancers. Who could this man from Giltlegard have been? Were there others? It did not make sense that it would be the stranger, but if not him, then who?

"When?" I asked.

"Couple days go."

"What city are we in now?"

"Cira Main."

"Are the people here free?"

"Whats?"

"Are you free?"

"Don't knows whats yas talksin 'bout."

During our inquiry, Aza-liel was caught up into the food and the music and the drinks. From her bar stool perch, she lost herself in the native dancers making sport of the night in the warmth of the air. The place, this little social house, reminded me of Giltlegard in its revelry, but there was a difference. I noticed a ritual about the people. When they danced, it was not as though they danced in order to live, but they danced because they lived. It was a culture. Although in Giltlegard custom was habit, I do not believe I would call it culture. In Cira Main, there was sincerity in the way they danced. I wondered to myself if they were truly free or if they too were merely deceiving themselves, much like we had for so long before the stranger came. The activity in Cira Main was what I imagined it to be in the social house of Giltlegard, but I could not imagine Giltlegardians dancing. I wondered

119

if this was part of the truth of which we sought. I wondered if this meant that we were getting close to Port Fectia. There were certain young ladies making eyes at me as they danced, but I dared not smile, for I was not sure if that would be appropriate. The music was pounding at my ears and tugging at my senses. Part of me wanted to dance since it seemed freeing. The natives danced in rows and congregations. I watched as they spun around and kicked their legs and I guzzled a strong drink from a glass mug sitting on the bar and the whole room seemed to flash like a flickering light and the music and the dancers and the music and the food and the music pounded at my brain and I looked, and there was Aza-liel with Cornelius, and they too were dancing. And after I swallowed my heart down my throat, I walked toward them and took Aza-liel by the hand and danced with her amongst the natives while Cornelius awkwardly stood to the side until he, in return, came back to her and took her hand and danced at which time it was my turn to stand there awkwardly. Then the dancers circled around me and the room was spinning and I remember feeling trapped in that boisterous establishment and I did not want to watch my friend dancing with the girl I loved anymore so I came to him and pushed him. To this day I blame the jealousy for my act of violence and wish now that I would have controlled myself. But I did not want them dancing together anymore. Cornelius retaliated by pushing me back, and the dancers kept dancing and the music kept playing and I noticed the men with black beards and knitted hats pointing towards us and laughing again from their round bellies. I swung my fist at Cornelius and he swung his fist at me and we collided together and rolled together upon the floor through the sea of natives and the people laughed and danced around us like we were a spectacle to behold. After a few minutes of clutching and grabbing one another, we stopped and rested and looked up at the happy faces all around us. Aza-liel looked embarrassed more than anything. Gingerly, we picked ourselves up off the floor and left the social house with Aza-liel, without looking back, into the night air which stung with shame. Without a word, we made our way back to the well to take our brownbacks and leave Cira Main. However, as we walked, I noticed in

120

the doorway of a dingy place, leaning up against a rail, a shadowy figure of a man, a dark man, like a dark cloud, like a shadow in the night, watching us. His presence was so vague and dark that fixing an eye upon him was difficult. He watched us as we entered the street. He watched us as we looked and noticed, to our astonishment, that our brownbacks were missing from the spot where we left them at the well. I turned toward the shadowy figure in the night, suspecting him, and he knew my suspicions. He lifted his demonstrative arm and pointed. He pointed up the street, toward the entrance of the city, toward the dilapidated horse stall off the edge of the road. There, ducking into the cover of darkness was the horse dealer with Danger Foot and Magic Healer tied and in tow.

Immediately, Cornelius darted down the street toward the horse thief and disappeared down the rocky path and out of sight. I stayed with Aza-liel. The dark man in the doorway eyed her precariously as I drew her close and led her down the street toward the city entrance. From somewhere in the darkness we heard a shout and a crash and the tramping of feet and a cry. It was a painful cry. It was the cry of pain and desperation. I could not suffer my friend in the throes of uncertainty, so I left Aza-liel standing alone in the stony street and rushed headlong into the perilous predicament.

The predicament was perilous for one certain man, to be sure. There, as a figure in the dark, was my friend with his sword drawn and held high. There, under his weight, was the horse dealer. As I approached, I could make out his eyes. They were wide and fearful and tired and moist. Cornelius brought the sword to his neck.

"Ize sorrys, Ize sorrys. Ize didn'ts knows theys yas. Ize promise. Ize didn'ts knows theys yas."

"You knew very well they were ours," explained Cornelius. "You're a thief, plain and simple."

"Please don'ts kills meze! Lets meze live! Have mercys!"

Cornelius pressed the blade more firmly against the man's neck. He stared at the man with those Giltlegardian eyes, those eyes of fire and steel. The pressure of the blade choked the horse dealer until he found himself gasping for breath. I said nothing. This time, I merely

121

watched. I watched Cornelius strike the man on the side of his head with a fist. The horse dealer closed his eyes. He ceased struggling. He could not breathe with Cornelius's knee in his chest. I had seen it before. My friend had patience, but his patience was a very weak bridge to cross. I thought of the guards pinned to the tree. I thought of that blade crashing down upon their skull. I remembered how even I had played that game. I remembered the emotionless look of the guard as I thrust my own knife into his side. I knew I was about to witness a terrible sight.

"I have a mind to kill you right now," Cornelius growled. "You are a worthless scoundrel - a filthy, vile weight upon my conscience. How dare you steal our brownbacks. I have no use for sorts like you. You are the vomit in my bowels. I have a mind to kill you right now."

"Thens does its!" came the voice, the sound like the squeaking of a pinch from a desperate man.

Suddenly, Cornelius surprised me. He relented. He pulled the blade off the man's neck. He loosened his grip and lightened his force.

"No, I will not kill you, though you certainly deserve it. I will not kill you because I am not a murderer...Not anymore, at least. I think I will take my brownbacks and go."

With that, Cornelius left the man to grovel in the dirt. We took our brownbacks and led them out of the darkness and into the street where Aza-liel still waited. However, she was not alone. Behind her, a shadowy figure stood. The dark man had emerged from the doorway of the dingy place and joined Aza-liel in the street.

He spoke in a soft, surly manner, "I hear that you're looking for Port Fectia."

Aza-liel turned and we all waited. He was tall and powerful, and his presence was profound in the darkness.

CHAPTER THIRTEEN
THE DARK MAN

The dark man's eyes were as dark as his countenance, hidden somewhere in the shadow of his figure. He was about as tall as the stranger had been, yet more muscular, more looming and mysterious.

"If you're looking for Port Fectia," he said, "I know about it. But tell me, what business have you there?"

"We're on our way to see the King," Cornelius answered, "We have business with him."

"With the King?" The dark man pondered the thought briefly before taking a step closer, his presence hanging over us like thick fog.

"Where are you staying tonight?"

"Actually, we were just getting ready to leave town," Cornelius answered.

"It's already late," said the dark man, "It's too late to travel...Too dangerous after dark. Come to my house and stay with me for the night. I'll tell you about this place they call Port Fectia, and, in the morning, you can be on your way."

"Why should we trust you?" Cornelius boldly asked.

"Because I'm a friend. Besides, I too wanted to find the truth once."

Tired, we reluctantly agreed.

We mounted our brownbacks and followed the dark man. He traveled on foot, but he traveled swiftly with such large strides he appeared to barely touch the ground at all when he walked. He was difficult to see in the night. He led us outside the confines of Cira Main and into the darkness of a winding, wooded trail. Without a word, he kept an aggressive pace, glancing back periodically to verify that we had not strayed.

"What do you make of him?" I said to Cornelius.

123

"Don't know yet," he answered, "He seems all right though."

"There's something odd about him. Remember, the stranger said not to trust anyone."

"I remember. But we need to hear what he has to say. And we need a place to rest."

"Yeah, I guess you're right."

We went along, side by side. Neither of us mentioned our behavior in the tavern. Aza-liel, fully refreshed, rode with her arms wrapped tenaciously around Cornelius' waist, resting her cheek against his back. It was not long before we came upon a modest, dimly lit cabin atop a hill. Behind us, the sparkle of Cira Main pressed through the quiet trees. After dismounting, we followed the dark man into his musky home, where darkness mixed with the aroma of wood and simmering meat. A smoldering fire glowed from a fire pit in the center of the room. The dark man took a moment to rekindle the fire and it burned brighter. The smoke sailed mostly upward through a vent in the ceiling. Warmth soon overtook us and the flames lit up just enough to cast exaggerated shadows upon the walls. It became difficult to identify the real dark man from his shadow as he stood and faced us like an image hanging from shadow to shadow. Finally, he broke the silence with a monotone voice, sleepy and deep, inviting us to sit down and eat with him.

We politely declined because, though it smelled delicious, we were no longer hungry, and even more so, we were too nervous to eat. The dark man had a large pot cooking over the fire. He slopped some stew into a bowl and sat down across the fire from where we sat and stretched his legs across the room and entertained his appetite. His presence flickered with the snapping of the flames. We rested while he ate, studying the man through the darkness and the pulsating glow of the fire and feeling a little bit lost.

"You were going to tell us about Port Fectia." Cornelius finally said. "So you say you've been there?"

The dark man set aside his nearly devoured bowl of stew and turned his attention upon my companion. A knowing smile crept across his shadowy face.

"You waste no time on small talk, do you young traveler? At least let me have your names first."

"I'm Cornelius. This is my friend Osgood, and this is Aza-liel. We're from Giltlegard. We were sent to find Port Fectia. What can you tell us about it?"

The dark man fixed his eyes upon Aza-liel through the smoky darkness. She was uncomfortable with his gaze.

"A-za-li-el," the dark man repeated, letting her name resonate for a moment before sliding the pronunciation off the end of his palate. "Aza-liel - a lovely name for a lovely girl."

"Thank you," she replied awkwardly. She forced a smile. The dark man's flattery was as strong as his gaze, and if Aza-liel had a flaw, it was that she was a glutton for attention. Her nervous smile disappeared and she returned the dark man's gaze with fascination through the flickering fire.

"Yes, indeed," the dark man continued, "A lovely, lovely face, certainly lovelier than the loveliest of all the cherubs' faces. If you are not careful, young lady, you may be in danger of becoming a cherub yourself."

With that, Aza-liel blushed amidst the smoky haze. She smiled a proud, spontaneous smile. She smiled a giddy, embarrassed smile. She placed her hand upon Cornelius's arm, but her attention was all over the dark man.

"So now that I know you," the dark man continued, "Back to your question. Have I ever been to Port Fectia and what can I tell you about it. Well, the answer is no and many things. I never said that I've been there, but I do know much about it."

Cornelius grew annoyed. "How can you know much about a place if you've never been there?"

"Because Port Fectia doesn't exist, Cornelius. It's but a story. A fable. An imaginary world. I know. I've searched for it myself many years ago, much like what you're doing now."

Cornelius and I looked in astonishment upon Aza-liel because we remembered her planting that seed in our minds around the camp fire eight days ago. Could she have been right? She was staring heartily through the fire at the dark man.

"How do you know it doesn't exist?" I asked.

"Because I looked for it. It wasn't there. It was supposed to be at the sea with a vast array of colorful flowers adorning the hillside. Sure, the flowers are there. It's a beautiful sight. But there's no village. It doesn't exist."

"What about truth?" I asked, exasperated. "We were told we could find truth. We have been living our entire lives believing a lie. If what you say is a fact, then where are we to find the truth?"

"It doesn't exist either," the dark man responded, "At least not in the way you think. Believe me. It took a long time for me to come to that realization. I want to save each of you the trouble and grief that comes by such a journey. By the way, if you don't mind my asking, where did you learn about this Port Fectia?"

We wished not to answer that question. We were embarrassed and confused.

"Was he, by chance, a tall man? Taller than me, even? Black boots? A skirt? Purple feathers in his hat?"

"Yes!" cried Aza-liel excitedly, "That's him! We never learned his name."

"He was a stranger," I explained. "He appeared in our city and spoke with authority and told all of us that we were prisoners in the city and that we led miserable lives and..."

"And he sent the entire city into chaos." Cornelius interjected. "But I know that part of what he said was true because I know myself and I know that I was a prisoner there and that I was miserable there and that I was missing something about which the stranger spoke. Are you saying he deceived us?"

"Have you ever heard of the Realm of the Unbelief?" The dark man was intense and the darkness around us at that moment seemed to squeeze us in that place and the fire crackled like it was trying to speak to us and I remembered that the stranger had warned us against the Realm of the Unbelief and just the thought of such a thing was too much for my mind to comprehend.

126

"Yes," Cornelius answered, almost methodically, like in a daze, like in a dream. "We have heard of it, from the stranger."

"Well," the dark man continued. "That man you call the stranger? I know him as Pirnoff. He's the leader of the Realm of the Unbelief. His sole ambition is to travel from city to city and convince the people that they are worse off than they really are and to send them into confusion and make some of them, people just like you, believe that there really is a greater existence which awaits them than that of which they have been accustomed until finally they torture themselves trying to find something which doesn't exist. He calls it truth. It's a dangerous, dangerous idea. I know. I believed him once. He still shows his face around here from time to time. But this was years ago that he infected Cira Main. We've since corrected ourselves. There are very few people alive who remember him."

Cornelius looked confused. "Are you saying he's a liar?"

"I'm saying he's a bad man. Well, yes, I suppose that means he's a liar."

"But I know from experience that I was a prisoner in Giltlegard. When the stranger spoke, I felt it."

"He speaks very well, doesn't he? He speaks with great fervor. Power. Authority. I know it all very well, but don't let the rhetoric fool you."

"Why would he warn us about a group that he is the leader of?"

"Young traveler, don't be so gullible. This man is a deceiver, plain and simple. He is bent on destruction and his greatest delight is to throw poor innocents like you into confusion."

"But his speech. The power in his words. I felt them..."

"They are mere words, nothing more. Believe me. I have been there myself."

As the conversation escalated, I noticed that Cornelius was growing more and more agitated.

"But, my mother. She's dying. My mother needs a magic healing potion. Is there no such thing? Is there no hope for my mother?"

127

The dark man simply shrugged his muscular shoulders before polishing off the rest of his stew. I was presently without knowledge or belief.

Suddenly, Cornelius, striking his baton against the cabin floor, rose in a fit and a fury shouting, "Damn him! Damn the stranger! I'll kill him, I swear!" Then he rushed out the door like a madman into the night. "Potion!" he shouted, "I need the potion! I just want to know the truth!"

His cries of indignation echoed from the hilltop and faded away into the surrounding forest. I raced after him, leaving Aza-liel alone with the dark man.

There we were, a week's journey away from home, and we were completely alone. We still had each other, but I was not even sure what that meant anymore. I was not even sure if we were still friends, but I could not let him go. With all of his rage and passion, I could not let him escape me, if not for his own good, then for mine. I needed him. The night air turned cold. I could feel the trail of insanity that Cornelius left behind him as he rushed off beyond the boundary of the trees. I called out to him, but "Leave me alone!" came the reply from somewhere beyond the darkness. My once unflappable friend was frightened by his uncertainty. He was more troubled than I had ever remembered seeing him. Even when I found him, just days before, weeping in the forest, there was humility. There was purpose. To the contrary, his present despair was unruly, altogether without method. There was merely madness. I could hear him tramping back and forth in the darkness of the night, roaming furiously and aimlessly, but I could not find him. He possessed the sound of a wild animal bent on destruction. I continued calling for him, but there came no reply. The sounds of his anger faded into silence. Despite my own fears and the recollection of the last time I navigated the forest at night, I ventured down the path in the direction I thought that he had run, but I felt helpless. Where had he gone? Should I try to find him once again? Or should I let him be? He could not have traveled far without Magic Healer. I thought he probably needed time alone. He embarked upon this journey thinking that he would find the magic potion to cure his

128

mother and now he was coming to grips with the possibility that his attempts were nothing but a part played in a cruel joke against him. Finally, after a few minutes, from along the forest path, I called him again.

"The stranger wouldn't want this! Come back!"

"Death to the stranger!" came the reply from somewhere I could not identify.

"Do not lose hope, Van!"

"The stranger is a liar!"

Then there was a movement in the brush. Slowly, Cornelius emerged from the shadows of the trees and came toward me like a monster. The rage in his eyes seemed to light up his path as he walked and he came to me and I stood still and tried to calm his temper but he would have nothing of it. Instead, he spoke a dagger into the heart of our friendship.

"Don't tell me what the stranger said," he growled from behind teeth clenched. "The stranger lied to us. If I find him, I'll kill him. Don't speak of him any more lest I kill you too. I was a murderer once. I am not afraid to become one again."

I was afraid of Cornelius at that moment in the darkness outside the dark man's cabin. I trembled from my fingers to my toes for I had witnessed his wrath before. I was afraid but mostly sad, and I cried in the depth of my bones but not in my eyes, because my tears were too frozen from fear to roll down my face, but I wanted to. Cornelius left me standing there. He turned and disappeared once again into the depths of the forest. He left me wondering who was true and who was false.

I followed the path back toward the cabin and noticed a window with the glow from the fire and two figures locked in conversation. Aza-liel and the dark man were talking and he was showing her something which he held in his hand, and he was gently touching her face with his shadowy fingers. I crept closer to the window, being careful not to be seen. It was the necklace. The dark man held the necklace I swore was the same one which she admired that day in the market square. I saw him hand it to her and I saw her take it and he

129

whispered something into her ear and I ducked down as he turned in my direction. When I looked again, she was wearing the necklace. It shimmered in the firelight, and I saw it clear as day. It was the same necklace, there was no doubt. I recognized the engraving of the cherub. I thought the transaction to be strange. How did the dark man come to obtain that piece of jewelry? Was it the original piece? And how did he know Aza-liel's taste? And why would he present her with such a gift? It did not make any sense. I could not think straight. Were my own eyes deceiving me? Then I had what you might call a revelation. Thark. Pestero said 'Beware of thark.' Thark. Dark. Thark. The dark. Beware of the dark. The dark man? I went back inside the cabin.

"He disappeared," I blurted, "I can't find him."

Aza-liel, startled by my entrance, spun around toward me and awkwardly stuffed what must have been the necklace into the pocket of her dress like she was trying to keep me from seeing it. She seemed flustered.

"I'm worried about him," she managed to say.

"What's in your pocket?" I asked.

"Nothing. Why?"

"I saw you stuff something in your pocket. I was wondering what it might be."

"Oh, that was just my handkerchief. I think I'm getting ill. I need to lie down. Sir, do you mind? I'm awfully tired."

"Not at all, young lady, not at all. There," he pointed, "The second door. You can sleep there. You will find everything you need."

"Thank you so much," she said, "You're very kind."

"What about Van?" I demanded.

"Cornelius? Oh, I think he'll be fine. He'll come back eventually. He gets this way sometimes. I just hope he doesn't get lost. Good night."

She scurried off, leaving me with the dark man, closing the door quickly behind her. She could not leave me fast enough, it seemed. The dark man added some logs to the dying fire while I stood stupidly in the entryway, bewildered at Aza-liel's lack of concern for the one she supposedly loved. It was a stark contrast to the first night when she chased after him through the forest begging him to return. It was almost as if she was trying to avoid him, as well as me, altogether. The dark man stood up from the fire. The moment was heavy with smoke and darkness and doubt. His shadowy face and the darkness about him bothered me, his eyes still hidden from plain view. There was a pride about him that I could not trust.

"I'm sorry to upset your friend," he said. "I hate to be the bearer of bad news. But I can't let you go along believing something which is false."

"False?" I snapped. "Did you say 'something which is false'?"

"Yes, false. Port Fectia doesn't exist. The idea is false."

"But if the idea of Port Fectia is false, wouldn't that mean that there does exist an idea which is true?"

"Nonsense," said the dark man. "If there is such a place, certainly I haven't found it."

I thought for a moment about what he had said, but I was not in the proper frame of mind to comprehend it. I simply thought that the dark man may have inadvertently conceded an idea of truth in his admission of an idea of untruth. I committed that notion to memory in order to revisit it at a later date. Presently, I was primarily concerned with who I should trust. The stranger? The dark man? Neither? I was certain I could not possibly trust both.

Suddenly, Cornelius barged back into the cabin. He stood straight and looked brave. He approached the dark man, passing me without a word or a glance. The flickering light from the fire danced across his face in the darkness of the room. I could not read his intentions. I just hoped he had not turned mad. The dark man greeted him with knowing eyes and a mischievous grin.

"Welcome back, Cornelius. I knew you'd return." The dark man spoke in a deep, soothing song.

"Where's Aza-liel?" He demanded.

"She's probably falling asleep by now. It's late, you know. Did you expect her to wait up for you?"

131

Cornelius extended his hand to the dark man across the fire. "I'll trust you if you can help me."

The dark man took his hand and shook it.

"Sit down," he offered, so we did. "What can I do for you?"

"We came here looking for the truth. I thought I would find it in the form of a magic healing potion for my dying mother. I had planned to meet with the King, he would give me the potion, I would go back home, and I would make my mother well. That's the truth which I sought. If there's no cure for my mother, then tell me so and I'll return to Giltlegard a failure and cast my lot with the rest of them and probably die still cursing the stranger in old age. But if you know of a cure for my mother, then tell me where I can find it so I can help her, and I'll be indebted to you forever."

I could not believe my own ears. Was my dearest friend in the world compacting with this man whom we have only just met? I could not allow it.

"Van! What are you saying? Don't be hasty, we must think this through!"

He faced me with undaunted fury. He spoke to me slowly and forcefully. "You are becoming a real waste of my time, Os. There must be at least some goodness in me that I don't put an end to you right here. I've come for truth and I am bound to find it with or without you."

I was speechless. That was not the Cornelius that I knew. He had never spoken that way to me before, or for that matter, to anyone else he loved. He was my friend, and my heart was crushed. I could feel it deep down. However, I just could not allow him to sell himself to the dark man. It did not seem right.

"No!" I exclaimed, and I shot up from my seat and he stood to meet me eye to eye. "You can't do this! Remember what the stranger said..."

Immediately, like the switch of the light, Cornelius struck my skull with the end of his baton and sent me reeling upon the floor, clutching my head. Dizzy, I scrambled to regain my composure when I felt the sharp edge of his sword pressed up against my throat, and I looked up, my vision blurred, to see my friend standing over me with the weapon he was given by the stranger, threatening my life. I dared not move lest his fury kill me.

"I told you already, never mention him again."

He returned the sword to its sheath. I lay in pain. My head throbbed mercilessly. My breathing was loud. I stayed on the ground and managed to crawl into the shadow of a corner and die inside. With my eyes closed, I listened to them speak as friends.

"So can you help me?" Cornelius asked.

"I know where you can find medicine," the dark man answered. "This 'truth' as you call it. It's a magical potion of life. It's kept in a secret place by a guardian in the mountains. It's sure to heal your mother."

"How do I get there?"

"I'm not positive. But there is one who knows. He is a hermit. I met him once quite by accident and he told me about the potion. He also lives in the mountains in some obscure, impossible place. But he gave me a map to his house in case I ever needed to return. He can take you to the potion. Here, let me find it."

I heard rummaging and the rustling of papers from my place in the corner of the room.

"What's your name?" Cornelius asked.

"Figsbi," was the reply. "Ah, here it is. This should be all you need."

I heard the exchange without opening my eyes. I was weary and broken. I heard something about gratitude and something about an easy journey, and after that, I must have fallen asleep, for the next morning, we were ready to go.

CHAPTER FOURTEEN
THE MOUNTAINS

The morning light caressed my tired eyes in the corner of the room and I awoke to the sound of a sweet, clear voice and the delight which came by finding the pleasant face of Aza-liel gazing down upon me, her smile warm and friendly and her hand gently dressing my wound. She smelled like a fragrant meadow. I wanted to grab her and pull her close for I felt like she was my only remaining friend.

"Wake up sleepy head," she cooed, "Unless you want to stay here forever. Cornelius sent me to get you. He says we have an easy journey ahead."

It took me a moment to realize I was not dreaming. She was well dressed and fresh and lovely and just what I needed to see first thing in the morning. She took my hand and helped me up. My head was heavy and aching.

"You really hurt yourself badly, didn't you?" she remarked. "That's quite a bruise you've got there. I'll put some ointment on it to help it heal."

She took my hand and led me outside where our brownbacks were fresh and ready and equipped with something called a saddle strapped over their backs, which was supposed to make riding easier. Sacks of bread and small barrels of water were fastened onto these saddles, and Cornelius was already waiting for me from atop Magic Healer, a rolled up map in hand. The dark man was nowhere in sight.

"Where's the man?" I asked.

"You mean Figsbi? He said he probably wouldn't be here in the morning and not to wait around for him. He gave us these supplies and said we should get an early start. Grab the reins. It's easier this way."

"You took supplies from a stranger?"

"Yeah, so what?"

Cornelius acted short toward me, annoyed at my inquiry. He took Aza-liel's arm and hoisted her up onto the back of the saddle. She locked her arms around his waist. She rested her head between the back of his shoulders. She smiled at me glowingly. She was unusually giddy, even for her. I mounted Danger Foot and away we went. I was not sure where we were going although I remembered vaguely from the night before the conversation regarding the magic potion, and I assumed we were headed in that direction. Already on the outskirts of Cira Main, we headed north into the mountains along a wide, smooth, dirt road. The road had obviously been frequently traveled. Cornelius and I said very few words as we ventured upward along the curving, gradual slope. Aza-liel made up some songs about cool waters and brown horses and whispering trees and cherubs. Her voice was sweet and restful. She sang like the morning light, like the winged creatures of the trees, cheerful and free. They went ahead. I followed closely behind. When I thought about being free, I thought about what the dark man had said the previous night. I took the opportunity, finally having time to think, to remember the words of the stranger, comparing them with our actions, comparing them with the words of the dark man.

It seemed like ages ago that the stranger had sent us on our way, but in reality it was little more than a week. I placed myself again in that dimly lit room and thought of his feathery hat and the authority by which he spoke. That is the thing which impressed me the most. It was his authority. His words held meaning, yet he insisted that he was merely a messenger. What would cause a messenger to speak with such authority and power? I supposed that authority and power is no proof that what he said was true, but it is still something nonetheless. It is something worth remembering at the very least. The dark man spoke with conviction to be sure, but he spoke for himself. The stranger spoke for another. And although both men were equally frightening, for some reason I did not trust the dark man like I trusted the stranger. Of course, just because the stranger spoke about the notion of peace and truth and beauty was no proof that it really existed, and therefore, maybe the dark man, although antagonistic toward our goal of finding the truth, was correct when he said that the stranger was bent on deceiving us. Still, as I recalled the stranger's words, I began to remember the excitement that was stirred inside the depths of my being and the hope came rushing back like the moment we stepped through that steel door and into the world of new experiences.

Trust no one, he said, not even ourselves. That was a scary thought indeed. I watched Aza-liel, riding so comfortably on the back of Magic Healer, so beautiful and seemingly pure, yet the stranger insisted that we not trust her. I watched Cornelius carry on into the mountains, my lifelong friend, so brave, so loyal, so passionate, yet the stranger insisted that we trust not even him. And what of myself? Could I at least trust myself? Not according to the stranger. What if *I* was the sinister one? Could it be that I was but a thorn in my friend's side? It was this whole concept of "trusting" that was all so confusing. The stranger clearly insisted that we trust no one, not even ourselves, and certainly no one whom we would meet along the way, but what of the stranger? Should we trust him? Could it be that he who insisted we should not trust be himself trustworthy? Is that rational? Or is that absurd? The answer to that question eluded me. There we were, in our supposed new found freedom, but was it really freedom? And if not, was there any freedom to be found? Or was the dark man correct in saying that we have been free all along and that our quest for truth was altogether built upon false notions? But the stranger spoke with such authority. Cornelius and I both agreed that what he said about our misery was undoubtedly true. That was undeniable. Or was it?

The stranger also prohibited us from accepting gifts. Cornelius took the supplies from the dark man, and Aza-liel took the necklace. He forbade us from making any allegiances with anyone outside of our party, but Cornelius did that as well. Travel west, he said, and we did that for a while, but presently we were headed north into the mountains, another forbidden place, all for the sake of saving Cornelius's mother. We entered the city of Cira Main after the stranger advised us that little good happens in the cities. I

136

remembered that he warned us to avoid the roads, that very convenience we were presently guiding our brownbacks along. Then I remembered that morsel of information which I tucked away in the back of my memory when the dark man intimated that truth did not exist while simultaneously insisting that the idea of Port Fectia was false. How could something be false if there is nothing to be true? Certainly something must be true. And if nothing is true, then how can anyone know anything? Can I ever know something which is not true? That notion seemed absurd. The existence of truth could not be disputed, of this I was sure. And I was quite certain that Cornelius would agree with me. But what is the truth? That was my dilemma. Should we trust the stranger? Should we trust the dark man? Or should we trust neither? As I contemplated around every bend, as I reasoned in the silence and the singing, something pricked my senses. The stranger insisted that the journey would be difficult. The dark man impressed upon Cornelius that the journey would be easy. Which is the way of truth? Easy or difficult? The answer to that question would point us in the right direction. Then a thought occurred to me. Answers! We all look for answers! It is knowledge we seek. Since the dark man denied Port Fectia and the notion of truth, I realized that he denied knowledge as well, because if truth could not be found, then how could we ever know anything at all? And if I could never know anything at all, then what assurance could I have that something is ever right? Or good? Or just? And if I could never have that, then how could I trust that our journey into the mountains to find some magic potion was going to make us free? It would save Cornelius' mother, maybe. But would it set us free?

I decided that one thing was certain - we could not trust the dark man.

"We can't trust the dark man," I blurted out.

"What?" Cornelius said, "You mean Figsbi?"

"Don't trust him," I insisted.

Cornelius brought his brownback to a sudden halt atop a rocky, narrow ridge and so I did the same. The coolness of the early morning was giving way to heat. It was penetrating the trees and the mountains.

I noticed I was sweating. Cornelius was too. He wiped his brow and Aza-liel squinted at the emergence of the great star. Then she frowned at me and then smiled and then frowned again like some child playing a game; she was beginning to act oddly. Cornelius looked tired. His exhaustion came not just from the heat of the day or from the journey or from a poor night's rest; he looked tired like a man who had been thinking too hard, like a man who had been wrestling with himself and had defeated himself. I think if he wanted to kill me, he had not the strength at that moment.

"Come on," he said calmly. "Let's keep going up the mountain and find some shade where we can rest. Then we can talk."

I took that as a friendly gesture, and I followed him further along the road. Aza-liel stuck her tongue out at me and waved at me and went back to her singing and she seemed like she was lost in some distant place and she rested against Cornelius with her head upon his back and stared off in my direction as if she felt it was necessary to keep a close eye on me. As I watched, her sweetness seemed to dissolve before my very eyes. I did not know what to make of it and I rubbed my eyes in case I was just sleepy or in case the heat was affecting my perception. She just looked different, gradually. As she sang and made faces atop Magic Healer, she seemed to be changing little by little as she kept that eye upon me. She made me nervous. I looked toward her pocket where she had previously stuffed the necklace and she knew what I was thinking and she scowled at me, making a gesture with her hands to go away, and I turned away so as not to look at her anymore because she was beginning to frighten me. Yet it was difficult because she was so perfectly lovely.

CHAPTER FIFTEEN
THE MADNESS OF AZA-LIEL

After a while we located shade and rested near a flowing creek. We let our brownbacks drink while I gathered water into the canteen and shared it with my companions who were sitting upon a patch of grass under an ancient tree.

The trees were broad and full of knowledge in that place along the creek, hovering over us with flourishing branches and rich leaves upon which the morning dew had yet to evaporate. We drank until we were satisfied. It was approaching mid-day as the great star dropped its rays through the foliage directly overhead, passing its warmth over our skin and displacing the mountainous morning chill. The elevation provided a far more pleasant climate than did the plains outside Cira Main. The dark man was right. So far, the journey was a little easier. I wanted to sprawl out and take a nap, but there was work to be done. Cornelius spread the map out on the face of a rock and studied it while I said nothing of consequence.

"This here is the house of the hermit," he explained. "This is the road we're on. We should be around here somewhere near the creek. There is that cliff we passed."

I watched his fingers glide from place to place across the map as he occasionally looked up to study his surroundings. I thought to myself how confident he appeared. No matter what the circumstances, he was always confident. Even when he was wrong, he was confident. Myself, I was never that way. It seemed that I was always doubting, or wrestling internally. Even when I was right, I still doubted. Aza-liel acted aloof, like she no longer wanted to be there. I studied her body language. She could not keep still. A few paces away, she occupied herself by stripping the bark from a tree and mumbling unintelligibly, maybe a song under her breath. She shifted back and forth talking to herself and took a moment to follow the tall path of the tree upward with her eyes until her head was fully tilted backward, and she held herself in that position for a few moments all the while her hands busily pawing at the bark. Then, as if that had grown tiresome for her, she plopped herself down upon a rock, oblivious that I was watching her. She began twirling the strands of her hair around her fingers, her face pouting, either bored or annoyed. She stomped her right foot like a child and stared up into the sky and twirled her hair and moved her mouth without an audible word. She kept that up while Cornelius droned on about turns and shortcuts to the house of the hermit. She made no sound except the shuffling of her feet in the dirt, drawing smiling faces with the toes of her boot. My mind began to drift away with her into her private world until Cornelius, without lifting his eyes from his map, said something which caught my attention.

"Os, I'm sorry I struck you. I had no right. Are you o.k.?"

Then he looked at me. I must have surely beamed with joy. I could have thrown my arms around him right then. It was such a simple phrase, but it was a phrase which made all the difference to a downtrodden spirit. I do not think he could have possibly known how important it was for me to hear those simple words at that moment. I tried to conceal my smile, but my world was bursting with new colors and optimism.

"Yeah, I'm o.k.," I answered. "It's not like it hasn't happened before when we were just playing." We chuckled lightly and rested in the shade like two old friends again.

"You're right," he said. "I shouldn't have made a deal with Figsbi. But I'm not sure we can trust the stranger either."

"Then why are we going?"

"I still have to see. I have to find out for myself if it's true. I need that magic potion. It's my mother's only hope."

"Van, you mind if I mention the stranger?"

"Go ahead," he said sheepishly.

"Remember how he spoke? It wasn't like Figsbi spoke. The stranger spoke with authority. Don't you think anything he said was true?"

140

"Yes I do. I know one thing was true. I know that you, me, and all the people of Giltlegard were prisoners there. We weren't free. And we were bad people. I know that to be true, because that was my experience. The stranger's words just clarified it. It was as if he took the things I already knew about myself and pulled them outside of myself so that I could see them. Either that or he just turned my eyes inward. But whatever it was, I saw myself, and I hated what I saw. I hated it with a passion. And I hated not being free. And even though we left that terrible city, I'm still not free. And I hate it still. And I'm still that same person who was trapped so long inside those four great walls."

Suddenly, Aza-liel called out from the rock. "Cornelius? When are we going to get married?"

Cornelius smiled awkwardly and ignored her question. She went back to drawing flowers in the dirt with her hands and stuck her tongue out toward Cornelius when he was not looking.

"Cornelius? Can you do this?" She stood atop the rock, balancing, albeit wobbly, upon one foot, arms extended for balance. She tilted her head back as far as possible until her back was arched, and she took one finger and placed it upon her nose and held it there until she toppled over onto the ground. She pretended that she was hurt by grabbing her ankle. She moaned and groaned and rolled around a bit, soiling her pretty dress. Cornelius was not impressed.

"Aza-liel, please. I'm trying to talk to Os."

"Watch me dance."

Healed, she sprung from the ground with miraculous vigor, kicking up a cloud of dust. She danced right there in the clearing. She danced awkwardly. She danced cheerfully. She danced boldly. If I had not known any better, I would have thought that I had filled the canteen with some sort of brew instead of water from the creek. She danced back and forth across the clearing and danced her way over toward where we sat and snatched the map from off of the rock, twirling around with the map held high above her head. Cornelius protested, but she pranced about, leaping from rock to rock in the direction of the creek until she spun one too many times and ran a tree branch right through the middle of the map.

"Enough, girl. Now you did it!" Cornelius rushed over and salvaged the map from the clutches of the tree. "Can't you see I'm trying to talk to Os? Keep that for another time."

Dejected, Aza-liel went back to her rock and sat back down and returned to twirling her hair.

"I was just trying to have some fun," she mumbled.

"So Van," I continued, "If you know the stranger spoke the truth about not being free, then why don't you believe him about Port Fectia?"

"Because it's hard. I want to, but it's hard. If there does exist a thing such as truth where all questions are answered and all knowledge is absolute, than I want to find it. But if there is such a thing, then I want my mother to find it too. I promised her that I'd be back for her. I know that for me, the truth is found in this magic potion, wherever it might be. And if it works, then I'll believe in truth. I'll be a different person. It if doesn't, then I'll return to Giltlegard and kill my father like I intended to. If the stranger had led me to the potion, then I'd find it easier to trust him. But he didn't. Figsbi is the one who told me about it. Whether I want to or not, I have to trust him. I just have to, that's all. And if I'm wrong, I'm wrong."

"I think you're wrong," I said. "I think the stranger had the words of truth. I think we should follow his direction a little more closely. I'm not sure if Port Fectia exists, but if it does, I want to find it."

"Well maybe we will. Maybe we will." We hung our heads momentarily, both our minds no doubt filled with a thousand ideas we wished to say but could not express, until I turned the conversation to my own interests.

"What about my mother?" I said. "What about my father?"

Cornelius looked at me, wide eyed and flushed, with a voice contrite when he spoke.

"You're right," he said. "I've been so selfish, I haven't even thought about your feelings. What do you want me to do? I mean, I'm sorry, Os, but what am I supposed to do? Do you want to go back for

142

them? Do you want me to let you go? You think I should finish this on my own? I'm sorry...."

"No, I don't want you to go alone. No, I'm sorry I mentioned it. This is your journey, Van. For some reason, it's your journey, not mine."

"But your family..."

"You're my family now. You and Aza-liel."

"Do you think I am wrong for wanting to find a cure for my mother? I've been waiting for this opportunity for what seems like my whole life. Should I forget about her? I promised her..."

"Van, forget I said anything, alright? Don't worry about it. Find the cure. Find the potion if that's what you feel is right."

I took a long drink from the canteen and passed it to my friend. I supposed I had to follow him, even if it meant going into the forbidden mountains and placing our trust in strange ideas. But then again, every idea was new and strange to us presently.

"Os, I've got to tell you something. I told Aza-liel that I would marry her once we found the truth, once we're all o.k."

"Marry her? Really?"

"Yes, Os, I promised her. She needs me..."

"But I thought you weren't the type..."

"I know. I thought so too. But she needs me. She has no one else. I need to take care of her, look out for her, you know? I promised her. She makes me happy, Os. I like being around her. I just wanted you to know that. So there's no surprises, I mean. I know you love her too."

First of all, I had no idea that Cornelius knew my feelings for the flower girl. I thought I had hidden them fairly well. Secondly, I felt something was amiss.

"Whose idea was this?"

Cornelius did not answer that question. He did not need to. By his silence and the way he turned his face from me and looked down, I knew the idea was not his. However, he was certainly fond of her. This, I had been sure of for a while, but there was another topic I

143

needed to broach, and since I presently had his repentance at my disposal, I took the opportunity.

"Van, let me ask you something. Don't take this the wrong way, but…"

"What? What is it?"

"Who made you the guardian of all the needy?"

I might as well have slapped him in the face, for my question garnered the same response. He was dumbfounded. He looked cross but confused at the same time. He turned his eyes upward the way one does when thinking, but his eyes were distant, shocked into stillness. As he gathered his composure, moisture formed upon his brow. I thought I would either have to fight him or hug him. When he finally responded, it was with further sincerity.

"What do you mean - guardian of all the needy? Is that what I am? Is that how you think of me?"

"Van, I only mean…I mean…Look at you. You are always willing to give of yourself. How can you call yourself selfish? You're the least selfish person I know. It's just that…well…you're always taking it upon yourself to be everything for everyone in need. That's not your job. You don't *have* to bear that burden. Your mother. Aza-liel. Me. We all need you, but we don't need you *that* much. It's like a source of pride for you. You can't go around marrying a girl just because she wants you to."

"Is it because you wanted to marry her?"

"No, not at all. I don't even like her anymore."

With that, Cornelius gave me a sour look, and I had to think quickly so as not to upset him.

"I mean, I'm not jealous. She worships you, it's plain to see. I'm happy for you. I really am. I just think you need to stop being everyone's hero. You're only a man, if that."

In my attempt at compliments, my words were getting in the way, so I stopped talking. Cornelius's sour look slowly turned pink. I think I was becoming a source of entertainment for him. He sniggered. He reached out his hand toward me. I shook it. Then we embraced. Then we laughed. Then he tripped me and threw me onto the ground

144

and jumped on me and wrestled me onto the road until we both grew tired, and we sat up in the dust and the rays of the great star, now tilting to the south.

"Van," I said, "Speaking of Aza-liel, do you think she seems a little bit strange today?"

"No," he said defensively, "Why do you ask?"

"No reason, I guess."

I still withheld the information about the necklace. I was afraid it might cause him more grief and confusion than it was worth. I looked over toward the rock where she sat, but she was not there. Earlier, while Cornelius and I conversed, I noticed her up and walking around the brush near the rocks, disappearing and reappearing from behind the trees like she was playing a game with herself. I hastily glanced all around, but did not see her.

"Anyhow, where is she?" I asked.

Cornelius called to her. "Aza-liel? Where are you?" No answer. "Come on. Come over here with us. I didn't mean to ignore you. I'm sorry." Still, no answer. "Stop hiding and come here. We need to get going." Again, no answer.

"Aza-liel!" Cornelius scolded.

Concerned, but not overly worried, we calmly got up and gathered the map and the canteen, calling her name without reply, and we headed down toward the creek thinking she might be there. I took the opportunity to fill the canteen while Cornelius adjusted the saddles on the brownbacks.

Aza-liel was not near the creek. Frustrated, we called out to her even louder and headed back to the shady clearing where we had sat. She was neither found at the road nor the rocks nor under the shade. We expanded our search beyond the clearing. We ventured off the road into the forest. We climbed hills and descended gullies. We split up. We searched in every direction. We called to her constantly. My voice fell faint with time and effort. The great star had dipped considerably in the sky, casting a cautionary shadow over the hillside. There was no sign of Aza-liel. The knowing trees kept the mystery to themselves. The stillness of the forest disclosed no secrets. The forest had swallowed her up. She had vanished like breath, without direction, without sound. She was nowhere to be found. As we searched and searched by the light of day, through forests and bramble and caverns and caves, we found not even a trace of her, not even a remnant of clothing or a footprint. We reasoned that maybe she was playing a cruel, cruel joke, but our reason only served to mask our fear that something terrible was about. Cornelius was without words. He was breathing heavily and sweating profusely. Did she run away because we were ignoring her? Did someone kidnap her? Did a wild beast devour her? It was all too weighty for even my imagination.

We were heavy hearted. As we reunited at the shady clearing, we were afraid to admit what we already knew, that Aza-liel was gone. Just like that, she was with us no more, and unless she miraculously dropped down from the top of the trees or the sky, we would have to leave that place and continue our journey along the road without her, and daylight was fleeting.

"What're we going to do?" I asked, hoping that somehow there was another solution left out there that we had not considered.

"We must keep going. What else? It's getting late. We don't want to get stuck traveling through these mountains at night."

"So it's just like that? That's it? We forget about her?"

Cornelius shot me a disapproving glance which said, "How dare you?" I knew my question was loaded. I did not mean to imply that he was uncaring. I just could not imagine moving on without Aza-liel. Cornelius recognized my quandary.

"Os, it's unexplainable. Some things are like that. What else am I supposed to do? She's gone. Should we stay the night and look for her all day tomorrow? What about the next day? Should we search for a whole week? We must keep going. My mother depends on it. You know that. I'm sorry. Maybe she went on ahead. Maybe we'll catch up to her."

Cornelius looked like death and spoke the same. I am sure his heart was shattered even worse than mine. I knew he was right, so we rode on and headed for the house of the hermit, sad and perplexed.

CHAPTER SIXTEEN
THE HERMIT

According to the map, the hermit lived in some remote place on the edge of Grey Mountain. We continued sadly up the dusty trail with hearts as heavy as the falling of the great star. We barely spoke. Around every bend we watched to see if Aza-liel was there picking flowers on the side of the road. With every breath of the breeze we listened for Aza-liel's voice to be carried across the trees in song. We waited for her to spring forth out of the bushes in jest and tell us what a good joke she was playing, but waiting is all it was. Darkness was creeping across the sky. Our path grew increasingly morose and winding and void of colors and flowers and flower girls.

Eventually, as the great star sank further behind the mountain, we came upon a rich ensemble of peculiar trees with sorrowful tops. An abundance of grey nuts weighed down the branches so that the trees looked old and tired and droopy. The nuts were shiny, almost silver. We took some and ate. We had to remove the shell to get to the nut. The shells were hard. We had to strike them with rocks to crack them. The nut was chewy and bitter, yet substantial. We ate them with the bread that we brought with us from the dark man's house. We finished the last of the water from the barrels that he gave us. We were beginning to tire from traveling all day, yet the dark man was not lying when he said the journey would be easy. Danger Foot and Magic Healer had no problems climbing the steep grade, for the trail wound so intensely that it barely felt like we were even heading uphill at all. The path was wide and cordial, and the higher we ascended, the cooler it became. We crossed a couple of bridges, one which carried us over a dry gulch and the other over a swift river, and came to a fork in the road at which moment Cornelius consulted his map and decided to veer right. The evening loomed patiently over the horizon as we emerged from the forest and came to a necessary halt at the edge of a frightening cliff. It was a marvelous sight which I will never forget. We overlooked a vast and beautiful valley with drops of dark green tufts and smooth, silky meadows strewn across the valley floor like a blanket. In certain places, homes dotted the valley floor like freckles, giving the impression of a community, and it felt like we were as high as the clouds and there was still enough daylight to cast an enchanting glow upon the plush world below. It nearly took our breath away as we savored the clear blue air with our nostrils. We had arrived at the east side of the mountain; looking down, it was an eternity to the bottom if we should happen to fall.

"Wow," Cornelius gasped, "Aza-liel would love this."

As I gazed eastward and directed my eyes slightly to the south, I noticed a peculiar settlement. Isolated in the deep green meadows was an ensemble of dark clouds hovering over a mass of grey. It was no bigger than my fingernail, but it could not be more familiar. The grey rose upward, disappearing into the thick of the clouds. It was a patch of darkness in the midst of the fertile meadows and tufts of orchards to the south.

"Look Van, over there," I pointed. "It's Giltlegard."

The grey was the Great Wall, jettisoning upward. Even from where we stood, high atop Grey Mountain, the Great Wall showed no intimation of finitude. The wall disappeared into the clouds and the sky. It was so distant that our eyes strained to see it, but there was no mistaking Giltlegard. It cast an enormous shadow to the north, a shadow so prominent that it carried across the great valley over villages and across rivers, as far as our eyes could see. Nightfall came early every day for all which stood in the shadow of Giltlegard to the north. We stared in the direction of the city for a few moments, and I looked at my friend, and his eyes watered, and I asked him what he was thinking.

"Of all the people," he said. "Of all the people who are stuck in that awful place knowing all the time that there is no way out. People without purpose. Without hope. Without help. If I think about it, I can still hear the terrible shrieks. Listen."

I listened, and I could hear the shrieks too - not with my ears, but with my memory. I stared at the steel wall that was but a blotch of grey and the dark clouds and I listened. I listened to the miserable cries, and then I looked again to the north, to that beautiful garden below, and I too felt the pain.

"Why?" Cornelius asked. "Why are we here while they're still there?"

I did not know the answer to that and I told him as much. He did not expect an answer, anyhow. For some reason, the stranger showed us the way of escape. Was it really because he wanted to further torture us like the dark man said? Or was it because there really is a King of Port Fectia who wants to set us free so that we might finally know the truth? I liked the second thought better, although I still could not be certain.

"We're going to have to go back there, you know," Cornelius reminded me. "That's where my mother is. I wonder what she's doing now. I wonder if anyone is helping her? I wonder if she's still alive."

With that thought, the water in his eyes made its way down his cheeks in the form of tears, and he wiped them away, hoping I would not notice.

"I know you miss your family, too," he said.

"It's funny...But not as much as I thought I would."

What I really meant to say was that I had very little desire to ever set foot in that dreadful place again, and if it was not for Cornelius wanting to make his mother well and rescue her from that miserable city then I doubt that I would have ever had reason to even look in its direction, let alone go there, even though my mother and father and brother were still there no doubt immersed in the cacophony of delirious cries. I would have liked them to escape and reunite with me, but as long as they were still there, I just thought of them in the same way that I thought of everyone else, that Giltlegard was the place where they unfortunately belonged. Looking back now, I know the errors of my thinking, because it was not by anything that I had done which

149

freed me from that place, but by a complete stranger showing me the way. I could have easily still been there with the rest of them, but I did not realize then the weight of such a possibility. I think Cornelius did, though. Although he may have been easily tempted by his own passions, it was that very realization which made him great in my eyes. It was because he understood that he was just as miserable as they that he remained humbled by his own confusion. If he was willing to go back to that horrible, steel city, then I was willing to go with him, family or no family.

"Van, I'm just thankful for the company I keep," I said. "I'm sorry about Aza-liel."

"Don't be. We'll find her."

He put his arm around my shoulder and we took one more look around. I wished that I could take that picture with me, but I hoped that I would carry it with me in my mind. I thought that if we ever found Port Fectia, how could it possibly be more beautiful than the scene from the edge of the mountain's cliff?

"Maybe you really do love her," I said.

He did not reply. He just stared off into the eastern sky.

"Van, if we make it back to Giltlegard, then how can you be sure that we'll ever be able to get back out again?"

"I don't. I'm not sure I really know anything right now."

Cornelius sat down at the edge of the cliff and unfolded the map and studied it. The great star began to cast its evening glow across the horizon, illuminating the tops of the trees with a tint of orange. Nightfall was in a hurry. It would not care to wait for a couple of lost boys at the top of a mountain. According to the map, we were on top of Grey Mountain at the edge of Dandy Nut Forest. The kind of nut that we had earlier eaten was decorating the ground from having fallen from the trees. Those which still adorned the trees were like a grey beard to a green head, stooped and wise, with the orange horizon as a bonnet.

"We are right where we're supposed to be," Cornelius said. His nose was buried in the map as if holding it close to his face would help him make out the details. "But where do we go now? Look, take a look. Am I not right? Isn't this where the hermit lives, right where we are?"

I looked and could not disagree. He studied it further, turning it left and right and holding it upside down and reading it from different angles and then studying his surroundings. He stood up and walked over to a thicket which rested firmly on the edge of the cliff, and, taking his stick, he poked around at the intertwining bramble, but it was like a fortress.

"The map has an arrow pointing right here," he said, poking and prodding without any luck. He just could not break through the tight fabric of foliage. He moved to the back side of the thicket. He poked and prodded further. He remained unsuccessful at breaking through. He took hold of his sword and tried chopping at the mass but found that it only tangled his sword in its thickness. I took a few steps backwards in order to gain a broader view of the situation.

"It looks purposeful," I suggested.

"So it does," he replied.

The branches acted as a barrier, like a fence, like somebody wanted it there. We could not see through it to the other side, but the thicket started right at the edge of the cliff and extended in toward the forest like a wall, so that it was impossible to gain access to the other side without cutting oneself on the jagged brush and probably getting stuck. Cornelius grew frustrated. He impatiently began flailing his sword aimlessly about.

"It's supposed to be right here!" he shouted, "Where is it?"

Suddenly, above all the commotion, a cantankerous objection cried out from somewhere on the other side of the thicket.

"Who's making all that noise? Noise, I say. Can't a body get some rest around here? You're driving me nuts. Ha Ha! I could have said 'mad', but I like nuts, so I chose to say 'nuts'. Leave me alone, will ya?"

We looked around, but saw no one.

"You there," Cornelius replied. "Where are you? Are you on the other side of this thicket?"

151

"I'm in no place of any real meaning," the voice snapped. "Now go away. You have no business here. Leave me alone."

"But I have a map. And it tells me that this is the right place. We're looking for the hermit. Do you know him?"

"First of all, if I knew him, why would I tell you? Second of all, if he's a hermit, he probably wouldn't want me to tell you where he is anyhow. Third of all, if you've got a map and it tells you you're in the right place but you still can't find the hermit, then maybe you're just not very good at reading maps. Fourth of all..."

"Mister," Cornelius interrupted, staring blindly into the wall of vegetation, "I know that you could probably go on all day, but we're really in a hurry looking for the hermit. We were sent by one named Figsbi. He said the hermit could show us the way to a magic, healing potion. Mister, why don't you come on out and show yourself that we might talk with you better?"

"I am out," said the voice. "You're just not looking."

"But we've looked high and low."

"You haven't looked low enough," came the reply.

Dumbfounded, we got down upon our knees. We looked all around us. We looked for any holes in the ground, but found none. We looked at the base of the thicket barrier, but we thought he must have been playing us for fools. We could not figure out where the voice was coming from. It seemed so distant. Suddenly, I was struck in the back of the head with one of the grey nuts.

"Ouch!" I cried. "Who did that?"

"Who did what?" my partner asked.

"Someone hit me in the back of the head with a nut."

"Then catch it next time," said the cantankerous voice.

Still on his hands and knees, Cornelius crawled over to the edge of the cliff and carefully peered over. I followed and did the same. There, about three body lengths down the side of the cliff on a ledge stood a smallish, wrinkled old man with a broad, crooked, smile and extremely large, white eyebrows below a mangy tuft of grey hair. His face looked like a dried lumpkus.

152

"It's about time, you fools," he cackled. "I thought Figsbi would have sent me some children with more brains. Come down here and we'll talk."

He disappeared into the side of the mountain. The ledge was barely big enough for the tiny, old man, let alone for the two of us, and it was more than just a casual jump down. In fact, it looked impossible.

"How do we get down there?" we called.

It was too late; he was gone. We looked around for an aid. One little slip could put us at the valley floor. This particular edge of the mountain descended straight downward. There were no jutting rocks, no dangling trees, no protruding angles or declensions upon which to smash our heads upon if we were to fall. The cliff was perfectly perpendicular, all except for this one insignificant ledge upon which we needed to descend.

Cornelius chopped a sturdy limb from one of the trees. He was explaining how he would hold onto one end and I would hold onto the other as he lowered me down onto the ledge when we heard a THUD coming from over the side of the mountain.

"A ladder!" we exclaimed in unison.

"Boys these days...They can't even figure their way down a cliff. You boys ought to be ashamed of yourselves...Ashamed I tell you... Useless...Absolutely useless."

The old man's voice faded into the mountain as he again disappeared. A ladder was propped up against the side of the mountain, almost vertical. It was not much safer than our own plan. One at a time, we climbed down. The feet of the ladder rested squarely on the perimeter of the ledge. It was a frightening descent. The ladder was made of tree branches, the rungs, those which were still intact, being tied together with rope. Cornelius went first. I held the top steady for him best I could. After he made it to the bottom, he had to carefully step off sideways being that the ladder was fixed against the back of the ledge, hanging for a moment from a rung, and swing himself onto the platform. Seeing his acrobatics, I was certain I would soon be dead. I started down. Cornelius positioned the bottom of the ladder closer to the side of the cliff so that it was completely vertical, holding onto it from the inside of the mountain, careful to keep the tension lest I fall to my doom.

Finally, we made it. We could not abandon that ledge quick enough. We disappeared into a cavernous opening in the side of the mountain where the old man had previously disappeared.

Inside was an amazing array of wooden chairs and benches scattered randomly throughout the spacious cave. They were dark and smooth, like the trunks and branches of the surrounding trees. The wood was warped and knotted and held together with rope in the same manner as the ladder. There were so many that I lost count.

The old man emerged from the shadows of the cave. His eyes were large and dull, as grey as the nuts on the tree. His nose was frightfully long. His lips were as distinctly crooked as his smile. His hair was a patch of absurdity, wild and gray. He was wide and short. His head was as wide as his chest, and his prominent, white eyebrows needed a thorough combing. His body was not so much round as it was lumpy, as lumpy as his display of furniture. He brought us a drink.

"Welcome to my dandy nut paradise. Drink up." His voice was as shrill as his stature was small. "It's dandy nut tea."

Not wanting to seem rude, we sipped on the tea as he curiously observed us. It was delicious, I must admit. It was warm and creamy and tasted like nothing I had ever experienced before.

"This is very fine tea," I commented.

"It's made from dandy nut milk," he replied. "It helps me live long."

"Are you the hermit?" Cornelius asked.

"Do I look like a hermit?" he snapped.

"Yes, sort of."

"Of course I'm a hermit. Are you a dumb fool?"

Our sips turned into gulps, and we devoured the tea simultaneously, clanging down our cups with a refreshing sigh. The hermit relieved us of our dishes, commenting on how inconvenient it was to have company on account of him having to be hospitable, and invited us to sit down, mentioning that he would return momentarily.

The wooden chairs were rather uncomfortable. They had no cushions. The seats poked us in places we did not want to be poked. The knots knotted us in one direction or another. We tried the benches, but they were so warped that sitting down comfortably on them was no easy task. We moved from seat to seat, but each one felt the same, so we decided to stand. The hermit returned promptly with three pipes in hand, already packed and lit as a testament to his inconvenient hospitality. Again, not wanting to be rude, we smoked with the hermit, and the cave began to fill up with a delightful aroma.

"Why haven't you sat down?" he asked.

"We'd just rather stand," I replied.

"Is it because my chairs are uncomfortable?"

"No," I said. "It's just that we can't stay long."

"Liar!" he snapped. "It's because the chairs are uncomfortable. I made them that way on purpose to keep me from sitting on them."

"What's the point in making chairs if you don't want to sit on them?"

"To prove to myself that some things which have been made serve no useful purpose," he replied.

"That makes no sense," I argued. "Why would you purposely create a problem which otherwise wouldn't have existed just to prove that it's a problem?"

"I don't know, young boy. I never really thought about it. Why don't you tell me? Besides, you can stay as long as I say you can. If you came to find the potion, and if I'm the only one who knows where it is, then you can stay forever if that's what it takes. Fortunately for you, I don't like company, so I am liable to excuse you at any time."

"What is it that we're smoking?" Cornelius asked.

"Dandy nut tree roots."

"It's good."

It certainly was good. I savored each and every puff of the delicacy. The aroma lingered in my nostrils like the morning air, and the flavor danced upon my tongue like a rolling flame. The longer we stood and smoked the more the hermit looked like an old relic. We relished the experience, forgetting our troubles for a time. The hermit

155

led us up another ladder, this one in the center of the cave that poked through a hole in the ceiling and out into the open air, into a clearing that we recognized was the other side of the thicket that we had previously attempted to access. From that spot on the mountain, we sat with the hermit upon the cool grass and took in a prolonged view of the dazzling, green valley below. The great star had since fallen and the parameters of our view faded into the dusky beginning of the night, so the hermit sparked his lantern and we polished off the remainder of our smokes and rested on top of his cave.

"What's your name, old hermit?" I asked.

"Gunther," he replied. "I'm quite fond of my name because I can't seem to think of anything that rhymes with it."

After thinking for a moment, neither could I.

"Pleased to meet you, Gunther. I'm Osgood and this is Cornelius."

"Why did Figsbi send you?"

"To find the magic potion," answered Cornelius. "It's for my mother. She's deathly ill and it's her only chance to live."

"We all have the same chance to live," he replied.

"Figsbi said you knew where the potion was, and that you could lead us there."

"Yes, I do know where the potion is, but I can't lead you there. I perfected the concoction myself through many years of labor, placed it in the care of a trusted charmer to ensure it is taken care of and well hidden. It's made from the shell of the dandy nut..."

"Is that what all these grey nuts are called? Dandy nuts?"

"Yes indeed. It is the all sufficient food. It's all I ever eat. It can be liquefied, mashed, boiled or whatever. For the potion, the shell's substance is extracted and blended with herbs from the dandy nut leaves. It cures illness if you believe. Why should I let you have it?"

"I don't know why except that my mother needs it. I'm desperate."

"Do you believe in its power?"

Cornelius hesitated. "I'll believe in its power if you say that I must. If that's what it takes."

156

"Yes, young man. That's what it takes. You must believe in the healing power of the dandy nut. It's all that I need. I'm four hundred fifty nine years old. I know that sounds old, but I don't think I look a day over two hundred thirty. I'm perfectly satisfied here in my own little paradise, smoking and eating dandy nuts until my heart's content. I watch the world change all around me, but my solitude remains constant. I'm truly free. Look at the world below. That view is my truth. I've found it and I'll enjoy it forever."

"Figsbi told us that truth doesn't exist," I blurted.

"Well, my friends. It does and it doesn't. What Figsbi meant was that truth doesn't exist as any one thing which could be grasped. There is no truth out there to be found. The truth which does exist is a truth to be forged. It's created. Like my little humble home. Like the wellness of your mother. Truth is finding satisfaction in the things which interest you. Everything else is false. You mustn't believe in a truth to be grasped. It's like water. It'll seep through your fingers until it's completely gone."

"Have you ever heard of a man named Pirnoff?" I asked.

Suddenly, the hermit's already smallish voice grew smaller, almost to a whisper. A breeze, a disturbing breeze, tickled the bare part of my skin, causing me to shiver. I could tell there was something evil in the air, and the night finally fell over the surface of the valley below, and the hermit's lantern was the only beacon under the blackened sky, and when he spoke he seemed much older than his four hundred fifty nine years.

CHAPTER SEVENTEEN
THE BLIND GUIDE

"Let me tell you a story," said the hermit.

"A long, long time ago...ages ago...two hundred years ago at least, this entire land was free. But now freedom can only be found in pockets of the country side. That's because the Realm of the Unbelief has deceived millions. Pirnoff is the leader of the realm. His chief aim is to trick free folks into believing that they're really not free at all, to throw them into confusion, and to lead them astray and eventually to their destruction. Slowly, city by city, he's spread his words of deceit. And he's led others to do the same. He's a dangerous, dangerous man. He attempts to impose his will upon others. He's destroyed the law of tolerance throughout the land, and he continues to do so today. He speaks of false notions of knowledge and peace, notions that no man has ever found to be true. It's a myth, for he tricks the whole world into giving up the life which we've held for generations, the ways which we've known long before he came to us with these preposterous lies. I know. He once came to my small village of Pogg, which existed about five day's journey north of here in the valley on the other side of the mountain. We were a self-sufficient people, but he came to us and spewed forth words of hatred toward our way of life. He told us that we weren't what we thought we were...that we were dependent upon our ignorance for our ways of life, that we needed law, that we needed truth, that we needed a King, and that the King existed in some far off land called Port Fectia. He told us that truth couldn't be found in any other place except Port Fectia. When he said that, I didn't believe it. Anyone who says that truth can only be found in one certain thing or one certain way, I cannot believe it. I was the only one in the entire village who didn't believe it. Everybody else wailed and screamed at the thought that their old way of life was really a deception, and they crumbled under the burden of not knowing the way of truth. So many Poggites killed themselves that very day. The others were scattered throughout the land, no doubt searching for this imaginary city of which he spoke."

"Did anyone ever find it?"

"No, of course not. It only brought more misery and disappointment. It made people hate themselves. It made people scared and confused. Myself, I made my way into the mountains and made my home here in this cave, and found my own truth, a truth which I had back in the days of Pogg. I've lived a self-sufficient existence, and there is no one telling me that I'm a miserable little hermit. And there is no one to tell me that I shouldn't smoke dandy nut tree roots. Stay away from that man Pirnoff. He's on the prowl constantly."

"But we've seen him," I blurted.

"So you have," he replied. "I was worried about that. Where did you see him?"

"He came into our city of Giltlegard. He spoke to the people and sent us into confusion, just like you said. But he let Van and I go free."

"Giltlegard, you say? Giltlegard is under siege now, too?" He hung his head as if a distant memory bothered him. "Giltlegard is a city of progress. A great city. A self-sufficient people." Then anger resonated from his quivering crooked lips. "That man will stop at no ends. He must be defeated! Oh my...Imagine the horror inside those steel walls as we speak."

Cornelius and I were speechless, for we knew the horror first hand. We saw for ourselves the people running and screaming and clutching at the steel walls and cutting off their own legs to escape the pelzors. And the dying. We already witnessed the dying. We did not need the hermit to remind us of the horrors within those steel walls, but when he spoke, he spoke with such compassion that I could not help but feel a resurgent pity for those who had been left behind.

The hermit led us soberly back down the ladder into his cave where he lit further lanterns. He invited us to spend the night, so we did, and in the morning when the first light broke through the hole in

159

the side of the mountain, he stood out on his ledge and called out into the forest with a foreign, whooping cry and a whistle. Before long, the strangest creature I had ever seen descended the side of the cliff and entered the cave. He handled the descent like an animal. He was much like a beast, but he was more so a man. The top of his head was flat as if a tree trunk had fallen directly on it. Scattered tufts of hair curled out from the surface of the flat. His face was hairy, but not compared to his back, and his arms were longer than the average man's arms ought to be. He had no eyes, only wrinkles where his eyes should have been, as if they had been sewn shut, so he used a walking stick to feel his way about the hermit's home, though he did so familiarly. He wore beggar's clothes, a tattered shirt and pants far too short while lacking shoes upon his terribly ugly feet. Despite his oddities, his facial features were quite like an ordinary man, even handsome considering his unfortunate hairs.

"Boys, this is Danxoumanxou. He's a friend. He knows these mountains like the flat of his head. He'll lead you to the potion. It's quite far from here, so don't be afraid. Just follow him."

"You can call me Dan," said the man-beast, his voice as clear and ancient as the trees. "I am glad to help, young travelers."

"I don't mean to be rude, Gunther," I said, "But is Dan here able to see where he's going?"

"Of course not, foolish boy! He has no eyes!"

Suddenly, both Gunther and Dan erupted into laughter, congratulating each other with slaps on the back, the former emitting a high pitched cackle and the latter a jovial snigger, amusing each other with my apparent ignorance.

"Well then," I shot back, "If he can't see, then how does he know what the top of his head looks like? How does he know his way around the mountains?"

"Young traveler," Dan replied smugly. "I simply feel my way around. I have had many years of experience that tells me that the top of my head is quite flat. It is the same with the mountains. Do you know what the top of your head looks like?"

"I suppose not."

160

"Then I already know more than you know, and you are supposed to be the one with the eyes!"

Again, the cohorts roared with glee. Cornelius and I watched, thoroughly annoyed. We were about to be led through the mountains by a blind guide who could not stop laughing about the fact that he was blind. Gunther seemed to take an excess of delight in our uncertainty.

"Well, young travelers," Dan finally managed, "It is imperative that we make haste. We are wasting daylight, though it has only just arrived. Follow me."

Follow him, we did. We bid farewell to the hermit, ascended the ladder at the edge of the cliff, and began mounting our brownbacks when Dan stopped us.

"No room for horses, young travelers. We are taking the most direct route where roads are obsolete. You must let them go."

Let them go? They brought us so far so faithfully. They had proven invaluable to our quest. Not only that, but they had become like friends, a familiar face each morning. I hated to leave them behind. I hesitated. I know that Cornelius felt the same way, but it was inconsequential to his earnest ambitions. He untied Magic Healer, swatting him on the back side, and watched him gallop down the trail from which we came, his eyes lingering upon his companion until he vanished out of sight. His eyes showed gratitude and finality. He was not the type to hold onto any obstacle which stood in the way of his mission, no matter how endearing it might be. His eyes shifted from the trail to the incline to the north, a fierce renewal of purpose. It was evident that the thought of saving his mother had become a reality within his grasp.

I untied Danger Foot. He looked at me with big eyes. If a brownback could cry, I think he would have then.

"Go on," I commanded, pointing back down the mountain, but he would not move.

"Danger Foot, Go on!" I slapped him in the backside but he only shuffled forward a few paces.

161

Cornelius and Dan had already started up the incline into the dandy nut trees, so not wanting to be left behind, I turned and followed.

"Go on now, scat!" As I retreated, I snatched a rock and flung it towards Danger foot, hitting him square in the side. He heralded a triumphant herald, one that had become so familiar to me whenever he sensed my will, and without further hesitation, he raced off down the path after Magic Healer. I wiped my dampened eyes and continued after Cornelius who was waiting for me just inside the edge of the dandy nut forest.

"I didn't realize what a comfort they've been," I said. "They've just always been there."

He knew exactly what I meant. Dan was increasing his lead on us, so we hurried to catch up. We followed our guide up along a crowded row of silvery trees and down into a steep, rocky ravine. The rocks were jagged and the dirt loosened as we began to slide, but we managed to balance ourselves well enough by grabbing tree branches and roots. Once at the bottom of the ravine, we turned west to follow its direction. Dan kept his walking stick pointed straight ahead the entire time, waving it purposefully about the ground as if it contained a nose, as if he meant it for sniffing out the right direction. How he knew where he was going, I had no idea, but we followed him nonetheless. Cornelius and I grew weary as the great star reached its highest point, but we were fortunate enough to move beneath the shade of the trees. Dan moved about like a wild animal, refusing to stop even for a sip of water, and my lips were parched and I began to taste the dryness of my throat. We continued down the ravine for a while. We followed our guide through a narrow gully and finally up onto an embankment that overlooked a swift and shallow river. We crossed it standing up. The cold water gnawed at my skin through my pants up to my waist, penetrating even my boots. The pressure of the current pushed against us, nearly knocking us over a number of times, but not Dan. He was stronger than the average man. He was faster and tougher. He was accustomed to the elements. While Cornelius and I grew fainter by the moment, Dan helped us along, lending us a powerful hand when we needed it and leading us through the waters safely. Finally, after we climbed up on the opposite side of the river bank, Dan allowed us to rest briefly. I wanted to sleep. I remembered the words of the dark man and supposed that the ease of the journey had ceased.

It was three days of that. Every so often, I heard the sounds of slurping and chattering that seemed to reside in the mountains.

Scaling large rock formations; blazing trails through forests; crossing narrow, rickety bridges; ascending higher and higher up sharp, mountainous inclines; sleeping in caves; we followed our guide as he felt his way feverishly across the mountain side, his walking stick in constant motion, never doubting his direction. I still found it incredible that we were following a blind man-beast, but we could almost smell the magic potion the further we tread. We had not spoken of the stranger in three days. We simply followed our guide, and we were exhausted, and our appearance bore witness to that. On the third day, just before nightfall, we stopped near a cluster of trees sprouting from the side of a dug out knoll to set up camp for the night.

"Go gather some wood for a fire," Dan ordered, "I will find us some dinner."

At his command, Cornelius and I took our weary bodies into the woods and began gathering sticks and logs. Then, from somewhere in the distance, we heard the desperate yelp of some unsuspecting creature, the breaking of bones, and the familiar victory cry of Dan that resembled a frightening howl.

"How does he do that?" I asked.

"I don't know. But we've never eaten so well as we have these past three days."

"I guess eyes are overrated," I joked. We hauled our firewood to our campground under the cluster of trees. "Van, do you believe Gunther?"

"Which part do you mean?"

"I mean his story about the stranger, Pirnoff, and how evil he is and about this village called Pogg. Do you believe any of that?"

163

"Have I reason not to? I'm beginning to think that this Pirnoff character is bad news. I think maybe he's responsible for a lot of death and tragedy in Giltlegard. The more I think about it, the more I realize that sure, things may have been a little mundane there, we may have had our bad moments, but was life really that bad that someone should come in and turn it all upside down and destroy us? Were we not at least living?"

I found that comment strange coming from the only one I knew who never really trusted the Giltlegardian way of life. Cornelius was the only one who actually contemplated a world outside of the four steel walls, and yet now my friend was talking as if he never wanted to leave in the first place. I could not understand him. Or maybe I could. I was beginning to doubt the stranger's words more and more myself. It seemed that the more we strayed from the meadows and ponds and the more we kept company with others from outside our party, the less the stranger's words seemed to be relevant. Our quest had now officially turned from finding the city of Port Fectia to finding the dandy nut potion and healing Mrs. Van. As we climbed over rocks and through caverns and up hills and in and out of forests, the stranger's words seemed increasingly like a distant memory. Yes, I too, began to doubt. I no longer believed the stranger the way that I had at the beginning. I still dreamed about the idea of Port Fectia, but it did not seem as necessary anymore. We were on a different journey now, and I must admit, I was growing accustomed to it.

Then, while I was overlaying the firewood and Cornelius was busy gathering stones to utilize in forging a spark, I looked up toward a clearing in the distance, astonished by what I saw. Darkness was creeping in. What I saw was clouded in the dusk. I looked into the clearing in the distance, but not so distant as to cause me to doubt what I saw, and noticed two figures, side by side, conversing. One figure, the taller one, was gesturing at the smaller. It was gesturing with a finger as if it was scolding the smaller figure. Then the smaller figure gestured back. A howling wind stirred among the trees. I stood up. I strained my eyes, mesmerized by what I saw. I crept closer, attempting to keep hidden. Night was descending quickly, so quickly that it seemed as if it was trying to hide this confrontation from my curiosity. The taller figure was Dan, to be sure. He was with someone, someone who wore a dress. The dress was blowing feverishly in the wind. A fog descended upon the clearing, dropping straight out of the sky. I emerged fully from the trees. I moved closer, quietly, but not quietly enough. The ground crackled beneath my feet. A face turned in my direction. It saw me. I saw the face. Through the fog, I saw the face and I realized for certain what I saw. Her dress was different. It was new. Her long, friendly hair and womanly figure brought pain to my stomach as I stood in the clearing, captivated. I could not breathe momentarily. In an instant, I regained my composure. I had no time to think, so I reacted, rushing like a madman in the direction of the two figures.

"Aza-liel, is that you?"

I have no doubt that it was. Upon my approach, she turned and dashed away from me, across the clearing, disappearing into a patch of fog.

"Aza-liel, come back! Van! Van! Come here! Come quick!"

No sooner had the words 'Aza-liel' left my lips when Cornelius burst forth from out of the woods.

"Van, it's Aza-liel! Hurry!" Together, we raced past Dan into the foggy night, but she was nowhere to be found. Where could she go? There was only field. The forest was a good dash away, but certainly Aza-liel was not fast enough to escape our advance. We stood in the clearing. We glanced desperately about. We started one way and then the next. Aza-liel again was lost, and this time I was persuaded that it was by her own intention. There was no tree to hide behind, no rock, no hole in the ground. She had simply vanished into the fog. She escaped once again, and the fog suddenly lifted, and it was exceedingly dark, and we stood there with the wind biting our faces.

"Did you see her?" I asked.

"Yes."

"I'm certain it was her."

"Me too."

"Where could she go?"

"Aza-liel? Where are you?" cried Cornelius. "Come back! Don't go! I need an explanation! Come back!"

There was no answer except for the empty sound of the night and the howling of the wind in the trees. We returned to Dan. He stood innocently with a furry, dead creature flung over his shoulder and a look of bewilderment upon his hairy face. I assumed he knew something we did not. Cornelius demanded an answer.

"Dan, what was she doing here?"

"Of whom do you speak, young traveler?"

"The girl! Now what was she doing here!"

"Young traveler, calm down."

"I won't calm down! I want the truth!"

"Truth? Truth, you say? What is that? I have not heard that word in a long, long time. Not since that man, Pirnoff came speaking of such things to my people so long ago. Girl? You want to know of a girl? Have you forgotten, young traveler, that I am what you might call blind? How can I see anything let alone a girl?"

"Or are you really as blind as you lead on? Shaking your stick all around the ground like you are going to bump into things, all the time jumping and darting and moving all around, moving so fast that we can barely keep up. You call that blindness?"

"Young travelers, have you seen my eyes, or are you blind too? Have you not noticed that my eyes are seared shut? This was done long ago by that man, Pirnoff. After he appeared to my people in the mountains, proclaiming our doom and his so-called truth, I resisted. I tried to lead a revolt against him. He was throwing all the Danxoumanxou into a frenzy. I could not have my people deceived by that imposter. I gathered some men, and we attacked him at the top of the falls. He captured me, and this is what he did. He put out my eyes with a hot iron. That is the kind of man he is with all this talk of truth, truth, truth. Look at me! And you think I am not blind?"

"I saw you speaking with her," I argued. "You were shaking your finger at her. She was doing the same to you."

"Well, young travelers, if you must know, I was speaking with the Spirit Queen of the mountains. She is the wisdom of the mountains.

166

She is the force of balance. She is the mediator of prosperity. I was simply seeking her guidance where she can be found. If that is what you mean by *girl*, then so be it. But she is no *girl*, I can assure you. Obviously, I have never seen her. But her wisdom is that of a queen."

"Why did she run off?"

"She will not let herself be seen by strange eyes. She is a spirit. She comes and goes as she pleases."

"That was no queen," I answered, "That was our friend. Aza-liel. The flower girl. I saw her with my own eyes."

"So there you go again. Your eyes. Maybe your eyes are not as reliable as you think they are. Besides, if she was your friend, then why did she leave you?"

"I don't know."

Truly, I did not know. I felt as if I could not know. I felt as though I could never know anything. Only weeks ago, I thought I knew so much. Now, I wondered if I could ever really know anything at all. Cornelius was speechless. Too much did not make sense. I was certain it was Aza-liel. At least, it looked exactly like her. If it was, how did she get there? Why did she disappear? Why was she talking with Dan? Was she the Spirit Queen of the mountains? Nonsense. She was a flower girl. She was the cart pusher from Giltlegard. She was the sweet, lovely, singing flower that had kept us longing for cherubs and rainbows. She wore a different dress, however. I began to doubt my senses. I wanted to strangle the blind man-beast, and I am certain that Cornelius desired the same, the way he looked at him with such contempt, but we did no such thing. We kept our frustrations under control. We were getting closer to finding the magic potion, and we needed Dan to lead us there. Without him, we were lost. Though we had eyes to see, we were blind. Danxoumanxou was our only hope. We returned to the cluster of trees sprouting from the side of a dug out knoll and started our fire and warmed ourselves and slept until morning.

CHAPTER EIGHTEEN
THE GIGGLING GIRL

We slept nestled in the dug-out portion of the knoll where we were protected from the wind and close enough together to feel one another's warmth, especially Dan's, whose hairy back provided the semblance of a blanket.

Though I slept, it was not well, for the memory of Aza-liel lay heavy on my thoughts. Maybe she fled because I knew that she accepted the necklace from the dark man. Maybe she was afraid. I should tell Cornelius, I thought. Maybe I was mistaken. Maybe my eyes deceived me. Maybe the Spirit Queen bore a striking resemblance to Aza-liel and nothing more. But Cornelius saw her also. Then again, the sighting was so brief. Could we really be sure it was her when things happened so quickly? Confusion was becoming our most intimate acquaintance. And what should we make of Dan's story? Was it as he said? Or did he know more than he was leading on?

That morning, we started early, at the first hint of light. We spoke very little. It took all our efforts to maintain Dan's rapid pace. The blind man pushed forward the way one does when finality is within reach. In brawlball, when nine points have been scored, the leading team never lets up; they push harder. They fight harder. They die harder. That is how Dan led us. Cornelius sensed it. It was motivation. We jumped rocks, we blasted through bushes, we scaled ravines, we ascended higher and higher, our pace steady and brisk. Our guide, with that walking stick constantly moving, dodged trees and jumped ridges as if he had the mountains memorized.

Looking at Cornelius, he was engrossed in contemplation. He contemplated while he moved about, and I wondered what he might have been thinking. He must have wondered why the girl was suddenly so bent on avoiding him. Maybe he noticed how Aza-liel had slowly begun to resent my company. Maybe he secretly blamed me for her disappearance. After all, he had barely spoken two words to me all morning, though it was not as if we had much time while trying to keep pace with Dan. When he did speak, however, he sounded angry. He sounded old and angry and worn. I had enough sense to leave him alone with his thoughts even though I wanted so badly to enter inside of his brain and see what those thoughts might be. I still found it difficult to understand his rush to find the potion instead of Aza-liel. I know he felt that his mother was dying, but his mother was still in Giltlegard. Aza-liel was somewhere nearby, possibly in danger. There was one thing, however, which I could never doubt, and that was Cornelius' resolve. It never deserted him. In fact, it may have been stronger than ever. Cornelius was the sort to feed off of his own will. The more passionate he became, the more focused he became. The more focused, the more resolved. The more resolved, the more stubborn. The more stubborn, the more crazy. But he was not crazy. He was tortured. He was tortured by the thought of a dying mother, a missing girl, and the slippery pursuit of truth.

After hiking all morning, as the great star lit up the sky directly overhead, forcing its rays of light into our dim forest, we came to a halt. We climbed a steep embankment which brought us to a flat. Across the flat was the place of reckoning, a dilapidated wooden retreat built into the hillside, tangled up in shades of green.

"Well, young travelers, this is it. We have arrived. My duty is done. I hope you find what you seek."

"What do we do now?" Cornelius asked.

"Go inside of course."

"Are you coming with us?"

"Sorry, but I will not."

Before us stood the resemblance of a house with steps leading to a porch and a door hanging half open. Around the porch and over it and growing up through it was dense foliage. The hillside, decorated with bushes and ivy, appeared to serve as its roof and walls. In fact, our destination was nearly hidden amongst the overgrowth of plants and shrubs and vines. We cautiously ventured across the flat. We came to the porch steps and ascended them carefully. The light from the great star was blotted out by the overgrowth. Plants sprouted from the hillside and drooped weepily upon the steps. The foliage was wild and waiting. It smelled of dampness and dark. The steps barely held our weight, rising from the dead with the sounds of creaking and moaning. Most of the floor boards were splintered or broken, some altogether missing. The front door hung by only one hinge, caught open between two warped planks on the porch. The railing, from what was visible out of the overgrowth, was falling apart. There was a window facing the flat that held the remnants of glass around its pane. Through the window was darkness like the night without the stars, like the nights of Giltlegard. Could anyone live in such a place?

Just then, I was startled by the familiar sounds of slurping and chattering that haunted me that first night in the forest, so I turned back towards Dan, but he was gone.

"Did you hear that?" I asked.

"Yes, that was weird."

"Dan's gone," I said. "I think they might have gotten him."

"Who?"

"The mountain creatures. Remember? They make that slurping noise. I have been hearing it periodically since we left the hermit. I don't know why we didn't think of it before. They've probably been stalking Aza-liel all over the woods, just like the night they almost chased her over the cliff. That's why she's so paranoid."

Something like a light must have switched on in Cornelius' brain, for his countenance changed.

"I think maybe you're right," he said.

I held my breath to keep from gagging on the stale air permeating the front porch. It was too dark inside to see anything, and outside, with all the overgrown foliage obstructing our view, we could not very well see past the spot where we left Dan standing. We failed to call out to him for fear of being too loud.

"Stay here," said Cornelius. "I'll make sure."

Cornelius hurried back down the entangled steps much quicker than we had climbed them, but when he reached the bottom step, the plank gave way under his weight, and his foot sank through the boards, slicing his flesh on the splintered wood. He yanked his leg out from the debris, causing him to tumble backwards upon the ground, crying out with a frustrated groan before rising to his feet and scanning the area around the flat. The commotion surely would have stirred anyone inside the little house so that our visitation was anything but covert. I could barely make him out from where I stood behind the foliage.

"Is he there?" I whispered.

No answer. He disappeared out of sight, so I followed after him, carefully navigating the dangerous steps. I found him hobbling about frantically atop the embankment, but the blind man was nowhere to be found. Blood was seeping through Cornelius' pant leg. He touched it, groaning, smearing it on his sash.

"Where's Dan?" I asked.

"You're right, he's not here."

He plopped himself down and stretched out his leg. I came to him and tore open his pant leg and removed my own sash and wrapped it around his wound. His laceration was long and deep, but of little consequence, I could tell. Knowing him, he may not have really felt it. It was everything else that caused his pain.

"Now, how are we supposed to find our way out of here without Dan? He should've come inside with us. He was supposed to lead us to the potion. What? Are we supposed to search for it ourselves inside that...that...place? I have my doubts about that. Guntheeerrr!! No, Figsbi did it. It's all his fault. I should have listened to you. He sent us on this wild extravaganza to get us lost in the middle of the mountains..."

"Listen to you," I interjected. "You're talking nonsense. We're here. Dan brought us here. So what if he's gone? This is the place that he said. We'll go inside and see if anyone's there; or if the potion's there. If it's not there, then we'll have reason to get angry. Besides, it's probably safer in there than out here if the mountain creatures are about. O.k.?"

"Maybe you're right. But then again, maybe not. Who knows what's inside there? But I suppose we better find out."

I helped him up. He limped some but walked it off. I was surprised at his momentary lapse in judgment. He seemed almost defeated for a moment. I guess it happens to the best of us. Anyhow, it made me feel needed, like I in some way helped him. I knew that he was braver than I, but sometimes his emotions got the best of him.

We returned up the front steps and slowly entered the darkened doorway where the musky air hit us tenfold like a sack of dirt in the darkness, groping us, inviting us to continue until the darkness surrounded us on every side and any light which fought its way in through the overgrowth disappeared at about five paces in. We crept forward unsure whether or not our next step would drop us through the floorboards. It was as if the darkness was darker than the light was light. We stuck close to each other. We felt our way about moving slowly, step by step. How were we supposed to find a bottle of potion in this atmosphere? It was crazy, but we had to try. We grabbed onto whatever was within our reach to give us a sense of direction. I felt a wall, and we followed it to another wall. The floor was unforgivably loud and unstable.

"Does it feel like someone else is here?" Cornelius whispered.

"It's strange," I answered.

"Stand still."

We stood as quietly as possible. The floor still creaked. Someone or something else was there. There was a presence with us. It moved about slowly, carefully, like it was stalking us, watching us in the dark, lurking without the need for eyes. There was a breath not our own. It was close and then it was not. It was someone else's breath in the musky darkness. We dared not move. I felt as helpless as that night in the forest. Surrounded. We huddled against the wall to give us a sense of bearing. We dared not speak. I was expecting to hear the sound of slurping and chattering and to feel the groping and grabbing, but it never came. It was worse. It was so close that it was distant.

"Let's go back," I said.

"No. We can't. There's nothing out there for us."

"There's Port Fectia," I said.

172

With that, a giggle like the giggle of a little girl, like a giddy little girl, like a little gem of a girl, erupted from somewhere in the midst of the darkness.

"Who's there?" Cornelius demanded, and the response was that of a very young, cheerful voice.

"Port Fectia? Did somebody say Port Fectia? I have not heard mention of that place in so, so long. Oh, how it sounds so nice. Port Fectia. Port Fectia. Port Fectia. Oh, let me say it again. Port Fectia."

There was silence again; only the creaking floor and the distant breath and the presence.

"Who are you?" I felt Cornelius clutching his sword as I pressed up against him. "Speak, you coward. Speak and show yourself."

A flicker of light caught our attention in the far corner of the room and went out as quickly as we could see it. In a moment's time I made out a table and a random assortment of chairs and a figure. A burning fragrance cut right through the musky air as if a candle or a match had been lit. Then the burst of light came again, this time from a different part of the room. We looked and saw a figure too briefly to comprehend. The light went out in a snap, leaving the mysterious sound of giggling in its place.

"Who are you and why do you want to play these games?" Cornelius asked. "Why not show yourself, if you're brave enough to do so."

"Because I like games," giggled the voice.

The giggling became incessant, moving about in the darkness. I heard it in one place and then another. It sounded near and then far. It came, froze, and drifted off again. It left us with the feeling of suspension in the darkness. Then the door closed and a light flickered in its place. It flickered on and off and on and off, each time revealing a glimpse of a figure; a chin, an arm, a frilly little dress; then the light held. A candle was lit and held by a little girl who could not have been older than eight. She appeared as a head floating in the darkness. Her eyes were pleasant and blue. Her cheeks were dimpled, her hair yellow and straight, the length of her chin. Her head was enormous, wobbling to and fro as if balancing atop her neck. Then it moved from

173

the doorway across the room, giggling as it went. The only light came from the broken window but stopped as soon as it met the darkness. It had not occurred to me then, but in that place, the darkness was stronger than the light.

"Oh, how I simply just love company," she said as she drifted. "It has been terribly too long. Too long. Too long. Oh, too, too long. Oh, so, so long..."

"What do you want with us, teasing us like this?" Cornelius asked.

"Want with you? Oh, you silly, silly boy. I was under the impression that it was you who was visiting me." More giggling occurred, and the flame was blown out, leaving even deeper darkness than before.

We cautiously moved away from the wall, our outstretched arms as our guide. We ventured toward what seemed to be the center of darkness where the girl's head floated only moments before. The giggling served as our compass.

"Show yourself." Cornelius demanded. "What's so funny that you can't stop laughing?"

"Port Fectia," she answered. "I heard someone say 'Port Fectia'. I thought that was funny." She giggled some more. The giggling moved toward us. We were converging. Then it stopped. And we stopped. I reached out to touch her, but nothing was there. Suddenly, she appeared in front of us like a ghost, holding the candle to her face, an illuminated, ghostly presence with large eyes and an expansive smile, giggling as if she had too much strong drink. Then, in a flash, a burst of light, stronger than a thousand candles, lit up the room and drove us backward in surprise, and the girl was there standing with a strange, black, furry creature draped around her neck and a stew pot dangling from her hands. The sudden brightness faded into a dim light, the light of a fire burning in the darkness, and the girl hung the stew pot over the fire, and we could see her, her entire self. She was little, a little girl indeed, but her head was three times bigger than that of a normal sized little girl's head. It wobbled because it was too big for her neck.

174

She wore a dainty red dress, but mutably so. Every time I looked at her after looking away, her dress was a different color in the light of the dancing fire. First it was red, then blue, then white, then a myriad of other colors too varied to remember. The dress remained unchanged as long as I kept my eye upon it, but if I glanced at the fire, or my friend, or the darkness around me, her dress would be changed as soon as I looked upon her.

"Sorry, big boys, I didn't mean to scare you," she giggled.

She was as dainty as her dress, and cunning, her smile wickedly delightful, and she was amusing herself at our expense. The creature around her neck had a furry, quiet face with beady eyes and pointed ears. It kept its menacing, glowing eyes upon us as we watched the little girl arrange an assortment of candles upon a table in the shape of a heart. Then, to our amazement, she reached into her fire and grabbed a pinch of flame between her fingers, tossing it onto the table and igniting the candles to form a burning heart. It added light to the darkness, but not terribly.

"How did you do that?" I asked.

"With great caution," she giggled.

She pulled the creature off from around her neck and cradled it in her arms, stroking its back and head and kissing the tip of its rugged, button-like nose. All the while the creature stared at us with mistrusting, green eyes and a mischievous grin. It purred while the girl gave it attention, but it would not look away from us. It waved its tail about the darkness as if to warn us, as if it intended to guard us like prisoners. The musky odor was displaced by the pleasant aroma of fire, but though it burned upon the floor, it produced no smoke, neither charring nor spreading.

"What is that thing?" Cornelius asked.

"This is a cat," she explained, "An animal perfectly adapted to the darkness in which I live. A most admirable and comforting creature. So soft. So soft. So soft. I call him Gregory. He is my friend. Tell me, big boys, what brings you to my humble home?"

"The healing power of the dandy nut potion. Gunther told us about it. Well, first Figsbi told us about it, and he told us how to get to

Gunther's house. Then Danxoumanxou led us here, though he seems to have disappeared. Gunther said he entrusted the potion to a charmer. Is it here? He said I could take it if I believe and I certainly believe. Is it here? Is it?"

"Oh, it's so delightful having visitors. It has been so, so, so long. I hope you're not angry with me. I was just having a little fun. I hope it's not too dark for you in here. Yes, I know why you've come. You're not the only ones who have come seeking the potion. Nobody comes here just to visit. They only come to take the potion. They take, take, take. Oh, but it's been so very, very, very long since anyone has tried. Yes, I can help you, if you believe, that is. Well, of course you believe, you already said that."

She began giggling uncontrollably. The cat, smug and grim, watched us intently as she held it close.

"Who are you?" Cornelius asked.

"It may seem silly, but I don't rightly know."

"Look little girl, if it's all the same to you, we're really in a hurry. Could you just tell us where the potion is so that we can get home before it's too late? My mother is dying. She needs medicine. We've come a long way for this potion."

"Silly boys, do you think I just leave the potion lying around like some frizbo you can just pluck off the tree? It is a very, very, very complex recipe. Give me a little time. First, tell me the password."

"What password?"

"I can't tell you, silly boy, you have to know it yourself."

"We weren't given any password."

"No password? No password? No password? Well, then, we will just have to make a deal. I don't just go around handing out potions like dandy nuts. Stand back."

The girl stood over the cooking pot. She set the cat on the floor at her feet. She waved her hands about the air and the pot began bubbling with a blue substance, emitting a blue haze into the shadows of the darkness. Then she gathered the candles, one by one, tossing them into the pot and the haze dissipated.

"What is it that your heart seeks most of all, big boys?"

176

"We're not sure what you mean."

"Why are you really here? Why do you want the potion? Is it for love? Is it for freedom? Is it for life? Is it for truth?"

Cornelius and I answered simultaneously. I said truth. He said love. The girl giggled uncontrollably, waving her hands about the air, stoking the flames, feeding the darkness. The more the fire raged, the darker the flames became until the fire turned black and the darkness purged the light and we could no longer see.

"Well, which is it? Love or truth?"

"We're looking for the truth," I said. "We just got a little sidetracked, that's all."

"Sidetracked? So you decided to follow love instead of truth? Let me tell you something, boys. You will never find love unless you find truth first, for how can you possibly know what love is unless you first know what is true? Then again, you love before you seek, for who dares seek for something he does not first love?"

"We are supposed to find Port Fectia. That's what Pirnoff said. He said we could find truth there, but my friend's mother needs help fast. It's the truth we really seek. We just want to know what this is all about. We don't know why we're here any more than you do, really. We seek truth because my friend's mother is dying."

"What about your other friend? Does he love her too? The one he left along the path? The one he was to marry? Is that love? Is that love? Is that love? Well, if it's Port Fectia you seek, you have come to the right place. This is it. Welcome to Port Fectia, my humble home. Gregory is the king. Bow to the king, big boys. Bow, I said! Bow, I said! Bow, I said!"

We did nothing of the sort. The darkness was growing more frightening and the little girl more confusing. She was attempting to make us feel guilty for leaving Aza-liel behind. How did she even know about her in the first place? Who was this girl, this charmer, this guardian of the potion, and why was she so intent upon confusing us further?

"You're not bowing, you're not bowing, you're not bowing."

Suddenly, a flash, like the striking of a match, ignited the entire room, accompanied by a monstrous crackling of the flames, and the fire was glowing once again, and we could see. The fire had been transferred from under the pot to inside the pot. The little girl with the enormous, wobbling head was standing before the fiery pot waving her arms about her head and reciting some unintelligible incantation. In each fist she held a dandy nut, squeezing with all the ferocity in her dainty little hands. Her strength was greater than any little girl's should be. As she squeezed the hard outer shell of the nuts, cracking them with her bare hands, a green gel oozed forth, covering her hands, running down her bare arms. As we watched, fascinated, mesmerized, she reached her hands inside the fiery pot and held them there. She held them in the fire. She held them longer. The flames climbed up her arms. Her face slowly changed. Her chin grew long and ghastly. Her eyes grew old, and her brow became wrinkled. Her cheeks sunk and her nose sloped and her hair turned wretched and grey. She was a little girl no more. She was older than the trees. She began to speak in a language we understood:

> Truth for truth
> Sea to sea
> Love for love
> Port Fectia be
> Sky to sky
> Dust to man
> Let these boys
> Now understand

Suddenly, the darkness lifted. Above us was sky. Below us was green. Behind us was the rolling sea, vast and beautiful. Before us were colorful meadows. The little girl, now an old lady, worked her magic before the fiery pot. She pulled her hands from the flames, unharmed. She held the shells of the dandy nuts in her hands. She took her fingernail and scratched the outer surface of the shells, causing the shells to flake and fall into the burning pot until they had been completely consumed. The charmer waved her hands once more, and, like the switch of the light, the scenery disappeared, and the fire returned to its place below the pot, lighting the room just enough to see that the old lady had changed back into the little girl with the wobbling head. She reached down and gently lifted the cat into her arms and began stroking its fur.

"There, there. Do you like that when I scratch behind your ear? Yes, I know you do. Tell me, boys, what did you see?"

"Beautiful meadows."

"And a sea."

"Was it Port Fectia?" we asked.

"Yes, big boys, it was as you say."

"So it really exists?"

"Of course it does. I already told you. You are already there. You just have to believe. Come here, let me show you."

We went to the girl. She told us to look into the pot. It was clear. It was pure. I was able to see all the way to the bottom where an image appeared. It was the same image we saw only moments ago, but it was different. The meadows were there; so was the sea and the sky and the lush, green ground, but there was something in the middle of it all, and we recognized it immediately. It was the little lodge in which we stood, only viewed from the outside. There was the hillside and the steps and the foliage; the broken window and the darkness inside.

"Port Fectia, big boys, Port Fectia. It exists, indeed. It exists here with me. It exists in this magic healing potion. This is it. This is it. This is it. This is the truth you seek."

Amazed, I was speechless. Cornelius shook with excitement. He reached toward the potion to touch it, but as he did, it darkened, and he refrained.

"Is this the potion that will heal my mother?"

She nodded. She giggled with glee, so playful, so coy.

"Then may I take it? How should we transport it? What must I do when I get there?"

"Not so fast, silly boy. What makes you think you can take it with you? How do I know that you really are who you say you are? How do I know that you are not trying to steal the potion?"

"Figsbi promised," Cornelius argued.

"I don't know this Figsbi. The potion belongs to Gunther. He did not tell me you were coming."

"Gunther knows Figsbi. And Gunther's friend Danxoumanxou led us here."

"Oh, *did* he now? Danzimanzi? Sorry, but I don't know him either."

Cornelius' excitement quickly turned to frustration. He was beginning to lose his temper. His eyes grew fierce, and his jaw clenched, grinding against itself.

"I think I can say with quite a bit of certainty," Cornelius continued, his tone showing his aggravation, "That Gunther is fine with us taking the potion to help my mother."

"That *is* the question, then, isn't it?"

"What's the question? That Gunther's fine with it?"

"No, on the contrary - that you think with quite a bit of certainty. What makes you so sure, that just because Gunther led you to the potion, that he wants you to have it?"

"How can I be sure that your concoction is the true potion?"

"Now you're catching on. You can't, of course."

"You're crazy." Cornelius was obviously losing patience with the wobbly headed charmer.

"Listen, big boy, you don't have the password. No password. No password. No password. I told you I'd make a deal, didn't I? You may take a vial of the potion with you on one condition."

"What condition?"

"Bring me the head of Aza-liel."

CHAPTER NINETEEN
THE POTION

A thousand questions raced through my brain at that moment, the most central being How does the little girl know Azariel? *And furthermore,* What does she have against her? *Something told me we were about to find out.*

The giggling little girl was giggling no more. Her countenance turned as cold as Giltlegard steel. She drew upon us with her eyes, her large, round eyes upon the face of her enormous head. The seriousness of her gaze caused shivers down my torso. I would have certainly believed she was joking if it was not for that gaze, and that gaze was directed most pointedly at my companion. He was not one to be shaken, even in the darkness of uncertainty. He returned her proposition with his own menacing glare. His fingers twitched, eager to strike. He was done with the craziness, done with the games. He wanted answers.

"What would a girl like you want with her head?"

"I could boil it in a stew, or maybe serve it on a plate of frizbos and dandy nuts. I could think of so, so, so many things to do with it. Gregory could even play with it on the floor. He likes to play with things."

"Little girl, I think I have been patient with you so far. I have come for the healing potion, and I will not leave here without it."

Cornelius clutched the handle of his sword, fastened to his left hip. From the girl's arms, the cat let out a low growl followed by a mean hiss. The hairs on the back of its neck stood up when Cornelius manipulated the handle of his sword. Silence. Darkness. The flickering of the flame. The potion. Those terrible, girlish eyes, frowning, narrowing, piercing.

"This is absurd," Cornelius argued. "I will do no such thing. Aza-liel is my friend."

"Then where is she, this friend of yours?"

"I don't know."

"You left her didn't you? You left her behind to fend for herself in the mountains – a girl, all alone, just like me – this friend of yours. I can hear her calling now. Cornelius! Cornelius! Yes, look, there she is."

The little girl's dress changed into the blue and white flower pattern that Aza-liel wore when we first met her. The little girl's face changed into an exact representation of the wonderful face of Aza-liel. She looked scared. She was wandering through the woods alone. She was tired and worn and mistreated. Her face was thinning, and her hands were bloodied and bruised. She looked as if she was trying to escape someone or something. The image faded. The little girl became the little girl again, and her giddiness returned, and she giggled.

"Is she still alive?" I asked.

"Of course, silly boy, that is why I want her head. It is not for her to live any longer."

"I will not do such a thing," growled Cornelius. "I will take *your* head if you don't watch your words."

At that, the little girl giggled and giggled and giggled some more. Her giggle turned into a cackle, and her cackle into a burst of laughter. She laughed and laughed at the thought of such an episode, Cornelius chopping off her head. But she temporarily lost her sense of humor when Cornelius acted upon his threat.

He drew his sword and, in a flash, rushed at the little girl, so young, so dainty, and he thrust his sword at her throat, pinning her against the back wall, holding her there with the tip of his blade nicking her skin. Undaunted, she began giggling again. The cat she called Gregory snarled, and the furry skin along his paws receded, and he flashed his claws, sharp and ready.

"Beware of Aza-liel," said the charmer. "She is one of them. She is part of the Realm of the Unbelief. She has led you astray. She is not fit to live. She wants to keep you from healing your mother. She ran away thinking that you would search for her. She was counting on your love for her being stronger than your love for the potion. But she underestimated your resolve. You have sought the potion. You have sought the truth. You have sought Port Fectia. She will stop at nothing to thwart your plans. She is the enemy. Bring me her head, and you can take the potion."

"You lie!" cried Cornelius. "You're a liar!"

"I tell you the truth. I swear by Port Fectia."

"She lies!" I cried, "Aza-liel is running from the mountain creatures."

"Mountain creatures? What mountain creatures, silly boy?"

"The ones that go around haunting people and making noises and driving them off of cliffs."

"There are no mountain creatures. I have never seen one. Silly, silly, silly boys."

She giggled uncontrollably. Cornelius thrust the sword a little harder, drawing blood, but the girl remained undeterred.

"Then where is she? Why did she leave you? Why did she hide herself from you? Why did she run from you in the clearing? She is one of them now. She is with the man, Pirnoff."

Slowly, Cornelius lowered his sword. Was the little girl telling the truth? Everyone we met was telling the evils of the stranger. But then again, why did the stranger have such difficulty trusting Aza-liel? Was it a ruse?

"I'm not sure what you're talking about," said Cornelius.

"Aha! Now that's a good start," she giggled. "Saying that you're not sure about something is a whole lot better than saying with quite a bit of certainty. You're already catching on."

"I will take the potion to my mother. Then I will know whether you are true or false."

"I want the head of Aza-liel – first."

Suddenly, we were at a standstill. Neither party was going to budge. The magic potion was sitting in a pot over the fire. There was no way to get the potion without interference from the opposition. I

183

looked at the canteen strapped around my neck. It was presently empty. Cornelius had his sword still drawn and the little girl cornered. I took the opportunity. My legs began shuffling forward. They brought me, slowly, to the pot that held the potion. I looked down inside. It was clear, just like before. Slowly, I lowered my canteen into the potion and filled it to the top. It was hot, almost scalding, but I was able to bear it for a moment. I looked and saw that Cornelius was playing along with me. He had raised his sword once again, pointing it directly at the little girl, so small, so dainty. The girl watched with wide eyes and a smile. She was not going to let us go without a fight.

Suddenly, the cat she called Gregory leapt from her arms to Cornelius's face, biting and clawing and hissing and gouging. Cornelius swung his sword wildly in vain, dropping it to the floor in desperation. He managed to rip the cat off of his head, tossing it across the room, but we looked, and the cat was no longer a mere cat. It had become large and fierce and powerful. It was still a cat, to be sure, but it was the size of a man, and its growl became a roar, and its hiss became a screech. With the potion secured around my neck, I darted to the open window where the light seeped through, trying to escape, leaping, but falling, falling in the darkness, caught from behind by the little girl, scrambling but seized. She pounced on me like a predator. She held me down. She sought the canteen, but I hid it under my curled body. She stood over me. She took both hands and grabbed the collar of my coat. She lifted me off the ground and tossed me across the room. I fell hard onto the wooden floor. I clutched the canteen, making sure I still owned it. The charmer looked like a little girl. She giggled like a little girl. She spoke with the voice of a little girl. But one thing was no longer in doubt. That was no little girl.

The cat-like beast and the charmer surrounded us, two fallen boys, desperate, beaten, cornered.

The little girl spoke no longer with the voice of a girl, but rather, with the voice of a monster. "Hand over the potion," she said. "It is what Aza-liel seeks. She seeks to become powerful. Immortal. I cannot let that happen."

"I swear by my mother's remaining breaths, I will not leave here without the potion."

"Then you will not leave here at all. Gregory!"

The cat sprang toward Cornelius to devour him, but this time, Cornelius was ready. He drew his brawlstick, the broad handled one with the flat trunk, and whacked the beast in the side of the head as it flew through the air, sending it sprawling across the floor. I joined in the fray. I took my own brawlstick, the one I obtained in Pattick's, and furiously beat the creature over the head and the back as it lay dazed upon the floor. Cornelius reached for his sword, but the little girl pounced on it first, holding it above her head, such a large sword for a little girl, but she had no trouble at all bearing its weight. She came at Cornelius and swung the weapon like she was chopping wood, but Cornelius escaped by rolling out of its way. Again, I tried to make my exit with the potion. The little girl came at me with the sword. Cornelius followed in pursuit. The fire went out. Darkness overwhelmed us. We heard the giggling from somewhere in the black. It seemed to be all around us. The giggling was constant, like a ringing in my ears, like the howling of the wind.

"You cannot win this game, silly boys. You cannot defeat the power of Port Fectia."

Suddenly, there was a furious commotion. There was the thumping of a body hitting the floor. There was crying and screaming. There was pounding and wrestling and beating and yelling. There was the sound of steel clashing with steel. I took a few thumps myself, but I crawled to the door. I found it. I pried it open. The sounds of abuse rose up from the rickety old planks of the floor. Suddenly, the fire ignited under the pot full of potion, creating a glimmer of light unto our path. The body of the little girl lay motionless on the floor. Her enormous head lay next to it, her eyes big and playful, her smile wide and welcoming. She reached out for her head. She took it and placed it back upon her neck. Cornelius jumped to his feet. He secured his sword in its sheath. He returned his brawlstick and baton to his sash. He joined me at the door and we hastily made our way outside, leaving the giggling girl lying upon the floor of her house. I felt the inside of my coat just to make sure the canteen was still there. I do not know how Cornelius made it out alive, but as we made our way across the flat and descended the embankment, heading east, we heard the echoes of a giggling voice carrying off with the breeze, "Be careful, silly boys, be good and beware of the Realm of the Unbelief."

CHAPTER TWENTY
THE FALLS

Leaving that dark, wretched place was like lifting a terrible mask off of the face of a young maiden only to find out that the real thing is far more hideous than the mask itself, for although we escaped, it was not without broken bodies and the looming anticipation of returning to Giltlegard, the most disturbing consideration of all, those four steel walls waiting, waiting, waiting for us somewhere in the distance.

We travelled feverishly into the early evening. When we felt as if we had distanced ourselves far enough from the dangers of the giggling girl, we relented, and rested under some trees. Though she had been beheaded, we knew her powers were great and refused to take our escape for granted. We had no idea where we were, but we thought about it. Gunther's cave was on the edge of the mountain cliff facing east with Giltlegard visible to the south east. Dan had led us north from the cave, further and deeper into the mountains until we reached the house of the giggling girl. We remembered that east of Gunther's cave was a vast valley which seemed to stretch north from there, curving west around the very mountain side upon which we traveled. Since the distance back to the cave was only a few days journey on foot, we figured that if we set out east from the house of the giggling girl that we would eventually locate the valley, and from there we could travel south toward Giltlegard, according to our calculations.

We had gone most of the day without water; our lips were chapping and our throats were dry. With the canteen filled with potion, we were hoping to rely upon mountain streams or rivers, but so far that day we found none. Even so, if we happened to find a water source, we had no means of carrying the water with us along our journey. It was a risk we were forced to make for the sake of Mrs. Van. So there we were, transients of the forest, tattered and worn.

Cornelius appeared like a surviving soldier emerged from a battlefield. How he made it thus far, I had no comprehension. His pant leg was ripped, my sash still draping his wound. He gingerly favored his right leg. Blood stained parts of his clothes, and the scratches on the back of his neck and the top of his head and his face still oozed, reeking droplets of blood mixed with dirt and sweat, courtesy of Gregory the cat and a hard day's journey. We needed a bath. We needed food. We needed to be loosed from that treacherous place and search for Giltlegard by way of the green eastern valley.

After resting our weary bones, we pressed on. The world was still. We crossed in and out of gullies and through thickets of brush. We were familiar with struggle by then. Our turmoil in the mountains caused me to reflect upon the beautiful meadows and ponds that once led us westward. Although it had not even been a week, it seemed like a lifetime ago. That was when the words of the stranger meant something. We had spurned those words. We had broken just about every instruction imaginable from the stranger. Yes, the words of the stranger. They seemed so distant there in the mountains. Somehow, our journey had taken quite a drastic turn. But for some reason, Port Fectia never left my mind. What was it? Where was it? Was it as the giggling girl had said? Was it there with the potion? Was it the potion itself? Was it the darkened hut in the woods? Does it exist at all? We were headed in the opposite direction of where the stranger said it would be. I wondered about it. The mystery. The truth. What was the truth? I reminded myself that this was not my quest. It was Cornelius'. What if the stranger was wrong? Why could I not make it *my* quest? If the stranger was wrong about anything, he could certainly be wrong about everything. I still longed for the western sea. I could part with my friend. I could leave him to Giltlegard, and I could go west. No. I could never make it without him. He may have little need for me, but I had great need for him. He was a survivor. Besides, as much as I wanted to find the truth for myself, as much as I wanted to find meaning for my own life, I felt more compelled to help my friend in any way I could. It was becoming evident that even though the stranger pointed both of us in the same direction and gave both of us the same rules and the same expectations and sent both of us upon the same journey together, Cornelius and I were searching for two completely different things. Even though we both knew Giltlegard, and even though we both felt its oppression, it seemed that we could not agree upon its solution. It was not my quest, I reminded myself. Cornelius was sent; not I. It was the King's edict - if there really was such a King. I wanted there to be one. I wanted it so badly. I had nothing else to want. I did not have a mother that was dying of sickness. Mine merely suffered from whatever it was that ailed all mankind, myself included, that meaninglessness and impending doom. I wondered about my mother and father and brother. I wondered if they had resumed their normal lives in that cold, grey prison or if they were scaling the walls or cutting off their pelzors. Was my father maintaining the light of the city despite the chaos? What would I be doing if I were there?

The journey east across the mountain was difficult. There was some terribly steep terrain. We were weary and only getting wearier. We were thirsty and only getting thirstier. We were dirty and only getting dirtier. The evening faded into night, and the night faded into cold. We continued until it became nearly impossible to see. We were forced to spend the night under some trees huddled together near a fire that we managed to build. We were so tired that we could not sleep. Suddenly, the world was not so still anymore, the forest coming alive with darkness and the sounds of darkness. I admit that we were slightly afraid. The fear of darkness is little more than the aching presence of the unknown, of the unseen. Presently, the unknown was the only thing we had to keep us company, day or night. But we did not speak of it then. We spoke of other things.

"Van?" I asked.

"Yes?"

"Do you miss the days lying on our backs in the grass and staring up at the walls of Giltlegard?"

"Haven't thought about it. Been too busy, really. But now that you mention it, no."

"Is this so unlike what you imagined?"

"Imagination could never produce this. This is completely original. Imaginations are like a copy, like a shadow. No one could have imagined this. No one. Our lives were so...so..."

"Small?"

"Sure. Small. I guess, small. Insignificant. Not even that. Worthless. I thought maybe it would be like Giltlegard, only no pelzors and no factory. And no fake smiles. But lots of brawlball. Wishful thinking I guess."

"Do you miss it? Brawlball?"

"Nah, but at least I got to use my stick anyhow." We laughed.

"Know what?" I asked.

"What?"

"I was scared back there. That little girl. No girl should have that kind of strength. And the way she put her head back on – it's like she's invincible."

"Yeah. She was more like a monster. I can't figure it out."

"What?"

"Whatever it was that she's all about. I mean, who's side is she on, anyway?"

"What do you think about what she said? About Aza-liel, I mean?"

"That she joined the Realm of the Unbelief? No way!"

"But what if she did?"

"Who is this Realm of the Unbelief anyway? I think she's truly lost. Whatever way she's lost, I don't know. But if it's true that she joined this – whatever it is – it wasn't of her own will. She wouldn't do that. She's one of us."

"She asked you a good question, though."

"What?"

"Why don't you try to find Aza-liel?"

"I will find her. That's why we must hurry. My mother needs me. I promised her. As soon as she is healed, I will find Aza-liel. I can't bear to think of her out here all alone. I'm afraid for her life. I just hope she stays safe until I get to her. Then I will never let her out of my sight again. I can't for the life of me figure out why she ran away from us that night in the field. It makes no sense. It burns me up inside. And where did she go? It's like she disappeared into thin air. Os, it might seem strange to you, but as much as I think she needs me, I need her too. She gives new meaning to my life. Her sweetness, her zest for living, it's a wonderful thing. It is so...so...contagious. I would give my life for her in a second. But I can't explain her, and I don't know where she is, and I love my mother, too. I promised her that I'd come back for her, and I intend to keep that promise. We just couldn't afford to spend any more time looking around for Aza-liel."

"I guess I know what you mean."

I thought again of telling my friend about the necklace, but refrained. I figured he had enough to worry about without adding more stress and confusion to his life.

"Van?"

"What?"

"Do you believe in Port Fectia?"

"I don't know. I think I do, but I'm not sure it's like the stranger said. I have my doubts."

"Do you remember when Aza-liel suggested that it didn't exist?"

"Yeah, I didn't understand at the time. Now I'm not so sure. I don't know what Port Fectia is. I just want to find truth, that's all. I just want to know the meaning of this journey. I want to know what we struggle for. I want to know what freedom really means. What about you? Do you believe in Port Fectia?"

"I just think it's possible, that's all. I want more than anything to find out. I want to go there."

"You know what, Os? I've been terribly selfish. I took us off the path against your better judgment. I made a pact with Figsbi. I led us into the mountains. I lost Aza-liel. All against your better judgment. And for what? For this potion that we don't even know for sure works. I've been blindly trusting the advice of everyone we meet because I don't know who else to trust. I don't know what to believe. And I've kept you from finding Port Fectia for yourself."

"Don't worry about it, Van. Your mother's more important. I just can't help but think that the stranger knows the path to truth, regardless of what everyone else says about him."

"Maybe you're right. Maybe I'm a fool."

"No. You're not a fool. You're the bravest boy I know. I could never do what you're doing. I could never carry the burden that you're carrying, having to care for your mother, having to decide what's true and what's false, having to make your way on this journey without really knowing who to trust. You're my hero. I can honestly say that. There's no one else like you."

"I suppose that only makes me a brave fool, then. The fact remains. If I don't find the truth, then I'm a failure, no matter how brave I might be. And if I don't save my mother, then I've broken my promise. And if I don't find Aza-liel, then I've lost my whole life. If I lose all those things, then what good am I out here? It'll be no different than life in Giltlegard. We just might as well return, for the misery will be the same. Only the scenery will change. In fact it will be worse, because we will never know if we are really prisoners out here. What if there is something better than this? What if there is another world outside of this one? We will never know. Not knowing is the greatest agony of all. Besides, I think you give me way too much credit. I'm not so brave without you, Os."

"You really think so? I was afraid I was more of a hindrance than a help."

"Absolutely not. I need you. If I didn't need you so much I might have the mind to send you off toward Port Fectia on your own. You'd probably do a better job of finding it than I would."

"Well, no matter what they all say, the stranger was right about one thing, at least. Giltlegard is no place to live. It's a lie. A fraud. Our lives were a fraud. And one thing I do know is that the truth will never be found inside the walls of that city. And when we do return, I don't think we could leave again soon enough. I'm almost afraid of going back there. I'm afraid of not getting out. How do we know that if we go back, that we will ever be able to leave again?"

"We don't, Os. We don't know. But we have to try. I'll tell you what. As soon as we get to Giltlegard, assuming we even make it out of these mountains alive, we'll give my mother the potion, we'll find our way back out of the city, assuming that's even possible, we'll find Aza-liel, and then we'll immediately start all over again toward Port Fectia to find out once and for all if it's really there."

That was a lot of ifs, but I agreed.

I was glad I had a friend in Cornelius. I trusted his character explicitly. I trusted his sincerity. I trusted his loyalty. But I quietly wondered if I could fully trust his judgment. Then I wondered if I could even trust my own. The two of us, still huddled together, still hungry and thirsty, surrounded by the mysterious sounds of the night, fell asleep. I was not sure, but I thought I heard slurping and chattering just before dozing off, and I took those frightening noises with me into my dreams.

When I awoke by the morning's light, the fire was smoldering, and I heard something I did not notice the previous night. It was the sound of trickling water. So I got up and followed the sound and found a water brook maybe only a hundred paces away.

"Van!" I called out. "Van! Come quick! Look what I found!"

In no time, Cornelius was beside me and we drank up the water like it was the truth itself. We did not waste our time scooping it with our hands. Instead, we bent over like beasts of the field and sucked it up straight from the brook. Then, cold as it was, we washed and refreshed our bodies and faces, and Cornelius cleaned and redressed his wounds and we were new again. We were spry, though still hungry, and we continued on foot throughout the morning. We crossed over another brook and eventually came to a larger stream flowing east, so we stayed along its banks, hoping that it would lead us into the valley.

The trees grew sparse along the stream, allowing the blue sky to become a cheerful covering for our heads, and we kept pace with the only two clouds which occupied it. We had access to more water than we could possibly drink in a lifetime and we kept an eye out for something edible as our stomachs continued to complain against us. The stream started out calmly and quietly but at some point caught us off guard by becoming a river. A roar began to resonate along its banks, and we looked up toward the east, and the blue sky met the plush green valley at the horizon, and we figured we must be nearing

193

the foot of the mountains, so our excitement raged like the rushing waters and our pace suddenly quickened and we forgot how hungry we were and we followed the rapid headway until we approached an impossible task. We came to the edge of a mountain cliff. The horizon opened up into a glorious expanse. The valley lay magnificently before us, but we were nowhere near the foot of the mountain. Before us was a waterfall, steep and straight, the perfect combination of beauty and power, crashing violently into a crystal clear pool before gathering itself into a pocket of serenity and dispersing with such poise that I wished I could dive down into its depths and cool my sweating head. Cornelius and I looked at one another with such curiosity and uncertainty that we stood speechless for a time while the beauty of the scene struck us, stealing the breath right out from our lungs. We were in a predicament. How were we supposed to get from the cliff to the valley floor? The mountain side was steep and treacherous with no sign of easing. We thought about heading south with the hopes of finding an easier incline, but we were both famished, and we had no idea how long it would be until we found food. We thought about throwing ourselves into the river and plummeting to the bottom of the falls, but we were so high, and even if we were somehow able to survive the drop, we had no idea how deep the pool of water was at the bottom. We spent some time standing there thinking and looking around and thinking some more. The safest thing to do was not necessarily the most prudent thing. We needed to get to the valley floor, and we needed to get there as quickly as possible.

"Grab that tree log," Cornelius ordered.

There behind us lay a fallen trunk from what used to be a smallish tree. It was heavier than it looked, but after some difficulty we managed to pry it away from its imbedded position in the dirt and carried it clumsily to the bank of the river, heaving it headlong into the flow of the current, holding our breath as it floated away toward the edge of the cliff. We rushed over to watch it plummet, and sure enough, it did. It was Cornelius' way of testing the fall. The log fell mightily, projecting itself only slightly away from the downpour, and in seconds plunged into the depths of the pool, popping back up

194

immediately and lingering there in the wake, struggling to break free. However, the log stayed afloat. After a few moments, it finally broke away and floated calmly to the banks of the pool into a harbor of wild limpets.

"It seems intact," Cornelius observed. Of course we could not tell for certain, but it did not appear to be splintered or gouged.

"I've got an idea," Cornelius offered. "We go over the side of the falls, just like the log. It's the quickest way down. If we wander around up here in the mountains anymore, we're liable to starve to death before we ever get down, and who knows what other creatures are waiting for us up here. If we go over the falls and survive, we've got an easier road in the valley."

"*If* we survive," I argued. "It's a risk."

"What isn't a risk? This entire journey's a risk. We don't know any one single thing for sure except that things aren't right and we can't stay here."

"You're right," I admitted.

"Listen. We need to share a log. Something big enough to hold us up, but small enough to take with us over the edge. We hold on to it. When we land at the bottom, assuming we're still conscious, we keep holding on the log until we're able to paddle our way to the shore. It's as simple as that. Ready?"

Ready? No, I was not ready. The drop was probably taller than the tallest tree on the valley floor. It was maybe twice as tall. It was not a matter of being ready. It was just a matter of doing.

"Sure," I said.

"Good. Let's find our floating device."

We searched around a little bit. Cornelius ventured into the woods until he found a log similar to the one we tested, only it was not buried in the ground. Together, we lugged it to the riverbank. It was solid and smooth with broken branches stemming from the sides, giving us something to hold onto. We were ready. We looked at one another as though we were parting, never to meet again. We shook hands and embraced.

"Hold on tight," he advised. "When we hit the water, make sure you hold yourself away from the log so it doesn't hit you, but you must not let go. There's no telling how deep it is. But it's at least deep enough to swallow up that log we tossed."

With that, we waded into the water. The current pulled us forward, slowly at first before quickening. My body tensed up. The cold water shocked my bones. We paddled to the center of the river, trying to position ourselves in the deepest waters. The log kept us afloat very nicely, my feet no longer touching the bottom of the riverbed. I shivered from head to toe, gripping the fallen tree like a shield in battle. The current lured us to the edge. I instinctively checked to make sure that the canteen filled with potion was secured around my neck. Then, as if a trap door had been released from under us, gravity yanked us downward, and we fell. I immediately lost perspective. I had no idea where Cornelius was because I could not see him. The downward force separated me slightly from the downpour. I was free falling. Looking up, I saw sky, blue and blurry, and I held my breath and suddenly it was not the sky anymore, but the clear jumbled splash of the pool. The landing felt rough at first and then soft. I was under the deep with my eyes wide open and my heart racing, plunging further and further into that watery tomb, still clutching the stems of the log as if they were a baby. Then I realized that what I was clutching was not half the amount of log that I started out with. The mighty impact had splintered our wood, and I was left holding the smaller piece. I finally came to a halt somewhere beneath the surface of the deep, so I kicked my feet, struggling clumsily toward the surface, my insides ready to burst, and when I finally broke through into the fresh air, I gasped for as much air as I could handle, struggling to keep my head above water in the magnetic force of the pool before realizing that somehow the canteen had become dislodged from my body.

"The potion!" I screamed between breaths, "Van! The potion!"

I tried to paddle out toward the shore, but the insignificant remnant of tree failed to keep me afloat, so I began to sink, the current pulling me under. I remember little else besides the flailing of my

196

arms and the strong grip of my friend. It was that grip that saved me. I felt it well. I would have died without it. Cornelius, still clutching the log, dragged me out of the deadly current, not letting go until we came to a place where my feet could touch bottom, and exhausted, we climbed ashore.

"The potion," I said, "I must go back and find the potion." I tried to go, but Cornelius stopped me.

"Don't worry," he said, "It's right here." I looked, and there it was around his neck. "After I went under," he continued, "I popped back up, and there was the canteen, bobbing up and down in front of me, so I swam towards it. That's how I found you. If it hadn't come off, I might not have known where you were."

We collapsed on the ground and rested. We rested in the plush green grass under the lovely sky, and we were alive and we were out of the mountains and we lay upon the valley floor. After a while, we managed to get up. At that point I couldn't care less how tired I was because I was alive and the mountains were behind us. We headed south. We helped ourselves to the bounty of fruit which decorated the surrounding orchards to satisfy our aching bellies, and we continued onward while it was still daylight. We continued that way for two whole days, the canteen full of potion strapped securely across Cornelius' shoulders. We found enough ponds to drink from and enough choice frizbos and blooms to keep us blazing the trail through the plush, fertile valley. Then, upon the third day after our plummet over the falls, just before dusk began to creep in over the horizon, we lumbered up a hill, our legs three day's worth of wobbly, our eyes fixed upon the distance, and we popped our heads up over the top of the grassy pinnacle, and there it was in the distance - the glorious walls of Giltlegard extending upward into the patch of gray clouds that always seemed to hover above, and we stared in awe. We were home. And suddenly we conjured a surplus of energy and immediately darted across the friendly golden meadows toward the city of inevitable doom.

CHAPTER TWENTY ONE
THE TRIUMPHAL ENTRY 1

As usual, I did well just to keep a generous stride behind Cornelius' heels as we ran. We laughed like children at play. The gangly grass nipped at my pant legs as we parted the meadow like the wind. I tripped a couple of times, popping up as quickly as I fell, but I doubt my friend even noticed. He was too excited to look back. He was too close to saving his mother to stop for anybody. It did not take long for us to tire.

"Keep going," Cornelius pleaded, "We've got to make it before dark."

Just watching my friend's determination was enough to keep me astride, but the harder we pressed, the less I felt like we were getting anywhere. Those great, steel walls just sat there on the edge of the horizon like a mountain of despair. I could not fathom how we could be so excited to be approaching the place we most dreaded to be. Finally, we had to rest, the city up ahead, as pronounced as a fortress, waiting for us between each burning breath. We could not rest long. Cornelius refused to let us.

"We've got keep going," he said with his steely eyes as glazed as the layer of cloud over Giltlegard.

The falling of the great star left a pink hue across the southern sky. We raced on for what felt like time standing still until, finally, the great walls seemed to grow taller before my very eyes. We were getting closer. Then, sometime in between my mind getting caught up in the beauty of the setting star and in feeling pity for my poor, throbbing feet, the city came upon us. The northern wall loomed over us like the wall of a prison. We could still hear the faint, desperate cries from the other side. As we approached the wall, it humbled me. In all of our days sitting under the trees at the outskirts of town and staring up at the great wall, it had never humbled me. It never made me feel as small as it did presently. It was humbling because it was so frightening. Furthermore, the thought that facing our worst nightmare could be the difference in saving Mrs. Van from death was enough to bring us to our knees. Coming full circle was a dangerously exciting horror, not knowing, once we got in, if we would ever be able to escape again. Then, before we could worry about how to re-escape, an even more pressing question presented itself. How were we going to get inside?

We headed the direction of the northwest corner and moved south along the great wall, all the time feeling for a possible secret passage and keeping aware of our surroundings, looking for clues that might lead us back inside. We finally came upon the area that we recognized as the place where we had ended up when we first walked through the magical door into the world around us where the bloom trees stood. Judging from the length of the wall, that was also the same general vicinity where, that fateful day, we first noticed from afar the stranger walking inside the confines of the walls along the pathway toward the city. We figured that there must be a passage way into the city around there somewhere, so we looked. We looked, and we kept looking. We searched all around, feeling the wall, looking for a door or anything to show us the way, but we found nothing. Maybe there was no way inside, after all. Maybe the stranger appeared magically. Maybe it was never meant for us to return. After a while, we grew frustrated, and I, exhausted from the events of the last few days, sat down upon a stump under the shade of a bloom tree to rest my sore feet, the same tree we first ate from when we escaped weeks ago. As I rested, Cornelius wandered aimlessly along the base of the wall, searching high and low, basically confused. Then I remembered what he said that day when we were first searching for a way out of the city when he suggested looking in the least obvious place. So I began, there under the shade of the tree, to look about me. What is the least obvious place? There was nothing around us but fruit trees and grassy meadows and a great, steel wall. I peered up into the tree under which I sat. There was nothing unusual up there. I looked behind the tree and around it. Cornelius was growing quite desperate, kicking and beating the wall until his hands and feet were sore.

"Maybe it's on the other side," he yelled.

I did not answer. I was too busy trying to climb the bloom tree. I hoisted myself up into the branches and disappeared amidst the leaves. When he looked, I was missing, but I saw him, and he appeared panicked for a moment as if I had found the way into the city without him, or as if I had disappeared in the same manner as Aza-liel. He cried out to me.

"I'm up here, Van. In the tree." He came over in a huff and looked up and found me and scolded me.

"You scared me, Os. What are you doing up there? There's no time for games."

"I'm looking in the least likely place," I answered. Suddenly, it was as if a light had turned on in his brain, and his countenance lifted.

"Yes, of course," he said. "I remember. The least likely place. You see anything up there?"

"Yeah."

"Well what? What is it?"

"It's huge. Bigger than I've ever seen. I can almost get it."

"What is it? Tell me. I'm coming up."

Just as he managed to find a solid enough branch to grab onto, swinging his legs over the top and dangling like a wild animal, I managed to take hold of what I was looking for.

"Look, I found it!"

"What? The way inside?" He hung upside down beneath my feet.

"No, look."

I managed to pull down the largest bloom that I had ever seen, pink and proud, at least three, maybe four times bigger than any other bloom on the entire tree. I held it down to show Cornelius.

"See what I told you? It's huge."

"It's a bloom," he said.

"Yeah, I know what it is. But look at it."

I bent down to give him an better look, and just as he managed to hoist himself up onto the fat part of the branch where my feet rested, I fumbled the bloom and it fell. I reached down for it and lost my balance. Cornelius tried to grab me, but I tumbled down past him, reaching out for another branch to break my fall and thud - I crashed down upon the grassy turf and laid there momentarily with the wind knocked out of me and a little embarrassed.

"Are you all right?" Cornelius inquired, jumping down from the tree. He rolled me onto my back. I was not injured, though I hurt. It was funny, so I chuckled. Cornelius chuckled, too. Together, we laughed at my mishap like we were suddenly without a care in the world in the cool of the grass under the shade of the bloom tree near the old stump upon which I sat only moments earlier, and I noticed something peculiar. As I rolled back over onto my stomach, my eyes met the base of the stump. I stopped laughing and looked. I observed its base. It was not flush against the ground. It appeared unrooted.

"Look at this," I said, reaching out my hand and running my fingers along the bottom of the stump.

Cornelius noticed the seriousness in my tone and stopped laughing and looked. Suddenly, I forgot about my aching body and scrambled to my feet.

"Here, help me lift this."

We both dug our hands in the crevice between the stump and the dirt, and we pulled. It began to budge. We pulled harder. We pulled with all our might. The stump was heavy to say the least, but it was loose. After struggling with it for a few moments, we finally yanked it away from under the tree and stared in astonishment at what was underneath. It was a hole. It was a hole barely wide enough to access with a knotted rope attached curiously to somewhere on its circumference, and Cornelius, never being one to waste time, grabbed hold of the rope with both hands and lowered himself down. His head disappeared into the darkness of the hole, and his voice encouraged me to follow, so I did. I failed to see a single thing down there. I could only feel the knots upon the rope. I feared that with each step downward I would slip and be left hanging, or worse, falling, but I tried not to think about it.

"Still there?" I asked.

"Yes, keep coming," Cornelius answered.

"Where do you think we're going?"

"Who knows? But we've got to find out."

"Still there?" I asked again.

"Yes."

"Can you see anything yet?"

"Not yet."

"Still there?" I asked again.

No answer.

"Still there? Van, can you hear me? Van? Are you there? Where are you? Van!"

I was alone in the hole, still descending. However, at some point, even though I was sliding downward, I must have somehow begun pulling myself and climbing upward, for my head came to an opening and there was light, and I lowered myself down one more knot and my head popped up from out of the ground, and I found myself caught up in a bush. I looked around. Behind me was the great steel wall, and before me was the hazy gray air of the steel city. Carefully, I attempted to dislodge myself from out of the bush.

"There you are," Cornelius exclaimed, "It's about time!" He bent down and lent me a hand. I stood up and brushed myself off. There we stood, together, inside Giltlegard, and the screaming, like a legion of madmen, echoed within the confines of the walls. We headed toward the city along the same path that the stranger took on that fateful day. The taste of death was on our lips. The sound of death rang in our ears. The stench of death lingered in the air. The appearance of death was more than we could stand. The city could have been mistaken for a battlefield, and for all we knew, that is exactly what it had become. Rotted bodies, mangled or dismembered, lined the fields and steel streets. An awful stench was held by the fog, hanging there, making me feel sick. The cries of agony had only increased in the last few weeks, and there was still an assembly of hopeless citizens with nothing better to do than clamor at the base of the wall and weep and wail and pound their fists and beat their already battered heads up against the steel. Some were still trying to climb. Some were falling from lofty places as they climbed. Others, barely alive, dragged themselves across the ground, their pelzors cut off at their shins, bleeding and groping each other. The scene was unforgettable. Oh, how I wish I could forget. To think that the mere words of a stranger could cause such distress! Oh, but those were no mere words! I reasoned right then and there that either the stranger must be the cruelest creature who ever lived or he must be true, for there was no other explanation for what we encountered. What if we became prisoners again? Why have no Giltlegardians discovered the hole in the bush? Suddenly, I trembled at the thought of getting stuck there.

"Wait," I told Cornelius.

I raced back to the bush where we emerged, and gasped in horror at what I did not see. There was no hole in the ground. It was just dirt. There was no rope. It was just a bush. The hole did not exist. I got down and began digging with my bare hands, hoping that maybe I somehow covered it up when I climbed out, but the dirt was solid.

"Van!" I called, "It's gone! It's gone!" He rushed over. He tried to calm me down. "It's gone," I said again, "There's no hole...Just dirt." I began to cry.

Cornelius examined the dirt beneath the bush. He was quiet. He appeared worried, but he refrained from becoming upset. I think he was puzzled more than anything.

"Calm down," he whispered. "It's all right. I led you here. I'll lead you out. Don't worry." His hand upon my shoulder was comforting. I knew he must have been afraid but did not show it.

"This is an awful place, Van," I muttered, choking back the tears, "I never wanted to come back here again. Never. Now I know why."

He pulled me close and whispered again. "For me, Os. Do it for me. We're so close now. My mother is so close. She needs us. We'll find a way out, just like we found a way in."

I nodded. I lifted my head.

"Then let's be quick," I said.

Together, we raced through the steel streets amidst the sound of clanging pelzors. It was louder than I remembered it. The air was as bitterly cold as ever. We passed the market square, now little more than a web of bodies. We passed the temple at the center of town where the stranger had once stood and the courtyard where the Ponderers surprisingly continued pondering in paths of eight. Then someone cried out to us from the distance, "Help me! Help me!" and as we looked, a guard, his yellow vest tattered, stumbled toward us across a street of rank bodies, his arms outstretched with a knife thrust into his back and he crumbled into a heap in the street and looked up at us, and I recognized him, and he begged for our help, but we kept going. We did not stop. There was a time when all the death and gore, like that of a brawlball match, was the most exciting event in all of Giltlegard, but things had certainly changed. After the pandemonium, the brutality of death and misery could be seen for what it really was - a tragedy. I could not fathom that I ever took delight in such madness. A brawlball match was a poor comparison to the chaos and torture that we saw as we hurried down those cold, hard streets. The light of the city still burned as dimly as ever. I figured that the light may have remained constant since that fateful day. It made me think about my own father, the lightmaker, and I shivered at the thought of what may have become of him.

Finally, we approached the Van house. Our entire journey seemed to consummate in that moment. I am unable to rightly explain my own emotions upon our arrival, let alone those of Cornelius. There was relief and excitement, pleasure and fear, and a pregnant anxiety, ready to explode. Wasting no time, we burst inside. Everything was still in order.

"Mother, I'm back!" Cornelius cried. "Mother, I'm home! I brought you some medicine!"

Cornelius pulled the canteen off from around his neck, heading straight for the bedroom where he left his mother only weeks ago. We looked. No Mrs. Van. He called out some more. Nobody answered. He rushed into the kitchen, but Mrs. Van's familiar place at the end of the steel table was empty. Cornelius panicked. He spun in circles. He looked as if he had never set foot into his own house before. I ventured further inside Mrs. Van's bedroom.

"Van!" I shouted. "Look! She's here, on the floor!"

Cornelius rushed in. Mrs. Van had somehow managed to get herself stuck on the cold floor between the bed and the wall where she could not be seen by a casual glance into the bedroom. Carefully, we grabbed hold of her steel laden feet and slid her out from her predicament, across the smooth floor into an open space in the bedroom. She was alive. There is no telling how long she had been wedged in that uncomfortable position, but she was breathing. However slight, she was breathing, still clutching the flaming sideon, now wilted, holding it, keeping it, with all the remaining strength of her fingers. Her face was engaged with imminent death, old and struggling. The food and drink we left for her had been completely consumed. Her blanket had been left on her bed. She was without anything in the world except for a single, struggling orange flower with red dots, the resemblance of a flame that still burned bright in a mother's love for her son. Cornelius cradled her delicate head in his arms.

"Mother, I'm back. Look Mother. Look at me." He warmed her cold face with his hands.

"Mother, wake up. I'm back. Mother, say something."

She turned her glazed eyes upward.

"Corn-nelius - my son, I - afraid. I - afraid. I - not - feel - well. Must - leave. That - man - scares me. Scares - me. So - cold. So - thirs-ty." Her breath was faint, her lips quivering.

"Mother, I brought you some medicine. It'll make you better. Here, drink." Cornelius held the canteen up to her lips, but she had not finished speaking.

"Your - far. Your - far's - sorry. He - said - sorry."

"Mother, look at me. You have to drink the medicine. It'll keep you alive."

205

She parted her lips slightly. Her breathing slowed. Cornelius drizzled the potion into her mouth, lifting her head so she could swallow.

"There you go. There you go. You'll be all better soon. Drink up. There you go."

I stood back and witnessed a son loving his mother. The problem was that she did not revive. Cornelius grew frustrated. She was still breathing faintly.

"Come on, work!" he yelled.

Mrs. Van faded off to sleep. Cornelius helped her drink more, this time pouring it into her mouth. She swallowed. She became motionless. Her breathing became barely noticeable. She looked as if death had already touched her. She made no more efforts to speak. Cornelius continued to administer the magic healing potion, pouring it, forcing it down, some spilling onto the floor. She spit some of it back up.

"Come on Mother, drink!"

I noticed her hand. She squeezed the flaming sideon as tightly as she could, with every last bit of strength in her dying body. She squeezed it. She held it. She squeezed it as if to say "You have done well for me, my son. Goodbye." It was her final effort. Cornelius poured the last of the potion over her lips.

"Come on, Mother. It's magic. It'll make you well. I promise. Drink, Mother, drink!" Cornelius began to panic. "Live, Mother! Live!"

She did not respond. Her breathing grew fainter, and fainter, and fainter, and fainter, and stopped. We watched for another breath, but there was none. She loosened her grip on the flower, and it fell to the floor. Cornelius was frantic. He believed in the potion, just like they said that he must. At that moment, he believed in the potion as much as anyone has ever believed in anything, but his believing was of no effect. Whatever was left of the potion ran down his mother's face onto the steel floor. She made no sound. She made no movement. She lay there in her son's arms, her face glistening from dandy nut potion, and she was dead.

Quietly, Cornelius wept.

Everything he longed for, his entire reason for suffering, at that moment, was crushed beneath the weight of his failure. He buried his face in his mother's belly, and he wept.

"Mother, don't die. You can't die. You can't leave me like this."

He cried that way for a while. Then, slowly, his sorrow evolved into something more dangerous. He pounded his fists upon the floor. He beat his fists upon his chest and upon his face, yanking his hair, abusing himself, wrestling with himself uncontrollably upon the bedroom floor as if he was going insane.

"Van!" I shouted, "Get a hold of yourself!" I grabbed him and wrapped him up in my arms and he pushed me away and stood up like a madman, pacing aimlessly across the room, his face twisted and contorted until he was practically unrecognizable. He was a man to be feared, I was sure, but I was not going to turn my back on my best friend no matter how crazy he became.

"I hate the potion," he groaned under his breath. He paced back and forth in anguish and confusion. His hands would not keep still. He pounded his fist into his open palm and he grabbed his face and pulled on it and then opened his hands like he was trying to clutch the thin air.

"I gave her the potion," he mumbled, "Why didn't it work?" Then, I watched him explode. "Why didn't it work! Why! Why, Mother, why! I told you I would find it! I told you I would come back! Why!"

He collapsed into a heap upon his mother's bed. I tried to comfort him by placing my hand upon his back. I knew that he would do the same for me. He lifted his head. He became quiet. He entered into some distant meditation. He closed his eyes. Then he retrieved the canteen, put it against his lips, and started to drink the final drops.

"Don't do it," I said. "You don't know what it might do to you."

Cornelius smelled the contents instead. Then he bent down to his mother and smelled the remnants upon her face and on the floor.

"Smells like dandy nut," he said. "I just can't understand."

"Maybe it's diluted," I suggested.

"Fool!" he shouted as he sent the canteen crashing to the floor in a rage. Then, from the depths of his throat, strange sounds emerged, like a man possessed, his nostrils flaring as if flames were about to ignite within them.

"It's that wretched girl," he growled, both fists clenched, "She tricked me somehow. That's not the right potion. She tricked me. She wanted Aza-liel dead. Well, I'll find her and I'll kill her instead, her and her talking head and her crazy cat. Vengeance is mine!"

"It's not just the girl," I insisted. Cornelius glared at me with his tortured face, but I boldly continued. "It's the dark man. It's Figsbi. And Gunther. It's not just the girl. It was them too. It was their idea all along that we come back here. They wanted us here. I don't know why, but they wanted us back in Giltlegard. Can't you see that?"

Suddenly, my friend understood. He calmed his temper yet remained ferociously stern.

"You're right," he admitted. "They all tricked us. They brought us back here for nothing except to watch my mother die. I swear that I'm going kill them all. I swear, Os, I swear. You're my witness. I'm going to crush them if it's the last thing I do. And don't worry. I won't forget about you. I brought you here, and I'll get you out. But first, I can't leave my mother's body."

We lifted Mrs. Van's body from the floor and draped her across her son's back. Together, we trudged back down the steely, lonely streets toward the center of town. I sensed a new resolve emerging from the sadness upon his shoulders, and I was afraid for anyone who would try to stand in his way.

CHAPTER TWENTY TWO
THE ENCHANTRESS

The custom in Tilllegard had been that whenever anyone died, the body was sent to the compactors, crushed into cubes, and filed away in the mausoleum. Cornelius had other plans. He could not bear the thought of destroying his mother's body, but neither could he leave her in the house and subject her remains to whatever cruel miser might happen on by. He was always thinking about things out of the ordinary. Sometimes he was right. Sometimes he was wrong. But he was never afraid to try. His convictions always went before him.

Thus was the case with the dandy nut potion. He believed in its power. His belief came not by means of considering the weight of some intellectual argument; he believed because he wanted to. He so much wanted to make his mother well that his passion affected his senses. As it turned out, he was mistaken. The dandy nut potion failed to work. Apparently, Cornelius believed a lie, but he believed it nonetheless. I remembered when the stranger told us to believe only that which was true and to believe nothing which was false. It seems that in our efforts to suppress his words into the distant archives of our consciousness we failed to see the truth in his commission. However, I could not help but wonder if my own personal quest for utopia was really any different than Cornelius' quest for his mother's healing. After all, I had yet to find fault with his loyalty toward his friends and loved ones. It just so happened that his plans did not work out. His belief was built upon faulty premises, his good intentions notwithstanding.

Cornelius bore the weight of his dead mother upon his shoulders, making the slow trek toward the hub of the city. I did not ask where we were going. I simply went along. Death was everywhere, but the city was beginning to adjust. Though multitudes still clamored at the

209

base of the Great Wall, and though many dead bodies still rotted in the streets, the city had begun reconstruction efforts. The market square was progressing in that the bodies were cleared away and many merchants were restoring their shops. There was even a new fruit merchant who stood where Mr. Gilactus once stood. I turned a curious eye toward the factory. Some men were entering the building. Was the city attempting production? Certainly, they could not linger forever if they had any intention of surviving. The factory lay not far from my own house. I gave thought to it, but I was afraid to investigate. I was afraid of what I might find.

I watched Mrs. Van's lifeless body, as limp as the wilted flaming sideon she once held, bounce roughly with every determined step that her son took, and it suddenly struck me that she could be my own mother or my own father. I was not sure if it was better that they live or die. Yet, that was the peculiar thing about our entire situation - everything was so unsure. Finally, we came to the courtyard of the temple at the center of town. The Ponderers pondered in paths of eight with their long, gray beards and white, flowing gowns and black, pointed hats. The people of Giltlegard were depending upon their thoughts to save them from their misery. What could they possibly come up with that would free these unfortunate people from their prison?

I followed Cornelius into the courtyard of the temple. There was no hesitation in his stride. He paid the Ponderers no attention. He did not stop to mock them, nor did he amuse himself with them; he continued straight away, pushing past their paths of eight until he reached the sacred temple doors. The Ponderers stopped and watched in amazement as we opened those doors and proceeded into the forbidden sanctuary. As the Ponderers moved toward us, Cornelius immediately turned to them, his fiery eyes stopping them in their tracks before they even crossed the threshold.

"Stop!" he commanded, "You are not allowed in this place. You are ruined! If you dare set foot in here to disturb this sacred body, I will annihilate you, every one! In the name of the stranger, I will do it!"

The Ponderers turned away. We continued into the temple. The rafters were ancient with dust and cobwebs. The high steel walls were decorated with archaic carvings, wonderfully made, most of which I could not fully understand. I did notice, however, a carving of a cherub beneath a rainbow, and stars all around it, and brownbacks and flowers and trees and flying creatures and other familiar creatures about the fields. Then I was struck by one particular creation. It was a danxoumanxou, flat head and long arms and hairy face. The temple was filled with magnificent carvings, things never to be found in Giltlegard, things proving the existence of a world long forgotten, of a world never even revealed within the four great walls. So there was a time when art was recognized in Giltlegard! It had been kept from us by those conniving Ponderers, and no doubt by a power much greater and much more terrible.

We climbed the steps at the head of the temple. I peered through the windows into the outside world, looking out over the chaotic streets. I tried to imagine afresh the scene of that terrible day when the stranger arrived, when the entire population huddled together in that one location, completely unprepared for what they were about to hear. If that day had never come, I would still be perfectly content in the ignorance that had for so long kept the city at ease. It amazes me even now how one small, powerful word can turn an entire civilization upside down. I thought about the hole in the ground that had disappeared. The prospect of never again setting foot outside the steel walls scared me to death. I looked at Cornelius. He was to me at that moment a living sculpture of adversity, one foot before the other, his outstretched arms wrapped tightly around his mother's body which was but a yoke around his neck, looking neither to the left nor to the right. He was driven. We came to the top of the steps where an altar stood erect, the steel dulled from years of misuse.

Cornelius lowered his mother's body atop the altar. He softly kissed her cheek. He closed her eyelids and brought both of her hands together upon her breast. He took the wilted flaming sideon that he carried in his pocket and placed it in her hands, closing her fists around it. She looked peaceful. She was no doubt loved. He removed

211

his cloak and smoothed it out across her legs and stomach to keep her warm.

"I will never forget you, Mother," he whispered. Then he turned to me, his sad eyes finding new purpose.

"Come on," he said, "Let's get out of here. Truth waits."

Though my heart was heavy, those words brought more relief to me than he could ever understand. They gave me a glimmer of hope in that dreadful place. We left the temple and headed up the street toward the small, dark alley to the side of the arena where we had first met the stranger face to face, hoping that the same door would lead us again to freedom. As we hurried down the terrible street, a voice like the sound of the wind called out from somewhere in the depths of the unknown.

"Cornelius," it beckoned, "Cornelius." We stopped and looked around.

"Did you hear that?" Cornelius asked me.

"Yes, but I'm not sure where it's coming from."

"Cornelius," came the voice, a sweet fantastic voice. We slowed to a walk. We kept our eyes about us, seeing nothing but a few beggars and lost children. We came to the familiar door which we sought. The alluring voice called out again, sweetly, softly.

"Cornelius, come here. I'm waiting."

Cornelius responded with a shout. "Who said that?" but there was no one about, no answer except for his own echo. The voice was strikingly familiar, yet otherworldly. It was compelling, mysterious, safe. It could not be the stranger, I reasoned. It sounded like a woman.

"Mother? Mother? Is that you?" Cornelius asked, hoping it was. It may sound strange, but we glanced behind us almost expecting Mrs. Van to be standing there, cured and alive. But it was not to be. There was nobody behind us. There was nobody in front of us either, or to the sides. We looked up, but the voice seemed to be coming from everywhere all at once.

"Cornelius, come inside. I'm waiting."

Curious, we entered the same door as we had weeks earlier. Could it be true? Could it be so simple to escape this city as to follow the path a second time? Sure enough, the room was dark and the doors were still present on the inside, one straight ahead and one to the right. However, there was no rod of light and no stranger. We went straight for the door facing us, the one which previously led us to freedom. We opened it. It was dark. We stepped inside and found ourselves in another room. No light. No meadows. No ponds. A sudden breeze whipped past us, dying as quickly as it had come, carrying the voice, the sweet, charming voice.

"This way. This way. Turn back. This way."

I felt a presence in the darkness, similar to what I felt before the giggling little girl. It was the presence of something cruel, something frightening. The voice called again. We stepped to the other door. We opened it. We went inside. Again, there were no meadows. No ponds. No trees. But there was something. There was a light. Brilliant light. There was bright, shining, almost blinding light, and through our painful gaze, there was the most beautiful creature we had ever seen. She was almost a woman, but not quite. Certainly she was no mere little girl. She was something in between. She was more than beautiful. She was enchanting. Her face lit up the room like a star all its own. Her hair was as white as her face and her lips were bold and her eyes were deep, like clear pools of blue. Her elegant gown beamed like a fire from her breath. Her feet hovered at least a hand's length off of the steel floor. I could not believe my eyes. She actually floated above the ground. She obviously had powers of which I had never before seen. She was a combination of glory and horror. As she hovered, she beckoned for us to draw near.

"Cornelius," she called, her voice like a whisper, like a lullaby. "Cornelius Van. Come to me." My friend started toward her, but I reached out to hold him back.

"Who are you?" I asked.

"I am no concern of yours," she scolded. "I have a secret for Cornelius. For his ears alone."

"Who sent you?" Cornelius asked.

213

"My dearest Cornelius," she continued, "I know you well. I know the stories that bear your name. There is none like you in all the world. There is no one as brave as you. I know about your journey. I am here to warn you. Stay away from the man named Pirnoff."

"I said who sent you!" he demanded.

"I come on behalf of the King of Port Fectia."

If she had not my attention before, she certainly did then. I wanted to hear more. Cornelius looked torn.

"What if I don't believe you?" he answered.

"You should first hear what I have to say. I have a secret for your ears only. Come to me, my brave boy. Come closer."

"Don't do it," I warned.

When she spoke, she barely opened her mouth. Her words were slow and deliberate, soft, yet programmed. It was almost as if she was communicating through her countenance. Her beauty acted as a magnet, drawing us in. Cornelius, almost in a trance, began creeping forward. I kept my hand upon him.

"There are no secrets here," I blurted. "If you have something to say, speak up."

"This is not your journey, foolish friend. My message is for Cornelius only. Come closer my strong, handsome boy."

"Cornelius, don't go," I warned. He brushed my hand away from his shoulder.

"Let me just hear what she has to say," he replied. "She says she's from the King."

"If you're from the King," I asked, "Then who is Pirnoff?"

"Pirnoff is an enemy to the King," she insisted. "He once served as the King's most trusted advisor. But he departed. He betrayed the King by one day luring His Majesty into the royal garden where the Realm of the Unbelief lay in wait, and they tried to seize him. Only through his great skill and courage was he able to escape, although not without a beating. His servant Pirnoff was never to be found again."

"Then why would Pirnoff want us to find Port Fectia?"

"He wants no such thing. He knows the nature of men. He knows you will covet an idea so perfect. But he also knows that you will try to obtain it by your own terms. He knows that if he gives you instructions that you will naturally be tempted to stray from them. He wants you to fall into the snare of the Realm. It is out there. It is waiting for you. Cornelius, come to me. Hear my words from the King."

"Who is this Realm of the Unbelief?" I asked, exasperated.

"If you fail to come to me now, you will almost certainly find out the hard way. Cornelius, I can take you to Port Fectia. I can take you in my arms. Come to me. Let me speak to your ear. Let me take you away. Come to me. I will take you there."

Cornelius went to her. Her seduction was more than he could resist. It was her voice. It was the way she called his name. I wanted to stop him, but I was not able. Her power was too great. She restrained me by her voice, by her beauty. All I could do was look at her. I wanted to believe her, but I dared not. I wanted her to take us to Port Fectia, but something was amiss. I refused to mistake her beauty for truth. I heeded reason instead. Reason told me not to trust her. She was far too familiar to make me comfortable. But I could not prove it. I could not prove she was wrong. So Cornelius went to her, mysterious as she was. She looked like perfection. But was she?

"That's it, my dear boy. Let me tell you a secret. The secret to a life worth living."

Cornelius came to her in a trance. His eyes never left her face. She pulled him close, floating, calling, floating. She put her mouth to his ear. It was then that I noticed something startling. I found my reason to doubt her. There it was, plain as the light of her face. I saw it around her. I knew her.

"Cornelius, stop!" I shouted.

She was already speaking into his ear, and I became terribly nervous. Cornelius looked back at me, but she steered his face back around and continued casting her charms. I knew that I had to act quickly.

I tried running to him, but her power kept me back. I tried punching and tearing my way through her spell, but it was no use. It felt like strong arms were wrapping me up, holding me in place, but there was no one around me. I shouted the only thing I could think of at the time.

"Aza-liel, leave my friend alone!"

Suddenly, she let down her guard. Her spell was cracked. She faltered. She frowned upon me in her old familiar way. Cornelius stepped back.

"What did you say?" he asked.

"I told her to leave you alone."

"You called her Aza-liel."

"She is Aza-liel!"

"That's absurd," he replied.

"Yes, absurd," she mocked. Then, somewhere from out of her clear blue eyes, evil lurked across the room. It was the same sinister look that she gave me along the path in the mountains when she realized that I knew what was in her pocket.

"Van, come here, quick."

I grabbed my friend and yanked him back through the doorway and into the previous darkness and back out into the street, where I slammed the door behind us, cutting us off from the enchantress. I muscled Cornelius up against the wall.

"Listen," I demanded, "I swear that's Aza-liel. I'm certain of it. Without a doubt. And I'm afraid she's working for Figsbi."

"How do you know?" he asked, eyes wide and bewildered.

"Remember that day? In the market square? With Aza-liel? Remember how she threw a fit?"

"Yeah, why?"

"Remember what she wanted?"

"A necklace."

"Not just any necklace," I reminded him, "A cherub necklace."

"Yes, so?"

"That woman, that thing... She is wearing the necklace. The same necklace. It's Aza-liel!"

"Os, you're insane. Even if it is the same, so what? What does it prove? Nothing."

"Van, you're wrong."

The voice came again, softly, sweetly, drifting, calling, everywhere all around us, "Cornelius, Cornelius, come back. Come with me. Port Fectia is waiting. Truth. Freedom. New life. Resurrection. Come, Cornelius. Come."

"Don't listen," I said.

Then there was a sound, an awful, desperate sound. It was the sound of desire and anger and loss. It was weeping. It was wailing. It was longing. It was hatred. It came from behind the door. It was a sound that Cornelius knew. He was drawn to it. He was drawn to the despair. Pounding began inside the place of darkness and inside his chest. I could hear it. There was pounding and wailing, wretched and wild. The soft voice resumed. It called for him. It pleaded. There was pounding and wailing and pleading. It was behind the door and next to us and all around us. It was the sound of the enchantress and the sound of every man's misery, like a friend, like a simple, waiting, treacherous friend.

"Van, there's something I didn't tell you."

Cornelius' eyes were intense. "If you've got something to say, then say it!"

"The night at Figsbi's house," I explained, "He gave the necklace to Aza-liel. I saw it with my own eyes. Through the window. She knew that I knew. It was the same necklace that was in Pestero's shop."

"Why didn't you tell me?"

His mind went someplace distant. His eyes glazed over with thought, drifting into another world. Suddenly, his contemplation turned to anger.

"Why didn't you tell me!" he shouted. I backed away.

"I didn't want to upset you. You were fragile then."

He breathed a heavy sigh. "So she's really alive," he concluded. He sounded relieved before a shadow of gloom crept across his face. "He has her under a spell," he continued. "He seduced her with the necklace and captured her mind. She's not right, Os. We must help her. We must bring her back. She's lost. That's not the Aza-liel I

217

know. She would never have left on her own. She's under a spell. I swear I'm going to bring her back."

The terrible sounds ceased. The beckoning faded away. Boldly, we stormed back inside. It was dark. The door which led to the enchantress had been shut. Cornelius flung it open. I followed him inside. There was no enchantress. Vanished. Neither was there darkness. We found ourselves standing once again outside the walls of Giltlegard. We were standing in the familiar meadow near the blume tree. It was twilight. Down the knoll, leaning against a tree, waiting for us, was the dark man.

CHAPTER TWENTY THREE
THE BATTLE

The dark man leaned up against the tree like a shadow. He was unmistakable, so tall that his head was nearly caught up in the branches. The great steel wall towered behind us. The enchantress was nowhere to be found. The bright colors of the meadow began to dim as the great star crept behind the orchard to the south. Slowly, we started down the incline, the faint cries from Giltlegard fading into silence. The only sound noticeable was the rustling of the grass as we marched in the direction of the dark man. He stood like a pillar of malice, waiting for our approach.

"Behold, Thark," I said softly.

"Thark?"

"Yes, Thark. Be bare thark. Beware of Thark. Thark. The dark. Beware of the dark man."

"You think he killed Pestero?"

"He had to get the necklace somehow."

"That devil."

"What are we going to do?"

"I'm going to kill him."

Cornelius strode ahead of me as we neared our adversary, his sword drawn and his jaw clenched. He already looked like a tattered soldier. Vengeance trickled down his forehead like droplets of sweat. We arrived at the tree where the dark man stood and presented ourselves. He straightened himself, his muscles accentuating his shadowy frame. He emerged from under the tree and loomed over us. He must have noticed me trembling. Cornelius, on the other hand, was crafted from Giltlegardian steel. Fearless, he stepped forward, his resolve so hot he could have kindled a fire with each breath he took. Figsbi spoke first.

"Have you come looking for a fight, young Van?"

"Have you?" he replied.

"I came to inquire of your mother. How is Mrs. Van? Well, I trust?"

"She's dead. But you probably already knew that."

"How would I? Am I all knowing? I am truly sorry to hear that. My sympathies. It appears you may have been a little too late."

"The potion didn't work. It's a fraud. And you're a fraud."

"No. You are wrong about that. It is because you did not believe."

"I did believe!" he shot back. "You lied to me! I gave myself to you and you lied to me! You lied and you seduced the girl! You're a fraud! You're a liar! You're nobody!"

"If I'm nobody, then why do you hate me so much?"

"What did you do to Aza-liel?"

"I have no idea what you are talking about."

"You know what I'm talking about. You turned her against me. You bribed her. You seduced her mind."

"I did nothing of the sort. You do not seem to understand, young Van. Aza-liel doubted Port Fectia, and because she doubted, she prospered. She realized what I tried to tell you the first time. Truth does not exist, at least not in the way that you want it to. You want it to make everything better. The potion is your proof. You say you believed, but what did it prosper you? Give up your ideals, young Van. They will only bring grief in the end."

"Stop it! You lie! You're a liar! Aza-liel would never leave! You stole her away! You seduced her with lies! I will kill you for it!"

At that, the dark man laughed. His laughter ascended into the evening sky like smoke, billowing and dispersing, rising and falling, touching every living thing until even the trees quivered under his spell, but Cornelius did not share the hilarity. At some point during the laughter, his patience reaching its breaking point, Cornelius lunged at the dark man, sword flying, but the dark man, as elusive as a shadow, darted away, producing his own sword, holding it high like a monument in the middle of the meadow. Then, as if to say, "Weapons are of no concern to me", he tossed it aside into the tall grass. He faced my companion with bare hands outstretched, beckoning his approach, an invitation to engage. So Cornelius came at him a second time, and again, the dark man stepped aside, this time striking Cornelius on the back of his neck with a closed fist, sending him face down in the grass. In reaction, I sprinted after the abandoned sword, but I did not get far. He was quick, and before I knew it he closed the gap and I backed away. He retrieved the sword himself, and in a show of strength, snapped it in half with a flick of his wrist. A knowing grin crept across his sinister face. He knew we could not beat him. It was a victory grin. However, despite the dark man's confidence, Cornelius picked himself back up off the grassy floor and faced the dark man squarely.

"I'm not impressed," Cornelius asserted.

"Well, you should be," the dark man replied.

"Fight, coward!" Cornelius demanded.

And the dark man began to change. It was a horrible, frightening sight. His head grew larger. His shoulders grew broader. His dark, shadowy frame solidified into a mass of gray flesh. Scales lined his backside. His eyes formed deep inside his skull. His forehead protruded like armor upon his face. His hands and feet expanded and his fingernails turned into claws. He was a different creature all together. He growled and hissed and gnashed his teeth and spat fiercely upon the ground. I trembled greatly, but Cornelius showed absolutely no emotion outside of his own determination. I do not think there is any form that the dark man could possibly have taken that could have frightened my friend out of his resolve. He was bent on destruction, and he was never one to back down from a fight.

"Who are you?" Cornelius inquired of the monster.

"I am Figsbi. Lord of the Unbelief. War is upon you."

Cornelius charged at him again, this time sliding into the grass just as the creature Figsbi swiped at him with his massive hands. The monster came up empty, and as Cornelius popped up, he thrust his sword into his enemy's side. As good a shot as it was, it did little more

221

than annoy the thick skinned creature. Figsbi swiped at Cornelius again. Cornelius blocked his claws with his sword, but the force sent him reeling backwards though he somehow managed to keep his balance. Then Figsbi flew into a full out assault, a violent display of evil rage, using his claws like multiple swords. Cornelius, to my amazement, blocked his advances with speed unlike anything I had ever seen. Still, the creature named Figsbi took the offensive, backing my friend into a tree and then slicing it in half with one mere swipe across its trunk. Cornelius took refuge behind it while he drew his brawlstick. Then he darted into the clearing to regain his composure, and Figsbi pursued him ferociously.

"Have you had enough, foolish Van? Or must I strike you dead?"

"I'll never bow to you!" Cornelius shouted.

He ran at the creature and slid again in the grass, this time popping up between his legs and piercing him in the inner thigh. Figsbi roared with displeasure as Cornelius emerged on his back side and sliced him again on the back of the leg. Figsbi stumbled, but did not fall. He lunged at Cornelius in an attempt to bite off his head, but my friend drew his baton and thrust it into the throat of the beast, causing him to roar with pain and momentarily back away.

"How does that taste?" Cornelius taunted.

Figsbi's anger only intensified. He bellowed forth a ground shaking protest before crouching and then springing himself, in the blink of an eye, upon Cornelius, suffocating him under the burden of his weight. Cornelius tried to escape from underneath the creature, but Figsbi had him with both hands. Cornelius wrestled with his opponent and attempted to turn him away with the sword, but it was no use. He had my companion firmly in his grasp, and I needed to do what I could to help. I charged Figsbi and threw myself upon his back, and taking my own brawlstick, I forced it around the neck of the beast in an attempt to choke him away from my friend. Yet, the more pressure I applied, the tighter the monster gripped, causing Cornelius to cry out in agony, crushing him with the force of his strength, until I relented. Figsbi brushed me away like I was but dust upon his shoulders. I tumbled backward onto the ground. The beast kept my friend in captivity, clutching, taunting, squeezing, threatening to slice him with his razor sharp claws unless he would submit. Cornelius kept fighting for his life. He would not submit. He would not give up. Then I remembered the horn around my neck. I had not used it since the first night in the forest. I figured if there was ever a time to use it, then this was it. I scrambled to my feet and stood in the vast meadow and brought the horn to my lips and blew with every breath I had left in my terrified body, and the sound trumpeted throughout the land and Figsbi looked in my direction. Cornelius sprung his sword free, flailing it about Figsbi's massive head, giving himself room to breathe, managing to wrestle himself free of the distracted beast.

There, in the distance, riding upon a horse as swift as the wind and leading two familiar brownbacks in his train, was the stranger. Upon noticing his speedy approach, Figsbi quickly turned his fury back upon Cornelius and tried to kill him with one thrust of his deadly claws, but Cornelius managed to turn, barely escaping, regaining his own feet before blocking further attempts with his sword. Time being short, Figsbi increased the fury of his onslaught. Cornelius blocked his advances brilliantly, but finally, the monster turned his fortunes by jolting the sword from Cornelius' hands and striking him with such power that he launched him across the meadow with a force that shook the ground upon his fall. Figsbi turned to me. He roared and spat and gnashed his teeth, and just as I thought we were about to die, the stranger arrived adorned in his impressive garb of purples and red. Dismounting in a flash, he drew his own sword and engaged Figsbi in a heated display of hand to hand combat, the likes of which the land had not witnessed before or since. As they fought, darkness descended over the face of the land. It was so intense that the trees and the meadows and the creatures of the night stopped and watched the brilliant clash. Figsbi and the stranger battled back and forth, ferociously, like two wild animals. They cut and clawed and scraped and scathed, and they hated one another through the dusk and into the night.

"Ride, my friends!" The stranger called to us through the sounds of sword and claw. "Ride away! Remember my words! Stay along the meadows and ponds! West toward Port Fectia! There's no delay! Ride, friends, ride! Remember my words!"

So we did. Relieved by our reunion with Magic Healer and Danger Foot, we mounted and rode. We rode west as fast as we could. As the battle became invisible in the distance and the night, we could clearly hear the clash of warfare echoing across the darkened sky. Eventually, the battle sounds faded into silence. Even now, it is impossible for me to shake the imagery of those two powerful forces colliding in the wary meadow outside the Great Wall. I shall remember it until I die.

CHAPTER TWENTY FOUR
THE OTHERS

We rode through the night and into the next day. Our eyes were heavy with fatigue, our bodies battered and worn, but our brownbacks carried us urgently, relentless in their retreat as if they understood the weight of our purpose and the nobility of their duty.

We passed familiar locations. This time we stayed along the ponds and meadows. We did not know what further dangers might lay ahead. We did not know who, if anyone, was trying to follow us. Our weapons had been left lying in the meadow. We were beggars at best. We fled with such haste that I had not even thought to retain the canteen that had been ripped from Cornelius during the fray. The stranger said Go and we went. No questions asked. We did not even stop to consider the validity of his command. We accepted his authority as easily as it came to us. I feared for his life. Figsbi was no doubt a formidable foe. I wondered if they were still fighting into the next day. I wondered if the stranger was dead. Upon daybreak, we obtained a clearer picture of our location. We stopped only briefly to guzzle down the pond water and clean our wounds. Our brownbacks drank, but nothing more. They displayed supernatural energy and strength. We rode all day. We stopped again for water. We rode through the night. We went sleepless for two days. We had not yet eaten. We continued that way through the next night and into the day. We still had not slept. Our brownbacks would not jade. I was so tired that I thought I was going to die. But I dared not complain. Riding with Cornelius gave me the willpower to continue. His determination was unflappable. I could not let myself be the reason that slowed him down. Finally, upon the third day, as the great star reached its pinnacle across the sky, Cornelius brought Magic Healer to a halt near a pond and some shade trees where the orchards grew thin. I was so tired that I let myself slide down from the back of Danger Foot, collapsing upon the shaded grass. I noticed that it was a bit parched.

"This is the last pond before Cira Main; I'm pretty sure," Cornelius said.

After he said that I recalled that Cira Main was a day's journey from our present location. As before, the great star burned hot upon our shoulders and our heads and the back of our necks. The cool grass felt wonderful upon my skin. Being drawn to the cool water, I forced myself up off the ground and stumbled over and dipped my scorched, thirsty head into the peaceful pool and promptly laid down on its banks in the shade of a tree, old and bent, hanging over the water like an old man, and dozed off to sleep while Danger Foot and Magic Healer grazed in the meadow.

When I awoke, evening had descended upon us. The world came alive with the peaceful sounds of the meadow in transition from light to dark. I had slept half a day. Cornelius was sitting by my side tossing pebbles into the pond, watching the rippling effect disappear like his dreams only a few days earlier.

"I'm sorry about your mother," I said.

"What's done is done," he replied. I realized that we had not yet exchanged sentiments of the tragedy. I needed him to know that I cared. I changed the subject.

"Van, just wondering, do you think Port Fectia is really there?"

Cornelius thought for a moment. He skipped another stone he found lying at his feet. He pulled at the tall grass that grew up along the bank. He put one in his mouth and chewed on it.

"Yes, Os, I suppose that I do. We'll find it."

"What do you hope it's like?"

"I hope Aza-liel's there."

"Do you think she will be?"

"I don't know. I hope so. I think about her all the time."

"Do you still want to marry her?"

Again, Cornelius took a moment before he answered. He chewed on that piece of grass. He took it out and wrapped it around his finger before tossing it into the pond and watching it float on the edge of the shallow waters, bumping into the grass that grew low and green. He smiled. He smiled for the first time in days.

"Absolutely, if she'll have me. I just need to help her. I just need to break her of Figsbi's curse. I think if I could get that necklace off of her, I think Figsbi's power might be broken. I need to get a hold of that necklace and destroy it. You saw how she looked at me. The enchantress I mean. If that really was Aza-liel. There's still good in her. I can tell."

"What if there's not?" I asked.

"I don't know. I'll figure that out if the time comes. I just know how important she is to me, that's all. She gives me a reason for loving life. It's her zeal. Her spirit."

"Van, what did she tell you when she whispered in your ear?"

"She told me how beautiful Port Fectia is."

"Van, we need to follow the stranger's words completely from now on. I'm glad we stopped here. I couldn't go much further. I know that once we reached Cira Main that I would be tempted to go inside for rest. It would have been too difficult in my weakness. I don't think I'd be able to pass the city without going in."

"I know. Me too."

"But you don't even seem the least bit tired."

"But I am. I'm tired and weak and hungry. My side hurts. My head hurts. My heart hurts. Your friendship keeps me going. And the hope of truth and saving Aza-liel. By the way, if you hadn't spoken up when you did, I would have gone with the enchantress. Thank you, friend."

I smiled. I was to be eyes and ears. My duty was difficult. I am not saying that to boast, but only because I wished I could have done my duty better. I suppose that the sum of all my failures amounts to something that I was too weak-minded to realize before, that the truth must be found in weakness before it points the way to strength.

"Come on," I said, "We're wasting time."

Somewhat rested, we continued westward upon our invigorated brownbacks. We crossed the thirsty plains riding through the night

227

and into the early morning at which time we approached the hill overlooking Cira Main. It was an oasis in a brown and barren land. It was a beast waking from its slumber. We did not hesitate. We veered south around the city, making haste, our brownbacks sensing our anxiety and speeding to an absurd pace, and I watched the city pass us by like a cloud, the stranger's words echoing in my memory.

"Don't look back," Cornelius cautioned, and I turned away.

As we ventured west of Cira Main, into unfamiliar territory, there were no trees and no ponds. There was nothing but golden fields as far as the eye could see except to the north, where the mountains loomed in the distance, the dreadful, looming mountains. I was hungry again. I was thirsty. I was tired. It did not take long for my senses to get the best of me. Even then it was tempting to turn right back around and go to the city. It would have been so much easier.

As we reached midday, time grew impossibly long and the hope of finding Port Fectia dwindled away to the back of my mind. At that moment, I wanted relief. I grew frustrated and restless. The constant riding was making me feel sick. I wanted to stop. But where else could we go?

"Forward," Cornelius said. "We'll keep pressing forward."

So we did. I thought about how much time we wasted in our previous detours in search of the potion. I was against it from the start. I began to resent my companion. If he had not been so foolish, we would have arrived at Port Fectia long ago. We would not be suffering as we were presently. It was shameful, but that is how I felt. I was not in my right head. My stomach ached. So did my side. I felt so weak. I turned my heat-drenched face to the side and watched Cornelius, so focused, so resolved, so regal upon his beast. I had to admit that his determination made me stronger - not in my body, but in my will. I fought against my malicious thoughts. As long as he pressed on, I could not fail him. But why did he have to be so rigid? Could we not at least rest? How could it be that he who was so easily led astray was now so untouchable? I respected him. I trusted him with my life, and he was killing me. I was going to die before I ever set eyes on Port Fectia. Oh, how I was hurting! I hated him and I loved

228

him. He took the flower girl under his dangerous wing, and he lost her. He lost the precious flower. He lost our daily song. Oh, how I longed for her daily song! It was blasphemy, what I thought, what I felt. Who was I? I was nobody. I could never have pressed on alone. I would have died long ago. It was as if he carried me on his back. I knew that he was hot and tired and hungry and thirsty, but he complained not a word. What thoughts turned in his steaming head? I wondered. Was he as broken as I? He just kept riding. It reminded me of when the other boys used to make fun of him as he walked along the way. He just paid them no mind. His strength was the fact that whenever he made up his mind to accomplish something, it was nearly as good as done.

As I discovered myself bathed in bitter sweat, something mysterious startled me out of my trance. Something emerged over the horizon, straight ahead in our path. It was dark, almost black, like a cloud, but it rolled upon us from the ground, rolling and rumbling. It grew louder and larger with each stride of our brownbacks, approaching quickly, approaching quickly, approaching quickly. It appeared as a storm, as a lost and careless storm, but as it came upon us, it revealed itself to be much worse. It was a stampede.

"Quick, get down!" Cornelius ordered.

Immediately, we dismounted our brownbacks, tugging the reigns, directing our beasts to the ground. They complied, setting themselves up as barriers. We laid low and tight, tucked behind them, snuggled in the crevice between them and the ground.

"We're gonna die!" I exclaimed.

"Stay low!" Cornelius commanded.

The pounding of the dark stampede upon the gentle meadow shook the foundation beneath our bodies. They came so fast and fierce that we could not make out what they were except that they were thin and wiry, nearly human and most certainly beastly, reminding me of Danxoumanxou.

They came upon us with the momentum of an avalanche, our presence notwithstanding. They barreled over us, they stormed passed us, and they rolled around us. Magic healer and Danger Foot provided our only means of protection from the violent migration. There must have been thousands. My insides quivered in the rhythm of their pounding feet. With my head pressed firmly against the floor of the meadow, I listened to the moanings and rumblings which rose up from the underworld, much softer than the garbled roar of the coming onslaught and the frightened cries of our brave, brown backed beasts. We stayed low. One wrong move and I knew it would be the end of us, though the creatures had no intention of harm. They simply moved over us with amazing speed and ferocity, unacquainted with our predicament. Finally, as the last of the herd vanished behind us, the roar faded into silence, and the silence was too much to bear.

Slowly, we stood up, surprisingly unharmed and pulsating with relief. The yellow meadow was thoroughly trampled upon, given over to a dull bronze. The sky was quiet. The ground settled back into place. Danger Foot, slightly bloody and shaken, managed to return to all fours. Magic Healer, however, lay still.

"What's wrong with Magic Healer?" I asked.

Cornelius tugged at him, but he was motionless. We examined his eyes. Lifelessness. Magic Healer was dead. He died laid out before us, as a shield. We hung our heads. Cornelius stroked the bridge of his nose while gazing off toward the west. If brownbacks could be heroes, he was certainly one, the truest form of magic we had found. He led us from the meadows to the mountains and from the Great Wall to self-sacrifice. My friend was becoming too acquainted with loss. Why must it be that way?

We could not bear to leave him in the open field, but we had very little resources for moving such a great beast. We tried dragging him, but we had not the strength. After much consideration, we removed his reins, tying them to Danger Foot's saddle, and walked with Danger Foot as he carted his most recent companion north toward the mountains.

When we finally reached the edge of the forest, we laid him under a shade tree between two large stones that had apparently tumbled down the mountain to their resting place. We maneuvered the heavy stones into a vague resemblance of a tomb, leaning them up against one another, coming together above Magic Healer. I tried not to think about what would become of his flesh, lying at the edge of the woods, open and accessible. The woods. The mountains. I curiously peered through the trees. I shivered. I backed away from the evil and the doubt.

We rode Danger Foot together through the night. Somewhere in the darkness, the dry plains blossomed into friendly meadows, for when the great star lifted itself over the morning mountain, the daylight revealed vibrant meadows, tall, green grass, and plenty of trees. Up ahead lay rolling hills. The air grew cool, a reviving feeling upon my face. We journeyed all day long, climbing and descending the hills and climbing again. The orchards became more plentiful. We came across a pond and stopped to bathe and drink. Soon, we headed westward again, tramping across the beautiful fields, feeling the breeze, basking in the warmth of the day. How much longer must we go on? I thought. It had been days upon days already. It is difficult going when you have no idea how long it will be until you get there. The stranger said Go and we went, but we knew nothing more. It could be one day. It could be a hundred days. Ignorance is a frightening place to be when you know it is ignorance. It was like we were told to wait, and we waited. And we waited. And we waited. What good is waiting if nothing ever comes? What good is going west if you never get there? Where is the sea? Where is Port Fectia? Must we ride this way our entire lives?

Finally, Cornelius said, "Let's camp for the night." I was quietly ecstatic. Then something up ahead caught our eye.

It was an orange glow in the night. We slowed to a walk. We neared what looked like the distant flickering of a camp fire. Our approach was masked by the darkness. Someone had pitched tents. Maybe they had food and drink. Or maybe it was a trap. It was worth investigating. We felt the warmth of the fire, even from our distance. It was difficult to see. "Hello there!" we called. No answer. After Danger Foot took a few more strides, we were met by five hooded figures, rising in unison from behind the fire. They drew their bows

231

and pointed their arrows directly at us. Most certainly, we came to a halt.

"Who's there?" one of them demanded.

"My name is Osgood, and this behind me is Cornelius. We're tired and hungry. We've been traveling for days."

"Where are you headed?"

"Port Fectia."

Immediately, upon hearing our destination, the five figures lowered their bows, and Cornelius spoke.

"We come in peace. We were hoping we might warm ourselves by your fire."

The five figures consulted one another quietly. One, who appeared the patriarch, stepped forward into the light, dropping his hood to reveal his face. A man of great years stood before us with a noble and wrinkled head, a kind disposition, and a full, aged beard.

"Please, come down from your horse," he said. "Welcome. My name is Jarvis." We dismounted and shook his hand. The others came up alongside him into the light, dropping their hoods as well. Jarvis continued. "We're from the village of Pogg, north of here, on the other side of the mountains. Let me introduce you to the others. This is my nephew Vergic."

A younger, bearded man with a tired face and deep, disheartened eyes stepped forward, shaking our hands. "Greetings," he said before returning to his place alongside his uncle. He looked like loss had come upon him, like something was stolen from him. He was broken. I recognized that look well.

Then, each in turn, followed the example. There was Cedric and Miles, Vergic's twin sons. Their faces looked sour. They did not speak. Their handshakes were halfhearted, especially Miles, who kept his eyes turned in the direction of our boots the entire encounter. Finally, there was Veritia, Vergic's daughter. Her voice was quiet and welcoming. Her green eyes came out of the fire as if they were born there, bright, powerful, and warm. Her scarlet hair shimmered by the light of the fire, like the fire itself, like the fire had jumped at her, and she blazed with a passion that I could not at first explain. She curtsied.

232

"A pleasure to meet you," she said.

"The pleasure is ours," we answered, and she, too, took her place with her family.

At Jarvis' invitation, we sat down at the fire opposite our acquaintances, warming our hands and faces and stretching our cramped legs. Veritia replaced the hood over her head, sinking into her veiled domain which cast a shadow across her face. Our eyes met once or twice. Hers pierced the darkness that veiled her face, smiling politely. I awkwardly returned the sentiment. I could not help but glance at her periodically from across the fire. Sometimes the flame would flicker in such a way as to cast a brief light upon her warm and pleasant disposition that my heart fluttered inside my chest. I could not pay the present conversation proper attention being that I was most certainly distracted, so my indiscretions were disclosed when I heard Cornelius mention my name.

"I'm sorry, I didn't hear the question," I explained.

"I said how long would you say that the stampede lasted?" Cornelius repeated.

I noticed Veritia take the posture of quiet laughter under the darkness of her hood, watching me, amused at me, as if she knew my thoughts, as if we shared a common thought.

"Well...Uh...Uh...not long, I guess. It happened so fast."

"No," Vergic said in a sad, distant voice, "We did not see it. We did not hear it. It may have come down from out of the northern mountains. Good thing."

"I'm amazed," said Cornelius, "I thought the whole world must have heard it."

"Well," replied Jarvis, "It's been quiet around here, I assure you. Now, young men, you mentioned that you're looking for Port Fectia."

At that, I witnessed Veritia's eyes set aglow and her head lift.

"That's right," Cornelius answered. "We're determined to find it."

"And where is this city supposedly located?"

"West of here. On the edge of the sea. Nestled in a plush field of beautiful colors the likes of which no one has ever seen."

"There is something you should know, then," Jarvis continued, "We are returning from that very place which you seek."

"So you've been there!" Cornelius and I were astonished, speechless, unable to conceal our excitement, but the old man's face was not so bright. His countenance was cold and displaced. Our joy dulled at the looks of him. The other hosts were the same, heads hanging low, a depression of spirit, all except Veritia. She kept her head up. She removed her hood as if to make it clear that she did not share the pessimism of her family, gazing pitifully upon them instead, ready to take exception with whatever it was that her great uncle was about to say.

"Yes, we've been there," Jarvis explained. "We've been to that very place of which you speak. I told you that we come from Pogg on the other side of the mountains to the north. That's a great journey. Tremendous. There were six of us when we started."

"Uncle!" Vergic interrupted.

"Nonsense, Vergic. There's no sense in denying it. Let me finish. Anyhow, there were six of us. My niece was with us, too. We lost her somewhere in the mountains. We were all together for the first few days, and although the terrain was rough, we hadn't encountered anything too severe. We were just tired. But as we approached one particular brook at the twilight hour, looking for a place to camp, a tall man emerged from the shadows to greet us. He said he was lost. He helped us pitch our tent. He was dark and muscular and mysterious."

Cornelius and I looked at one another knowingly while the old man continued.

"He asked where we were headed and we told him 'Port Fectia', and he shook his head at us. He told us it didn't exist. We told him how we heard the stories about how great this place was - how peaceful, how happy, how free. He told us that he also once looked for it, but that it was only a myth, that it was false. He advised us to turn back, but we didn't. We continued. Then the next day a wild creature - a frightening creature - hungry and prowling, came upon us to hunt us, and we all ran. This creature was tall and broad, like a monster,

234

with scales up its back and long claws. We shot him with arrows, but they either bounced off or barely penetrated his skin. It was useless..."

Vergic interrupted. "I protected my daughter by hiding her in the bushes, but my wife escaped my sight. I couldn't get to her in time." Vergic couldn't continue. "I'm sorry," he said. He buried his face into his hands and cried.

"Yes, we couldn't save Belza. The creature found her in the clearing and pounced on her and devoured her alive, in plain sight, and we all watched her get eaten, slowly, feet first, and she screamed and pled for our help up until that very moment that she disappeared inside the creature's mouth."

Jarvis' graphic depiction tormented the others around the fire, yet he spoke with truth and conviction. He spoke like it had to be said, and I suspected that he felt that it needed to be said for our sake even though it further tore open the wounds of the others. We listened further. We were certain he was speaking of Figsbi. Figsbi was the dark man to be sure, and, by the description, was probably the creature as well. Veritia, now in tears at the retelling, fled the fire. The others let her fly. She disappeared into her tent.

"Still," the old man continued, "We kept going. We didn't believe the dark man. Even though we were frightened by the prospect of being eaten by another vicious creature, we believed in the city and wanted to find it. So we kept going."

"Good for you," Cornelius said, but he was met by a line of motley expressions.

"No, it wasn't good," said Jarvis, "That's why I'm telling you this. I want to spare you the sorrow. We kept going, like I said. We made it through the mountains. We headed west, just as you're doing now. And finally, we made it to that beautiful place on the edge of the sea - with the most beautiful array of colors adorning the hillsides and meadows. We've never seen anything so gorgeous in all our lives. But there was one thing missing."

"What?" I asked.

"Port Fectia," he said. "It wasn't there. There was no village. It was just like the man told us in the mountains. We came all this way for nothing. And now one of us is dead. I'm sorry to have to tell you. I don't want you to be as devastated as we were when we arrived."

Cornelius and I were again speechless, this time for a different reason. Their story was heartbreaking. The twins just stared off into the night sky, hopeless, like so many of the wandering people in Giltlegard during the pandemonium, hopeless, emotionless, and no doubt tormented under their skin. At least their father was able to cry about it. And Veritia. I wanted to go to her and tell her that it would be alright. The old man, the family patriarch, was strong. He was sad but strong. I knew it was difficult for him, but he did it for us. I believed that. However, I hoped that he was somehow mistaken about Port Fectia. Cornelius broke the silence.

"The dark man in the mountains. We've met him too. He told us the same thing. But I'm going to prove him wrong. I'm sorry for your loss. I really am, but I plan on proving him wrong."

When Cornelius said that, my heart skipped a beat. I looked toward the tent and there was Veritia, standing and listening. She saw me. My heart went to her. Cornelius was not one to waste words. I knew that he meant what he said. It lent no comfort to the family. It was not meant to. He meant no disrespect, but he just did not fully trust them. He could not afford to. It was just like the stranger commanded us. Trust nobody, not even ourselves. Trust only his words. It was not their story that was the problem. It was their experience. It was their perception. He did not trust their perception of the beautiful meadows by the sea, and neither did I. And when I looked at Veritia, I realized that neither did she. The way she stood there listening. The way her eyes grew brighter at the mention of Port Fectia. I sensed that she believed in it, even though she could not see it. I sensed that she believed in us and our quest. I sensed that it was still her quest too. We were going to find Port Fectia, despite this old man's words. I believed it then more than ever because Cornelius believed it more than ever, and he does not make promises lightly.

"Well," Jarvis explained, "Don't say I didn't warn you. You're young and naive. You'll do as you please. I wish you well. Please, join us for the night. Stay warm and get some rest. You've only got three more days journey ahead of you. Maybe only two with the horse. Eat, drink, make yourselves at home."

"Thank you," we said.

We did make ourselves at home. We sat around the fire and ate like kings. Veritia, who had dried her eyes, rejoined her family around the fire. They had freshly cooked meat. They had soup. They had smokes already rolled. They had sweet, hot drinks. We warmed ourselves and told them about Giltlegard and they told us about Pogg. I asked them if they had ever heard of Gunther and they said no. I asked them if they had ever heard of Pirnoff, and they said no. I asked them how they heard of Port Fectia and they said from old, old stories, stories older than any living man. We told them how old Gunther was, and they said that he must have been alive when the stories were born. Their family was tired and sad. They spoke with a sadness beyond remedy. We spoke until late into the night. Eventually, one by one, our acquaintances retired to their tents until only Jarvis remained. When Veritia retired to her tent, she went hesitantly. I needed to speak with her, so I excused myself and caught her arm before she went inside.

"May I speak with you for a moment?" I asked.

"Did I give you permission to touch my arm?" she replied.

"I'm sorry," I said.

"What do you wish to speak about?" she asked.

"Would you mind stepping over here?"

"Wait," she answered.

She ducked inside her father's tent. I heard soft conversation. I could not make it out. Finally, she emerged.

"Alright," she said.

I led her away from the light of the fire to a place where I could barely see her face. Her great uncle kept keen watch upon her from the fire. Her father, Vergic, emerged from his tent and stood at its entrance, watching, listening. They would not trust the two young strangers in their midst. I felt their eyes. I needed to speak. I spoke quietly.

"Veritia," I said, "I'm sorry to hear about your mother. Really. Only a few days ago I watched Cornelius' mother die in his arms. Death is all around us. I don't mean to be crude, but I want you to know that Cornelius and I are determined to find Port Fectia. Is it true that it doesn't exist.?"

"Sir..." she started, but I cut her off.

"What I mean to say is...well..."

"Sir..." she said again, but again I interrupted.

"What I mean is...I don't want to seem presumptuous..."

"Sir..."

"I know you're grieving right now, but..."

"She spoke sharply, "Osgood."

"Yes?"

She raised her humble head and our eyes met through the darkness. I sensed that she knew me too well. For a moment, I listened. Her spirit soared. She was so far above her circumstances that she could have flown.

"Osgood," she said, lowering her voice below a whisper. "I saw you looking at me through the fire. I've wanted to tell you something all evening. I believe you and your friend about Port Fectia. I believe that it's really there."

She spoke so softly that I could barely hear her. Her father stepped away from the tent. I watched him out of the corner of my eye as he watched me shamelessly. He was a fragile, fragile man. Jarvis studied us from the fire as he drew a puff from his smoke and narrowed his careful eyes. Aware of my watchers, I returned to my need.

"Did you see it?" I asked.

"No. But I didn't have to. The place was perfect. Beautiful. Serene. There is a civilization there. If it's not there now, then it will be. It has to be. I want to tell you a secret."

"All right," I said, "What is it?"

She whispered, careful not to be overheard by her caring father.

"The death of my mother torments me. It was devastating. It took us all by complete surprise. We wanted to go back, but my uncle

238

wouldn't let us. He was convinced Port Fectia was true. But that's not why I left the fire crying. Well, maybe it was in a sense. I mean, his graphic recounting of events was not pleasant, though he felt they were important for you to hear. My uncle is a noble, good man. He would never purposely deceive you. But the death of my mother is not what torments me the most. It's their doubt that torments me. I just know that they're wrong about Port Fectia. I have been bottling this up ever since we arrived. I just had to tell somebody. I can't explain it, but there's something about that place. It has to be true, it has to be..."

"Veritia," her father called. "Come back to the tent now."

"Yes, Father."

"Veritia..." I blurted, "Wait. I know."

"You know?"

"I know." The loudness in my voice indicated my excitement. She looked embarrassed and motioned for me to speak quietly.

"I know," I continued, "I could see it in your eyes. The way they light up every time someone says the word Port Fectia. You're completely devoted to the idea, I can tell. That's what I wanted to ask you...but I didn't know how. Do you want to come with us? I mean...Is there any chance that you might be able to come with us?"

She glanced toward her father who was now sitting upon the bottom of an overturned cooking pot outside the opening to his tent. His expression was one of compassionate impatience. Veritia appeared flustered.

"No. That's not possible. I can't leave my family. Especially now."

"But they're keeping you from the truth!" I said aloud.

"The truth isn't going anywhere, Sir."

"I couldn't stand to leave here tomorrow without you. If you believe as much as we do, I could never leave you behind. It's not your fault they don't see it. Don't punish yourself over their unbelief. Talk to your father. Maybe he'll understand. I'll talk to him. I'll assure him that I'll take good care of you. Nothing bad will happen to you as long as I'm around."

I turned from her in the direction of her father, still waiting, peering through the darkness, straining his ears to hear. Before I could get away, she took my hand and reeled me around to face her.

"You don't seem to understand, Sir. I want to go with you, but I won't. It's not just my father. I refuse."

"Veritia, let me tell you something. I can honestly say that I have never looked upon the face of any girl, any woman, and seen the purity of heart and mind and the faith that I find upon yours. I intend for you to find the truth, just as I will. It's not right that you be left behind."

"Sir," she said in her gentle, convincing way. "I don't mean to contradict you, but if you really do find Port Fectia, and it really is a place of peace, and truth, and beauty unsurpassed, then please don't mind my saying that it will still be all those things for you without me there. It is good of you to think of me, but the fulfillment of the hope will be all sufficient for you. The promise itself is enough. If you're truly in bliss, what more is there to want? Please," she continued, "Go and find Port Fectia. Prove them all wrong. Vindicate my mother's death. But let me go with my family. They need me right now. And someday, if you ever think of me again, then come find me. Please. I would like that very much."

She left me there in the darkness and went to her father and they disappeared into their tents. Cornelius and I slept out under the night sky near the warmth of a dying fire and a few borrowed blankets.

"Van, I don't believe them about Port Fectia," I whispered. "I think it's really there."

"I know," he said sleepily, "I told you we'd find it."

"I wonder if there's loneliness there."

I fell asleep to the soft breathing of my best friend in the world.

240

CHAPTER TWENTY FIVE
THE TRIUMPHAL ENTRY 2

We awoke the next morning at the first sign of light. Veritia was already busy packing a sack for us with items useful for our journey. There were blankets, extra meat, a new canteen of water, and knives, one for each of us. Her face, the face of light itself, glowed in the morning dawn. When she saw me stir, she laid the sack by my side. I took it and fastened it to Danger Foot's saddle.

"I don't want you going back through those mountains," I said. "It's too dangerous."

"It's not your decision to make, Sir," she replied. "I won't stop believing, even though I'm far off. Please know that I'll think of you often."

I watched her walk away again, and it pained my stomach to see her go. It was like losing a glimmer of the truth of which we so passionately sought. She paid me no mind as she began chopping sweet smelling herbs for the morning stew atop the skirt of her dress, sprawled out across the ground as she sat. The others began packing their tents and other supplies. We ate with them before saying goodbye. We offered them our thanks. They bid us farewell. I feared for them as I am sure they feared for us, suspecting that we too, in a matter of days, would be making the same regrettable return that they were making with the same defeated countenance. Veritia, however, smiled as we rode away, her green eyes sparkling bright, though not without longing. A tear crept down her cheek as we parted, glistening, glowing. Was it for sadness or hope? She waved proudly, so brave, so loyal, and before long, her figure disappeared out of sight.

"There's no reason to keep looking back," Cornelius reminded me. "We're going forward, remember?"

How could I forget? I doubted that I would ever cross paths with Veritia again. I wondered if she thought the same.

Danger Foot was well rested and fed. So were we. We rode swiftly throughout the morning and into the warm afternoon. The sky was bright and blue. The meadows were swimming with a multitude of brilliant yellows and blues and pinks. We passed ponds like old familiar friends. After such toil and disappointment, it was difficult to imagine that in just a couple of days our journey could end. I was confident that our anticipation in the existence of Port Fectia was presently stronger than ever. We had our periods of madness. We passed through the depths of darkness and doubt. We had been beaten. We had been confused. We turned on one another. We loved. We lost. We nearly died. Everywhere we turned, throughout our adventure, the stranger's words were threatened, but it was not always outwardly that they were threatened. It was inwardly as well. We had to wrestle with them over and over again for them to make sense. And they still did not necessarily make sense, nor were they always true to our experiences. But without them, we always seemed to find ourselves in danger. We even discarded his words altogether at one point, giving them up for dead. But we were wrong. Those whom we hoped would be for us were against us, and in the end, we were alone. In fact, as we rode Danger Foot across the gorgeous meadows in the warmth of the day and our dreams, we were utterly alone in the world. Then it occurred to me that even though I had my friend at my side, and even though we were committed to one unified goal - the pursuit of truth - that even then I was completely and utterly alone, for I was not he and he was not me. We traveled together, yet we traveled apart. It was his journey, to be sure, but was I to gain nothing for myself? I had asked myself that very question before. I was content to be a second. I was content to merely follow. That was my answer before. But something was changing inside me the further we pressed on. Was it not also my journey? Was not I also pursuing the truth? Was not I also hoping in the reward? Was not I also stricken by the unbearable life of Giltlegard? That is, after all, why we made it this far. It was our disdain for Giltlegard and the hope of something better. But even so, as we traveled together with the same purpose, we did so individually. It just so happened that our journey was the same, and that, according to the stranger, there was no other road upon which to ride but the road that we took. Yet how could it be that our five new friends had not seen Port Fectia when they stood in the very place it was supposed to be? We would know soon enough I supposed.

"Do you think the stranger's alive?" I asked.

"Os. He's not a stranger to us anymore. His name is Pirnoff."

"You're right." I laughed. At least, I hoped he was right. But I laughed not only because I hoped he was right but because Cornelius essentially called him a friend, this after having discarded his credibility on the road in the mountains and forbidding me to ever mention his name. Cornelius, by correcting me, did not answer my question, so I left it at that.

We continued riding until night fall, and we camped near a pond, building a fire and resting. I could not sleep right away. I lay upon the soft grassy field and listened to the sounds of the quiet night air. Cornelius could not sleep either. The anticipation of finding Port Fectia was too great. He paced back and forth near the edge of the pond and I could barely make him out through the darkness. I closed my eyes, but my mind was racing, images flashing back and forth so fast that I could not make sense of them or dwell upon them for any length of time. But it was the image of Veritia's confident, green eyes, the way they illuminated under her hood that kept popping into my head. I made a conscious effort to slow my thoughts, slow the anticipation and focus upon something certain, something that I knew for sure was true. As I lay gazing upward into the night sky, there she was, in the stars, her face clear as day, her hair as fiery as her confidence. Stars came together in the formation of her mouth and eyes and nose. It was if she was there. Maybe I should have been bolder. Maybe I should have been more demanding in my invitation. It would not have mattered, I concluded. She was too resolute. Who was I to tear a young thing away from her father and her brothers? Who was I to intrude? But it was her willingness to give up everything for her family that made it so difficult to leave without her. I will come for you, I told the sky. When I find Port Fectia, I will come for you. Her illusion faded out of the stars, just as Cornelius asked who I was talking to. As her face disappeared, I felt a strand of her hair tickling my face, but as I turned my head I found that it was nothing but a long blade of grass blowing in the breeze. Then I must have dozed off, for the next thing I remember was awaking to the sound of whispering in a clamor of voices.

I got up and went down to the edge of the pond to check upon my friend and found him there, still pacing back and forth along the bank of the water, his head down, mumbling to himself. I realized that the clamor of voices was but one single voice projecting a variation of sounds. It was Cornelius wrestling with himself, rubbing his hands together, holding a conversation with himself, a dialogue. I watched him for a moment. He paced with anguish. He was nervous.

"What's wrong?" I asked. He looked up. He looked tired.

"Can't sleep," he said.

"What are you doing?"

"Thinking."

"'Bout what?"

"What if it's not there? What if we get there and it's not there, just like they said?"

"Van, you're doubting."

"You're right I'm doubting!" His eyes burned with fire in the dark of the night. "What if it's not there? What do I do then?"

I went to him. "Sit down," I suggested.

We sat down together on the bank of the pond, tossing pebbles into the water and listening to the plunking sound.

"If it's not there, then we keep looking."

He seemed to be satisfied with that. He took a deep breath and laid himself down upon his back and tossed all his remaining pebbles into the pond, listening to the splash.

"You know what I'm afraid of?" he asked.

"You? Afraid? I thought that wasn't possible."

"I'm afraid that I've misplaced my hope. That in my pursuit of the truth, I'll somehow miss it. I'm just like you Os. I want to find the

244

truth. I want to be able to know that the things I believe really are. I want knowledge. That's all I want. Knowledge. We left Giltlegard with the sole purpose of finding that knowledge. Our whole existence has been a life of deception. That fact was the beginning of all of this. But I'm afraid. What if we never find it? I thought that saving my mother was that one thing that would lead us to Port Fectia. To the truth. Now I want nothing more than to save Aza-liel from the power of Figsbi. I want her to be free. I want her to be there with us. I want so many things. How am I supposed to know for sure that the things which I seek are the things in which truth can be found? I'm a mess right now, Os. I can't help but wonder that if we do find this place that it, too, will slip through my fingers just like everything else. That scares me to death, because without a final resolution, I will be worse off than before. The only thing worse than being bound by ignorance is knowing that you are bound by it. That scares me to death."

I was not sure how to answer that. I realized that the reason Cornelius was so much more tormented by this journey than myself was because he was so much more honest than I. I just wanted to find a beautiful city. Cornelius wanted to find something so much more. But the more I thought about it, the more it struck me. He was right. There had to be something more to finding truth than simply finding Port Fectia.

"Van," I suggested, "You need to stop worrying about how you can save people all the time. When we find the truth, we'll know it. Plain and simple."

"But what is it?" he cried, exasperated and restless.

"The King, remember?"

"The King? Oh, the King."

"Yes. The King. He called you, right?"

"You're right. I forgot. The King. He has the answers. The King."

Cornelius sat up more relaxed. He pondered that for a moment.

"It's not the place, it's the person," he said to himself. "Hey Os."

I looked at him. We tossed more pebbles and blades of grass into the waters.

"Did you know that today's my birthday?"

"Your birthday? Oh! I can't believe it. How could I forget? I'm so sorry, Van. There's been so much going on. I should have remembered."

"No, not at all, don't worry about it. Besides, it's been sorta hard keeping track of the days lately. The reason I bring it up is 'cause I was just thinking that if none of this had happened, that I'd be getting fitted for pelzors right now. Can you imagine that?"

"Never. You'd be playing brawlball, that's what you'd be doing."

"Well, even so, that's really not much better. I can't believe I used to think that way. It seems like a lifetime ago now."

"Do you ever wonder what happened to your father? You were about to kill him, remember?"

"Sure, I wonder."

"Your mother said that he was sorry. Do you think she was right?"

"I don't know. I used to hate him. I kind of feel sorry for him now, stuck in that awful place with no way out. If I saw him again, I wouldn't kill him. Strike him maybe, but not kill him."

"What are we doing here?" I asked.

"You're right. I'm not tired enough. Let's go."

We gathered our belongings and made haste. The faster my heart beat, the harder I took the reins, and the faster Danger Foot flew. We rode all night. Night turned into morning, and morning gave way to the afternoon. The flowers of the fields were growing brighter and brighter. The air smelled fresher and fresher. Over each grassy knoll, our heartbeats increased at the thought that Port Fectia would be there on the other side. We stopped maybe once all day, briefly. We kept on. Then, as evening drew near, as the blue sky became a deeper shade of blue, and the light over the horizon glorified the spacious sky like the glory of the fertile fields, in pink and red and gold, we smelled a fresh, sweet aroma like we had never experienced, and we hoped that it was the legendary smell of the sea, and I pushed Danger Foot even harder. It was as if he knew the fragrance, as if he had been there before. He ran like he was running home. The meadows grew brighter the further we rode. It was still light enough to cast long shadows across the flowery floor. Danger Foot raced up hills and down hills, each one more spectacular than the other. Finally, he carried us up one particularly vivid hill, grassy with the greenest grass we had ever seen, accentuated with bold, flowery fields, with sideons, and daggles, alive and calling, colors screaming across the ground like the most fantastic blanket, like the horizon melted and fell upon the world's floor. This hill was no ordinary hill, for as we reached the top and sped right on down toward the bottom, we were stunned by the most beautiful sight, a sight more dazzling than we had ever dared imagine. There, at the end of the world, was the open seascape, calm and still like endless glass, reaching to eternity, flaring out and kissing the deep sky at its horizon. There were bright and bold colors, fields, flowers multiplied a hundredfold, a curtain of flowers draping the long hillside, a beauty which practically defies description, mesmerizing, articulate, just begging us to fall down in the meadow and roll and play and laugh and sing. The meadow fell and flattened into a valley of plush perfection. It was wide and deep and long. We raced through the valley, headed for the sea, parting the tall meadow like we were opening a door into the future. Near the sea there was sand, fine and smooth and white, beyond our experience, beyond the danger of dreams. Danger Foot carried us to the sea and across the sandy beach and back through the meadows and across the glorious expanse. The air was both warm and cool. There were a thousand colors and a thousand fragrances. It was vast. It was beautiful. It was incomprehensible. We knew that it must be the place. The stranger told us that we would know, and we knew. There was no denying it. It was the place at the edge of the sea nestled in a bed of flowers so vivid and beautiful that I began to doubt that I ever really knew what beauty was before then. We were there. We were finally there. I brought Danger Foot to a halt in the middle of the dancing valley so that he could catch his breath and so that we could catch ours also since it had been siphoned away by the shock of our amazement. We gazed at the magic. There it was. It was all there, better than we had ever dreamed. Except for one important thing. There was something

247

missing. The village of Port Fectia. It was just as we heard. It was just as we feared. The village was nowhere in sight.

CHAPTER TWENTY SIX
THE CAVE OF DEAD
BONES

We rode back toward the beach where the meadow faded into sand and dismounted. We gazed out across the monstrous body of water that lay to the west. Not too far to the north was a forest leading up into the mountains. To the south were vast orchards decorated with their colorful produce and other dazzling trees with rich green leaves, some brown and some purple, some tall and proud and some crooked and bent. To the east were the hills from where we had presently traveled. All around us, together, was a kaleidoscope of sweetness for our eyes.

I ventured across the submissive sand toward the sea in silence. The tide rushed in over the beach in slow rhythm, leaving tiny gifts upon the sand as it was sucked back into itself. Little shells. It pushed shells and pebbles. It brought plant life from its depths and moments later took them back again, moving things around, shifting the sand, building and then destroying. I bent down to investigate the phenomenon. I held some in my hands, so coarse in small quantities, yet so smooth all together, like tiny balls rolling in unison under my touch. I remember feeling but the size of a grain of sand as I stood before the gigantic sea. It was even more humbling than the Great Wall had been upon our return to Giltlegard. And it was warm and welcoming. I took some of the sea into my hands to taste, and it was sweet, like the juices from a blume, only more satisfying.

Where were we? What was this amazing place? Certainly it must be Port Fectia. But how? There is no denying that we were standing in the very location where the stranger sent us, but there was no village. There was no civilization. There were no people, no creatures, and certainly no King. It was just as we feared. It was so beautiful, yet so empty. The great star hovered above the orchards, ready to cast its final glow across the sky unto which Cornelius lifted his gaze, standing alone in the meadow. Evening was about to gain a foothold on us. One of us needed to make a decision before darkness fell.

"How can this be?" Cornelius cried.

Cornelius began staggering across the meadow as if he was drunk. He looked to the sky for answers. He looked to the horizon for the same. He fell to his knees and beat the ground with his fists and then looked up again into the empty sky, crying out in desperation.

"Why? Why me? Why, Pirnoff, why?"

I went to him. I tried to comfort him, but he pushed me away. He darted up the hillside through the long shadows of dusk, his ardency falling from his shoulders like his dwindling hope. I chased him. He climbed to the top of a small knoll on the south end of the valley and stood upright scanning the meadows for any sign of civilization. He was a monument, a cold, lonely piece of rock. I stopped and watched him from his shadow in the valley below.

"Where is Port Fectia?" he called.

I could not answer. Apparently, Port Fectia was not there. I tried to think. I tried to remember the stranger's words. What did he say? My mind was so foggy even though the air was so clear. Clues. I needed clues. I needed to remember. But I could not. I just could not think straight right then. Cornelius gazed out over the daunting sea. Anxiety crept across his face like the impending darkness. He resembled a lost child looking for his mother in a crowded street. I hurt for him. This was his journey. His face imbued brokenness in droplets of sweat forming on his forehead – anger, sadness, confusion, devastation. He was unpredictable. I waited for him to come back down and gather himself and talk. Slowly, he turned in a full circle, carefully studying his surroundings, thinking, probably doubting, and most certainly dying inside.

"It's not here, Os!" he yelled. "They were right! We were wrong! It's not here!"

He was consoling himself by stating the obvious, for what else was there to say? We came all this way. We expected to find a village, or at least some people, maybe even an entire city. Anything besides nothing. He not only lost his mother, but also the one thing that would make his mother's death bearable. What had he left to do? I know that is what he was thinking. But what could I say? His mother was dead. Aza-liel was gone. And Port Fectia was nowhere to be found. We had come out of ignorance into a world of doubt only to find more doubt and probably more misery than we ever had before. At least in Giltlegard, we did not know any better. Ignorance is somehow a comforting thought. If I must be miserable, then at least let me believe that I am happy. Having knowledge of my misery was the only thing more dreadful than the misery itself. We could not give up. There was nothing left for us if we gave up. I would rather die than lose hope in ever finding Port Fectia. Even if it was not a real village with real houses and real people, it had to exist. It just had to.

"Van," I yelled from across the valley floor, "Come back down here. Let's talk about this."

"There's nothing to talk about," he answered. "It's not here. It's over. I'm done."

He descended the flowery knoll, cutting across the meadow toward the sea. I ran over to meet him. The sky turned golden pink as the great star continued to descend. We stood together on the sandy shore.

"Come on," he said, "Let's get out of here." He tramped over to Danger Foot who was waiting beside the quiet sea.

"Wait, let's think about this," I suggested.

"There's nothing to think about. It's not here."

"But there must be another way, I mean..."

"Stop it!" he blurted, "Don't be an idiot! It's not here! Can't you see? Look around! Stop waiting for something that's not true!"

"But...But maybe we're looking in the wrong place. Maybe there's somewhere else...One similar to this one...Maybe..."

"Listen," he demanded. He came at me with impatient eyes. He was furious. He was resolved to his fury, to his hopelessness, but this time I was not afraid.

"I told you I'm finished," he continued. "There's nothing here. Figsbi was right. They're all right. Now I'm only going to say this once more. I'm leaving. If you want to stay here and live by the sea, then fine, but not me. I'm gone."

He turned away. I could not let him go. "Let's think about this," I pleaded.

He refused to listen. He mounted Danger Foot. I froze in place. I did not want to leave. It was too soon. I could not give up so easily. But I could not stay there alone either. He waited for me briefly, without a word, and I still could not move, so he began to ride away.

"Stop!" I cried, and thankfully, he did. "What are you going to do?" I continued. "Steal my brownback? Please, come back. Get down. Let's talk. We can't give up so easily."

I went to him. He backed the beast away.

"I'm not staying, Os. Come on. I'll help you up."

He extended his hand. Hesitantly, I took it. He tried to pull me up onto the saddle, but I did not cooperate. Instead, I grabbed his arm with my other hand and yanked him right off the brownback and wrestled him to the ground.

"Get off of me," he shouted, "Before I kill you right here! I swear I'll do it! Let go!"

But I would not let go. I had him with all my strength. My arms were locked solidly around his neck as I drove his face into the sand. He swung at me vainly, his arms flailing about the air and the sand. He scooped up a handful and tossed it up, scattering and falling and landing in my hair and on my back, but I pressed him hard into the ground. He mumbled a few words, but his mouth was so full of the beach that I could not understand what he was trying to say. I had not come this far to let him run away now. We were in this together. I refused to let him leave, at least not without me, and I was not going anywhere, not until we found the village of the King. Until he saw

252

things my way, I was content to keep him there, his head locked inside my arms, the whole weight of my body barreling down upon him.

The problem was that my arms began to tire. We struggled. Cornelius would not give up. I was unable to fully subdue him. I could only hold him. Finally, his voice broke free from the sand, gasping, choking.

"I said get off of me!"

I was wearing down. Slowly, Cornelius managed to roll over onto his back with me still clutching his neck. I was losing my grip. We were face to face. Then, in a burst of strength, he kicked me away and sprung to his feet, leaving me lying in the sand. Before I could get up, he pounced on top of me, returning the gesture by driving the back of my head into the sand. He left me there.

"Now leave me alone!" he shouted. He turned away. He went to Danger Foot. But again, I refused to listen. I popped up and rushed at him, kicking up sand as I went. Just as he took hold of the saddle, one foot already in the stirrup to hoist himself up, I caught him and swung at him, striking him in the back of the head with my fist, knocking him to the ground at the feet of the brownback. In a flash, he was up and facing me, staring me down with that familiar, steel look in his eye, and we said not a word. He came closer. I thought that he really might try to kill me. We circled each other. He came closer. We circled each other. I would not give in. He came closer.

"You can't leave," I said.

No reply. His fists were up. So were mine. He was not himself. He was a monster. We circled each other. We held no weapons. It was skin on skin. He came closer.

"Did you hear me, Van? I said that I won't let you leave. Don't be so weak. Don't forget we've been set free. Don't leave this place without finding what you came for. I won't leave it. And I won't let you leave it either. You'll have to kill me first. Hear me? I said you'll have to kill me first."

"Just let me go," he said. "It's not here. Just let me go. Listen. I'm going to turn away slowly. Just drop your hands, and let me go. I don't want to have to kill you."

Slowly, he turned around toward Danger Foot.

"I said stop stealing my brownback!"

I rushed at him. He turned and struck me in my left jaw. I fell back. Then he came and walloped me across the face. I went low and rushed at him, grabbing him around the waist and lifting him up off the ground as he kept pummeling me with both fists as best as he could in the sides of my head. Undaunted, I drove him back to the ground and stood above him, our fists flying, but very few swings connecting, and he kicked me away and jumped up out of the sand. We circled each other upright. He came closer. We circled each other upright.

"Have you had enough?" he asked.

"Not even close. Have you?" I asked.

"No way. I can do this all night if I have to."

"Then why don't we?"

"Maybe we will."

"Yeah, maybe we will."

He came closer. We circled each other some more. A hint of darkness crept across the sky. The great star had fallen. Our shadows had disappeared.

"Come on, make a move," I said.

"No. You make a move. What are you? Scared?"

"Kill me then," I said. "If you think you really can."

Slowly, Cornelius reached down and pulled a knife out from the inside of his boot. It was the gift from Veritia's family. He held it up. He came to me. I backed away. He walked right passed me. He walked across the sand to the edge of the sea. He sat down. He stuck the knife into the wet sand beside him. He took off his boot. I came over to where he sat. The knife left cuts up and down the side of his ankle. As the tide came in, he let the sea run over his leg, cleaning the wound. He sighed.

"You're right. We should at least think it over."

I sat next to him. I took off my boots. I let the warm sea run over my legs. It soothed my sores. We dressed our wounds with sea water.

We doused our faces and arms and the top of our heads. The sea was growing as dark as a shadow.

"Well," I said, "This isn't exactly what I expected either."

"Sorry I lost my head," Cornelius replied. "I was just so angry. So disappointed. I really believed it would be here."

"I know. Me too."

"But why? Why would Pirnoff lead us here for this? Is this it? Is this really what we're supposed to find? Maybe we're supposed to live here and wait. I don't know."

"But there's no King," I replied. "He specifically said we were chosen for this journey by the King of Port Fectia. I see no King. And there's certainly no Port Fectia. And if those things aren't in place, then how are we supposed to know what's true? How can we know anything at all?"

"We make it up?" Cornelius suggested.

"Then we'll just end up creating another Giltlegard."

"You're right. Port Fectia has to exist. But where?"

"I wish we'd written down the stranger's words. I think he may have told us what to expect when we got here."

I tried hard to think. I tried to remember. I searched my memory for any clues, any information, anything at all. I went back to that secluded room in the center of the city, the stranger's presence towering over us in the dark. Aza-liel was there, her sweet disposition, the way she used to be. The stranger commissioned us. He gave Aza-liel the wreath of flowers which she lost over the side of the cliff. He gave Cornelius the sword which he lost in the battle with Figsbi. He gave me the horn. Of course, the horn. It worked twice before in times of danger. I thought maybe if I blew it again that Port Fectia would magically appear before our very eyes.

"I'll blow the horn," I said.

"The horn?"

"It's worth a try."

"Good idea."

I stood up and blew. I blew with all my might. The sound echoed throughout the land, just as it did before, and we waited. The sea was calm. Night was falling fast. Danger Foot stood still. There was no movement anywhere around us. We waited. Nothing happened.

"Try it again," Cornelius said. So I blew it again, just as loudly. Still nothing. We waited. Nothing came. Nothing appeared. We were alone. It was getting difficult to see across the meadows.

"I need to think," I said.

I put my boots back on and walked into the meadow, thinking. The stranger's words. They were not a riddle. He spoke plainly. A difficult journey. Did it. The Realm of the Unbelief. Saw it, at least I thought so. I tried to think. So much had happened since we left that place. It's Cornelius' journey. The stranger was clear about that. Maybe that had something to do with it. But what? Should I have let him go alone when he wanted to leave? But I was supposed to be a true companion. A true companion would not allow let his friend to leave without finding the reward, would he? No, there must be something else. There was something about being enticed by our own passions. Saw that. Do not trust anyone. No gifts. No allegiances. Been there already. There must be something else. Travel west. We did that. Ponds and meadows. Port Fectia rests against the sea. Found it. Lush fields. Exuberant colors. It was coming back to me now, clearer than ever. That dark room, the stranger's hat, his powerful voice, his rod of light. It was as if I was there again. You cannot miss it. He said you cannot miss it. It is more beautiful than anything we have ever imagined. But first...But first...Yes, there was a 'but first'. We were there, I was certain.

"It's right here," I said.

"What? Are you crazy?" he answered while putting himself back together.

"It's here. It's right here. He said we can't miss it. This is it. We're in the right spot. No doubt. But first, there is something we must do. Remember? He said 'but first'. It's here, we just can't see it." Suddenly, it came back in an instant. "Of course," I said, "How could we forget?"

"What is it?"

"The cave of dead bones. We must first enter the cave of dead bones. Remember?"

"I guess so." He was trying to think, and a smile crept across his face; a grin so big that he looked like a different person altogether.

"It's near the village to the north," I said, "So it should be right over there." I pointed to a hillside which marked the entrance to the northern forest and the foot of the mountains.

"Let's go!" Cornelius shouted, and we jumped on Danger Foot and rode toward the north side of the meadow and came to the edge of the forest where, sure enough, at the base of the hillside, surrounded by trees and bushes, barely noticeable by the nightfall, was a small cave, large enough for only one person to enter at a time. We had to enter on our hands and knees.

"How do we know this is the right one?" I asked.

"We'll find out soon enough," Cornelius replied, so I stopped asking questions. I simply followed him in. Once we made it through the entrance, the cave expanded into a large cavernous tunnel with lit torches resting on ledges protruding from the walls of the cave. They put off sufficient light so that we were able to get our bearings once we were upright. However, it was still too dark for comfort.

"Now what?" I asked.

"We keep going," Cornelius said.

As we continued, I realized why the stranger called it the cave of dead bones. Bones were scattered randomly on the floor of the cave. Bones and skulls littered our path. Some appeared human while others seemed anything but. They were not skeletons. It was far more savage than that. The bones were no longer attached to any other bones. They were disassembled bones. Creatures did not just die in that place. It appeared they were eaten, and terribly so. I wondered what kind of horror might be lurking there, hidden within the hillside.

The cave we followed broke off into other openings, some wide, some tight, but we went with the torches, always looking, always watching, moving our eyes rapidly from left to right, turning our heads from front to back. We walked cautiously, stepping over the dead bones like we were ignoring some warning. At some point, from out of the darkness, a figure emerged up ahead, coming toward us, a living, breathing specimen. As it emerged from the darkness into the light, it became clear. It was Danxoumanxou. At least I thought so. He had the same flat, bald head and long arms and hairy face, but he had two glowing yellow eyes. He came at us. We stopped and waited. Then he passed us as if he did not even see us, disappearing into the darkness behind.

"Dan!" we called, but it was in vain.

As we crept forward by the light of our path, another creature emerged just as Danxoumanxou had. In fact, it was Danxoumanxou again! Just like his previous self, he came upon us with yellow glowing eyes and an apparent disinterest in our being there. Just as he did previously, he passed right on by.

"What is going on?" I asked.

Then it happened again and again. Danxoumanxou appeared before us and passed right by us. We called to him, but he heard us not. We tried to grab him, but he pushed right through us. Then the sounds emerged, quietly at first, then louder and louder and louder. It was the slurping. It was the chattering. It was the whispering. It was the sounds of the forest and the mountains. It was the sounds of the darkness which frightened me previously. It was the sounds we heard as Dan led us to the retreat where the potion was kept. It was the sounds we heard when Dan left us there. It was the sounds of the mountain creatures. The sounds drew near. Then we saw what we heard. It was Danxoumanxou, but not really him. It was many Danxoumanxou coming at us from the darkness of the cave, coming from the front, coming from behind. We tried to walk on. I followed my friend. He kept his head. He kept his courage. Surrounded by yellow eyed Dans, he kept his wits. Suddenly, one came to him and struck him in the neck with a mighty blow which sent him to his knees, clutching his throat.

Cornelius cried out in pain. I helped him up. Before he could regain his composure, another one punched him across the face, whipping his head backward and to the side. Then another knocked him from behind, sending him to the floor atop a pile of bones. Again,

I helped him. I was deeply afraid. Slowly, the creatures backed away, hiding themselves in the darkness. I still heard the noises.

"What was that?" Cornelius asked.

"I'm not sure," I answered. He stood upright, this time bracing himself, ready for a fight, but he was confused. So was I. Then, in a blur, another Danxoumanxou rushed at us from out of the darkness, striking both of us in the face quicker than we could react and disappearing into the darkness behind us. Then another came and did the same, this time striking us in the knee. Then another struck us in the chest. Then another struck us in the side of the head. They were too quick. They raced at us from the tunnel ahead, but they were upon us before we could even react.

"Come on!" Cornelius shouted, "Come on! One more time." His voice echoed down the corridor, but there was no answer. My body throbbed with pain. Cornelius persevered onward, so I followed. He was fearless and determined. As for me, I was trembling in my boots. I feared that I would soon join the others who rested permanently upon the floor in a pile of dead bones. But my friend pressed on through the darkness, through the evil, through the doubt. He did not flinch. He did not cry. He moved forward. Only forward.

"Port Fectia," he said, "I'll meet the King. We're close. I know it. Aza-liel, I'm coming. I know she's here. I just know it."

Suddenly, the Danxoumanxou showed themselves again. They surrounded us. I realized that these were the same creatures that barreled over us in the stampede.

"Keep walking," Cornelius said, "Don't let them scare you. Don't let them hurt you. Just keep walking. No matter what, just keep walking."

The creatures came upon us. Evil accompanied their every move. They slurped and chattered, their long tongues slapping feverishly against their lips as they closed in on us. Still, we pressed on. Their eyes glowed at us. Still, we pressed on. The creatures surrounded us so tightly that I could feel my arms rubbing up against them as we walked. Still, we pressed on. They danced and jumped and pranced about like wild animals, like unrestrained monsters, forcing cackling noises from their throats while they slurped and chattered and danced. They began groping us, just as they did to me that night in the forest. They poked and prodded and groped. We had nowhere to run. I barely had room to breathe. Still, we pressed on. Again, they attacked us - hitting us, beating us, poking us, gouging us. Still, we pressed on. We fell down from time to time, but we got back up. They could have killed us. I was waiting for them to do so, or I was waiting for them to eat us alive. However, for whatever reason, it was not their purpose. Finally, through the suffering and ridicule, we pushed forward until we reached something that stood in our way. It was a door. A large, round, wooden door.

CHAPTER TWENTY SEVEN
THE REALM

The mountain creatures hovered around us, waiting, as if they knew our imminent fate, but they harmed us no further. Was Port Fectia waiting for us on the other side of the door? I could only imagine.

I imagined a king, with a sparkling, red robe and a magnificent crown propped upon a noble head, strong and royal, with soft, understanding eyes and a kingly beard. I imagined perfectly disciplined guards, armed with silver swords and shields and coats of armor, proud and silent, protecting the throne and the majestic king. I imagined gardens of shaded fruit trees and fountains and beautiful maidens dancing and playing before the throne and singing with inspired faces and voices. Oh, the voices! I imagined a lot of things in that brief moment standing at the great, round door, but they were things already acquainted with my fancy, having thought about them numerous times along our turbulent quest. I had my own opinions about what Port Fectia would be like as I am sure Cornelius had his own opinions. One thing, however, I know for certain - that no matter how many times we had laid awake at night staring up at the stars and fantasizing about Port Fectia, no matter how many times we shuddered in our sleep as we dreamed of finally pacifying our every noble longing, no matter how much pain we endured, no matter how many conflicts we resolved, no matter how much deception we suffered for the sake of this one perfect thought, I am certain that it came nowhere close to preparing us for what waited on the other side of that round, wooden door, for as soon as Cornelius pushed, swinging it inward, it became obvious that there was nothing beautiful at all waiting on the other side, but rather, another cavern, a dim, evil cavern. We were still somewhere beneath the mountain. We had not entered another world at all. As soon as we stepped inside, the mountain creatures wasted no time in shutting us in. But by that time, whatever remained behind us was of little consequence, for it was that which waited before us that made my heart sink and my blood turn cold. The dark man, Figsbi, in his original form, his shadowy figure barely noticeable against the dark wall, was standing behind a stone table, and he was not alone. Others sat to his right and to his left. There was Gunther, puffing away at his dandy nut pipe, raising smoke rings to the ceiling and greeting us with a quirky, familiar grin. There was the giggling girl, still giggling, and Gregory, her monstrous cat, growling by her side. There was Danxoumanxou, the blind guide, his flat head and hairy face and wrinkled eye sockets. My first thought was that the stranger was dead, that Figsbi had defeated him outside the walls of Giltlegard. My second thought was that we were doomed.

I felt the warmth of a fire. I saw dancing shadows upon the wall, shadows of three figures, shadows which did not originate from anyone around the stone table. They originated from somewhere inside, but I knew not where. The cave contained drops and turns and hanging rock, so I reasoned that the source of the three shadows must have been hidden somewhere behind the elements.

"Congratulations," said the dark man. "You made it. You are here. Welcome to your precious Port Fectia."

"Where's Pirnoff?" Cornelius demanded. The dark man shook with laughter, a laughter that echoed throughout the cavern. The others joined his laughter. The giggling girl giggled in her girlish manner.

"Well?" asked Cornelius.

"You will find out soon enough."

"You lie," said Cornelius. "We all know this is not Port Fectia. Where are we?"

"Of course," explained the dark man. "Because that's what I do. I lie. Surely you must have figured that out by now, being that you made it this far, and being that you are a boy of impeccable intelligence. No, this is not Port Fectia. You are correct in saying so. But it is, young Van, a very special place nonetheless. So let me be the first to welcome you to the Realm of the Unbelief."

262

Everyone around the table stood up to take a bow. Gunther took a long drag from his concoction. He offered a smoke to each of us, but when we failed to acknowledge his gesture, he begrudgingly sat back down. Cornelius and I were unsure of how to respond. Should we run? Should we fight? Why did the stranger lead us here?

"So what do you think?" the dark man asked. "Do you like what you see? Or are you still infatuated with finding some utopian idea of truth? Remember, I told you that truth did exist, just not in the way that you thought it did. Pirnoff filled your mind with false hopes and good intentions, but what good is it if you can never find it? You're both more than welcome here. I mean that. You're both young and brave and adventurous. So are we. We could certainly use you - if you are willing, of course. You were meant for us. You cannot deny it. You are volatile. You are unpredictable. You have conviction. You are everything that we are. You belong to us, young Van. We are the same. In fact, like you, each one of us wanted to find the truth once. Each of us at one point recognized the misery of our existence and sought to change it. We sought knowledge. We sought peace. We even sought love. And we realized what you are about to realize - that it does not exist. Whatever exists is all relative. You can be perfectly happy if you only give up the vain notion of Port Fectia. You promised, remember. We have a deal."

"That was in exchange for the potion," Cornelius countered. "The potion didn't work. It was a fraud."

"On the contrary, I think your faith was a fraud!" His booming voice shook the very foundations of the mountainside. "I have something to show you. Come."

Figsbi led us down into a sunken portion of the cave, between some jagged rocks, where the sole light of the darkened den glowed and cast those three shadows upon the cavern wall. There were three large stones set up along the edge of a ravine. Each stone was occupied by a mysterious figure. Each figure wore a black robe, and a black sack bound up each head. Furthermore, each figure was bound at the hands and feet, the hands being tied behind their backs. The one appearing on the left was medium height and build. To our

263

astonishment, pelzors peaked out from under the robe. The figure sat frightfully still. They all did. The figure in the middle was much taller than the others. The figure on the right was small.

"I'll make another deal with you," the dark man said, "Since I am such a fair dealer. I will cancel our previous agreement. Gone. Done. There is a new deal upon the table. Young Van, under each of these sacks is a face that you will certainly recognize. I will reveal them to you one at a time. But first, look over the edge."

We went to the edge of the ravine and looked down. Flames came up. It was a fiery pit; no, much more than a pit. It was an abyss. The heat alone singed my ears and my face. I had to back away. Across the ravine was a rocky ledge that formed a pathway against the far wall of the cave. There was no way around the ravine. The only way to get to the other side would be to cross it. And crossing it was impossible. The dark man motioned for us to return and continued his proposition.

"I want to make sure you understand the consequences of the choices I am about to give you," he said. "As I stated, I am willing to make you a new deal. If you join us in the Realm of the Unbelief, then all three of these faces will go free. If you refuse to join us, then that is your choice, but two of these faces will be thrown down there." He shifted his eyes in the direction of the fiery abyss. "Do you understand?"

"What if I don't agree to play?" Cornelius asked.

"Do you really think that you are in a position not to?"

"How do I know that you'll keep your word?"

"Know? Have you learned nothing, young Van? You cannot know anything for certain."

"Fine. Let's see the faces."

"Very well then. Very well." Figsbi, his muscular, shadowy frame, lurched across the flickering den toward the figure on the left, the figure which bore the mysterious pelzors. He untied the sack and ripped it away from the head to the applause from the stone table.

"Father!"

264

Cornelius turned pale with dread. Immediately, he rushed over toward Mr. Van, burying his head in his lap. There was no hatred. There was no killing. There was no punching. The foremost emotion was relief. He just buried his head in his father's lap and cried. Since Mr. Van's hands were tied behind his back, he was unable to return the affection. His mouth was gagged so that he could not speak, but his eyes filled with tears as Cornelius begged his forgiveness.

"I'm sorry Father. I'm so sorry. So sorry."

Cornelius pulled the gag cloth down so that he might hear one sweet word from his father. Even though Mr. Van could not reach out for his son, he embraced him with every affection from his welcoming face.

"Oh, son, my son. Don't be sorry. It is my fault. I've failed you." His breath was hard. His face was shaken. Emotion rose from his throat as he spoke, his voice cracking and quivering. Cornelius wrapped his arms around his father like he wanted to hold him for the next eighteen years.

"Have you seen your mother?" asked Mr. Van.

Cornelius shook his head, but Mr. Van knew. I could tell by his face. He knew by looking at his son. And he closed his eyes in pain. Then he whispered something into Cornelius' ear that I could not discern, and Cornelius held him a moment longer until the dark man could stand it no more.

"Enough!" he roared, tearing Cornelius away from his flesh and blood and stuffing the gag cloth back into Mr. Van's mouth before moving on to the tall, middle figure, where he ripped the head covering away in the same manner as before, revealing a terrible, yet comforting face. It was the stranger.

"You're alive!" I cried. I wanted to run to him. I wanted him to make everything better, but he was a captive, he was no better than I, and he sensed my intentions. Though he was bound and gagged in the same manner as Mr. Van, he spoke to me with his stern, fierce eyes as if to say, "Stand Back! This is not your decision."

Cornelius, however, did not rush at him. He did not go to him at all at first. He just stood there. The stranger watched him with knowing eyes that barely peeked out from the shadow of his hat. I knew that Cornelius was never terribly fond of the stranger, often doubting him, other times disdaining him, but I also knew there was respect. And he believed him now. After a moment, Cornelius walked over to the stranger and gently pulled the gag cloth down out of his mouth.

"I'm in a difficult spot, Pirnoff," he said.

"Do not worry about me," came the reply, "I am only a messenger, remember? You do not need me anymore."

At that, Mr. Van tried to interject, but his words were muffled. The dark man struck Mr. Van across the face to silence him as quickly as he tried to speak. Mr. Van glared at the dark man with dangerous eyes.

"Remember, Cornelius," the stranger continued, "The last thing I told you before I set you free..."

"Enough!" the dark man roared, again putting an end to the conversation and quickly resetting the gag cloth in the stranger's mouth. I thought about the stranger's words. What was the last thing he told Cornelius that day in the center of town? I thought I knew. I wondered if Cornelius could remember on his own. One more face to reveal. I waited nervously. How could we all escape together without anyone having to die? Was I plotting in vain? The situation seemed impossible, I admit. For the first time, I felt completely helpless, stranded, like I was watching the entire scene unfold from some distant mountaintop. The dark man towered over the final figure before revealing the most terrible face of all, so terrible yet so beautiful. There she was, the way we used to know her, sweet and desperately sad and broken, the way we found her on her knees, alone in the steely streets. Cornelius' knees buckled at the sight of her, but he kept his composure, and his face lit up like a lantern in the dark.

"Aza-liel!" he exclaimed, "I knew I'd find you. I just knew it." He ran to her and pulled down her gag cloth and stared at her in awe while her lips quivered with emotion. She did not speak, but she longed for something with her eyes. She longed for finality and reconciliation, but something was not right.

266

"Bring me her head!" cried the giggling girl. "Her head! Her head! Her head! I want her head!"

"I'll get you out of here," Cornelius said. "Don't worry, Figsbi's got you under his spell. I'll find a way to save you, I promise."

He touched her cheek, but he must not have noticed that the necklace was still dangling from her neck. She may have looked like the old Aza-liel, but I did not trust her, not with that necklace in her possession. She was one of them, I just knew it. But how could I get Cornelius to understand? I needed to try. This decision was too great.

"Van, stop!" I shouted. "Look at her! She's got the necklace! Don't let her trick you."

Cornelius pulled away and noticed the necklace. He took hold of it and ripped it from her neck like he was plucking a piece of fruit from its branches. He held the medallion in his hand.

"What are you doing?" she wailed. "My necklace!"

"Breaking the spell," he replied. He took the medallion and tossed it. He tossed it into the fiery abyss. Aza-liel glared at him in shock, but Cornelius failed to notice her contempt. He simply thought that he was setting her free.

"Silence!" the dark man roared. He pointed directly at me. "How dare you intervene? Seize him."

Immediately, Danxoumanxou was upon me. He bound me and set me down beside the other captives, gagging me as they were gagged. Before I could resist, I was counted among the doomed. Horrified, Cornelius watched, unable to act. He was as helpless as the rest of us.

"Because of your friend's stupidity," the dark man explained, "Your choices have just increased. The conditions remain the same, however. If you join the Realm of the Unbelief, they all go free. If you refuse to join us, then you will go free with the person of your choice. You have heard and seen them all. Now make your choice, Cornelius. It is time."

Cornelius looked lost. I just hoped he would think clearly. Just remember the stranger's last words to you. Victory will be found apart from the sword. That is what I was worried about. Cornelius was so used to fighting his way out of situations. He usually forced his own way. He willed it. But he could not will himself to win now. He had no weapon. His determination was useless. All he had left was his faith. What was he going to believe? Was he going to believe in Port Fectia? Did he value the truth more than his friends? Was his affection for one lost, lonely girl going to cloud his vision at a time when he needed it most? To me, the choice was clear. Choose the stranger and walk away. That was the only rational option. That was the only way to preserve the pursuit of truth, the only way to gain knowledge, the only way to defeat the Realm of the Unbelief, even though it meant that Mr. Van, Aza-liel, and myself would have to die. I was ready for it. I was ready to die so that Port Fectia could be found, even if I could never be a part of it. My companion's face glimmered with sweat. He looked upon us, one at a time. None of us could speak. We spoke best we could with our eyes, but I am not sure whether or not he understood. Come on, Cornelius. Get it over with. Whatever you do, do not join the Realm. I was so afraid he was going to join the Realm in order to save his friends. I nodded at him. Choose. Come on, choose. Choose the stranger and walk away. It is the only rational choice.

Little did I know that Cornelius had already made his choice. He must have remembered the stranger's last words and understood them better than I. Little did I know that there was another option, one that had already been planned by Cornelius and his father.

"I'm ready," Cornelius said, "I've made up my mind."

"So what is it?" asked the dark man. "What have you decided?"

"I've decided to join the Realm of the Unbelief and save my friends." My heart sunk as deep as the sea. I wanted to die. I looked at the stranger. He had failure upon his countenance.

"Good choice," said the dark man, "That is how I know that you will make an outstanding member of the Realm."

"On a couple of conditions," Cornelius interjected. Suddenly, the game was not over. All eyes were focused upon the young man in the center of the cave. The dark man looked surprised.

"Conditions? I do not think that you are in any position to make conditions to me."

268

"On the contrary," Cornelius replied, "I think I am if you want me to join you. Otherwise, I'll leave this place with Pirnoff, and you better believe that we'll find Port Fectia."

Cornelius was bold again. He found strength from somewhere. I do not know where, but he found it, and he was just as determined as ever. He was not going to give up without a fight, sword or no sword.

"Very well then. What are your conditions?"

"I want them all freed before I join the Realm. I want to know that they're all safe outside the cave. I want to see you free them yourself. Untie them one by one. First Osgood. Then Pirnoff. Then my father. Then Aza-liel."

The dark man hesitated. The request to untie them personally may have seemed strange to him. It certainly did to me, but why did it matter in what order we were released?

"Very well," he agreed, "But I will do it my own way."

The dark man released the binding around my feet and mouth, but he left my hands tied. He had me stand up and ordered me to the stone table.

"I will not untie their hands until they are outside," he explained. Cornelius could not argue.

The dark man did the same to Pirnoff, albeit more cautiously, releasing his feet, removing the gag cloth, and leading him, hands still bound, to the stone table. He approached Mr. Van. Cornelius was anxious. His eyes widened expectantly, like he knew the cave was about to collapse or the fire was about to rise up from its slumber. The dark man removed the gag cloth from around his mouth. He knelt down to untie the cords binding his pelzors together.

"Forgive me, son," said Mr. Van.

Just then, as the dark man stood erect, Mr. Van shot up from his seat and spun around facing the dark man, his hands somehow free. In one concise effort, he lunged at the muscular enemy with all the force of his pelzor laden frame, driving his shoulder into the dark man's stomach and wrapping him up as solidly as he could. The sudden surprise caught the dark man off guard, and he was unable to keep his balance. Mr. Van had not far to go. He held on with all his might, pushing the dark man backwards. In a blink, the members of the Realm leapt up onto the stone table, roaring their displeasure, unable to react quickly enough, and the dark man fell. He could not recover. All he could do was grab hold of Mr. Van as he fell. Together, they fell. They fell down into the ravine, into the fiery abyss, and we heard the desperate cries of the dark man, the sound of one being burned, rise up, echoing throughout the chamber, monstrous at first, then fading, growing smaller and smaller, fainter and fainter until the unfortunate sound disappeared somewhere in the depths of the fiery hole. Mr. Van fell silently, but fall he did, down, down, swallowed by the burning abyss. Mr. Van and the dark man were no more.

During the commotion, Cornelius cut the ties which bound the hands of myself and the stranger with the knife that he had strapped to his wrist, hidden beneath his shirt sleeve, setting us free, though our predicament was far from over. Immediately, at the fall of their leader, the Realm of the Unbelief let out a monstrous roar from somewhere deep in their throats. Then, just as we had witnessed the dark man change when we fought him outside Giltlegard, his comrades began to change. Their heads grew larger. Their shoulders grew broader. Their bodies became a mass of gray flesh. The scales along their backs. The eyes deep inside the skull. The foreheads protruding. The hands and feet expanding. The fingernails becoming long claws. Eyes fierce and teeth sharp. Gunther changed. Danxoumanxou changed. The giggling girl changed. Gregory changed. Each of them changed. Aza-liel changed as well. She broke the cords which bound her, snapping them as if they were but twigs. If there was any doubt about her loyalties before, then the doubt had presently come to an end. She was most certainly one of them. They were monsters. It became impossible to tell them apart. They were frightening, angry creatures, and they were bent on our destruction. Cornelius, however, had a plan. It was simple. Follow the stranger.

"Jump!" the stranger cried, "We must jump!"

"Jump?" I said.

"Jump!" Cornelius said. "It's the only way! Across the fire!"

In a flash, the stranger raced toward the ravine, leaping from the edge, sailing toward the narrow path on the opposite side, gliding across the mouth of the fiery pit like a winged creature in flight, and landing, in one magnificent stride, upon the safe ledge. But that was the stranger. He was tall and strong. I knew for a fact that I could never do it. I even doubted that Cornelius could do it. The monsters came at us.

"We can't do it!" I cried.

My companion tugged at my shirt, prompting me to flee. We bolted toward the ravine. Enemy claws came crashing down behind us so closely that I felt a force of air molesting my back as I pushed forward. At the edge, we jumped. Together, we jumped. We jumped as far as we could. I think that I jumped farther than I ever had before, farther than I ever thought possible, and Cornelius jumped even farther than I. But it was not far enough. We fell far short of our goal. We fell downward into the fiery abyss. I saw the stranger, reaching for us from the narrow ledge, but even he could not save us, and down we fell. Down, down, we fell.

CHAPTER TWENTY EIGHT
PORT FECTIA

Into the fire, we fell. In a moment, the stranger's face disappeared out of sight and we plummeted into the burning abyss. I never felt such agony in all my life. The flames engulfed me like a net, probing me and pulling me further and further into a lake of burning despair. We fell, and we fell. We continued to fall, never landing, never stopping, only burning, only falling. The hot flames consumed me. The pain was unbearable. I screamed in silence.

Suddenly, I became unconscious to anything outside of myself. There was only me and the terrible burning sensation of the fiery lake. And I fell so slowly. The strange thing is that as much as the flames scorched my flesh, gnawing at it like a sharp toothed beast, I never burned up. I was still there. I wondered if this is what it meant to be dead as I screamed inside myself. I was not even sure if I was still falling. The only thing I knew is that my flesh was on fire. Then, suddenly, without warning, after what seemed like a timeless suspension amidst the flames, it came to an end. The fire disappeared, and I dropped from the sky, landing upon the surface of the ground with a heavy thud.

Where was I? My bones ached. My skin burned. I wanted so desperately to drown myself in a pool of water. I lifted my head. It was no longer dark. Blue sky hovered above. I recognized the entrance to the cave of dead bones. I was lying at the mouth of the cave. I tried to push myself up, but I was too weak. Then I turned my head and noticed my dear friend, a flushed face and limp body, lying motionless nearby. I had to go to him. I forced myself up, but fell back down. I tried to crawl. It was so hard. I reached for him, but he was too far away. My skin pulsated with heat as I struggled to reach him, but I could not. I let my body rest. My head fell back down upon the dirt.

"Van," I said. "Wake up. Are you awake?" He moaned, reassuring me at least that he was alive. "Can you move? Can you get up?" His exposed flesh looked blood red, so I shifted my eyes and examined my own arms and noticed that my skin was red as well, red and burnt. "Van, say something." Slowly, he lifted his head and looked in my direction. He smiled. I knew he was alright. "Say something. Say anything," I pleaded.

"I need to sleep," he answered.

I began to laugh at him, lying there, all sprawled out like a large piece of burning ash, like the ember from a smoldering fire, just waiting for someone to come by and step on him and put him out, or pour a bucket of water over the top of him. I laughed because I knew that I probably appeared just as comical. It hurt to laugh, but he laughed with me. It was good for us. We made it through the fire, and we were still alive. Now, if only we could muster enough strength to get up and walk.

Suddenly, Cornelius stopped laughing. He looked up and stopped laughing. His face became frozen with awe. He saw something behind me, something that lifted his head and dropped his jaw. I was afraid to turn around.

"What is it?" I whispered, but he could not speak.

His fixated eyes told me I needed to see for myself, so slowly and painfully, I turned my head to see what lay behind. It towered over us. It was frightening, yet beautiful, dangerous, yet meek. It was a beast, a most perfect beast. It had wings, great, feathered wings. I counted six of them. It had five beastly legs. It had human feet upon its legs and the arms and the hands of a man. It carried a great many fingers upon the end of its hands and a snout upon its face. Its snout was sloped, unlike a caroo; more like a cat, only longer, with a caring smile upon the end of its snout. And the eyes. It had eyes upon its face certainly, but so many more upon its wings. Each of its wings was covered top to bottom and inside out with eyes, telling, fluttering eyes, eyes which held the story behind the history of the world. Each eye carried a different emotion, a thousand different emotions working together, seeing, feeling, knowing. It carried every emotion, every suffering, every joy known to man. Every possibility of living being wrapped up in the haven of its wings. It was a cherub. It was a wonderful, mesmerizing cherub.

It reached down. It took both of us under its wings. It held us. Our bodies suddenly cooled. Our true complexion returned. The heat faded away into the bosom of the cherub. The aching subsided. Energy altogether new started in the warmth of the creature and entered my body inside out. I was fresh. I was whole. I was healed.

The cherub turned and held us facing a cluster of trees at the edge of the forest which led back into the beautiful valley by the sea. The cherub breathed. His breath caused a gentle wind. Two trees that came together at the tops, forming an archway, parted in the breeze. A brilliant blossom of light radiated through the opening, revealing a magnificent sky and a sight more wonderful than the dreams of the world. We saw a civilization, and we were awestruck. I was afraid. I was afraid to speak, but I could not stop looking. Finally, Cornelius spoke for me.

"Can you believe it?" he said. "Look at it. Just look at it."

Cornelius said it all. I had nothing more to add.

The cherub set us on the ground upon our feet. Without hesitation, we went, hearts pounding, eyes fixed upon the promise that waited. Together, we burst through the cluster of trees to the top of the north embankment, enraptured by what we saw. Port Fectia. Suddenly, the journey seemed as easy as if we had begun only yesterday. The scene was just as we left it. The sea was like an expanse of glass, lined with the same white sand, glistening in the daylight. Bright and colorful meadows adorned the valley floor. The grass was lush and tall with deep shades of green. Everything was there again. The flowers. The hills. The sea. The beach. The valley. The meadows. The expanse. The great, great expanse. Everything was in place, but there was so much more. A rainbow, a vivid, arching, towering rainbow stretched across the sky over the orchards to the south. There was a village. In the village, there were buildings, marvelous buildings, each one uniquely crafted, scattered across the valley floor. Oh, if Giltlegard could only see! What I counted for so many years as a worthwhile existence in that cold, steel, city became death to me upon the first glimpse of Port Fectia. It became trash, like the trash so neatly compacted and stored away in cubes, out of sight, out of recollection. Ever since the stranger visited Giltegard and denounced us all on the temple roof, I wanted nothing to do with that city, but I had nowhere else to turn. Even outside the walls, I was nothing more than a wanderer. My disdain for Giltlegard was predicated on everything that I had not, everything that I was not, nothing concrete, nothing real. My regards for Giltlegard were vain escapes until contrasted with the glory of what presently lay before me. I realized what was really meant by being a prisoner, and it made me eager to know more. Seeing Port Fectia made all my previous strivings fall like scales off my back, like the scales that crusted and clung to the backs of the monstrous beasts in the Realm of the Unbelief. Looking out upon the vast, motley, expanse from atop the northern hill, we gathered and savored the feast that spread out before us across the valley floor.

The epicenter of the festive arrangement was a palace beyond just description resting off the beach where the sand became meadow and rainbow sideons dotted the landscape like a myriad of smiling faces, of true, smiling faces, the very same patch of land where we had sunk into despair only one evening before. The palace sparkled in the light, reflecting the rays of the great star back up into the blue sky, casting a golden hue over the village. The village fluttered with colors as the fields waved and shimmered in the breeze. Stone walkways weaved their way throughout the valley, crossing fields, widening, narrowing, and ducking behind buildings. Stone huts adorned the valley, solitary and humble, spaced by fruitful farmland.

"I can't believe my eyes," Cornelius said. "I mean, actually, yes I can. I can believe it. It's real. I've been such a fool. Look at this. How did I ever think that the truth would be found in a bottle of some magic potion?"

We raced down the hillside into the valley of meadows. The purples and yellows and blues and greens, some soft and some bright, bowed to us as we forged our way down the embankment. I felt so new, so real. That mixture of warm and cool air carried us to the valley floor. Freshness blew in from the sea. We picked up one of the stone walkways and followed it toward the village, coming upon a clear, blue pool near an assembly of fruit trees that was beckoning us to drink. I dipped my hands, my arms, letting them dangle for a moment before Cornelius pushed me in, immersing me in the water, laughing and pointing. I pulled him in. We frolicked about like little boys, like the way we did the first few days. We ran. We played. We basked in the warmth and rolled in the cool grass. We had a newly found energy. We took to the pathway again. An assortment of tame beasts pranced about, most of which were new to us. Two legged, four legged, six legged beasts scurried about the fields, some hiding in the grass, some scurrying up trees, some hopping about, some flying. Some larger animals worked in the fields. Every creature had its purpose. Every beast had its place. There was order. There was peace.

As we walked, we came upon a delightful pair of young ladies in the meadow, under the shade of a tree, picking flowers and conversing. I called to them.

"You over there! What are you doing, might I ask?"

"We're picking flowers for the King, of course."

"For profit?" I asked.

They laughed. They thought I was making a joke.

Further on down the path, we came upon a man working feverishly in his field, hacking away with a sickle.

"Excuse me, sir! We're strangers here. May I ask what you're doing?"

"I'm harvesting wheat. It keeps the people fed," he answered. Work in Port Fectia? I never would have imagined. He seemed so contented about it. His smile was genuine.

As we moved along we happened upon men and women, young, and old, sitting together near a twisting creek, vigorously singing. Upon our arrival, they greeted us.

"May I ask what you're doing?" I said.

"We're practicing a song for the King," they replied. "We understand that there is going to be a great ceremony today." I wondered what about.

The more we walked, the more we saw. The more we saw, the more people we met. Some were working. Some were playing. Some were visiting with neighbors. There were more fields being harvested, more flowers being gathered. There were children running and playing and singing. There were more cottages being built, some stone, some wood, some large, some small, some with brilliant gems bordering the doorframes and window frames. And there were more pathways leading one way or another and everywhere. Everything that was done was done with purpose, and everyone we asked had the same response - they were doing it for the King.

As we entered the marrow of the village, business was taking place. The shops were homes, much like the ones we found along the path, except they were closer together and formed rows separated by streets like we had in Giltlegard, only smaller and less crowded. The village was sparse. Alive, but sparse. There was business in trades and trading, but the marketplace was friendly, and quiet. Yes, everything was quiet. It was a peaceful rest, even in the bustle. The people were good mannered and quiet, a laughing people, a watching people. There were breads and cakes and meats and juices. There were no jewelry shops. No trinket shops. No brawlball to be found. Everything was good. Everything was decent. Some people walked. Some rode brownbacks pulling carts. Everyone greeted everyone else.

Finally, we came upon the courtyard of the palace, containing flowery gardens and manicured hedges. The broad walkway led to a circular, grassy sitting area. From there, the path narrowed, coming to an end at the enormous palace steps. There were streams snaking across the courtyard with small waterfalls and shooting fountains. The courtyard was a picture of serenity. Circular towers, reaching to the sky and coming to a majestic point at the tops, marked the palace on each side to the north and to the south. Twelve stout pillars stood erect from the platform holding the weight of the second, third, and fourth stories of the palace. The palace itself glistened of gold and precious stones lining the eaves and draping the archways, setting a tinge of pink against the grand monument. Each level was tiered, reaching its finality at a platform roof cradled by a parapet and housing a living garden. It was the most beautiful structure I had ever seen. It did not compare in sheer size to Giltlegard's factory, but it was a true work of art, a dwelling fit for a king. We passed the courtyard and climbed the steps and were met by two regal guards as we approached the great palace doors.

"What business have you in the King's palace?" we were asked.

"We'd like to see the King," Cornelius answered.

"Have you been invited?"

"I think so. By Pirnoff."

"Well then, you must be Master Van."

"My name is Cornelius." Upon hearing this, the two guards immediately bowed the knee.

"What do you mean by this?" Cornelius asked, but they would not speak. "Stand," he ordered. We were astonished at their compliance. "Why do you bow to me?"

"I will tell you why," said a familiar, booming voice. It was the stranger. He was alive and well, and he ascended the steps behind us. When he reached the platform, he knelt and bowed. The stranger bowing to us! Upon his knees, he matched our height, his tall, purple hat giving the appearance of supremacy.

"They bow," he continued, "Because they know who you are. You have been summoned by the King. He is expecting you. He is eager for the ceremony to begin. May I rise, Cornelius?"

"Of course," said Cornelius, "You must never bow to me."

"What ceremony?" I asked.

"You will see."

There was so much I wanted to ask, so much I wanted to say, but I could not even begin to speak it. I wanted to know how he escaped. I wanted to know about the fire. I wanted to know if there was more for us to accomplish. I wanted to know if there was anything else for us to learn. I wanted to know what became of Mr. Van and the dark man after they fell. I wanted to know about my family. I wanted to know more than I could possibly understand. I wanted to know, but the stranger eyed me knowingly, and then I realized. It was not about the stranger. It was not about me. It was not even about Cornelius. It was about the King. Suddenly all those wants and lingering questions were caught up in a fit of anticipation, and I wanted only one thing. I wanted to lay my eyes upon the one who called us there, the King himself.

The stranger led us through the palace doors and into a place where every new sensation was greater than the last. I am completely inadequate to describe what was beheld inside the confines of the palace. It nearly brought me to my knees. Golden floors. Glass walls. Sparkling mirrors. Stone hallways. Emerald, spiral staircases. Hanging gardens. Floating clouds and stars. And cherubim. Terrible, gentle cherubim. We followed the stranger up the staircase, stepping off onto a crystal floor lined with jewels and mist. We came to a great red door. My mind flashed back to the door in the cave and the disappointment that came after the expectation. How could I control my excitement now? Would we be disappointed again? It was not in me to resist. I had no caution left in my judgment to curb my anticipation. I had only myself to give. I had only risk and danger. If we opened this door to further confusion, I knew that I would rather die. By this time, my imagination was useless. I quit trying to think. I only wanted to see. Cornelius faced the great red door confidently. As for myself, I could not keep my hands from shaking.

"There's nothing to be nervous about," he whispered.

I clasped my hands together to keep them still. The great, red door must have had a will of its own, for it swung open without aid. Upon doing so, we were struck with a brilliant light, a light so powerful that it bent us over so that we had to hide our eyes in the cleft of our shoulders. It took us a moment to adjust. It was if we were unaccustomed to the light, as if we had spent our entire lives up to that point in darkness. Slowly, we looked up. Everything was blurred, as in a fog, as if our eyes had not the capacity to see clearly, but what I did see amazed me.

The source of the light was a splendid, golden throne. A red carpet ran from where we stood to the foot of the throne. Two guards stood at attention, one on each side of the throne. The throne was so grand that a giant could have sat upon it. Its back soared almost to the ceiling. Its arms reached out to us, curling down at the ends. Its feet sprawled out across the crystal floor like the roots of a tree. It sparkled in its own light. The longer we looked, the more acquainted we became with the light until, finally, we could see clearly. We saw our surroundings as if we were part of it all. However, once acquainted with the light, it became apparent that something was amiss.

"Where's the King?" Cornelius asked.

"What do you mean?" the stranger replied.

"There's nobody on the throne," Cornelius said. "The throne is empty."

"Nonsense," replied the stranger, "Look."

We looked. No King. There was a beautiful throne, but no King. There were noble guards, but no King. There was impeccable light, but no King.

"There's no one there," Cornelius complained. "There's no King. What kind of fool do you take us for?"

"The King certainly is on the throne," replied the stranger. "Look again. Where else would the light be coming from?"

"But he's not there. I'm looking right at it. There's no one there."

Cornelius grew anxious. Could it be a trick? I sensed tension in his voice. It was as if we came all this way, finally resolved as to what to believe, only to be deceived once again. I felt the same way. I was beginning to think that this whole thing was a charade. If they could not produce a king, then maybe the Realm...I caught myself. I was about to think that maybe the Realm of the Unbelief was right. But I knew that was not possible. I realized then that we did not know as much as we thought we knew, even in Port Fectia.

"The King is right there," the stranger said, "And your reaction is not what I would expect from a humble servant."

Suddenly, a voice, older than sea, mightier than the wind, and louder than a herd of Danxoumanxou, boomed from out of the light. It sent us reeling upon our knees, our faces buried in our hands, afraid. It spoke with the power and authority of a thousand strangers.

"Stop doubting, Cornelius!"

We did not dare look up for fear of being killed. I trembled. I whimpered. I cowered. Then the voice spoke gently, like a father to his contrite son.

"Lift your heads," it said.

The throne appeared empty still, although I knew it was not.

"Rise up, young men!" Immediately, we obeyed. "I have brought you here by my own decree. How dare you doubt me! Cornelius, you must never doubt me again. But I know that you will. It is the way of you. It is your weakness and your strength. My knowledge is yours, Cornelius, but you must defend that which you know. Your conviction is strong, but your passions make you weak. Pirnoff has already instructed you to control your passions. You will learn to do that increasingly in Port Fectia. I have brought you here for a reason. You will serve me well. And welcome, young men, welcome to the Kingdom of Truth."

I felt shame and fear, but unsurpassed joy, for the words of the King rung in my ears the same way his light bore upon my eyes, and I had never been so certain about anything in my entire life. Cornelius spoke out.

"Your Majesty," he asked, "May I say something?"

"Oh Cornelius, it is your boldness that makes you great. You may certainly speak."

"I was just wondering...if I may do so...I just thought maybe you could tell me whatever became of my father."

"Your father is alive and well. And you will esteem him when your time comes. As for now, go out. There is a ceremony you must attend. Pirnoff will show you the way. I have made you the Governor of Port Fectia."

Cornelius was astonished. We were speechless together. The stranger led us back into the courtyard outside the palace doors. Mr.

281

Van, happy as a frizbo, waited for us in the garden. He looked well. He skipped along the path, leaping and twisting, pointing at his feet, kicking them into the air. He had been freed from his pelzors. There was so much that I could not comprehend, but I was learning. Truth came to us rather than the contrary. Sure, we may have had to search for it, but I realized then that we never would have found it if it had not been revealed to us by the King. We would still be flailing in the ignorance of Giltlegard, in the misery, in the prison. We would be trudging along the steely streets in our pelzors, pretending to smile and eating dirt. The King brought us out of that, and we learned that in our pursuit of knowledge, it is impossible to know something which is false.

Cornelius embraced his father. They shared no remorse. No regrets. For them, it was over. Neither did they mention Mrs. Van, although I know they both missed her. The only thing they spoke of was the dark man.

"What happened to Figsbi?" Cornelius asked.

"He burned up."

"How? Why him and not us?"

"The fire wasn't death to us. It was life. To those who don't believe the truth, it is death. So it was with Figsbi."

I understood. Cornelius did also.

"Now come on," said Mr. Van. "We have a ceremony to attend - Governor."

I grabbed my friend as he turned to leave.

"Van?"

"Yes, Os?"

"I've been meaning to ask you, - You didn't think we'd make it over the fire, did you?" He shook his head. "Then what made you think that the fire was the only way out?"

"Sometimes you have to look in the least likely place, remember?" At that, I smiled. "And besides," he added, "Pirnoff told us to jump."

"Of course. The stranger's words. I should have known."

"Os, he's not a stranger anymore, remember?"

282

My dear reader, there it is. That is the story of how we found Port Fectia. That is how Cornelius became Governor. Things were so much more certain then. Cornelius made me his Chief Advisor. Mr. Van became the Captain of the Guard until his death many years ago. Cornelius soon forgot about Aza-liel, finding love in the companionship of a village maiden who would sing in the royal courts and weave clothing for the officers in the King's service. They were married in the palace and named their firstborn Osgood. I was honored. As for me, I never forgot Veritia. I swore that one day I would find her. I knew that somewhere over the mountains she believed in Port Fectia from a distance. So one day I went for her. I took some companions from the village, and together we set off on a long, terrible journey to find Veritia and bring her back to Port Fectia. Needless to say, we made it safely. But that is another story altogether.

As for now, the armies of the unbelief are nearly upon us. We are going to have a battle on our hands. It is quite possible that Port Fectia will be lost. As for Cornelius, there is no time for a funeral. His body is now safely in the ground. He is gone. But the truth lives on. And we will fight for it best we can, just as he would have wanted.

THE END